$\mathscr{D}$UCHESS

DUCHESS

DAUGHTERS of FORTUNE

Susan May WARREN

summerside
PRESS™

New York

Duchess

ISBN-10: 1-60936-771-5
ISBN-13: 978-1-60936-771-8

Published by Summerside Press, an imprint of Guideposts
16 East 34th Street
New York, New York 10016
SummersidePress.com
Guideposts.org

*Summerside Press™ is an inspirational publisher offering fresh,
irresistible books to uplift the heart and engage the mind.*

Distributed by Ideals Publications, a Guideposts company
2630 Elm Hill Pike, Suite 100
Nashville, TN 37214

Cover design by Lookout Design, Inc., LookoutDesign.com
Interior design by Müllerhaus Publishing Group, Mullerhaus.net

Printed and bound in the United States of America
10 9 8 7 6 5 4 3 2 1

For Your glory, Lord

PART ONE

1929
RED CARPET

Chapter 1

Tonight, if only for three hours, Rosie Worth would glitter. Like a star plucked from the sky, hot and glowing, she would light up New York's Fiftieth Avenue and burn a path into stardom, her name in white neon emblazoned across the marquee of the Roxy Theater.

And hopefully, her past would flicker out, eclipsed by the glow of her future.

"Darling, you look smashing." Dash emerged from his bedroom into their shared sitting quarters in the Taft Hotel, holding a highball of something amber, the glass catching the glamour of the room. Gold brocade sofas, dark rose velvet chairs, a white marble fireplace and, under the dripping chandelier of teardrop crystals, an enormous bouquet of yellow and white roses blanketed the center of the dining table. New York City certainly knew how to welcome a prodigal in style. Except, well, her studio bio, the one printed in *Photoplay*, hailed her as being from a small farm in Kansas.

Some days, she longed for it to be true.

"You clean up pretty well too, big boy," she said, letting the filmy curtain over the Palladian windows drop. She held her long, white gloves in one hand and slipped over to him, smoothing his gold ascot, the lapels of his tuxedo. "A real studio mogul."

He drained his glass and set it down on the cherry desk. "Think they'll be at the premiere?" He lifted her white fox stole and settled it around her shoulders.

"Mother? Never. She might be a society queen, but she is also a devout Episcopalian. She wouldn't set foot in a theater."

"Not even to see her daughter, Roxy Price, on the big screen?" He picked up his beaver top hat. Yes, he looked every inch like he could be a leading man, with his dark hair slicked back with pomade, his wide football-player shoulders, a little danger in his eyes. A gal could fall in love with Dashielle Parks. And Rosie had—too many times. First in Paris, and then again nearly a year ago when he offered her a steady, seven-year contract with Palace Studios.

Probably that accounted for why she'd said yes to his marriage proposal.

And why she kept hoping that he'd fall in love with her too.

"Don't call me Roxy," she said, folding the stole around her shoulders then slipping her hands into the long gloves. She stopped again at the window, looked down upon the street seventeen stories below. Somehow Palace Studios had figured out how to splash daylight along Fiftieth Street, turning the grimy pavement of New York into a wash of brilliance. A crowd amassed under the marquee of the theater, and already the street was jammed with Model As and Rolls Royces, dark and shiny in the light.

"You're going to have to get used to it," Dash said. "You're Roxy Price now."

"Remember when you laughed at me in Paris, that night when I told you I wanted to be an actress like Sarah Bernhardt? I still do. With a name like Roxy, no one will take me seriously. It feels like a made-up character, a fantasy."

From here she could see the Dakota, where her mother lived with Bennett, her stepfather, and her half brother, Finley.

He'd be twelve by now.

Time moved too quickly. Her daughter Coco would be nearly two. A toddler. She longed to look past the New York skyline, all the way to Montana, where Coco lived with her cousin, Lilly. A world so far away it seemed untouchable, as if she hadn't really lived that life, hadn't really had a child, given her away, or even held the man she loved as he died in her arms.

This life gave her a fresh start.

Rosie pressed her hand to her roiling stomach. Yes, maybe Roxy fit her well.

Dash gave what sounded like a laugh, and she turned.

"Red, this isn't the stage. We're in the *movie* business. We create fantasy, a world of glamorous make-believe. Stars, not actresses." He tugged her arm, pulled her toward the ornate floor mirror. "Look at yourself and tell me if there is one smidgen left of Rosie Worth, former showgirl and widow, in that mirror."

Palace Studios had bleached her hair to starlight white, plucked her eyebrows clear off her face, and penciled in a line of black. They'd framed her lips in a bloodred cupid's bow and honed her figure into something that added mystery and allure under her teal blue satin evening gown. The garment hugged her like a negligee, dripped down to the floor, and trailed behind her.

"This is what you wanted from me when you appeared at my door two years ago, wasn't it? To make the world fall in love with you? This is how we're going to do it. By creating Roxy Price, bombshell blond. This is how the world will fall in love with you. They're not going to love a tragic socialite who lost her heart—they'll love a small-town girl from Kansas whose dreams came true in Hollywood."

"But it's not—it's not real. It's not me."

"Make it you, doll. If this is what you want, you'll have to become Miss Roxy Price."

The actress in the mirror found a smile for him. Nodded.

"C'mon, gorgeous. This is your moment." Dash pressed a kiss to her cheek, spilling the odor of bourbon over her, and offered his arm. "Smile. Be brilliant."

He led her through the service entrance, into the alley, just like they'd planned, and she climbed into the open-air backseat of a studio limousine. The studio had shipped the car from Hollywood just for tonight's premiere, because of the way the seat faced backward so the stars could wave to their fans.

Dash's idea.

The odors of the city marinated in the heat of the July night and were captured in the grungy alley. The tall buildings suffocated any breeze. She leaned back into the leather seat as Grayson Clarke slid in beside her. "A doozy of a night for a premiere," he said, sweat across his brow. He dabbed it away with a handkerchief.

Indeed, heat slithered in under her fur, a line of sweat dripping down her spine.

And sitting next to her young, attractive costar didn't help.

Dash climbed into the limousine passenger seat and tapped on the window separating them. "Just remember to wave!"

She smiled, nodded, and wished he might forget the studio for one night. But Dash never let love get in the way of business.

Not that love was what they had.

"You look stunning, Roxy," Grayson said. He winked.

If anyone could take the crowd's breath away and turn them to frenzy, newcomer Grayson Clarke had that power. With those dark, devil-may-care eyes, his rogue smile, the way he could kiss a woman on screen… Even she had forgotten her name a few times in his embrace.

And he always smelled good, despite being covered with the sweat of the day, as if he'd just run in from some football game, showered fast, and left the exertion still clinging to his body in a mix of soap and strength. Grayson's bio suggested he'd played college football, came from a small town in Idaho, and that Palace Studios Director Fletcher Harris had plucked him right out of a Central Casting line and added studio polish until he sparkled.

In reality, he'd been hoofing it around Hollywood for two years, working odd jobs until he'd had the luck of chauffeuring Dash home from the studio one night. He somehow talked the producer into giving him a screen test.

Grayson's hometown-hero face filled the darkened screening room until it drained the air from the set. Fletcher cast him in the first movie he could find—*Star for a Day*—and proceeded to turn prophecy to reality with a script penned with the ink of destiny, because when Roxy's male lead broke his leg mid-shoot, they recast the role with Grayson.

If she had to choose between kissing Grayson Clarke or the boozed-up silent film has-been John Drake…well, she'd thrown herself into her role with new luster.

The B movie became a studio bonanza. Because of the hype filling the pages of *Photoplay* magazine and the previews screened at locations around the country, every woman in America longed to be Ivy Waters, Rosie's character in *Star for a Day*, loved by a boy with nothing to offer but his rakish good looks and a promise, who has to choose between true love and stardom.

In truth, the story felt too close to Rosie's.

She wanted to shout at the screen and tell Ivy to run. To choose the life that couldn't break her heart.

Love was just too dangerous.

But Hollywood…well, Rosie could admit to spending a few long hours pining for a man like Grayson—at least the on-screen Grayson—while waiting for Dash to return home from the studio. Apparently Hollywood had the power to crush her too, if she let it.

Maybe tonight after the premiere, when the applause subsided, Dash would decide to shake off the demands of the studio, take Rosie in his arms, and make her his wife.

After eleven months, it might be about time.

Not that she loved him either, really. She thought so, long ago. But then she'd known real love, and their business arrangement didn't quite match the definition. Sometimes, however, the night got too cold, the voices of the past finding her. And it might be nice to hold on to someone who knew the real Rosie.

The limousine pulled out of the alley and headed around the block so they could make their Fiftieth Avenue entrance. The roar of the crowd rumbled under her skin as they neared the street. Grayson slipped his hand over hers, squeezed.

"Smile, darling."

They turned off of Sixth Avenue onto Fiftieth, and flashbulbs exploded, the pop and sulfur seeping into the sultry air. The crowd lined the sidewalks, five and six deep, women waving with handkerchiefs, men watching her with a smile.

"They love us," Grayson said, his grin genuine as he waved.

Perhaps. The cheers heated her through, like a blaze in her chest. She waved and blew kisses, both hands extended to her public.

Yes, Dash had kept his promise—at least the one to make her a star.

The limousine pulled up to the red carpet that spilled out under the marquee of the Roxy Theater—Roxy at the Roxy, Dash had said when he'd chosen the venue. And her name.

But now it blazed right beside Grayson Clarke's, and it seemed like it belonged there, in lights.

The orchestra Dash had hired played the theme song from the movie as the white-gloved attendants opened her door and ushered her out. She landed on the red carpet, blinded by the pop of lightbulbs, shattering and showering the night with glass and filament.

Dots flickered against her eyes, even as she scanned the crowd.

Just in case.

But no, her mother, Jinx, hadn't found a place on the sidelines to cheer for her daughter.

Fans shouted Roxy's name, a cacophony of screams as she turned and slipped her arm through Grayson's.

Clutched it, really. He tugged them up the red carpet, waving as the crowds surged toward them. Security pushed them back, and she pasted on a smile.

The adoration thundered behind her.

Doormen held open the double doors to the theater and the entourage promenaded inside to more applause, more fans lined up inside the rotunda, curled around the circular carpet, packed up against the arching colonnades. Police cordoned the crowd behind red velvet ropes held up by brass stanchions.

Grayson led her up the stairs to the second-floor balcony, and she looked down to see Dash at the door, shaking hands with Fletcher Harris, his studio partner, and director of *Star for a Day*. Fletcher could terrify her with a look, censure in the crease of his dark eyebrows, the thin, puckered moustache, his sharp eyes. With thinning hair and a wiry frame, only his studio power could account for the redheaded trollop who hung on his arm.

A bimbo from one of his B movies, no doubt.

Dash stuck out his elbow for his secretary, Irene Marshall, a dishwater blond with sad eyes and a little too much padding around the middle to be a star. She'd shown up at the last two premieres— B movies that the studio produced to fund *Star for a Day*. Dash showed his rare soft side with Irene, who'd arrived on the Palace Studios lot as an extra only to fetch coffee and run errands. She'd girl-Fridayed herself right into a desk chair outside Dash's mahogany office door. She seemed to have a crush on him, and for that Rosie pitied her. Dash loved the studio first. Maybe only.

Irene looked frumpy tonight in a black two-piece overcoat dress and a black cloche hat, but she smiled as if she belonged.

Maybe the girl—Rosie placed her at about twenty-one—did have acting ability.

Dash put his hand on the small of Irene's back as they started up the stairs, and Rosie bit back a flare of heat in her stomach. It died when he grabbed the railing and turned away from Irene, waving for the crowd below. He joined Rosie and Grayson at the apex of the stairs, where the balcony overlooked the foyer.

"Ready for the show?" He whispered close to Rosie's ear, his lips brushing her neck. Almost like a kiss.

"Isn't this it?" Rosie said and winked at him. He smiled and slipped his hand over hers, ever so briefly.

"See, I told you that you'd be brilliant."

Yes, tonight Rosie glittered.

* * * * *

"Don't jump."

The voice found Rosie on the balcony of the presidential suite of the Taft, where Fletcher had taken rooms in the name of the studio. Inside, through the open French doors, a small orchestra played tunes from the show, and white-gloved waiters passed golden champagne around in fluted glasses to the few remaining guests. Rosie cradled a glass in her hands, nursing it really, planning to leave it untouched.

Her stomach had enough trouble staying calm.

She turned and frowned at the man entering the balcony. "What?"

He looked about thirty. He wore a tuxedo but had taken off his jacket, turning up the sleeves, opening the collar, as if to be done with the nonsense of formality. Still, he had a regal bearing about him, and when his eyes caught hers, something shifted inside her, a sense that she might know him.

But she couldn't place him as he smiled, raised an eyebrow, nodded. "You were brilliant. And beautiful. I've never seen anyone transform on the screen from small-town girl to starlet quite like you did. You're an amazing actress. Which is why I would hate to see you as a splat on the pavement."

She moved away from the edge of the balcony. "Don't be silly. I wasn't going to jump."

"You looked like you might be gauging the distance to the street."

She rubbed her arms, gave a tinny laugh, and it sounded as if she'd had more than a sip of that champagne. "No, I'm just tired. I want to go to bed." She cast a look inside and spotted Dash sitting on the arm of the gold sofa, gesticulating with his hands.

Concocting a new movie deal for her, she had no doubt. Good. She wanted to get back to work. No more cheesecake publicity photos. No more posing at the Brown Derby over a chicken salad sandwich or at the Coconut Club, being dipped in a tango by Valentino or that handsy John Barrymore.

And if the studio made over her boudoir one more time, she might take to sleeping at the Roosevelt Hotel.

She turned back to the balcony railing, wrapping her hand around the edge. She'd long ago kicked off her shoes, untied the fur stole from her shoulders, and left them with Dash's coat on a chair inside.

"So that accounts for the forlorn look. You're waiting for Parks." He leaned over and braced his arms on the balcony. The wind reaped his smell, sent it back to her, a mix of exotic cologne and cigar smoke. He wore enough of five-o'clock shadow to temper the look of aristocracy, but she pegged him as one of her mother's set, New York Society. "I hate to break your heart, but he's got a reputation with the ladies."

Once upon a time, yes. But he'd changed.

Except, he hadn't told the press that, had he? Why he wanted to keep their marriage a secret, she couldn't understand, despite his claims that it wouldn't look good for her career for her to be married to her producer.

She shrugged as if she didn't care. "I'm just trying to figure out who that woman was I saw on the screen tonight. I sat there in the theater, a cold sweat down my back, trying to comprehend that the person on the screen was really me."

"Is it?"

She frowned at him, something quick.

He raised an eyebrow. "I thought you were brilliant." He raised his glass to her. "To the woman on the screen."

She clinked her glass, forced a smile. "To her."

"Your fans seem to love the woman they see. I think you shut down all of Fiftieth Street. They were still lined up after the premiere."

She glanced at the bouquet of orchids a male admirer had thrust at her. No, it just didn't feel real.

"Are you a school chum of Dash's?"

He laughed and glanced at her. "No."

"What's your name?"

"Rafe. Rafe Horne."

He had blue eyes, so blue they contained a magic. Enough to steal the words from her mouth.

She took a sip of the champagne. Regretted it, although it helped her forage up her voice. "Your accent tells me you're not from around here."

"Europe. But I have family on this side of the pond. I'm visiting. And doing some business."

"And what business is that?"

He carried what looked like a glass of orange juice in his hand. "The movie business," he said, but he winked at her.

Oh, so that's how he knew Dash. Maybe he'd been around the studio.

She set down the champagne, before she succumbed to the urge to gulp it down, and ran her hands up her bare arms. Up here, the rank stew of the city's street couldn't reach them, and a light breeze tempered the heat. She'd had enough of the studio talk of Dash and Fletcher and of watching Irene follow the pair around the room taking notes.

Her only friend, Grayson, had disappeared with Fletcher's red-head halfway through the party.

"The city seems like a blanket filled with stars from here," Rafe said, staring out over the darkness.

"It's nothing like that during the day, I promise."

He glanced at her. "You know New York?"

She lifted a shoulder. "Over to the southeast is the *Chronicle* Building. My Uncle Oliver is the publisher. And to the north, just off Central Park is the Dakota. My mother and stepfather have a seventh-floor apartment there with my little brother, Finn."

"You're from New York City? I thought you lived in Kansas."

She smiled and twisted the diamond band on her right hand. Dash never let her wear it on her left, even though the magistrate legally married them. A business arrangement. Not even the press knew.

She doubted even the studio knew, other than maybe Fletcher.

But her marriage to Dash meant that she had more control over her contract, and he got her at a bargain rate—one that included shares in their fledgling studio. Someday when Palace Studios began to make hits, her paltry weekly salary would pay off in spades.

"Sort of. I married a baseball player from Kansas. Fletcher adopted his story when he created mine."

Rafe frowned. "You're married?"

She refused to look at Dash. Drew in a breath. "Guthrie died about two years ago, at the hands of a mobster here in New York."

Rafe stilled, and she looked away. Yes, it sounded terribly, dramatically tragic when she just said it out loud like that. Which she hadn't, not for two years.

And she didn't follow with the rest. Like the fact that, at the time, she'd carried his child.

"I'm sorry," Rafe said softly.

"It's in the past. So long ago, it's hard to remember." Except, sometimes Guthrie visited her in her dreams. Sometimes he took her in his arms.

Sometimes she woke sobbing.

"You never forget your first love," Rafe said quietly. She glanced at him, found compassion in his face and a shifting of pain through his eyes.

She couldn't bear to ask.

"Yeah, well, I'm with Dash now, and that life is over." She shook her head. "I'm not the Kansas girl. Never was."

"Now you're a star," Rafe said, but she couldn't read his expression. Was he mocking her? Or...

He raised his glass to her. "I hope you get everything you dream for, Roxy Price." Then he took her hand and kissed it through her glove.

She watched him return to the party and had no words to chase him.

Dash looked up, caught her eye. Smiled. She pressed her hand to her stomach. No more champagne for her.

She didn't look for Rafe as she returned to the party. Irene stood behind Dash, furiously scribbling notes. Yes, Rosie might call her pretty in a small-town way, with those hazel eyes, delicate heart-shaped lips. And if the studio added a little bleach in her hair...

Rosie sat on the edge of the sofa, pressing her hand into Dash's shoulder. He looked up at her.

"I'm tired. Can we go?"

He covered her hand with his. "Of course you are. I'll have one of the footmen see you home."

"It's only five flights down, Dash. I can manage." *But I don't want to.* She tried to put it into her eyes. *Come back to the suite with me.*

But he only glanced at Fletcher and then behind her to Irene, as if he needed the permission of either. His voice lowered. "Red, I have studio business."

"At one o'clock in the morning?"

Oh, she didn't mean for her voice to rise. But it hung over the conversations in the room, and eyes turned toward her.

Including Rafe Horne's. His lips tightened into a thin line.

She produced a smile, something for her audience, and patted Dash, laughing. "Of course you do. Get me a fabulous role, Dashielle. I'll run and get my beauty sleep."

Dash caught her hand as she turned away. "You're beautiful enough, darling."

That earned him laughter, and she winked at him, for their public. The fussy star placated by the studio mogul.

She picked up her fox stole, slung it over her shoulder, found her shoes. A footman stood at the door, but she put her hand on his tuxedoed chest. "I can make my own way, thank you."

She glanced at Rafe out of the corner of her eye. His gaze burned her neck as she left. *"I hope you get everything you dream for, Roxy Price."*

* * * * *

To my Red Star. Fondly, Dash.

Oh Dash. Rosie let the note drop on the bed and picked up the pearls. The bulk of the necklace hid behind a velvet cardboard pad. As she picked up the necklace and let it drip between her fingers, she discovered a choker with a diamond brooch in the center and two long pearl tails that hung off the clasp.

She slipped her dress off her shoulders, pinned the choker around her neck, and wandered into the bathroom, flipping on the light.

The brooch settled in the well of her neck, glittering like starlight. And when she turned, the long tails dripped down between her shoulder blades.

She shouldn't have doubted him.

Unbuttoning her dress at the side, she let it fall to the floor then scooped it up and draped it over the chair before her dressing table. She went to the closet and pulled out a filmy dressing gown, white ermine at the neck and wrists. She knotted it at her waist then returned to the bathroom and dabbed on a refresher of Moment Supreme at her wrists, behind her ears.

Turning off her bathroom light, she curled up in the center of her bed, upon the silky coverlet, her fingers trailing over the pearls.

Tonight, she'd leave her doors unlocked.

* * * * *

Rosie couldn't account for why the summer sun woke her early, slipping through the drapes and across the room to where she lay curled on the bed, her hand still at her pearls. Or why she bathed, washed her face, dressed in a pair of high-waist, wide-leg trousers and a black shift, slipped on an oversized straw hat and headed outside. Why she walked the seven blocks to Central Park and took the loop past the skating rink to the boathouse and then finally sat by the lake, watching ducks paddle and a little boy float a boat, his mother holding him by the scruff of his sailor suit.

Once upon a time, long ago, she'd taken Finley to float his toy boat in a pond in France while waiting for Dash to find her. To propose.

He'd broken her heart that day too.

Her gaze trailed to the bridge, and she closed her eyes against the images it scoured up. Pressed her hands to her ears.

She shouldn't be here.

Not yet.

She got up and found herself headed toward the Dakota. Probably they wouldn't yet be up and she'd only be disturbing them.

Most likely, they didn't want to see her, after what she'd done.

Still, the ache pressed her to the doorstep and she identified herself for the doorman with a name he'd know.

He called it up and announced her.

Miraculously, the housekeeper buzzed her in. Despite the years that had passed, she recognized the voice of Amelia, the woman who had served her mother for over three decades.

The lift stopped on the seventh floor, and Rosie had hardly stepped out when the door opened. Amelia stood in the frame, smoothing her white apron, smiling. "Miss Rose."

"Amelia." She wanted to hug her, but one didn't do that with the help—on either side of the country. "Is Mother in?"

"Indeed. Breakfasting with Mr. Bennett. And Master Finley—"

"Rosie!"

The voice stopped her in the foyer. Finn strode toward her, looking tall and wide-shouldered, his blue eyes bright, so full of welcome she wanted to crazily burst into tears.

He looked so much like her missing big brother, Jack, it put a fist through her chest. Dark hair, a smile that could turn her to mush.

And her mother, Jinx, had to live with this reminder every day. Rosie had no words as her brother wrapped his arms around her waist. "I can't believe it!"

"Nor I," said Jinx. Her mother stood behind him, a smile at her lips, her hands clasped before her, so much society in her frame she couldn't break free to embrace her prodigal daughter. She'd aged, wisps of white streaked into her hair, a little more padding around her middle. As Finn untangled himself, Jinx came forward and took Rosie's hands, pressing a kiss to her cheek. "I've been worried," she whispered. Then she leaned away. "Was that you who caused such a consternation last night by Times Square? I was just reading about it in the *Chronicle*."

So she knew. Rosie drew in a breath. Nodded. Jinx pressed her hand to her cheek. Met her eyes. They glistened. "I am pleased you visited us."

"Your picture is in the paper!" Finn said. "Are you really in the movies?"

"Just this one, but yes." Rosie tousled his hair just as Bennett emerged from his office. Sometimes, like now, her stepfather could take her breath away with his likeness to her father, same tall build, same green eyes. His blond hair had darkened also, just like her late father's. But Foster never bore kindness in his eyes like Bennett did when he smiled at her.

"You get lovelier every time I see you," he said. Someday he might be anything but awkward with her. Maybe it would help if he knew she'd forgiven him.

"Thank you, Bennett."

"We're having breakfast. I'll instruct Amelia to set you a plate."

"Not much for me, Mother. I—"

"Even movie stars need to eat." Jinx caught her hand, the other reaching for Bennett's. Rosie couldn't ignore the look that passed between them.

A quick smile, something that resembled relief.

She should have written.

But surely Lilly had told them the story, betrayed her sins?

The breakfast room, with its creamy white French furniture, overlooked Central Park—the lake, the boathouse, the lush forests. And beyond that, the homes of Fifth Avenue. She searched for Oliver's but, of course, it had burned that night.

Amelia set a poached egg and a piece of toast in front of her, a small bowl of raspberry jam. "Coffee, ma'am?"

"Please."

"Have you met Rin-Tin-Tin?" Finn pulled up his chair.

"Warner Brother's trained dog?" Rosie laughed. "No."

"Is Dashielle treating you well?" Bennett said. "I see his father occasionally at the men's club. He tells me that Dashielle runs the studio you work for."

She salted her eggs, her stomach growling. "He...yes. We have an agreement." She glanced up, found Bennett's eyes on her. "We're partners."

Bennett raised an eyebrow and she glanced at Finn, who was watching her with a grin.

"I—I have some stock in the studio. And when the studio grows, so will my salary." She didn't know why she suddenly felt as if Bennett might track down Dash, maybe pin him to the wall to extract promises.

It all felt very...fatherly.

"Dashielle is my biggest fan," she said, and tried to mean it.

His room remained untouched this morning. She'd checked. Which meant that he'd stayed with Fletcher, discussing business all night.

Or he'd found another place to catch some shut-eye.

Or...

"I hate to break your heart, but he's got a reputation with the ladies."

She kept her smile. "These eggs are delicious, Mother."

"I have a new chef. From France." Her mother's hand curled around Rosie's wrist, however, stopping her mid-bite. She glanced at her then at the boys. "A moment, gentlemen, with my daughter?"

"C'mon, Finn," Bennett said. "It's time for classes anyway."

Finn got up. "Rosie, can I come out and visit you sometime in Hollywood?"

"Absolutely, Finley. Anytime."

Jinx watched them go, a softness in her eyes, then turned to Rosie. "Are you all right?"

Rosie's throat tightened. "Of course. I mean, you read the paper. They loved me."

Jinx glanced at the *Chronicle* folded beside Bennett's plate. "That is not what I'm referring to."

Oh. Rosie stared at her plate. Bit her lip. Drew in a breath. "I dream about him sometimes. And—and Charlie."

"They call her Coco. I have a picture they sent." She got up, but Rosie grasped her hand.

"I—I can't look at it, Mother. Please."

Jinx sank back into the chair.

"You have to understand…it simply hurts too much to be reminded of everything I lost. It's like Finn."

"I do understand. The older he gets, the more he becomes Jack. The more the ache burns. And yet, Finn is one of my greatest joys." She pressed her hand to Rosie's face, turned it. "As are you, daughter."

Rosie looked away, toward the picture window overlooking Central Park. "I have a different life now. I can't look back. I can't—I have to forget Coco."

Jinx said nothing.

Rosie drew in a breath. "I married Dash." She looked at her mother.

Jinx had drawn in a breath, her face tight.

"It's a business arrangement."

"But you love him?"

"I don't have to. It's just business."

Jinx closed her eyes.

"Dash is good to me. And I love him enough."

Jinx looked at her, shook her head. "Dash is good to Dash. You've always known that. And it's not enough to tolerate each other."

"I'm not going to look for love, Mother. It costs too much. Besides, I had it once. That is enough."

"Is it?"

Rosie nodded, stared at her eggs. "I am going to be a star. I won't need love. In fact, I don't even want it. I'll never replace what I had with Guthrie."

Out of the corner of her eye, she saw her mother watching her, her lips a tight line.

The doorman buzzed, and Rosie heard Amelia's steps across the foyer.

She took Jinx's hand, squeezed. "I promise. This is not your marriage to Foster, Mother. I know what I'm doing."

"So did I, when I married Foster. And he nearly destroyed our lives."

"You were young and naive. I control my own destiny. I will never let a man steal my future from me, trap me into a life I despise." *I won't become you, Mother.*

Amelia appeared at the door. "Ma'am. At your pleasure, Dashielle Parks is requesting to see you and is inquiring after Miss Rosie."

Jinx glanced at Rosie. She nodded.

"Allow him entrance," she said.

Rosie took a sip of coffee. "He must have realized I'd left our suite."

"Didn't he offer to accompany you?"

She couldn't meet her mother's eyes. "He didn't come home last night. In fact—" She closed her eyes. "We haven't yet—well, we are husband and wife in name only."

Jinx's mouth opened. "Rosie—"

"There's my starlet!"

Dash didn't appear exhausted, his tuxedo mussed, a five o'clock shadow. No, he looked rested, shaven, and bright, even as he came over and pressed a kiss to Rosie's cheek.

The man even smelled good. Clean. Exotic.

She tried not to let that curl a fist inside her.

Her mother had risen. "Dash. I suppose congratulations are in order."

"Thank you. I always knew Rosie would be a star."

"I was referring to your marriage into our family."

Rosie glanced up at Dash just in time to see his face redden. His smile fell, and he frowned at Rosie. "Red?"

"She's my mother. She should know."

Jinx knew how to hold a man captive with a look, and Dash couldn't escape as he stood there, hat in hand. "I—we—it's not what you think."

"It sounds like exactly what I think, Dashielle. I hope you're not just using my daughter to further your position."

Rosie stood. "Mother—"

"Shh. I know this isn't any of my business, so I'll say only this. You hurt my daughter, Dashielle Parks, and you'll live to regret it."

Rosie put a hand on his arm. But she didn't temper her mother's words.

"Yes, ma'am," Dash said, and Rosie almost felt sorry for him. Almost.

"I'm afraid we have a train to catch," he said softly, maybe to Jinx, maybe to Rosie. He glanced at Rosie. "Rosie has to get back for the West Coast premiere. Her public awaits." He winked at her. "Our car is waiting downstairs."

Oh. So soon.

She turned to her mother just as Jinx caught her in an embrace. Rosie ducked her head and held on, breathing in her mother's powdery scent. The woman still wore a corset, still bathed in rosewater.

"If you ever need anything, we're right here," Jinx said softly and then released her.

Her mother offered her hand to Dashielle, who kissed it then nearly fled the apartment.

He turned away from Rosie when she climbed into the limousine.

"We're leaving?"

"I had the valet pack your cases. I'm sorry—I thought I told you we'd have to leave in the morning."

The streets were already filled with horses and carriages, trucks, and cars logjamming through the city. "Hurry. The train won't wait," Dash barked.

Now he sounded tired.

"What's wrong, Dash?"

He took off his hat, ran his hand along the brim. Barely looked at her.

"It's nothing. Just studio business." But the smile he gave her didn't touch his eyes.

"I'm part of the studio business," she said.

"You *are* the studio business, sweetheart," he said.

Her stomach began to churn again. She should have eaten more, perhaps. "Dash, don't you dare loan me out. We have an agreement. I work for Palace Studios. Not MGM, not Warner Brothers. I swear, if you make me work for Jack Jr.—"

30

He took her hand, squeezed. "Shh, darling. I haven't auctioned you off. You're still the property of Palace Studios."

Property. But he didn't mean it like that. Just studio jargon. Still, his grip stayed on her hand as they drove through the congested streets of New York.

They pulled up to Grand Central Station, and the driver let them out. "Are you sure the valets packed all my things?" Rosie watched as the driver unloaded Dash's traveling case.

"I told them to get it all, even the kitchen sink." Dash grabbed her elbow and hustled her through the doors, and she couldn't help but shoot a glance at the waiting area.

Five years ago, right there, she'd waited for the man she loved to show up and save her life.

Dash hustled her through the ticket area and flashed his tickets to the gate attendant. The train had already pulled up, and Dash led her to the end, the cars reserved for the studio.

He helped her up and followed her into a private car, shut the door behind him. The red velvet, fringed shades over the window shuttered the light, casting shadows over the green brocade chairs, the desk, the canopied bed.

Dash sank down onto the bed and cradled his head in his hands.

"Dash, you're scaring me."

He sighed. Then, suddenly, "I'm sorry, Red. I'm so sorry."

Sorry? For what? It was the defeat in his voice that made her sink to her knees before him. That made her reach for his face, lift it in her hands. "What is it, Dash?"

His eyes met hers, dark and husky, a hint of danger in them, not unlike Grayson's so many times on screen. He caught her hands, drew them from his face. "I should have come back with you last night,

Red." He cupped her chin. "I'm sorry," he said softly, almost with a catch. Then he kissed her. It started sweetly, as if he might be afraid, but in a moment it changed. It wasn't a movie kiss, nothing chaste or staged about it. He had a darkness in his touch, something almost desperate as he curled his hand around her neck, pulled her closer.

As if he meant everything he put into the kiss.

Sorry. She hung on to that word and believed it as she kissed him back.

He pulled her up, onto his lap, and then turned her onto the bed, finally lifting his head as the train lurched, starting its movement west. "I—we—" He licked his lips, swallowed, as if not sure how to ask. But she saw it in his eyes, the way his gaze raked over her, as if seeing what he had in his arms for the first time.

And it filled her up, right to the brim. "Dash." She flattened her hand to his chest then curled it around his tie, pulling him closer, whispering into his ear. "Make me your star."

Chapter 2

"It's show business, Roxy, nothing more. If the studio wants it, the studio gets it."

Clara Bow lay in a reclining chair as Daisy, her hairdresser, penciled in her perfectly arched brows.

Outside on Sunset Boulevard, the August breeze tickled the towering palm trees. Sunlight draped like a curtain down the street, over the red-and-black awnings of the Hampton boutiques, the white-washed Westside Market and Mermaid Club Café, and through the picket fence that cordoned the parking lot of the Café Lamaze. Shiny Rolls Royces caught the gleam as they motored by, others parked at the curb, probably to attend services at Blessed Sacrament Church. Maybe someday she'd have a shiny white convertible Rolls Royce to drive to her Sunday appointments at Jim's Beauty Salon.

"The important thing to remember in this business is that it's fickle. And through it all, you gotta keep ahold of your heart, or Hollywood will break it to pieces."

Rosie glanced at the silent-film star, her dark locks burned and curled to perfection, her face powdered, her lips in a perfect heart-shaped contour. She wore a dressing gown and had toted her own hairdresser with her for today's treatment at Jim's, in preparation for tonight's party at the Coconut Grove.

A party Dash insisted they attend. Rosie could still hear his voice echo through the tiled hallways of their bungalow on Palm Drive. *"You're going to be there. End of discussion."*

"I just don't understand why tonight's shindig at the Grove is so important."

She could feel the peroxide bleeding into her scalp. Please don't let her walk away with burns again. Jim had layered cotton around her face to keep the drips from her skin, but last time she'd exited the parlor out the back, hidden under sunglasses and a headscarf to conceal the red chemical splotches.

It took her two days to escape the headache.

Jim leaned her back to attack her brows. Thankfully they hadn't shaved them completely off. Yet.

But any day Fletcher might decide to upgrade her regimen. He already had her on cottage cheese and celery. Just for once, she'd like to eat a full meal.

"It's Louis Mayer's birthday party. MGM expects Hollywood to pay their respects," Clara said.

"It just seems like we could stay home one night. We've been out every night since the West Coast premiere. I'm exhausted."

Clara laughed, and Daisy chided her. "Shh. You're making a mess of this."

Rosie liked Clara. Her New York accent made her seem real, not at all like the larger-than-life It Girl portrayed on the silent screen.

And no one had made Clara a star. She, like Rosie, headed to Hollywood with a dream, armed with nothing but determination, and acting chops.

No one played an on-screen flapper like Clara. The public loved her—hopefully all the way into her next movie, her first "talkie."

"Just remember, they're all snobs, Rox. You just have to play their game, and then you'll get what you want," Clara said as Daisy began to work on her lips. "And you know the line, darlin'." She raised her voice into a singsong. 'The show must go on.'"

Daisy flipped the chair upright and went to work teasing her hair. "And the studio is just getting started. I saw your name on the billboard coming into town. *Star for a Day* is a hit."

Maybe. The West Coast premiere doubled the size of the New York opening, and she'd charmed the crowd at home by talking into the radio mic of KFWD radio, while Dash stood on the sidelines, grinning at his creation. She'd worn the pearls, a purple dress, and long, white gloves under a chiffon wrap.

He'd sat with Irene in the darkened room of Grauman's Chinese Theater. Next to her, Grayson wrapped his arm around the redhead, a girl named Sally O'Neil.

And after the premiere, they'd gone to a party at Fletcher's estate. Dash made the rounds with Irving Thalberg and Jack Warner, talking shop. Rosie took the limousine home alone.

Rosie ground her jaw tight, her eyes closing against the pain as Jim tweaked out the wayward brow stubble since her last appointment. Her eyes watered.

"You thought the publicity machine was rolling before the show. Just wait until they have you attending everything from beauty pageants to the Horned Toad Derby at the Ambassador Hotel," Clara said. "All so that the public won't forget you before you start shooting another movie. And then the studio will leak stills of the new movie until the next publicity run. Forget about your life being yours, sweetie. The best you can do is keep smiling, looking beautiful, and keep a tight hold on your heart. They can't take that from you."

Rosie winced as Jim finished plucking and grabbed a pencil. A thin man with graying hair and round spectacles, he seemed like a professor rather than an artist as he squinted, applying her paint. She always had the sense that he might suddenly lecture her on the invasion of Bonaparte or ask her to recite her sums.

"You know, Roxy, it could be that Dashielle wants you there because of Rooney Sherwood."

"Who?"

"The billionaire from Texas. Came to Hollywood to be a big producer. I hear he's going to be there tonight. He's still making that movie about the war heroes, *Angel's Fury*," Clara said. "They say he's spent a couple million dollars already. He built a huge sound stage inside the lot at Paramount and hired a new screenwriter to add in dialogue. He shot the whole thing as a silent movie, and now he wants to make it a talkie. Can you believe it?"

"Why would Dash want me to meet him?"

She glanced at Rosie and caught her eye. "They say he's looking for a new leading lady."

"For his film—or his life?"

Clara shrugged. "Maybe both. He's cute, really. Brown eyes, a little danger in them. I never see him without a dame."

Rosie ached to spit it out, right then. *I'm married to Dashielle Parks. Really married.* But it seemed he'd forgotten that over the past two weeks since the premiere. He'd slept at the studio office more often than not.

She hated that she spent so many evenings waiting for a knock at her door. She shouldn't care. Wouldn't. After all, he'd never really made her promises.

In fact, on the day she married him, she told him not to expect her to love him. He promised the same thing back.

Clearly, he'd meant that vow.

Still. "I'm not looking for a date."

Jim raised her chair and, indeed, her brows looked cleaner, more pronounced.

"Of course not, silly. Dash may be looking to loan you out. They make a bundle and don't give you a dime," Clara said as Daisy starched her hair. Not a curl out of place. She puckered into the mirror, angled her head to look at the 'do. Nodded. "And if Rooney is looking to make a talkie, he might be trolling for cheap actresses with star potential."

"They can't loan me out—"

"Of course they can, Roxy. This is show business and the studio owns you. They can do anything they want."

"But Dash said he wouldn't loan me out without my say…." She didn't want to work for Rooney, or worse, someone like Jack Junior of Warner Brothers. Besides, she wasn't just another cheap blond bimbo from Central Casting. She was the star of Palace Studios.

So what that she only made a hundred and fifty dollars a week? She was part owner of a studio. On paper, at least.

"He might have said it, but he certainly didn't mean it." Clara slipped off the chair. "Listen, sweetheart. It's a game. And you gotta play by their rules. But it doesn't mean you can't make your own destiny." She winked. "You're an actress, aren't you? If you want the world to love you, you gotta give them what they want. Doesn't mean you gotta love them back." She tied a scarf over her hair. "If Dash wants to loan you out, then make something of it. Find yourself a good leading man, at the very least. It'll help you forget about Dashielle Parks."

Rosie shot a look at her, and Clara smiled. "It's plain as the gorgeous nose on your face that you're smitten with him. You're just a commodity to Dashielle Parks. Don't forget that. If you give him your heart, he'll own you."

She slid on her sunglasses. "See you at the Grove."

* * * * *

"Mr. Parks said he'd meet you at the Ambassador Hotel."

Rosie stared in the mirror, at the perfection Jim had created. Arched brows, sculpted ruby-painted lips, hair the color of the moon. All of it set against the siren red satin dress that Dash had left hanging in her room. Her costume for their show tonight.

Like a beacon in the middle of the nightclub for someone like Rooney Sherwood to see.

Her housekeeper and lady's maid, Louise, a woman in her late forties who reminded Rosie of her mother, stood behind her, fastening the pearls around her neck. She touched them, turned, and watched them dangle down her back.

"You're beautiful, ma'am."

She turned, smiled at Louise. "Thank you."

"Your car is waiting." Louise handed her a white cape, draping it over her shoulders. Rosie fastened it at the neck and let it drag behind her out of her dressing room.

She loved this house, the long hallway between her and Dash's room, the two-story living room that overlooked the back patio, the lush green lawn that framed the pool then rolled down to a small pond that the studio had stocked with swans for a photo shoot and left behind. The house was unassuming from the street, a two-story Tudor with cypress trees in the front yard.

The studio Rolls waited for her outside, and she gathered her dress, dragging her cloak on the stone steps.

She had a good mind not to go at all.

But if Dash thought he could simply auction her off—or sell her to Rooney Sherwood…

She conjured up too many conversations in her head for her own good as she rode to the Ambassador Hotel.

Her driver parked at the entrance, helped her out. She heard the band even as she walked under the long awning toward the nightclub and then inside, down the corridor, past the shops, now closed for the evening.

Two palm trees loomed over the door, a footman in white gloves holding it open for her.

The place buzzed with conversation, a tropical paradise with arching palm trees, gold-painted ornate columns, and a dance floor surrounded by two hundred round, white-clothed tables, all out in the open for the magazines to photograph the stars with their studio bosses or in the arms of a potential costar. The smell of cigarette smoke hung in the air.

She stood at the entrance, watching the white-gloved waiters, the cigarette girls, the dancers on the floor. And she spotted familiar faces, the ones she'd read about in *Photoplay*: Louise Brooks, Lina Basquette, Charlie Chaplin, Douglas Fairbanks, Lionel Barrymore, Mary Pickford. She scanned the room and recognized some newcomers sitting with their studios—Betty Grable, Paul Muni.

Clara spotted her and waved from her table, where she sat with Dorothy Arzner, a director from Paramount. Trust Clara to come without a man on her arm.

Rosie lifted her hand in a quiet wave.

"There she is. Roxy Price." Dash was coming up the stairs, a smile on his face, as if he hadn't seen her in years and had waited breathlessly for this moment.

"Why didn't you wait for me?" she asked under her breath, smiling as she let him kiss her on the cheek.

"I had business. Shh, you're here now." He reached for her cape, helped her remove it, and handed it to the hostess. "Please bring me the tag." Then he took her arm, wove it into his, and led her down the stairs. "I have a table for us near the floor."

On the front stage, Gus Arnheim and his Ambassadors played the Tiger Rag. A handful of dancers had the floor, but soon it would be too full to do anything but sway.

She smiled at a few faces she remembered from the Palace lot and stopped to kiss Myrna Loy, who'd helped her with a few dance steps while shooting *Star for a Day*.

Dash had a firm grip on her arm, though, and directed her to their table.

Fletcher Harris stood up to greet her, leaving his slimy kiss on her cheek. She extended a hand to Irene—of course the secretary would be here. Irene smiled, but it didn't reach her eyes. The young woman looked like she'd gained weight, however, and kept her jacket around her shoulders.

"You look lovely tonight," Fletcher said as Dash pulled out her chair.

"Thank you."

"I love your pearls," Irene said.

Rosie touched her neck. "Dash gave them to me."

Irene flicked her gaze to Dash and smiled.

"He's very generous with the studio's money," Fletcher said. "But we thought you deserved it after your performance in *Star for a Day*.

They're saying that it might be nominated for best picture at this year's Academy dinner."

A waiter came by and handed her a menu.

"She'll have cantaloupe," Dash said and handed back the menu. "And a piece of chicken."

"Dash, I can order for myself."

He smiled at her as he might a child. The band switched to a waltz.

"Would you like to dance?"

She drew in a breath. "Absolutely."

He helped her up, and she didn't glance back as she headed toward the dance floor. He caught her hand and swung her into his arms.

"'The studio thought you deserved it?'" She hissed into his ear, smiling for their audience, setting time to his lead.

"Red, don't be sore. It was my idea."

"I thought they were from you."

He twirled her around, moved her through the crowd. "They were."

"And Fletcher, it appears."

"Mostly me, Red."

She ran her hand up around his neck, hating that he smelled good, clean, alluring. And tonight he wore a tuxedo, a black bow tie. Smart. "We need to talk, Dash. I talked with Clara today, and she said you were thinking of loaning me out—"

"Don't believe anything that Clara Bow has to say. She's a troublemaker, at best. She has no manners, and she's on her way out of Hollywood."

"But is it true?"

He twirled her out, back in again, then dipped her slowly. She tilted her head back, and a flash popped.

Dash was smiling as he brought her back to her feet. "C'mon, I want you to meet someone."

He took her hand and moved her through the dance floor then abruptly swung her again into his arms.

"I thought—"

"Just dance." He held her close, turning her in a soft sway as a singer got up, crooned out a romantic jazz tune.

"What are we doing here, Dash?"

"Is this the girl, Dash?"

The voice came from behind her. But instead of releasing her, Dash turned them, kept dancing. The man had his hands in his pockets, was considering them with a smile, something of mischief in his expression. He had brown eyes that lingered on her, dark blond hair slicked back, a dandy tuxedo that belied his youthful face. She'd put him as younger than her, but he gave a tiny flicker of his brow that suggested he liked what he saw.

"Can I cut in?"

Rosie tightened her grip on Dash, and he seemed to consider it for a moment.

But no, this was the game, and she knew it the moment he released her. "Roxy, I'd like you to meet Rooney Sherwood."

Rooney was about her height, and she could look him in the face, with her heels. She narrowed her eyes at Dash one moment before she lost in him the crowd.

And then Rooney had his arms around her.

Yes, he was young. Nothing of the smooth moves Dash had honed, but maybe she could like him a little for that.

"Nice to meet you, Rooney."

"You too, doll. Dash says you're looking for a new part."

She was going to murder him with her bare hands. "What's this, an audition?"

He smirked. "I like you already."

She looked away, but he twirled her deeper into the floor, the mass of people. "I suppose Dash told you I am making a movie?"

"Are you now? How novel. In Hollywood even."

He smirked. "Yeah. And I have to reshoot the entire dang thing. Most epic war movie ever made and not a pip of sound. Who knew the talkies would be so popular?"

She leaned back from him, met his eyes. "You're saying it's already shot?"

"Almost all of it. We'll keep the aerial sequences, maybe add some new ones, but yes, we have to start over, with a star who can speak English." He smiled and it contained such a boyish sheepishness, she couldn't help but laugh.

He reminded her, in a way, of Jack, the way he stirred up with an idea, let it catch fire. He could catch her on fire too.

"Where are you shooting this epic, Mr. Sherwood?"

"I have a set built at the Paramount lot, but we have to go on location for the runway scenes. I have a fleet of airplanes parked up in Oakland."

"A fleet."

"Oh honey, you have no idea."

He turned her again and tried something fancy, twirling her fast, moving her with her back to him. He put his hands on her waist, moved with her. "Think you might be willing to do a screen test for it?"

From this vantage point, she could see Dash, sitting at the table, his eyes on her. Irene had leaned forward, was talking in his ear, but he never took his gaze off Rosie, so much hunger in it, she missed a step.

"Who's in it?" she said over her shoulder.

"Just a couple of chaps. You might know one, Grayson Clarke?" He twirled her back around, and she caught his grin.

"Grayson?"

"He dies, sadly, but there's a regular tear-jerker love scene on the runway before he goes off to war."

"I can't wait."

"And another fella, a man named Lyle Hall. He's on loan from Paramount."

"You're taking out lots of scripts, it seems."

He turned her out, did a little step, twirled her back in. "I don't care what it costs. I need a bombshell, sweetie, someone who can add sparkle to our show." He pulled her close, whispered in her ear. "I saw you in *Star for a Day*. I'll make you a star for longer than a day."

She pushed away from him, smiling. "Oh, you're smooth, Mr. Sherwood. But I'm not a bombshell. I'm an actress."

He wore a gleam in his eyes. "Honey, with those legs, that hair, you're so much bombshell a man might have to take shelter."

She kept her smile, but heat burned her cheeks. Oh. Well. "But I can act too."

"Of course you can." His eyes roamed her face.

She moved her mouth close to his ear. "You're a lot older on the dance floor than you look. Can I ask, how old are you?"

He put his hand at the small of her back. "Twenty-four."

Twenty-four going on twelve. She moved away, and his hand rose up her back. Still, he had enthusiasm; she'd give him that. "You have a lot of ambition for a man of twenty-four."

Something flickered in his eyes, a flash of sadness. "Life's short. Can't waste any of it."

The song ended, and she stepped away, clapping. He slid his hand down her arm, caught her hand. "Come, have dinner with me, and we'll talk."

"I don't know."

"Please?"

It was the way he said it, enough of a boy in his voice, that swayed her. So much like Jack she felt as if she were seeing her lost brother in his eyes, his smile.

Maybe Jack had been a scamp with the ladies too.

She let him pull her off the dance floor toward a large, round table. Grayson looked up from where he was huddled in conversation with a brunette and smiled. "Roxy!"

He stood, and she let him kiss her.

More flashbulbs, but she ignored them.

Dash's gaze burned her, and she sent him a scowl.

Across the table, two men in tuxedos turned their attention to Rooney.

"Rosie, I'd like you to meet my dialogue director, Luis Fishe." Fishe rose and extended his hand. He had the good looks of an Englishman, white hair, dark eyes that considered her with a flick of his gaze. "Miss Price," he said.

Clearly, this meeting wasn't a surprise to him.

And then her gaze settled on the other man.

And for a second, it jarred her, seeing him here, dark hair slicked back, in a tuxedo, wearing an expression she couldn't place. Something of a frown, she might even call it disapproval. "Rafe."

"Hello, Roxy," Rafe said. "Good to see you."

Rooney looked at her. "So you've met my consultant."

His consultant. She looked at Rafe, then Luis, and back to Rooney.

And then across the short distance to Dash, who'd risen from his chair, his expression stricken.

Because she got it then. The subject of the all-night meeting in New York City. Dash's heartfelt apology.

Even the way he'd held her on the train, as if trying to make up for his betrayal.

"Oh, I see how it is. This isn't a birthday party. It's a horse auction."

She glanced at Dash. He was making his way toward them, and she shook her head just a moment before pasting on a smile. "Well, boys, how does it go? Do you want to examine my teeth perhaps? See how I trot? Check my hooves for rot?"

"Miss Price, I'm not sure I understand—" Rooney glanced at Grayson.

"Oh, please, Mr. Sherwood. You're not quite that smooth." She leaned down. "And Grayson, I'm surprised at you. Although, maybe I should take it as a compliment you missed me so much."

His smile dimmed. "It wasn't my idea."

"Should have been. You might have gotten a commission." She stood up, looked at Dash, who had reached the table, fear in his eyes. "What is a bombshell blond going for these days, Dash?"

"Roxy, please."

She smiled. "Fear not, Dashielle. You chose well. I come from good society stock, even if you did turn me into a floozy." She leaned close to him, spoke in his ear. "But remember, I'm my mother's daughter. I have a long, very specific memory."

She leaned away and straightened his bow tie. "I'll leave you men to figure out my future." She patted his cheek. "I'll be home, packing. What's the temperature in Oakland these days?"

"About seventy-five," Rooney said and sat down, pulling out a cigarette. He met her eyes as he lit it, nothing of humor in them.

"How'd I do, Mr. Sherwood? Enough drama, enough sass for you?"

He drew in on the cigarette, something of a game in his eyes. "I think you're exactly what we need."

She turned back to Dash. "See, Dash? I have this all under control. See you at the races, boys."

She floated past them, past Fletcher, Irene, and even Clara, who met her eyes and winked.

As she gathered her cape, wrapping it over her shoulders, she turned, looked at Dash, puckered, and threw him a kiss.

And the lightbulbs flashed.

* * * * *

It wasn't that she didn't want the part, although who wanted to be in the middle of a war movie, the only woman, ogled by a company of men?

Or that Grayson and she didn't have on-screen chemistry destined to make them stars all over again.

Or that she didn't want to work on location. She wasn't some sort of princess, unwilling to do the job.

It simply galled her that Dash had sold her like chattel.

"You're just a commodity to Dashielle Parks. Don't forget that. If you give him your heart, he'll own you."

Clara's words ticked around in her head as she dangled her feet in the swimming pool, the water refreshing to her ankles. She wasn't sure why they'd purchased a house with a pool. She didn't know how to swim. Still, the surface sparkled brilliant diamonds under the blue-skied day and the sun baked her shoulders, seeping into her skin after a sleepless night.

She'd waited up too long, just in case Dash returned.

Just in case he might be sorry.

She flung a hand over her eyes, blotting out the sun, and let her memories balm her.

Too easily Guthrie walked in, even two years after saying good-bye. She never pictured him on the floor of her uncle's home, but always in his baseball uniform, usually the White Sox, because she was happiest in Chicago. She could see him coming off the field, glove in hand, searching for her under the brim of his hat. He'd take it off, shake off the dust, his blond hair showing fire in the sun. And when he found her, the look in his brown eyes could steal her breath from her chest. *"Hey, Red."* He always had a strength about him, a fierceness, the kind a fighter carried around inside. But he directed all that energy at the game—and at loving her.

She ran her hand over her stomach, still remembering the feel of the child inside her, sometimes how Guthrie would loop his arm over her belly at night, kiss her neck. *"We'll call him Charlie."*

"And if it's a girl?"

"Charlie."

She ran her hand over her eyes.

Silly. So long ago, she should be over it by now.

I miss you, Guthrie.

Sometimes, if she listened hard, she could hear him answer her. "*I miss you too. And Charlie. I miss Charlie.*"

He had a right to miss their daughter. She, however, didn't. She wished she had the courage to ask Lilly to stop sending her pictures.

Or writing her stories of how Coco had her first tooth or rode on a horse with Truman, her new daddy. Or how she could speak.

Because, although Lilly didn't write it, Rosie only had to guess who Coco might be calling Momma. Still, despite the reminders of her loss, despite her mistakes, she couldn't stop herself from cherishing every mention of her daughter.

She'd done the right thing; this wasn't the right life for her daughter. But she couldn't help but wish...

No. Wishes were for children and naïve showgirls. She was neither anymore. Besides, Coco had a life—a good life—with a mother and a father. She couldn't destroy that.

Rosie sat up and wiped her eyes again, reached for her sunglasses.

Kicked her feet through the water, dislodging the memories from the silence. See, maybe working would do her some good, keep her too busy to think, to remember.

She got up, grabbed a robe, wrapped it around her, and went over to the lounge chair where the script lay open. A messenger appeared this morning with the package, along with a bouquet of orchids.

The boy director/millionaire was learning fast.

She'd spent the morning seated in her chaise lounge reading the cumbersome tome. The script would have to be cut in half before it might be suitable to show in a theater without some sort of picnic lunch. Still, the story of a woman caught between two heroes, both of them winning her heart only to lose their lives had made her cry.

Whoever wrote it knew about loss.

She picked it up and reached for her iced tea.

"Is it a good script?"

She looked up. Dash stood at the edge of the portico, mostly in shadow, wearing a linen suit, a straw boater.

"What do you care?"

"I care." He stepped out into the sun and pulled a bouquet of white roses from behind his back.

She shook her head. "Pitiful. Put them next to Rooney's offering." She gestured to the orchids wilting in the heat on the table under the portico roof.

He glanced at them then came over to sit on the lounge chair opposite her. He put the roses on the table beside her. "Don't be angry."

She sighed. "It's not a terrible script. Quite moving, in fact. And apparently, all I have to do is show up and sob occasionally. In between kissing all the boys."

"It's a role."

"I didn't know I was desperate."

"The studio is desperate."

The way he said it caught her breath. He was serious—she saw it in the way his eyes darkened, and met hers. "I didn't want to tell you, but *Star for a Day* drained all our resources. We need cash flow to make even our current run of movies. And frankly, darling, you're it. I know it feels like I sold you, but…Rooney paid top dollar for you."

"Isn't that nice—"

"It is! Don't forget your name is on this partnership, and if Palace Studios goes down, so do you."

That stopped her. She sat up, slid her feet into her sandals. "If it's a partnership, then I should have known about Rooney. I should have known we needed money."

He considered her a long moment then swallowed and looked away. She pulled the robe around herself, feeling suddenly naked.

"It's not a partnership, is it, Dash? Not really. You wanted a cheap actress, and you got it in me. Yeah, my name's on a few shares, but that's it. You're not really interested in letting me in on the studio business. Unless, of course, it brings in the bucks you need."

"You don't know anything about making movies, Red."

"And you're brilliant. You came out here with your daddy's money hoping you could become a big studio mogul. Please don't tell me it was so you could turn your casting couch into a—" She gritted her teeth, looked away from him. "This marriage is a joke, isn't it?"

He drew in a breath. Didn't answer her.

"What was—" She put her hand to her mouth. Closed her eyes. "What was the train?"

He ran his finger and thumb into his eyes, hung his head. "I'm sorry about that too."

Mm-hmm. "Did you ever care about me, Dash?"

"You know I did. I do. I'm just not cut out for marriage. Not the kind you want."

"Could be you're reading too much into me, Dash. I never said I loved you. In fact, if I recall, we pledged something about *not* loving each other."

He looked up, his jaw tight.

"But please, do you think you could keep from humiliating me?"

"No one knows we're married."

"And maybe we shouldn't be."

"Like that won't make the papers? We're in this now, Red. And it's gotta stay that way. For both of us, whether we like it or not."

His last words stung. "What have I done to you, Dash, to make you not like it? Like me?"

His mouth opened. "Red—"

"Forget it." She moved to stalk past him. "You know. This movie is a godsend after all. I can't wait to go to Oakland. I may buy a house there and never come back."

He reached for her, caught her arm. She yanked it away, nearly tripping into the pool's glistening deep end. "Don't touch me."

"Red, we're friends. Business partners. We've always known what we wanted from each other. It's never been about love."

Her chest burned, as if his words were daggers. She rounded on him, her voice lethal. "I didn't need you to love me, Dash. But frankly, occasionally, I do need you to hold me—and mean it."

He swallowed, his eyes hard in hers. "I meant it."

"Not enough," she said. "You didn't mean it enough."

He stared at her. "What do you want from me, Rosie? What do you want?" He stood there his dark hair gleaming, slick and smart and clean, his eyes sharp, the sunlight against his back so bright it washed tears into her eyes.

"Guthrie," she said quietly. "I want the life I should have had."

Then she turned, and before she could break, stalked into the house.

Chapter 3

She looked like a movie star now.

Rosie figured that she probably had grime in her ears. Shooting on location on a lonely strip of airfield in Oakland, surrounded by potato patches, bean fields, and chicken farms, only the slightest fragrance of the ocean to temper the heat of the day. California took on new misery under the August heat. Especially with slave master Rooney Sherwood at the helm of the movie, his eyes shielded with sunglasses, zinc oxide on his nose to keep it from peeling yet again, as he stared heavenward at his fleet of actors.

Stuntmen. Aviators. She didn't know what to call the crew of men who pirouetted through the sky in the World War I biplane replicas he'd built for his multimillion-dollar epic—or fiasco, depending on the one you talked to.

Already, Rooney had killed one stuntman. She'd heard the story shortly after arriving on set, of how he'd set up a plane to crash but forgot to tell the mechanic, who'd been stuck in the fuselage creating fake smoke. The poor mechanic went down with the plane.

Rooney nearly died himself just a few days ago while trying out a new kind of airplane, a prop plane that he took out as the sun sank behind the far horizon, beyond the sunbaked hills. She'd stood beside one of the many nameless crewmen and saw her salary go up in smoke.

Rooney had the luck of a cat, walking away from the wreckage. This time.

He'd just wanted to know if they'd gotten it on film.

After two weeks of shooting, she wanted to turn around and go home, where she'd strangle Dash for loaning her out to a madman.

"Your lemonade, Miss Price?"

The male assistant handed her a sweaty glass of lemonade as she sat in the canvas chair, holding an umbrella. What she wouldn't give for a palm tree. A beach. A role that saw her as more than just a swell face on screen.

The assistant stood to watch the spectacle with his hand braced over his eyes. "Is that him?"

"Who?" she asked. She likely had a pile of scripts waiting for her. And certainly *Photoplay* had called.

However, it seemed they didn't lack for material from Palace Studios. The current issue lay on her lap.

"It's Rooney's consultant. He's a real war hero. He shot down Germans over Paris. He's supposed to arrive today."

Perfect. And she thought she'd escaped Rafe Horne.

She had no doubt Rooney would ask her to kiss him too. It seemed she'd kissed every sap going up to "die in battle."

"Do you need anything else, miss?" the assistant asked. Jerry, she thought his name might be, an extra turned into lackey, still hanging around in the wild hope he might be needed to sacrifice his life on screen. She placed him at about nineteen. Handsome, but not so much he'd be noticed by the camera.

"Thank you. No."

She took a sip of the lemonade. Already warm, the ice cubes nearly dissolved. She set it on the table and picked up the magazine. Her eyes watered, but they did every night they shot under the klieg lights. The carbon powder and ultraviolet burned her eyes. At least her headache had subsided. She'd sat up most of the night with a wet cloth over her eyes, rubbing her temples.

Not that Dash cared. She held up the photo taken of him at the Coconut Grove and tried to make out the woman with whom he might be dancing. The caption didn't list the woman's name.

Probably she didn't have a name. Just another face from the casting line.

Still. Rosie ran her thumb down the profile of his face. She knew that smile—had it shine on her once upon a time.

Her throat burned.

"Miss Price!"

She sighed and turned at the voice. Another assistant, this time with pages. He thrust them at her. "Mr. Sherwood wants to retake the runway scene tonight. He's rewritten it."

"Of course he has," she said. She took the pages, scanned them. "Oh good, another kiss with Grayson."

The assistant grinned at her. Rosie sank into the chair, reading through the lines, the words of Mr. Fishe going through her head. *"It's a love scene, be seductive."*

She closed her eyes. She couldn't even figure out how to do that with her own husband. Not unless they were trapped in a train car for three days.

Occasionally, I just need you to hold me—and mean it.

She just wanted to erase the memory of their trip home. And their fight.

"What do you want from me, Rosie?"

She hadn't meant her answer. Or, maybe she had. But really, she couldn't go backward. She had to take hold of what she still had.

Her career. Her public.

Her name. Bombshell Roxy Price.

As if to confirm everything he'd said, Dash hadn't even come from the studio to see her the last time she went home. Three nights he slept at his office.

Not that he hadn't called. Apologized. Sent her a bouquet of orchids.

But Dash was right. Their partnership had never been about love, and if she wanted to keep her career, she had to figure out how to play the sexy bombshell Rooney wanted.

She lifted the lemonade and pressed it to her forehead. She had no idea how to be seductive.

"Ah, so you're the beautiful oasis in this barren landscape. I knew I landed in the right place."

She turned and shaded her eyes at the voice and found it in a man dressed in khakis, a short-sleeved shirt. A bomber jacket hung over his shoulder from his hooked finger. He wore an aviator cap and sunglasses.

She nearly didn't recognize Rafe Horne. Not until he smiled.

It moved something forbidden inside her, despite her fury. "Come to check on your spoils of war?"

"Still pouting, I see?"

"Why are you bothering me, Mr. Horne?"

He pulled off his glasses. Yes, those blue eyes still had the power to unsettle her. She turned away.

"I came to make peace. I don't know what happened between you and Dashielle Parks, but it sort of felt like I was in the middle of a dog-fight without any ammo."

"Funny. It was nothing. A miscommunication."

"Rooney says you're fabulous."

"If he thinks that, maybe he'll stop shooting scenes over and over."

"He's just a perfectionist. Wants to get it right."

"He's young and idealistic."

Rafe smiled. "He is that."

She considered him a moment then took her feet off the canvas chair opposite her. "What kind of consultant are you?"

"I'm working with the stunt pilots. I flew a Sopwith Camel during the war, and I'm going to be showing the stunt pilots a few tricks."

"You're full of surprises."

"I was eighteen, and it seemed the most romantic thing to do." He sat in the canvas chair. "I've never been so terrified in my life."

She didn't know what to do with that kind of honesty. Nor his disarming smile. Nor the way he took off his hat and let the air riffle through his hair. He had tanned forearms and strong hands, yet he held his hat as if he might be shy and needing something to hold on to.

She glanced at Rooney across the dusty tarmac, huddling with a group of garbed pilots. "It seems so long ago, doesn't it? The war? I was in Paris in 1923, and I remember so many soldiers wandering the streets, still shell-shocked. Seems strange to make a movie of it."

"Maybe people need to remember so it doesn't happen again."

She stared at him. Nodded. "Maybe."

A biplane taxied by them and lifted into the air. She watched it go. "Are you studying your lines?"

She looked at the pages. "It's a love scene. I don't do those very well."

"I'm sure you're lying."

Oh. She sent him a coy smile, however. "Grayson hasn't complained. Even if Rooney has."

"Maybe you need some help?" Rafe winked at her.

She probably should be offended, but it only stirred something inside her. Still, her words faltered and came out more real than she intended. "I—I don't think that's a good idea, Mr. Horne."

He chuckled. "Call me Rafe. And let me see these."

She handed him the pages. He read them over, shook his head. "No wonder the scene feels stilted. These lines sound like they've been written by a man."

"They were. Rooney Sherwood, as a matter of fact," she said. She put her hand to her chest, mimicked the lines. "Oh, please don't go, Joe. I don't know how I'll live without you." She shook her head. "Even if she meant it, a woman wouldn't say that to a man going to war, fighting for her country."

"What would she say?"

She shrugged, but he didn't fill in the silence, offer her suggestions. He just sat back and looked at her, as if studying her.

"I—I had someone who left for war. My brother, Jack. I watched him pack, and, yes, I begged him not to go. I was young and scared. And he was angry. But—but that was different."

Rafe still had his gaze on her, the tease gone from his eyes.

"He wasn't going off to war so much as he was running away. I—I think maybe a wife would say something different."

"I heard a dialogue coach say once that everyone brings a piece of themselves to the stage. Find that piece. And you'll be able to play this scene. What would *you* say?"

She closed her eyes and saw Guthrie, beaten, bloody, sprawled on her uncle's foyer, searching her eyes. "I'd say, Please stay alive. Please come back to me. I refuse to breathe until I have you in my arms again."

She heard her words, felt them run through her, grab ahold of her bones. Yes. Her voice softened. "If I had to, I'd give my last breath to you to make sure you come home."

She opened her eyes.

Rafe wore a strange expression, his forehead drawn into a frown. He said nothing for a long time then finally licked his lip and sighed. "Yes, that works. If I were your husband, I'd make sure you never forgot me."

He handed the pages back to her. Stood. Looked away from her. "Good to see you again, Roxy."

Rosie. But she held the name in as he walked away.

No, not Rosie. Roxy. Roxy Price, actress. "You too, Mr. Horne."

* * * * *

"He's going to die."

She stood with the crowd of extras, her hand cupped over her eyes as she watched Rafe's plane stall and arrow toward the ground.

"No, he's not." Rooney stood with his hands on his hips, still looking every bit the twenty-four-year-old millionaire at the helm of a project too big for him. He wore director's pants, a white shirt rolled up at the elbows, argyle socks, and he held a megaphone in his hand.

All the better to shout your name in humiliation, dearie.

Rooney was brash and, yes, terribly handsome when he wasn't running around on the set, perfecting every shot. Obsessed, even.

But he was also dangerous. Sometimes Rooney actually climbed into the cockpit, donned goggles, and took to the air to show off his directions.

At least he'd finally put the seductive runway scene in the can. She thought of Guthrie and saying good-bye and even talked Rooney into letting her rewrite some of the lines enough that they seemed real. Then she'd kissed Grayson off to war in the backseat of a Model A and had the set crying.

Even she felt like crying.

Which meant it must be good. Oh, she hoped.

It didn't make playing the scene any easier with Rafe Horne standing in the shadows beyond the klieg lights, watching. But she didn't think of him.

Much.

"He's going to hit the ground!" an extra screamed from behind them.

"I'm not paying him to crash," Rooney said.

Please, God, no. Rosie couldn't breathe as she watched the plane plummet.

"Pull up," Rooney muttered.

Suddenly, the plane nosed up, and miraculously, to the gasps of the crowd, Rafe buzzed the airfield.

Rooney turned to his cameraman. "Did you get it?"

The cameraman nearest him signaled a thumbs-up.

Rosie though she might faint. She'd been feeling woozy all day anyway.

"That's a wrap. Reel it in, boys." Rooney headed out to where Rafe now landed his plane, the wheels spitting out dirt. "We'll take the night off."

The night off. Perfect. A night alone in her hotel room. She gathered up the pages for tomorrow, her sunglasses, and then headed toward the hangar, where a driver would take her back to the hotel.

The extras were assembling at the craft service table for a quick bite to eat, but Rosie headed for her convertible, tying a scarf under her chin. She'd change out of costume in her hotel room and take a long shower. Occasionally, the press camped outside the Sands Hotel, where Sherwood had purchased rooms for the duration of the shooting. They'd like her showing up in her filmy dress, and probably the studio would add some sort of pre-movie caption under it to start the publicity wheels turning. Always a photo op.

She climbed into the backseat. "The Sands," she said to the driver.

"Roxy!" She heard the voice but didn't turn. She didn't want Rafe to see the fear that still flushed her cheeks.

Rafe put a hand on her door, jumping on the running board, a little out of breath. He bore the raccoon eyes of an aviator, and he grinned at her, windburn on his chin. "Where ya going so fast? What about dinner?"

She picked up a bamboo fan. She couldn't look at him, not at his tan forearms, not the way he grinned at her.

She was a married woman. Sort of. On paper, at least.

Oh brother. Dash didn't even return her phone calls anymore.

"I'm tired and hot, Mr. Horne. I'm headed back to the hotel—"

To her surprise, Rafe hopped into the seat beside her. "No, you're not." He leaned forward to the driver. "Take us to Neptune Beach."

"What? No. You can't just kidnap me."

"Watch me." Rafe leaned back, spreading his strong arms across the edge of the seat, taking up too much room as the driver pulled out of the hangar and into the sunset. A mild September breeze fanned through the towering palm trees as they drove along the shore, the waves calm, almost languid. The sun hung low on the horizon, a simmering ball that licked her skin.

She narrowed her eyes at him. "Where are we going?"

"Don't tell me you've been here for nearly three weeks and haven't been to Neptune Beach."

She didn't want to tell him how she spent too much of her time reading her script, trying to figure out how she really felt about delivering the lines.

He'd taught her something that day a week ago, even if she'd never tell him. Finding that real emotion brought life to her scene. Made her into a real actress, if only for a moment.

A real actress with a bombshell body and brilliant platinum hair. Perhaps she shouldn't forget the real reason why Rooney—and probably Rafe—wanted her on set. Not that she blamed Rafe for his attention. Rooney dressed her in little more than a nightgown. That made sense—the silky dress, the white fur in the middle of war-torn London.

"I have lines to read. And—"

He looked her over then. "You're a funny one, Roxy. You're all siren and lights on the outside, but inside, you're quiet and even shy."

She was? She glanced at him as he lowered his aviator sunglasses.

"It's time to teach you how to have some fun."

"I have fun."

"Yeah. I see you sitting on your balcony at the Sands, reading while the rest of the cast is out by the pool. You're a real troublemaker." He smirked, and she wanted to smack him.

But she smiled and the fight left her as they turned out of the airport toward Alameda.

She leaned her head back in the seat and closed her eyes. He hummed beside her, not talking. But she could smell him. A hint of airplane exhaust, sweat, sunshine. And sitting next to him felt easy. As if she could breathe, finally, the ocean-soaked air.

She must have fallen asleep because he nudged her awake in the parking lot as the driver drove them to the curb. "We're here."

She sat up, cleared her eyes. A Ferris wheel loomed before her, in front of an enormous building maybe three blocks long, with a red-tiled roof, stuccoed exterior. She smelled hot dogs and cotton candy, heard music, the bells of a carousel.

"It's an amusement park," she said as he got out and came around the car and opened her door before their driver could manage it.

He gave the driver a bill. "We'll be back in a few hours. Make yourself comfortable." Then he took her hand. "C'mon. I'll buy you a swimsuit."

"I'm not going swimming," she said, but he pulled her into the entrance, a looming tower with a red cap on the top. Beyond the striped red awnings, she spied an enormous swimming pool, patrons kicking through the glistening water.

Inside the pavilion, Rafe steered her toward the gift shop and found her a black swimsuit, a bathing cap, a robe. He purchased a pair of trunks for himself.

"Meet you on the deck," he said as he steered her toward the ladies' dressing area.

She couldn't believe that she found herself changing, donning the suit, the cap, the robe. Or that she obeyed him and found him cordoning off two beach chairs in the sand beyond the pool, grabbing an umbrella to shade them. He waved a waiter over to order drinks.

"Just an orange juice for me," she said.

"And me. I promise, there will be no champagne." He winked at her.

The sound of frivolity filled the air, from the shrieks of children, splashes in the pool, music from the carousel, and an announcer calling out something from the high-dive area.

"In the summer, they have water polo tournaments and boxing matches and later, if you want, we can go over to the dance pavilion and cut a rug to the band."

She drew in a breath, the air salty from the ocean combing the shore just beyond the oak trees. He stared at her, smiling, an odd look on his face.

Right then she had the strangest sense that, yes, she knew him.

"Where are you from, Rafe? France?"

He shook his head. "Belgium, actually. It's a little country south of Holland. But I spent a lot of my life in England. Studied at Cambridge. Flew for the RAF."

"That's where you got your flight training."

"Where I enlisted, yes. I fought for England then went back to Belgium to get married."

That stilled her. "You're married?"

"No."

She leaned back, remembering the pain in his eyes on the balcony in New York City. She didn't want to ask—

"It didn't work out. She didn't want me."

She closed her eyes. "I'm sorry."

He said nothing, but she felt his hand brush hers.

She leaned back in the chaise lounge, closing her eyes. Breathing deep. Yes, this felt nice.

Water sprayed across her legs. She let out a shriek and opened her eyes.

Rafe stood over her, dripping. "C'mon. You're getting wet." Then he leaned down and scooped her up into his arms.

"Rafe!" But she laughed and tried to hate the idea of being in his arms. But why? He had strong arms, a toned body, an infectious smile. She looped her arms around his neck and clung to him as he lowered her into the water. "It's cold!"

"It's perfect. Stop being a pansy."

He let her go, but she held on to his arm. "I can't swim."

"Okay," he said and looped his arm around her waist, swimming with her through the pool. The buoyancy of the water seemed like flying, and she laughed then gulped in a mouthful of water and came up sputtering.

He caught her up, held her by the arms as she coughed. "You okay?"

She nodded, still coughing.

Then she covered her mouth with her hands, giggling. "Imagine if the press saw me now. Nearly drowning." And in the arms of another man.

Not that, to anyone else, it might be anything torrid. After all, no one knew she was married.

She didn't feel married. Hadn't Dash made it clear he didn't consider their vows, well, vows?

She hooked her arm around his neck. "Take me to the deep end."

"Are you sure?" He put his arm around her. Tucked her into the curve of his body.

She nodded.

"Don't pull me down," he said. "Just let me hold you up."

Yes.

He took her into the deep end, and she tried not to let her heart climb into her throat. "Just let yourself float. You can kick to keep your balance. Don't panic, though. I've got you. I'm not going to let you sink."

The sun was in his eyes, and he watched her with a smile as she kicked, held herself afloat. "Where did you learn to swim?"

"My father taught me. We have a lake on our estate."

"Estate?"

"More like a farm," he said. A diver jumped in not far from them, and he winced as the spray hit his face. "Ready to get out?"

No. "Sure."

He swam with her to the edge of the pool, helped her climb out, then grabbed a towel from the attendant and wrapped it around her shoulders as they reclaimed their lounge chairs. He took a towel and ran it over his head, turning his hair wild.

He looked like some Roman hero standing over her, blocking the sun. Fletcher should be here to frame the shot.

And maybe the studio doctor to restart her heart.

If it weren't for his accent, she'd peg him as an Old West cowboy, maybe from Montana.

Their drinks had arrived, and she drank hers through a straw.

"How did you meet Rooney?" she asked.

"He was in Europe, buying old RAF Sopwith Camels and trying to hunt down a German Gotha. He finally ended up creating a replica. That was the plane I flew in today. We met at a party in Austria, through a mutual friend who knew I was interested in movies."

"You are?"

He glanced at her. "Isn't everyone? Half of America goes to a movie on the weekends. They want the fantasy. The world we create of drama and glitter and glamour."

"Is that what you want? To create the fantasy?"

"I want the reality." He smiled. Met her eyes.

She looked away, the sun hot on her skin despite the late hour.

"I'll never forget the first time I saw a movie. It was in France, after the war. *The Three Musketeers* with Douglas Fairbanks. I was mesmerized. He made it looks so…easy, so real. And for an hour I forgot what I'd seen, forgot the men I'd buried." He took a breath. "Forgot the day the Germans marched onto our property and murdered my mother."

She glanced at him, watched him run a thumb across his glass.

"Movies can make us forget," he said. "But they can also inspire us to be better, be more. That's what I want. To make movies that change us. That's why *Angel's Fury* is important, Roxy. So we understand exactly the cost of war. So we make sure we do everything to stop it from happening again."

She knew the cost. Had spent years trying to forget it. She stared at her glass and suddenly wanted to give a little of herself. "I lost my brother in the war. He simply vanished, and we never knew what happened to him. My mother still thinks he's alive, somewhere. She hasn't stopped hoping."

"And you?"

She took a sip of her juice. "I think that if a person wants to be found, they will be. And if they want to hide, start over, then maybe we should let them. Maybe what he left behind is just too terrible to remember."

He sat up, braced his hands on his knees, his shoulders wide as he considered her. "What's your real name, Roxy?"

Oh, he was handsome. And sitting so close, she could nearly feel his eyes caressing her. A warm shiver went through her, and for a moment she realized just how easily it might be to trust him. To even give him her heart.

To find herself right back where she'd been after Guthrie. Lost. Alone. Broken.

She couldn't go back to Rosie Worth. Couldn't let him see the woman she'd been.

She drew in a breath. "Roxy is my real name, Rafe."

* * * * *

It was too easy to enjoy Rafe Horne. To laugh with him.

To relax into his embrace on the dance floor, in the soft jazz of the music that pulled her arms around his wide shoulders and pocketed her into the curve of his embrace.

He read her lines with her and didn't laugh when she got them wrong. He helped her work out the crazy retakes Sherwood demanded.

He told her about his life in Belgium, growing up in the country, the village he grew up in. She listened, wrapped herself into his world.

Made him believe that she hung on his words.

Maybe she did, a little.

He made three weeks of tireless shooting fly by, sitting at night with her by the pool or on her balcony, rubbing her feet, making her laugh.

And he didn't even try to kiss her.

Strange.

He did, however, give her the sky, taking her up in one of Sherwood's biplanes, over Oakland and the frothy waves of the ocean. She expected terror and white-knuckled the sides of the plane. But Rafe sat with his arm around her, held her tight, and she relaxed into him, surveying the surf, the matchbox houses, the road curling like a ribbon along the shore.

They flew over Neptune Beach, and she waved to the riders of the Ferris wheel.

Rafe touched her back down just as the sun dipped into the sea, and then he took her walking on the beach, his hand bumping hers.

She wanted to take it, to hold on.

She walked barefoot, her toes digging into the creamy sand, feeling decadent.

"We're just waiting for the clouds," he said into the night wind.

"What?"

"Sherwood. He's waiting for the skies over Oakland to grow cloudy. Then he's going to add scenes to his aerial shootout. He's thinking by next week it'll get stormy."

"Are you going to fly?"

He nodded. "He needs extra fliers for the stunt."

She drew in a breath. "You could get killed."

He stopped, turned, caught her hand. "I flew over Germany, nearly got shot down so many times, I lost count. Nothing is going to happen to me over the skies of Oakland, California."

His thumb ran over her hand, sending tingles up her arm, through her entire body. His eyes met hers, and they turned her inside out.

She turned away, shaking, heading up the beach, away from Rafe.

She didn't want this, the feeling of teetering at the edge of something she couldn't have. Something that would only end up destroying her. Clara's words had bounced around in her head for the past week, *"You gotta keep ahold of your heart, or Hollywood will break it to pieces."*

Rafe Horne would break it to pieces.

Besides, it was all a fantasy. As soon as they finished shooting, he'd fly away.

She'd return home to reality. To Dash and the Studio's mechanisms.

And, Dash was right. She couldn't divorce him. The press would find out. Her public would turn on her. Would think she slept her way to a role via the casting couch.

Thank you, Dash.

Even if she did divorce him, he'd keep the studio *and* her contract. Who knew where he'd loan her out next. Mozambique, maybe, for a Tarzan remake. He'd put her in a sarong and make her swing from vines.

Rafe's hands slid over her shoulders, wrapped around her, and he began to hum. She recognized the song.

"Love me or leave me, let me be lonely. You won't believe me...."

"I love you only," he said into her ear, his voice turning her body hot under the cool breezes of the evening. The waves rolled onto the shore like applause in the swaddling of the night.

She hooked her hands onto his arms, let the rest of the song seep into her, whispering the words. "I'd rather be lonely than happy with somebody else."

He hummed a few more bars. Then, "There'll be no one unless that someone is you..."

She closed her eyes, let them burn, and tasted salt on her lips.

"What's the matter, Roxy?"

She shook her head as she opened her eyes and stared out into the ocean. On the other side of the bay, the starlight of San Francisco glittered.

She sighed against the loneliness hollowing her through. No, no, she couldn't let herself fall for Rafe. Not really. "The movie's nearly in the can. I—I don't want it to end."

He turned her. Met her eyes. Oh, he had the power to unravel her, especially with the waves reaching for them, the cool ocean breezes tickling her skin.

He tipped up her chin and kissed her.

She should have put her hands to his chest and pushed him away. Should have listened to Clara's words.

Maybe should have even remembered that she vowed to belong to another, in word and deed, and that briefly, she and Dash had become man and wife.

But it didn't feel like it.

She forgot it all as Rafe wove his hands through her hair, angling her head, deepening his kiss.

Rafe.

She wound her arms up around his shoulders and sank into him, letting herself relax, letting his arms curve around her back, pull her to himself.

He tasted like the wind. And the night. She wanted to hide here forever.

He lifted his head, found her eyes. "Roxy—I—after this movie, I want you to come away with me. I want to marry you."

Marry. The word slapped the sense right back into her. Marry. See, this was what happened when she let her heart venture too far out of her grasp. She backed away, pressed a hand to her face. Shook her head.

His expression fell. "What—I'm sorry. I'm moving too fast—"

"No—" She held up her hands. "Just…"

"What is it?"

She stared at him, the moonlight on his face, enough of a five o'clock shadow to turn him into a bona fide war hero, so much emotion in his eyes, he could make her hand over her heart.

No.

She couldn't do this again. Not only was she not free, but a man like Rafe, a stunt pilot, just might end up in a fiery wreckage.

And then she'd have nothing left of her heart. She couldn't be the girl who cared about marriage or a family or a ring on her finger. That was her life with Guthrie.

That was the life of Rosie Worth.

She never needed Roxy Price more than right now.

"No, Rafe. You don't want to marry me." She flicked her hand across her cheek, found a dangerous smile. "Trust me."

He stood in the sand, frowning as she walked toward him. The wind had her hair, pasted her dress to her body.

"I—I think I do," he said, his gaze travelling over her.

Yes. She smiled. "No, darling. Besides, the studio wouldn't let you. Dash has me on a leash. You saw that."

Mostly true, and she reached for him, ran a trail with her finger across the well of his throat. Her heart thundered.

"I could talk to him. Buy out your contract—"

"You can't afford me," she said, winking. "But that doesn't mean we can't have some fun."

He caught her hand. "Roxy, what are you doing?"

She stepped close, wove her hand around his neck. "Shh." She kissed his neck, took the opportunity to smell the wind on his skin. Yes. Enough of her silly vows. Dash hadn't kept his, had he?

They had a farce of a marriage. And maybe she wouldn't give Rafe her heart, but perhaps she could find something close enough to it.

"Roxy." Rafe's voice rumbled beneath her hand. "What are you doing?"

"Isn't this what you really want, Rafe? Roxy Price, all to yourself."

She wound her arms up around his neck, plastered her body to him. Urged his neck down for a kiss.

And for a second, the briefest of moments, she had him. She heard him groan, a soft surrender in the center of his chest as he wrapped his arms around her, catching her up, kissing her back, as if she might be right. As if she belonged to him, his mouth on hers, hungry, even amazed.

And in that moment, she let Roxy vanish and became herself. Needing Rafe. Surrendering just a little of her heart into his arms.

"No."

Then, as if she might be made of fire, he let go, shoved her away, held her at arm's length. He was breathing hard, shaking his head. "No, Roxy. What's going on here?"

"Isn't this what you want? The fantasy?"

He let her go, stared hard into her eyes. "No. I told you. I want the reality. I want the real Roxy Price."

She pressed her hand to her lips, as if to wipe away his touch. "This is the real Roxy Price."

"But it's not the real Rosie Worth!"

She stared at him, the words like a slap, stealing her breath. "How do you know my real name?"

"I know a lot more about you than you think." He stepped close to her, reaching for her, even as she yanked her arm away from him. His voice softened, so much it could wound if she let it.

"Rosie, you don't have to play a part with me."

She stared at him, his words undoing her. What did he know? And how much? "I'm not—"

"Don't." His tone silenced her, but his expression softened as he came close, cupped her face in his hands. "Okay. I get it. For now. I've waited this long. I guess I can wait until you're ready."

Then he kissed her again, this time so gently, she thought she might cry.

No, she was already crying. Weeping because, yes, Hollywood could cost her everything.

Chapter 4

Rooney Sherwood would get her killed yet. Rosie ached everywhere, down to her toes as she lay in her hotel bed, reliving the moment when, in an effort to get a realistic final shot, Rooney perched a cameraman on the wing of a taxiing Sopwith Camel, catching her and Grayson in a kiss as she sat on his lap.

Which, of course, made it nearly impossible for Grayson to steer the plane, his rudimentary pilot talents turning into folly when he drove them off the runway and into a ditch, turning the plane over on its nose.

Really, they hadn't been moving that fast. But she'd flown from the cockpit and landed eight feet away in the dirt.

Grayson had hung up in the cockpit and broken his arm.

And Rafe, well Rafe nearly lost his head.

Perhaps, if anyone would lose his life, it would be Rooney, because four men had to pull Rafe away from Rooney and hustle their director off the set.

They'd taken her to the hospital, just in case, but she'd only sported a few bruises and hadn't stayed overnight.

She still suffered from a backache that could cross her eyes. She groaned and curled into a ball under her cotton blanket. Outside, the October Sunday sunshine beckoned and the voices of the cast drifted up from the poolside area.

Clearly, Rooney hadn't returned. He'd probably gone to Los Angeles to scrounge up more extras for his next change in script.

At this rate, the epic might be finished sometime in the next century.

At least they had a day off. Her head pounded, and she put a hand to her forehead. Hot, as if she had a fever.

The breeze drifted into the window, and she closed her eyes, trying to relax through the spasm in her back. She let herself smile at how Rafe had scooped her up, muscled her to his convertible, and driven her himself to Oakland's Highland Hospital.

It would probably make the papers, her hanging on to his neck as he carried her into the emergency area. The look on his face had scared her, though.

He loved her too much for her own good.

A knock at her door jerked her free of where her thoughts were spiraling her. Like into his arms. Like abandoning everything and running away.

Yet again.

No. She groaned as she sat up. "Yes?" Probably Rafe, coming to check on her. She reached for her robe.

"A telephone call for you, ma'am. At the front desk."

She winced, flopped back. "Take a message."

"He called twice yesterday, ma'am. The clerk forgot to deliver your messages."

He. She had an idea who that might be. Still, Dash rarely chased her down. "I'll be right down."

She got up, pressed her hand to the small of her back. Leaned on the white wicker bed frame. Maybe she'd spend all day in bed. She had more pages to read, thank you, Rooney.

Maybe Rafe would read with her. Make her laugh. Help her live in the fantasy before it crumbled and she had to tell him the truth.

I'm married to Dashielle Parks.

Yeah, she could wait on that conversation. But it was the only defense she had left.

The only thing keeping her from giving in, letting him inside Roxy Price to the woman he made her believe she was, letting him steal her heart.

She knotted the gown then gripped a chair as another spasm flared in her back. She shot a look in the bureau mirror. Maybe she needed a turban before she headed out in public. And some lipstick.

Sufficiently attired, even for the press, she headed downstairs, a strong hand on the railing as the pain in her lower back fisted her again.

The clerk held the phone out for her when she finally descended. Unfortunately, the cord didn't reach over to the whitewashed rattan chairs. She stood at the counter, a hand pressed to her spine. "Hello?"

"Please tell me that the pictures in *Photoplay* aren't the reason you didn't come home this weekend?"

She opened her mouth, had no words. Hello to you too, Dash.

"Rosie?"

"Please, are you serious? I'm not the only one making a splash in *Photoplay*. Besides, what photos are you talking about?"

"There's one with you sitting with your feet on a man's lap. Another with you sitting on a lounge chair, it looks like at some amusement park. What's going on up there? Are you having an affair?"

"What? No. Nothing's going on, you dope. Not that you would care, but that's Rafe Horne. He's a consultant on set for Rooney—

who nearly killed me yesterday, by the way. You might see a picture of Rafe carrying me to the hospital, although who knows what tripe *Photoplay* will print as the caption."

Silence.

"Dash?"

"I—I know you don't like our agreement, Red, but—"

"Agreement? Since when was what we have an *agreement*? Convenient, perhaps. As long as we're talking about *Photoplay*, who is the brunette that I keep seeing you with?

"She's no one."

Rosie didn't expect it to hurt, for his words to wrap around her like a claw, digging into her. "So there *is* a she."

He drew in a breath over the phone line, and she could imagine him, on a Sunday, in his linen pants, a cotton shirt untucked, maybe barefoot as he paced the tile floor of their hallway, one eye on the pool, the other on the driveway, trying to decide his next destination.

"I wanted you to come home this weekend, so we could talk."

"About what? Our marriage? Our *partnership*?"

"Yes. Red, the last thing we need is a scandal right now. We can solve this without drama."

"Solve what? Wait. Are you going to ask me for a *divorce*?"

She glanced at the hotel desk clerk, aware that her voice had ricocheted through the room. He turned away.

Their clandestine marriage wouldn't be secret for long. She imagined the clerk taking down her every word.

"Please, Rosie. It's not—I just need to talk to you. Face-to-face, like old friends."

"Have we ever been friends, Dash?"

"I thought we were."

She rubbed her forehead. She still had a fever, her brow sweaty.

"Just come home, please. Soon."

"Do whatever you want, Dash. I don't have a home anymore."

She banged the receiver onto the cradle with such force the phone shivered, the bell resounding through the lobby.

And she'd attracted an audience. She turned to storm back up the stairs and saw the crew watching her from their table outside on the patio.

And then Rafe. He'd risen and stood by the open doors, wearing the face she'd seen at the Grove. Shock. And a little horror in his blue eyes.

Oh. He'd heard.

He took a breath.

Nothing but the fan breached the silence.

"I can explain," she said softly, taking a step toward him.

"You're married?" The way he said it, a little tremor in his voice, she wanted to weep.

She shook her head. Then nodded. Then shook it again. "I... It's not what you think."

"I think you're married to Dashielle Parks," he said, this time less shock, more finality, more anger.

The crew turned away, shuffling cards, their voices deliberately raised. She pressed a hand to her back, which spasmed again. She closed one eye in a wince and reached for the edge of a rattan chair. She missed and hit the palm tree in a pot beside it. Even as the spasm passed, she righted herself, finding her aim on the chair.

"Are you okay?" Rafe came toward her, concern tempering the anger written on his face. Good, kind Rafe. She loved him then.

And it made her want to weep. "No. I ache everywhere. But that's beside the point. Here's what you don't understand." She took a step toward him, cutting her voice lower. "Dash and I got married a year ago—a business arrangement. We… He doesn't love me."

"I know." Rafe growled.

"What do you mean?"

"Let's just say I know. A man doesn't love a woman and then—then—"

"Cheat on her? Trust me, that's standard behavior for Dash. He ramped it up when he became my boss. Or should I say, owner. I was such a fool— Oh!" This one seemed to wrap around her entire body, clamp down. She clasped her hands over herself, bent into it.

Rafe grabbed her arms. "You don't look so good. You need to sit down."

"I'm fine. I just need rest." She met his eyes. "Listen, Rafe. I never meant to hurt you. I don't love him. I'm just… It's just a business arrangement."

He searched her face, as if testing it for the truth. She put it all right there into her eyes, hoping he wouldn't ask for more.

And then something kicked her, right in the back. A blow, but from the inside, as if something unlatched, broke free.

Her body spasmed and her legs buckled. "Oh!" She reached out for Rafe, and he caught her as she went down.

Wetness streaked down her legs. The room tilted, her body feeling suddenly hot. Heavy.

"Roxy, you're bleeding!" Rafe said.

Bleeding?

And then her entire body began to convulse, drawing in on itself. And she knew.

Even as Rafe yelled for help, even as she put her arms around her waist, breathed through the pain. Through it all, she called herself an idiot for not recognizing the symptoms. She'd been here before.

Baby number two, lost to miscarriage.

* * * * *

Rafe stood with his back to her, at the hospital window, staring out as she shifted herself awake. Her body ached, and she felt raw and empty under the cotton blanket of the metal bed. They'd put her in a private room—probably Rooney's doing. Or, more likely, Rafe's, arranged while they'd taken her into surgery.

She remembered Rafe's face at the door as they wheeled her away, pinched with fear.

Clearly, between then and now, the doctor had told him exactly why she'd lost so much blood. Why she'd fainted in his arms on the way to the hospital.

Why he could never believe her when she claimed she and Dash weren't really married.

"Rafe?"

He turned, and with the glow of the daylight behind him, she couldn't see his face. Just the outline of his shoulders, the way he shoved his hands into his pockets, as if defeated.

Then, he sighed and walked into the light.

He may have been crying, betrayed in the red cracks in his eyes. He hadn't shaven, although he'd changed his shirt, probably soiled with her blood.

She couldn't look at him. A bouquet of flowers sat on the table at the end of the bed. Orchids.

"I had to stay to make sure you were okay." He put on his hat, a brown derby. "I guess you are."

Rafe moved to the door.

"Just like that? You won't let me explain?"

He stopped at the foot of her bed his head down. He closed his eyes, wincing. Then, "What's there to explain, Roxy? You were pregnant. Maybe you should be glad I'm assuming it's Dash's and not someone else."

Her mouth opened.

He lifted his head, met her eyes. Shook his head. "Sorry. I'm just... I—I believed you. Or I guess I just wanted to. I wanted to believe that you were more than what I saw. Believe that you weren't the type of girl to marry the studio director to get a role—"

"That's not what happened."

He held up a hand. "I should have known Dashielle Parks would win in the end."

"What are you talking about? Dash didn't win—"

"He married you, didn't he? I call that winning. Or, at least I did."

She ground her jaw. "Listen. Dash and I have known each other for years. We started the studio together. He needed an actress, and I wanted to become one. So I married him. He gave me studio shares, and I gave him control of my contract for the next seven years, and we agreed to share the profits."

"That's not all you shared." His mouth tightened in a dark, unforgiving line. "I suppose I should be offering my condolences. But it sounded from your phone conversation that maybe you weren't expecting to start a family together."

She looked away. But out loud the plan, their so-called marriage did sound so...foolish. Even, naive. "I just wanted to start over. To be someone else. And marrying Dash seemed to be the way to do that. He gave me security."

Rafe gripped the end of the bed, his knuckles white on the metal frame, and nodded. "Why would you want to be someone else, Rosie? What is wrong with being you?"

There went the use of her name again. She frowned at him. "What do you know about me, Rafe? I don't understand—how do you know my name?"

He drew in a long breath, and the light of the room cast a glow over his face, the chisel in his chin. His eyes, so dark, even fierce on hers as the sunlight cast over his face.

And suddenly, she knew. "We *have* met. We met in Paris, seven years ago. You helped my brother Finn get his boat out of the pond at *Jardin Tuileries*."

He took a breath. "You were waiting for Dash. He came up while we were talking."

"You left without saying good-bye."

"I saw the look on your face. You were in love with him. Probably still are."

"No, I'm not. I—I wanted to run away with him because my mother was setting me up to marry someone I didn't know. A duke from some European duchy."

"I know." He met her eyes, a sorrow in them. "I know."

"What do you mean, *you know*?" and then, "Wait. No."

"Rolfe Van Horne, Duke of Beaumont, only son of Frederick of the duchy of Beaumont-Belgium."

She stared at him, those blue eyes—how could she have forgotten them? And his chivalry, yes, she should have spotted that right off. She could see the snapshot in her mind, the memory of him dripping wet as he waded into the cold pond after Finn's boat.

"Don't tell me that you were the duke my mother wanted me to marry...."

"I came to Paris to meet you."

Their conversations shifted back to her. "You said you moved back to Europe after the war to... Oh no. You weren't planning on marrying *me*, were you?"

He shrugged. Smiled, but it didn't meet his eyes. "I hadn't quite imagined catching up with you in Hollywood, but perhaps fate thought it had a future for us."

Past tense. "Rafe, please. Wait—"

"The name is Rolfe, I guess. His Serene Highness, Duke of Beaumont would work also." He said it without humor. As if...

"You're serious."

"I'm not sure what I was thinking. It would never have worked for me to marry Roxy Price, bombshell actress, to manage the duchy." His eyes flashed. "She's a far cry from Rosie Worth, heir to the Worth family fortune."

Rosie sat back, suddenly feeling soiled. Her throat burned. "Get out." He flinched, and she turned away. "Please. Get out."

She pressed her hands to her eyes.

"Good-bye, Rosie Worth."

She heard the door close behind him.

Fate could not be this cruel.

She lay on her side, curling into a ball.

God could not be this cruel.

Not to show her the man she seemed destined to marry only to break her heart with her mistakes. Her failures.

Rolfe was the duke her mother had planned for her. She closed her eyes, remembering their brief meeting so long ago in Paris. She'd remembered him as kind when he rescued Finley's boat. Kind and handsome and with a longing in his gaze she now understood.

She wished for that longing on his face to return as she watched the sun fall into the horizon, a star dying into the magenta of evening.

The nurse came and brought her a plate, but she didn't look at it. The room fell into darkness, shadows cascading across the floor, over her body.

The moon rose, an eye in the sky, watching her, unblinking.

Another nurse came into the room. She looked about fifty, with dark, salted hair, brown eyes. Despite being thin, she had a presence to her that reminded Rosie of her mother. Commanding. Her tag read G. House. She reached around the bread and captured Rosie's arm. Took her pulse, timing it with her watch.

"You're going to live, Miss Price."

"Thank you for that insight."

The woman reached out, pulled up a chair, sat down.

"What are you doing?"

"Did you know there is a mob of people outside, and I had to wrestle my way into work tonight?"

She wanted to put the pillow over her head.

"People care about you, Miss Price. You should eat something. Losing a child is difficult, but you and your…you can have more."

Roxy lifted her head, stared at her. "No, I don't think I can, thank you. And it was my husband's baby, contrary to what you're insinuating—"

"I wasn't—"

"And that was my second miscarriage. I had one with my *dead* husband. The one who died in my arms two years ago. But no one knows about him, because that's a secret. And then there's the child I left behind—his child, the one I sat in bed for six months to carry. I left her, my daughter, in the care of my cousin in Montana, who is raising her to think she is her mother. So no, I don't think I'll be having more children."

She grabbed the pillow, tucked it in front of her, lay back to look at the ceiling. "And the worst part is, the man I love is *not* my husband. He's the man I should have married seven years ago. Which means that, maybe, I would have had his baby instead and never had my heart broken at all."

The nurse didn't move. Didn't speak. Finally, Rosie looked at her. Her head was bowed.

"What are you doing?"

"Praying for you."

"Well, stop. I don't need your prayers. What I need is for God to show me some mercy."

"He has, Miss Price."

"Were you listening at all?" Rosie rolled over. "Here's the really sorry part. After saying good-bye to the man I didn't want to marry, I meet him again, seven years later, and fall in love with him. But guess what? I'm already married, to a man who doesn't love me. And I don't love him."

The nurse bowed her head, started praying again. Rosie could see it in the movement of her mouth. "Are you a nurse, or a nun?"

"A nurse." She looked up. "But there are some wounds I can't tend. You know what your story tells me, Miss Price? That God has a destiny for you that you can't escape."

"Don't say that to me. I just need God to leave me alone."

"God has no intention of leaving you alone. He loves you too much."

Rosie stared at her, wanting to slap her. "He just took my baby."

"Your accident took your child."

"And God doesn't have control over that?"

"He has control over everything—"

"No." Rosie shot out her hand, closing her hand over the word. "Not over me. Or my destiny. Never has and never will. My life is *mine*."

The nurse's expression seemed filled with sadness. "You might consider that it is *because* you took your destiny into your hands that you find yourself here today."

Rosie leaned back against the bed. Dug her fingers into the pillow in front of her.

"Jesus said, 'Blessed are the meek: for they shall inherit the earth.' Do you know who the meek are, Miss Price?"

"The cowardly? The quiet?" Not her.

"The ones who hope in the Lord. The ones who wait for Him. Those who allow God to set their course. The Holy Word says that they will inherit the earth. It means they will inherit everything God has for them. His blessings, His love. His destiny."

Rosie looked away, out the window at the trail of moonlight across the sky. The stars pinpricked the velvet night.

"Your destiny may be more glorious than you think, Miss Roxy. You just need to let go of it. Be meek and find your inheritance." She got up to leave, but Rosie snaked out a hand and grabbed hers. She didn't look at her.

"Please, don't tell anyone—"

The nurse squeezed her hand. "I'm not a nun, but I will keep your secrets."

Roxy didn't let go. "Perhaps you could keep praying too?"

The nurse sat back down. "On the condition that you eat your dinner."

* * * * *

She wasn't going to let Rolfe fly without saying—well, Rosie couldn't quite wrap her mind around what she might say. But outside her hospital window, clouds assembled on the horizon, and his words rippled through her.

Today they'd fly, the dangerous dogfight, complete with Rafe's aerial stunts. And at the rate Rooney's luck seemed to be holding out, someone would get killed.

She shoved her hair into the turban and waited for the nurse to call her a taxi. Two days sitting around the hospital only awakened her to how she'd endured enough grief in her life.

No more letting go of her life. Her destiny. She couldn't let Rafe—no, Rolfe—fly without telling him... Okay, she'd start with *I'm sorry*.

Then, she might go to, *You were right*.

And, finally, *Can we start over? Pretend we're meeting again in the garden in Paris...and I don't turn away into Dash's arms but walk with you instead?*

She couldn't seem to escape the nurse's words. *"You know what your story tells me, Miss Price? That God has a destiny for you that you can't escape."* They sat in her thoughts, churning.

Maybe she had brought all this on herself. Maybe she'd created her own nightmare by taking hold of her destiny instead of letting God deliver His chosen destiny to her.

Imagine the life she'd have if she'd married Rolfe.

Except, then she wouldn't have known Guthrie. She couldn't bear to choose, but perhaps she didn't have to. Not anymore.

Maybe destiny *had* brought them back together. She just had to help Rolfe remember that.

She wouldn't do it as Roxy Price, however. Rolfe had never made her feel like a tramp, a sex symbol, until two days ago when he walked out of her hospital room.

She wouldn't be Roxy, not for him. Not anymore.

She'd waited all day yesterday for Rolfe to return. Watched the press assemble outside. Backed away from the curtain before they could snap a photo.

She wondered what Rooney and Dash might be telling the press. No doubt spinning something about her accident on set.

"Your cab is here," Amanda said. One of the studio extras Rooney had assigned to her during her convalescence, she'd arrived yesterday with Rosie's makeup and a fresh change of clothing. She'd stayed all night.

Poor girl. Just wanted a chance to be noticed, to be discovered.

This morning, Rosie sent her back to the hotel with specific instructions. Her white sundress, light blue linen jacket, a ribbon for her hair, a pair of pearls, low socks, and her white oxfords.

She spent an hour penciling in her eyebrows, adding rouge to her still wan cheeks, but she left off the heavy lining around her eyes, refrained from painting on a pout.

Not quite so much Roxy, please.

Then, Rosie donned her jacket, her gloves, a smile, and pressed out through the throng of reporters, photographers, without answering their barrage of questions. The convertible and her driver were waiting. "Good morning, Eddie." She slid into the seat. "Take me to the set."

"Rooney said you could take the day off. They're shooting the aerial sequences today," Amanda said.

"The set, please," she said.

She had to feel a little sorry for Eddie, watching his jaw tighten. He was a good kid, and Rooney didn't like to be disobeyed.

"I promise I just want to watch. I won't get in the way."

"You should be resting," Amanda said. Rosie glanced at her. Blond. Blue eyes. Pretty, not striking, but she could stand in for Rosie if she suddenly couldn't perform.

"I feel marvelous," Rosie said, flashing her a grin.

They drove through the heat, the wind tearing at her hair, her hand white on the frame of the car. Nearing the airfield, the rage of the airplanes thundered through the sky even before she spotted them, dropping from the bulbous clouds, hiding again, spinning, rolling, some with black smoke trailing their fuselage.

"How many planes are up there?"

"Forty or more," Eddie said. "And Rooney's going to crash the Gotha today."

The Gotha. The big plane Rolfe flew, with the double wings, made to look like a German bomber. "Who's flying it?" she said, trying to keep her voice even.

"Horne. The stunt pilot. He's supposed to bail out before it hits the ground."

She kept her smile. Searched for it in the sky as they pulled up to the set. Rooney ran from camera to camera across the tarmac, checking shots as the airplanes waged a mock war, the peril ubiquitous. Already she saw smoke drifting up from destroyed planes, now nothing but a rubble of wood and fabric on the ground.

"Stop here," she said as they reached the edge of the tarmac. The last thing she needed was Rooney seeing her, sending her home.

She slid up to the back of the car, cupped her hand over her eyes. Spied the Gotha bomber lumbering through the sky. A plume of black smoke curled from it. German Fokkers and Sopwith Camels waged a dogfight like flies in the sky.

She might be over a French countryside, watching the Germans and the Brits, for the intensity of it. She fought the urge to put her hand over her eyes and peek through her fingers.

"Look, he put the plane into a spin!"

Her driver pointed to the Gotha. She pressed her hand over her mouth as the double engine bomber began to spiral toward the earth.

"Do you see a chute?" Amanda said, now getting out of the Rolls, standing away from the plane, her hand to her brow.

Please, Rolfe, bail out.

Planes buzzing around the Gotha as it plunged obscured her vision. Two Sopwith Camels suddenly collided, exploded in midair.

Men hung in parachutes across the sky.

"I don't see him," Amanda said.

The Gotha spun like a drill toward the earth.

Bail out!

But no one appeared above the beast as it disappeared behind a rise in the terrain.

The crash rent the air, terrible, brutal, shaking through her, turning her brittle.

She couldn't breathe.

"Did you see him bail out?" she whispered.

Eddie didn't speak, his hands on the steering wheel as he bent his forehead onto it.

On the tarmac, a group of men—maybe medics—jumped into a truck.

No...no...

"Drive me over to the set," she said, her voice shaky. She slipped down into her seat. Amanda climbed in, her hands shaking.

This would be just like God, at the helm of her destiny. What was she thinking, believing she could trust the Almighty with something so delicate as her heart?

Rosie wrapped her glove around the door handle, holding on as the car bumped toward the set. Rooney looked over at her then frowned and dismissed her for the directions he leveled at his crew. The dogfight in the sky, oblivious to the flames and smoke from the debris of the Gotha, now blackened the sky.

She got out before the car stopped moving. "Please tell me that no one has died," she said to Jerry as he came toward her. "Please tell me that Rolfe bailed out."

"We don't know," Jerry said, coming up to her, his face whitened. "It's possible. What are you doing here, Miss Price—"

"Don't give me that. You know what I'm doing here." She stood, hands on her hips, refusing to let panic have her.

But she wanted to weep when she saw more men hop on a truck and head out to the smoldering mess on the horizon.

"No, I mean, didn't anyone get ahold of you at the hotel?"

She looked at Jerry now, frowning. "What are you talking about?"

Jerry blew out a breath, glanced at Rooney, who was now stalking toward her. "You have a message from Fletcher. You need to go home right away."

Oh, Dash, that dope. He just wouldn't leave her alone. "No. I'm not leaving."

Rooney came up, sunburned, his eyes fierce. "What are you doing here? You gotta go back to LA. Sheesh, Roxy, what are you thinking? Dash is in a coma, and you're here on the set?"

She stared at him. Trying to fit his words into her head. "What?"

"Don't you read the papers?" Jerry signaled to someone behind her. "Dashielle Parks shot himself last night."

She couldn't move. Just stared at Rooney. Dash—shot... "What are you talking about?"

She pressed her gloved hand to her chest. She—couldn't—breathe...

"Aw, Roxy. Ya didn't know." Rooney looked immediately sorry, his rare compassion budding forth. "Eddie, take Miss Price to the hangar."

He came up, touched her cheek. "We'll take care of this, darling. I got a plane for you. You go home and be with Dash." He kissed her on the cheek.

She caught his hand. "Why did Dash—are you sure? But I just talked to him—"

"I don't know, doll." He squeezed her hand then turned back to the dogfight.

And what about Rolfe?

Eddie slipped his arm around her waist, turned her back to the car. But...

She climbed in, her legs nearly numb. Kept her eyes on the wreckage on the horizon as Eddie pulled away toward the hangar.

She said nothing as she watched the plume of black smoke as fire destroyed the final remains of Rolfe's warplane.

"I found him on the patio. We were supposed to have lunch, and when he didn't answer the door, naturally, I thought he might be on the telephone. I didn't expect—I didn't—Oh Roxy, there was blood everywhere.... How could he...?"

* * * * *

Fletcher sat on the wooden chairs in the hallway of St. Vincent's Catholic Hospital. Somewhere, through the wooden doors of the ward behind him, Dash's body lay in a coma, a ventilator pumping air into his body, a hole next to his heart where he'd pointed a Colt .45 at his chest and pulled the trigger.

She still couldn't get Fletcher's words into her head, her heart.

She stared at him, exhaustion bleeding through her. She still heard the buzzing of the prop in her ears, pretty sure that the flight in one of Rooney's warplanes from Oakland to LA had jarred free her teeth from her head.

Thankfully, a representative from the studio met her, but he'd abandoned her at the hospital door to plow through the gauntlet of press on her own.

Only to find Fletcher distraught and unraveling, pacing outside Dash's hospital room. He took one look at her and sank into a chair, wearing his age on his gaunt face.

"How bad is it?" She glanced through the window in the doors of the private ward. Nurses, the sisters of St. Vincent Catholic hospital, moved in and out of the ward carrying supplies, occasionally offering her a condolent smile.

"It's bad. He shot himself in the chest. If I hadn't shown up, he would have bled to death."

"And his heart?"

"He had surgery to fix a tear, his lung collapsed." He ran his hands down his face. "They told me that it's not looking good. They'll be surprised if he survives the night."

She walked up to the window and peered in. Dash lay in a bed beyond her view, a curtain pulled for privacy.

Probably so the world didn't have to watch him die.

She turned away. Tried to get ahold of how everything had suddenly careened so wildly out of control.

"I don't understand; why would he do this?"

She looked up to see one of the studio agents manhandling a photographer from his stealthy perch in the hallway.

Rosie turned her back to him. She was still dressed in her sundress, ready to take back her destiny with Rolfe, who may or may not have perished in a flaming crash for Rooney Sherwood's epic motion picture.

Oh, she had just about enough of the stench of death, of the sense of her life slipping through her fingers.

"Fletcher, I talked to Dash two days ago. He seemed fine, if not angry. Typical Dashielle Parks, just wanting his own way. Are you sure this wasn't some crazy accident?"

Fletcher looked up at her, nonplussed. "Please don't tell me that the events of the last few days mean nothing to you?"

She frowned at him. Even Dash didn't know about the baby—she put her hand to her empty womb. "Of course they do. Do you think me heartless?"

It might be true, however, that she hadn't given enough thought about the child she'd lost. Dash's child. Her child. Someone with Dash's dark eyes, rogue good looks. A scamp of a little boy, or a darling, sassy girl.

Oh. She sank down onto the bench beside him. Maybe Dash *had* cared for her—and just didn't know how to show it. Maybe she shouldn't have been so unkind, so angry with him. "I—I didn't know what to say. I didn't know, Fletcher. And then it all happened so fast." She folded her gloved hands together. "I never expected him to care."

"Not care? How does one not care about losing two million dollars?"

She stilled. Looked at him. "Two—million—dollars?"

"Maybe more." Fletcher ran his hand into his thinning hair. "He told me he'd invested the studio funds, but he didn't tell me how much until the market fell on Friday. Then, this morning, when he got the news of last night's market crash—"

"What crash?"

"*What crash*? Do you not follow the news at all, Roxy?" Fletcher stared at her as if she might be a child. "The stock market in New York City. It crashed this week. First on Friday, and then—well, Dash put everything Palace Studios had into the market, hoping to revive us."

"I know things were bad—that's why Dash loaned me out to Rooney. But I thought—"

"They're worse than bad. We have nothing left." Fletcher sighed, covered his face with his hands. "I don't blame him for trying to escape it all."

Escape? She stared at Fletcher, something hot rising inside. "Well, I do." She stood up. "I think he has a lot of nerve. He's not the only one with something at stake here. We were supposed to build the studio together. That's why we—" She closed her mouth. Glanced over her shoulder. Yes, press congregated at the end of the hall, near the nurses' station, probably tuning to her every word.

She turned and marched to the swinging doors.

"You can't go in there—"

"Watch me."

The scent of ammonia and iodine smarted her eyes as she entered the room. A nun rose from her station, but Rosie held up her hand. "I'm his wife," she snapped and headed toward Dash.

"Visiting hours aren't—"

"I won't be long," she said, beginning to tremble.

Dash lay in a metal-framed bed, an oxygen cannula under his nose, tubes connecting him to fluids being pumped into his body. A white cotton blanket outlined his strong, lean body. He'd only grown more handsome over the years, with those high, regal cheekbones, his dark hair that simply wouldn't behave, the five o'clock shadow of a bona fide playboy. No wonder she'd fallen in love with him, over and over.

Why she still loved him now, really.

He didn't look like himself today, the dashing and dark studio executive. Or even the college boy she'd met and fallen for in Paris.

She didn't know this man, gray and broken, too many bandages and tubes to be Dashielle Parks.

She pressed a hand to her mouth, her eyes blurry. No, this couldn't be Dash. Dash laughed and teased and made her feel beautiful.

Dashielle Parks didn't give up. He took the world by the tail, tamed it, made it his own. He lived by his Technicolor dreams, believing in the impossible.

Made her believe in the impossible.

"How dare you." She drew in a quick breath. "How dare you do this? We had a deal, Dash. A *deal.* You'd make me a star, and I'd make you rich. I'm *trying,* for Pete's sake. What do you think I'm doing up there, week after week? Rooney nearly killed me—and then you go and do this?" She clenched her teeth, cut her voice to low. "Why didn't you wait for me? I would have kept my word."

She was shaking even as she moved toward the bed. Someone had pulled up a vigil chair and she grabbed the back of it. Leaned over it to talk into his ear.

"We were supposed to be partners. To build something. To show the world that we didn't need to play by their rules, that we could write our own futures. "

She wanted him to open his eyes, but she would have settled for a twitch, even a glower. But he couldn't even keep that part of his promise. The one to rise to her accusations, to keep up with and even tame the temperamental bombshell Roxy Price.

She bowed her head, both hands on the chair. No. This was not right. "Listen." Her voice trembled. "Just wake up. I forgive you, okay? I just—I need you to wake up, Dash."

Please respond. Please...

Her breath turned to fire in her chest as she watched his face. Nothing moved on his countenance, his lashes dark against his cheeks.

She looked away, blinking fast. "You're so—you're so stubborn. Arrogant, really. You just always have to have things your way. I should have figured that out in Paris, when you told me I wasn't the marrying kind." She turned back to him. "Then why did you marry me, Dash?" She wiped her cheek, drew a faltering breath. "Why did you marry me?"

She came around, stood in front of the chair. Touched his hand, remembered how he'd held hers, first in Paris then before the justice of the peace in Hollywood. She wove her fingers between his. Swallowed. "Oh Dash. You can't break my heart. Not like this." She lifted his hand, pressed it to her forehead. "Please, Dash. Don't leave me. You have no right to leave me."

"No. He has no right to leave *me*."

The soft, even angry voice made her turn. Irene Marshall stood at the end of Dash's bed, her face white, looking drawn and exhausted.

And she looked very, very pregnant.

She wore a long-sleeve, drop-waist, navy blue dress, with lace at the neck and cuffs. And a string of pearls at her neck.

Rosie's gaze went to her belly, and Irene curled a hand over it, as if to protect it.

No...

She looked back at Dash. Oh no. "Please don't tell me that Dashielle Parks is the father of your child."

Irene's breath hitched, but Rosie heard venom in her voice when she finally said, "We were going to marry the moment you two were divorced."

Rose swallowed. Closed her eyes. "Of course you were."

"We were!"

She turned to her. "Is that what Dash told you?"

Irene's mouth opened, closed. Her eyes sharp, despite her grief. She turned away, pressed a hand to her mouth. "Why do you think he loaned you out to Rooney? It wasn't for the studio. It was so you'd be out of the way."

Rosie swallowed, her chest closing in on itself.

"I think he was hoping that you'd find someone else." Irene turned back, her eyes red. "You did, didn't you? That stuntman?"

Oh.

She glanced at Dash. Oh, that scoundrel. He'd probably even sent the press to hunt up a scandal.

Irene's voice softened. "He told me that you'd be upset, but that maybe you'd understand."

Understand.

Rosie glanced at Irene through her peripheral vision. The woman clung to the end of the bed, stared at Dash as if she might shatter, so much love, so much fear on her face, it could skewer Rosie through.

Yes, she understood exactly how it felt to lose the father of your child. To want and believe in something so much you didn't stop to consider the consequences. To hope that love might be enough.

Oh Irene.

Rosie couldn't breathe. She put down Dash's hand, tucking it back onto the bed. Then, she bent over and gently kissed his forehead. Her lipstick left an imprint as she pulled away. Good-bye, Dash.

"He's all yours, Irene," she said, backing away from the side of the bed. Irene stared after her.

Rosie offered her a sad smile.

Irene pressed a hand to her mouth then moved over to the chair, sat, and bent her head toward his hand. Began to weep.

"I'm so sorry for your loss," Rosie said quietly. Then she left them there, the ventilator wheezing out his last breaths.

* * * * *

The scent of the funeral flowers chased her out of the house and into the November sunshine. A glorious day with the sun high overhead in a cloudless sky. Seventy degrees, a slight wind caressing the palm trees, rippling the pond, the feathers of the swans.

Not a day to bury a friend.

Rosie unpinned her hat, removing the long black veil and setting the pillbox on the patio table. Even here, she couldn't escape the sympathy bouquets. White hydrangeas, lilies, roses.

She pulled out a rose from the bouquet, walked with it to the edge of the pool.

"You have to make a decision, Roxy. The bank won't wait."

She smelled the rose, ran her fingers along the silky petal. Fletcher would probably follow her to the bottom of the pool if she flung herself in. "Why today? Can't we wait one day after we bury poor Dash to sign away his dream?"

"Because the buyer won't wait. Because it's four million dollars, Roxy. And because, if you don't, then it'll all be on you to make it work. You'll have to pay the bank, roust the studio back into the black."

"And I'm just a silly blond starlet who doesn't know a thing about running a studio?" She glanced over her shoulder to Fletcher. And oh good, Marley stood behind him, the studio's lawyer, a man built like a bull and ready to trample right over her.

She brought the rose to her nose. "Who is this buyer?"

"He doesn't want his name given out. Not until the deal is signed."

She stared at the pool. "What makes this deal different from the one Warner offered us? Or Louis Mayer?"

"He's independent. You wouldn't be absorbed into another studio and join their cast of stars. You'd stay on as Palace Studios' lead actress."

"And give up control of my life, my contracts..."

"You'd get to stay in your home."

It seemed the longer Dash had lingered, the more word escaped of his financial woes. The press simply couldn't escape the tragedy of a life cut down in the prime.

The studio tried to spin it as a tragic accident. Probably Fletcher's handiwork, or better yet, Leo, the studio's press agent. But she read the faces of the congregation at today's funeral. Hunger.

Even Rooney had pulled her aside at the wake and suggested she sell him her contract before the bidding started.

She didn't have the courage to ask about Rolfe. Thankfully, she didn't have to because he showed up at the funeral.

Without a scrape, as if he hadn't crashed in a fiery pyre. Apparently he'd bailed out, but she hadn't seen it behind all that black smoke.

Rolfe had sat in the audience, third pew to the left of the First Methodist Episcopal Church, not meeting her eyes as she delivered Dash's eulogy. One of her best performances, she thought.

She made Dash practically sound like St. Peter.

Rolfe had escaped before she could leave her pew, disappearing into the throng outside the church.

She ran a finger between her eyes, rubbing away the dark throb there. "And Irene, what happens to her and her little boy?"

Silence behind her made her turn.

Fletcher was frowning at her. "What do you care?"

Irene had given birth to a healthy seven-pound baby the day before Dash died of sepsis. Roxy couldn't bear to look at her at the funeral, sitting with the studio as if she might be just one of the legion of secretaries.

Especially when Rosie found Irene's picture on the bureau next to Dash's bed while trying to find something of Dash's to give to the undertaker.

So, Dash had loved someone other than himself.

She felt like the other woman when she looked at Irene trying to soothe her newborn.

"She should go back to Ohio," Marley said. "It's not the studio's concern."

Rosie stared at her reflection cast across the pool, a long, looming shadow. Go back to Ohio.

"What if she doesn't want to leave? What if her home is here?"

"She has nothing here."

Except her memories. Her dreams.

"I remember when Dash showed me this house. I'd landed on his hotel room doorstep and asked him to make me a star. He could have closed the door in my face, made me get in line at Central Casting, but he didn't. He gave me a place to stay, gave me a screen test, and groomed me for a part. He even made a place for you, Fletcher, gave you a chance to make movies. And he had the screenplay for *Star for a Day* written for both of us. To give us what we wished for." She considered the rose then tossed it into the pool, watched it drift on the clear water.

She turned. "What would it take to keep the studio?"

Fletcher stilled. "Four million dollars."

"You know I don't have that."

"You can't keep the studio—"

She held up her hand to Marley. Looked at Fletcher.

"A loan, I guess, to cover production costs. A string of B-budget movies made fast, to keep us afloat, and then a few big-named stars to put together a smash hit. And lots of luck."

But Marley was shaking his head. "You don't have that kind of luck. Or time. Face it, Roxy. The game is over. Dashielle knew that— that's why he hocked the house, drained his bank account. That's why he took his life—"

"No. That's not why he took his life. He took his life because he was selfish and afraid. He took his life because he didn't trust the people who cared about him."

Her voice had risen, but she didn't care. "Dashielle Parks died because he saw everything he loved falling apart, slipping out of his hands. And he couldn't hold on."

"And neither can you," Marley said. "It's over, Roxy." He met her eyes with something of steel in his. "Sign the papers, before we all lose everything." He pulled out a file folder and set it on the patio.

"I've already lost everything," Rosie said, but Marley had walked away.

Fletcher gave her a pinched, hollow look, but followed him out.

She stood in the hot sun, in her black mourning dress, sweat dripping down her spine.

No.

But she picked up the sheaf of papers. The buyer listed himself through a corporation, Essex 315. She flipped the pages, read through the terms. Her eyes caught on a clause about retaining the current contracts of Palace Studios. Which meant she would be sold right along with Palace Studios.

No.

She folded the papers in half, carried them into the house, and dropped them on the long dining table, black and gleaming in the sunshine.

On the center of the table, beside an overflowing bouquet of purple tiger lilies, lay a pair of Dash's gold cuff links.

She scooped them up, examined them in the palm of her hand. They bore the Parks family's crest—a knight's helmet, surrounded by laurels.

He had no family at the funeral, his parents deceased.

And he hadn't legally passed on his name to an heir.

Oh Dash.

She closed the cuff links into her hand and wandered down to his room, pushing open the door.

She'd instructed Louise not to touch the room, to concentrate, instead, on scrubbing the blood from the patio, the hallway. Now, she stood in the door frame of the expansive suite, watching the sun part the heavy green velveteen drapes and graze over his desk, cluttered with papers, books, scripts.

Someone had made his bed, drawing up a chenille coverlet over the sheets, tucking them into the carved mahogany bed, the curved footboard, the ornate, scrolled headboard. She walked over to the high dresser, noted his watch curled into a tray on top. She set the cuff links in the tray.

He'd left his shoes sitting out next to his butler's stand rack. His tuxedo coat and pants hung on it. She walked over to it, ran her finger down the seam of the jacket.

Dash.

She could smell him, the enticing splash of his cologne permeating his room.

And, if she closed her eyes, she heard his steps in the hallway, could feel his hands on her shoulders, his breath on her neck.

Yes, she'd loved him. Or rather, she'd loved his dreams. The hope he had in her.

She slipped the jacket off the hanger, pulled it over her shoulders, slipped her arms through it. It dwarfed her, but she stood at the mirror and rolled up the sleeves. Reached over to grab his white scarf and wound it around her waist.

Stared at her profile. Studio mogul, indeed.

Oh, what was she thinking? She couldn't take over the studio. Hadn't the foggiest idea of how to run something so massive.

Four million dollars in debt.

She sat on the bed.

Once upon a time, she'd been the daughter of an heiress.

In fact, once upon a time, she'd been bequeathed a fortune. But she'd turned it down, wanted to find her own life.

Her own destiny.

She lay back on the bed and stuck her hands into his pockets. Something brushed against her hand, and she pulled it out.

A playbill from the *Star for a Day* premiere. The photograph depicted her wrapped in a fur, Grayson sitting at her feet, staring up at her, as if love struck.

The fantasy of show business.

That's all this was—a fantasy. Maybe, like Irene, she should give up, head back to Montana. Be a mother to Coco.

She laid the playbill on the bed and got up.

Dash had his own private liquor store on the bureau. She uncapped one of the decanters, sniffed, pulled away.

But she filled a glass anyway, two fingers high, and capped it.

She turned and held it to the mirror. "To your dreams, Dash." She swallowed the heat in her throat as she threw the drink back.

Oh. Everything trembled, the room turning woozy, and she reached out for the dresser. Oh.

Her throat turned to fire, her stomach spasming.

She might be ill.

Pressing her hand to her stomach, she left his room, going back to the dining room. Picked up the contract.

No, perhaps she didn't belong here at all.

She walked out to the patio. Sank onto a lounge chair. Spread the contract out on her lap as the sun began to drift toward the horizon.

Maybe it was time a girl stopped fighting destiny.

* * * * *

"Mama!"

How many times did she let herself curl into the dream? Rosie didn't even bother to nudge herself, to hold back.

Not this time.

This time she let her heart tumble into the fantasy, allowed herself to stand at the end of the road and breathe in the Montana air, the tangy smell of the sagebrush, the bitterroot flowers. Listen to the sound of cattle ranging over the hills. Laugh at the prairie dogs that watched her as she headed toward the big white house, the red barn.

Everything she remembered about Lilly and Truman's home.

She spied Lilly on the porch, her body rounded with pregnancy, her dark hair long again and plaited. And Truman, tall and dark, emerging from the barn, wiping his hands with a cloth, probably working on the engine of their Cessna.

But Rosie's gaze settled on Coco, the little girl with the auburn hair tufting out in curls, just like her daddy's. She wore a pair of britches, a floral shirt, a bonnet to shade her nose from the sun, and she played on the dirt and grass, holding a doll.

Always holding the doll.

Rosie had picked it up in a shop off Sunset Boulevard.

Her heartbeat quickened at the sight of the little girl, the sun kissing her nose as she laughed. Yes, she had Guthrie's blue eyes.

She was near enough now to— "Coco!"

She expected the little girl to raise her head. Maybe glance down the road. Rosie lifted her hand. "Coco!"

Lilly came down the steps. Sat on the end of them. Held out her arms.

Coco stood up, waddled toward Lilly, starting to run.

"Coco!"

But the little girl never turned. She picked up her pace then tripped.

She skidded into the dirt with a wail.

Rosie began to run toward her.

Lilly also came off the porch. She reached the little girl first, swooped her up in her arms. Held her close, soothing her.

Her sobs lifted into the sky, coiled around Rosie's heart, and squeezed.

Truman came up and lifted Coco into his embrace. Tall and lean, he looked like a flier, and now he raised Coco above his head, soaring her through the air.

Coco laughed, and he brought her back down, nuzzled her neck. She tried to squirm away, but Lilly tickled her.

She screeched and kicked.

"Not too high, Tru," Lilly said.

He was making airplane sounds.

Maybe they didn't see her.

"Lilly!" She picked up her pace, could see now Lilly's expression, the softness on her face.

Neither of them looked up at her.

Lilly put her hand on his arm. "Dinner is ready," she said. She reached over for Coco. "Wash up."

Truman surrendered the toddler, kissed her on the cheek.

Then he got up and almost walked right through Rosie. She gasped, stepped out of his way, nearly losing her balance.

Lilly propped Coco on what remained of her hip and headed inside.

"Lilly!"

The sound of her voice woke Rosie, and she shook herself awake.

She'd fallen asleep on the lounger, the crickets serenading her in the darkness. Overhead, the stars sprinkled across the velvet sky, watching.

Seeing.

The dream felt so real, it might have been a memory. But she hadn't returned since that day she'd left her daughter with Lilly.

She'd only dreamed about it.

But she didn't belong there. Not anymore. Coco had a mother, and it wasn't Rosie.

If she started over, where would she go?

She closed her eyes, and too easily Rolfe appeared, the way he'd held her on the beach.

"I've waited this long. I guess I can wait until you're ready."

But he hadn't, had he? And even if he had, she couldn't give away her heart. Not anymore. Not when she had nearly nothing left to give.

No, she couldn't start over again.

Behind her, in the house, she heard sniffing, the sound of whimpering. She got up and turned to see Irene standing in the living room.

She held her infant, rocking him, her face shiny. "I—I didn't know where—they won't let me stay at the boardinghouse."

Oh. Rosie spied the suitcase by Irene's feet. "I see."

"I didn't know where else to go—"

The baby began to fuss, to squirm. No wonder she'd heard crying. Rosie walked over to them, cupped her hand over the baby's downy head. So soft. "What's his name?"

"Dash said he always liked the name Sammy."

"He did. That was the name of his dog, growing up."

Her expression fell.

Rosie watched the baby squirm, one tiny arm snaking out of the blanket, his hand fisted. "I think Sammy Parks is a fine name."

Irene looked up at her, her smile trembling. "I didn't know you two were married until—until I got pregnant. And even then, I didn't tell Dash. I stayed away from him. And then that night at the premiere in New York City, I couldn't hide it anymore. He found out, and... he was so upset. I thought he was going to put me on a train back to Ohio. And then—then things changed. He told me we'd be together, but that he needed to get a divorce first."

She didn't bother to wipe her face.

"I didn't know, Roxy. I really didn't know."

Roxy stuck her hands into the tuxedo pockets. Nodded. "Dash has never loved anyone but himself. I think maybe you changed that."

She bit her lip, bent to soothe the fussy baby.

"He looks hungry."

She nodded.

"I'll show you to Dash's room. You can stay there."

Irene's eyes turned on her, so needy, so afraid, that the crazy urge to wrap her arms around her rose up inside Rosie.

Instead, she picked up the suitcase. "It's a big house. And they can't evict me immediately."

Irene followed her down the hallway. "What do you mean, evict you?"

"Palace Studios is broke. Lost everything in the stock market crash. We have to sell."

"Why?"

She glanced over her shoulder. "Because, although I can probably come up with a loan, I haven't the foggiest idea how to run a studio. Dash did all that."

"*I* did all that." Irene had stopped, the shadows half illuminating her face. "I was Dash's secretary for the last two years. I might be young, but I wrote every letter; I took notes on every business deal; I arranged every phone call; I went to every business dinner. Dash made the decisions, but I watched how he did it. I know the business side of Hollywood, Roxy."

Roxy stopped at Dash's door. Opened it. The moonlight fell over his bed.

"I've never been in here before," she said. "Dash always—well, he said this was your home. He didn't want you to feel betrayed in it."

How thoughtful. But, oddly, she didn't feel betrayed. Not as she watched Irene walk in, set Sammy on the bed. He was sucking on his hand, rooting for something to eat.

Irene stood over him, unbuttoning her shirt.

"Irene, do you think you could help me run Palace Studios?"

The woman sat down on the bed, scooped up Sammy. He began to nurse. She looked at Rosie in the moonlight. Smiled. "You are everything Dash ever said about you."

Rosie frowned.

"Brave. And gracious. And kind."

Had Dash known her at all? "I don't think—"

"Dash loved you. And he loved me. And I think the fact that he'd betrayed us both is what killed him." Irene ducked her head then swallowed and looked away, into the night.

No, what killed him was that, after everything he'd been given, it wasn't enough.

Rosie closed the door behind her then walked through the house, back out to the patio, onto the lawn. Her toes slid through the blades, cool against her bare feet. She walked past the pool deck, all the way to the edge of the pond.

The white swans had disappeared for the night. Only the moonlight parted the darkness, silver on the rippling, dark water.

"I don't know why you abandoned us, Dash. But I'm tired of starting over. I'm tired of running."

She pulled the contract from the tuxedo pocket. Ran her thumb over her signature. The wind ruffled the pages, threatening to ease it from her grip, toss it into the darkness.

She tore the contract in half and dropped it into the pond. Let the fish eat it.

Then she looked at the stars, rubbing her arms against the goose-flesh. "My destiny belongs to me, thank You. I don't need Your help."

And fantasy? Fantasy was for dreamers. For stars. For blond bombshells.

For Roxy Price.

Not for the heiress of the Worth Family fortune.

Not for the head of Palace Studios.

PART TWO

1937
STARLET

Chapter 5

If she could, Rosie would climb into her double bed, pull the gauzy white curtains around the four posters, pull the silk coverlet to her chin, and lose herself in the cloud of her sheets. There, she'd tuck herself into a quiet place, no sound stages with directors haranguing her, no klieg lights to burn her eyes. No diet masseuse to prod her into shape, no hairdresser to pencil in her eyebrows, no studio publicist to drag her to a cheesecake photo shoot, not even a lunch at the Brown Derby with one of Fletcher's newest Central Casting leading men to tempt her.

No, she'd close her eyes, maybe drift back to Paris, so many years ago, to her impressionable youth, to the moment when she stood in the window watching the funeral of actress Sarah Bernhardt, longing to live the life she'd left behind. In that moment, perhaps Rosie would whisper a different truth into the ears of that twenty-year-old flapper.

Maybe she didn't want to be famous. She just wanted to be happy.

But fame was what she'd procured after eight years and twenty-six films, two musicals, and an unauthorized biography. That—and a studio that could nearly pay its bills. A studio that she helmed.

A studio that might weather the storm of the Great Depression if they could hang on. MGM had already posted millions of dollars in losses this year, and she doubted the Warner Brothers, despite

Jack Warner's legendary miser economics, fared any better. With the Depression in full swing around the country, people simply didn't have the income to flock to the theaters.

Despite the public's need to keep the fantasy alive.

B movies, budgeted down to the bare bones, with cut-rate extras and stars—like Roxy—who would work for the privilege of her name above the title on the movie poster, kept Palace Studios in business.

That, and the fact that Rosie wore two hats. She'd moved into Dashielle's office, added Irene to her staff, moved Fletcher to head producer, and given him the reins on the budget. She didn't blame him for his tight control of the directors, or the fact that he usually chose the cast. He'd cut production schedules down to seven weeks, worked the extras nearly around the clock, and made sure every costume landed back in the costume department. He even instructed Irene to bill actors for their bottled water consumption and made them appear at wardrobe and makeup by 7:00 a.m.

No MGM royalty at Palace Studios. Actors worked for their dimes, smiled when the cameras flashed, and belonged like cattle to the hand that fed them.

The fantasy life of a movie star.

Reality was the nuts and bolts that went into a movie. The reading of thousands of plays and books and treatments to discover a story, the rewriting into a script, then the selection of a director.

Rosie could barely keep up with the stack of material on her desk or the new faces sent over from Central Casting.

She should recommend to Fletcher the fellow who played Turkey Morgan in the new Curtiz movie, *Kid Galahad*. He had a rugged, almost wounded rawness about him that America would find appealing.

Okay, she could admit that, maybe, she should let Fletcher choose his cast, and she too often prowled the sound stages they rented from the nearby MGM lot to supervise the costuming, the lights, even the makeup on a current production.

And yes, occasionally, she might change actors' lines, handing them new pages mid-production.

But that's what it took to run a studio, even a tiny one. She didn't expect to ever host the grand star lineup of MGM or Paramount, but she still had to compete in the world of Jack Warner and Samuel Mayer.

Especially if she hoped to take Dashielle's place and keep their little production studio in the black.

She held out hope that, someday, she might stumble across a blockbuster script.

But first she had to nail her lines.

"Roxy, I hate to interfere, but you won't mind actually remembering your blocking and hitting your mark on cue, would you?"

She looked up, her eyes burning. Her scalp itched, and her skin blistered under the hot lights. It might be eight hundred degrees in here. They hadn't eaten since lunch. But no one would move until Fletcher got his shot.

And she'd thought Rooney had been a tyrant. He might have been reckless, but at least he'd fed her.

She blinked against the glaring lights, seeing spots. "Sorry."

Fletcher came into focus, standing in front of the lights, a dark shape of anger. "Okay, that's enough for today." He waved his hand, and the entire sound stage seemed to exhale, grips and gaffers, extras hanging around on the fringes, some playing bridge, others hoping for a line. Grayson leaned up from his perch on the café bar, where she was supposed to walk in and steal his drink.

He shot her a look, shaking his head, then headed over to the wings.

She followed him with her gaze, squinting at the woman waiting there. Stared. No—

Fletcher approached Rosie, his shirtsleeves rolled up, his tie loosened. He smelled of cigarette smoke and a bourbon lunch.

"What is Joan Crawford doing here?"

Fletcher said nothing, and she looked at him.

"It's a good role, and we're only a week into shooting."

Her mouth opened. She glanced back at Joan, young and smiling up at Grayson, who'd only matured into the years, his dark hair lazy over his blue eyes, the way he smiled turning the average farm girl to a puddle of swoon.

Yes, he and Joan looked good together, her with her blond hair perfectly coiffed, those enormous brown eyes that stared up at him, her movie-star smile. He held out his arm, and she took it.

"This is my role, Fletcher. *A Man to Hold* is *my* movie."

"I'm not giving it away." But his frown suggested more.

"We can't afford her." She cut her voice low. "She's temperamental and difficult to work with. And her last movie was wretched. Did you even see—"

"*Love on the Run*? Yes. It wasn't wretched and you know it. She and Grayson had real charm. Put them together again and we'll have a hit."

She looked away. Heard laughter as Grayson led her away.

Fletcher held up his hands. "Do you want to make money, or do you want the adoration of the public?"

She drew in a breath. "I'll see you in the morning."

"Don't you want to watch the rushes?"

She ignored him, her head pounding as she walked back to her dressing room, a tiny canvas-walled cubicle with a table and chairs, mirror, and dressing screen. She changed, leaving her costume, a blue pinstriped dress, hanging over the top of the screen, and headed to her office.

Irene had already left. But Sammy and his nanny, Myrna, were due home today.

No wonder Rosie couldn't think.

The sun hung over the lot, casting long shadows between the exterior props, the tall castle façade where Rooney shot his *Sherwood Adventures* epic, the cityscape where gangsters and cops fought out the uncensored ending of *Face of Scars*.

Across the lawn, the production crew from the other closed stage, 2B, began to emerge, grips and gaffers, the craft team, wardrobe, the cameramen, and sound team streaming into the June heat. They headed toward the cafeteria or out through the whitewashed gates onto Santa Monica Boulevard.

She walked into the offices of the producing units, the ground floor of the executive building. Their staff writers, Jacob and Harry Epstein, brothers from New York she'd discovered four years ago, lifted their heads as she passed their office. Jacob nodded at her. She'd heard he'd had a son not long ago. Harry and Grayson occasionally liked to leave a trail of headlines at the Coconut Grove.

She took the elevator up to her office, noticed that, yes, Irene had left, her own office dark through the glass, the door closed.

Rosie kicked off her shoes and let her stocking feet drag through the carpet of her office. Lamplight glowed upon a sheaf of papers on her oak desk. The daily production and progress reports of their other two movies. One of them was a B movie that Rooney was shooting out on location in Kauai.

She might have liked to work on that film. If Rooney hadn't signed up to direct it. She still hadn't quite unwound from the shoot in Lake Isabella, by the Sequoia National Forest, where Rooney had her covered in dust for a month as he shot, and reshot, and reshot yet another gunslinger showdown.

They weren't making *All Quiet on the Western Front,* for pity's sake. No one would nominate *Riders of the Sagebrush* for an Academy Award. But Rooney couldn't be deterred from his epic mind-set.

Even if he had to risk her life on the top of a runaway stage. Or nearly get her trampled by a cattle stampede.

No, she wouldn't mind a few months—maybe a year—away from Rooney Sherwood, and especially away from his idea that the fewer clothes she wore, the more tickets she sold.

Whoever heard of a rancher's wife cavorting around in a white nightie as she held off rustlers?

It wasn't the era of the bombshell any longer. America wanted morals, and with the "Motion Picture Production Code" passed down by Congress, a bombshell didn't have a place on the hometown theaters. Not in today's films.

And it wouldn't help to turn her into a redhead, regardless of how Fletcher and Rooney tried. She wanted a role that actually turned her into an *actress.* Something that, well…wouldn't it be nice if the new Academy noticed?

She'd settle, however, for something that America noticed. Something that changed lives. That made her an icon.

Unforgotten. Beloved. Brilliant.

She picked up a script on her desk, considered it a moment, then tucked it under her arm, grabbed her bag, and stopped by the mirror to tie a scarf around her head, her neck. She slipped her shoes back on and flicked off her light.

Tonight, she'd make it home before dark.

She lifted her hand to the studio security officer as she pulled out onto Palace Boulevard in her white convertible Rolls. The sun heated her face on its downward slide over the ocean.

The script lay on the seat beside her, the pages fanning up in the wind. She waved with a gloved hand at a couple of young girls camped out on the sidewalk, fans hoping for a peek at Grayson or any of the other studio actors.

They ran after her, however, calling her name, waving a studio photograph, wanting an autograph. She nearly stopped at the corner, but her throat ached, and she just wanted to get home.

To see Sammy. How he would have grown, his dark hair curly upon his head. And his blue eyes dancing for her, even if she couldn't quite surrender to picking him up, hugging him to herself, inhaling his little boy sweetness.

Maybe someday—when guilt loosened its grip.

She turned onto Rodeo Drive and let a summer breeze lift the day from her chest. The fight with Fletcher, the budget numbers on Rooney's latest film, the news from the trades of MGM's financial straits—if they went into receivership, then they'd certainly raise the rent on the Palace rentals.

Even the studio's masseuse had left Rosie more bruised than relaxed.

She wouldn't even think about Grayson's flirting with Joan. Not that she cared, but…

She pressed her lips together. Refused to remember their laughter.

At least he wasn't focusing his aim on yet another starlet who would be his mood of the weekend.

And, she didn't want a man like Grayson. A man at all, really. She had her fans.

But, Joan Crawford? *"She and Grayson had real charm. Put them together again and we'll have a hit on our hands."*

Sometimes she hated this business and the jealousy it too easily churned inside.

Rosie turned down her street, oak-lined and shady, trapping the fragrances of summer among the ivy-lined homes, the plush lawns. Two miniature cedar trees flanked the marble pillars of her drive. She beeped, and Rogers opened the gate for her. She didn't stop as she drove up the brick driveway, seeing the gardener had finally tied up the hydrangeas and peonies that overflowed the bed by her front steps. The lilac tree dropped nearly all of its purple buds onto the lawn. Tonight, she'd open her window and savor the aroma.

She stopped and got out. Stood in the driveway, breathing in the smell of evening, the fresh-cut grass. She was reaching for the script as Louise came out.

"Are they home?" She handed the satchel to Louise, slipped her handbag onto her arm.

"Just thirty minutes ago. Shall I tell Cook to wait for dinner?"

"I'm not that hungry."

But Louise had that look, the one that reminded her of her mother, Jinx, when Rosie had arrived home after Dash's funeral.

I need my trust fund, Mother. And a loan from Bennett.

For a long moment, right then, with her mother's sad look, Rosie had considered staying. Considered rebuilding her life in New York, perhaps on Broadway. But she had promises to keep on the West Coast.

Now, with Finn grown at twenty and off at college, perhaps her mother would come west. Especially after Bennett's recent heart attack. Her stepfather could use life near a beach, something away from the pressure of his shipping company.

Louise closed the front door behind Rosie as she entered, and the house captured the stillness of a long day. The faintest scent of Dorian's cooking, parsley, chives, tarragon, and oregano drifted down the hall. Maybe lamb, or even ratatouille.

Her stomach growled, the Cobb salad delivered from the Brown Derby to Stage 1A long forgotten. Maybe she could manage some food.

She toed off her shoes, her stockings hot and sticky on her legs, the tile cool against her bare feet. She could hear laughter, high and sweet in the next room, and it filled her soul like a breeze off the ocean, deep and thick and salting every pore with a tangy heat.

She couldn't admit it, not really, but Sammy's laughter was what echoed in her heart, reeled her back home no matter where she wandered.

"Rosie, is that you?"

Irene came around the corner, her blond hair in tight waves, dressed in a blue work dress, belted at the waist. Obviously home just moments before her. "I'm glad you made it home before midnight. Or at all."

Rosie dropped her handbag onto the entry table. "I fell asleep last night looking over the latest production sheets. Who knows what Rooney's doing?" She shook her head. "I knew we shouldn't have let him talk us into it."

"It's a beach movie. Set in Hawaii. With soldiers and hula girls. It'll be a hit."

"Let's hope that it actually pays for itself. Is Sammy here?"

"Finishing up a sandwich in the kitchen—"

"Aunt Rosie!" Rosie tried to hide a smile at Sammy and the way he skidded into the room.

Times like this, oh, Rosie wanted to hold out her arms to him, to scoop him up, to mold him to herself. But she had long ago schooled those urges into submission and now, at seven, he'd only squirm away. "Hello, Sammy," she said.

Lanky and already handsome, he had Dashielle's dark eyes and dangerous good looks. Thankfully, he still had enough little boy in him to make her breathe relief.

He grinned at her, his cowlick standing straight up. She had the urge to lick it down. Instead, she reached for her handbag. "There might be a surprise in here for you," Rosie said and handed him the handbag.

Myrna, tall and robust and enough of a matron to mother them all, appeared behind him, her brown hair tied up in a predictable bun. "He's tired after the plane ride from Ohio. It's been a long trip."

His once-a-year trip to see his grandparents. Rosie never asked why Irene didn't accompany him.

He grabbed it, grinning up at her as he opened it, found a package inside, something wrapped in tissue.

"I have one guess," his mother said, but Roxy looked up and winked at Irene.

"Maybe he'll be a detective someday," she said softly as Sammy unwrapped the package.

"Another Hardy Boys!"

"*A Figure in Hiding*—their new one. I saw it in a shop and thought of you."

"Aw, this is just swell, Aunt Rosie." He grinned up at her, and then, suddenly, wrapped his arms around her waist.

She startled, but put her arms around him. Oh, she should have known that a child of Dashielle Parks would possess too much charm for her own good. Too bad he'd never know the identity of his father.

Irene made that clear and warned everyone in the household from breathing the truth.

Irene didn't have the heart to blight Dash's name, even now.

"I'm glad you like it," she said.

Irene picked up the handbag, snapping it closed. "You spoil him."

"Not enough," Rosie said, watching him go. He strolled out into the lawn, the fireflies blinking in the twilight, and settled on a chaise lounge, cracking open the book.

In this area only, Irene won. She had the prize, the one thing Rosie would never have. She'd never told Irene about the miscarriage, not wanting to put that between them. But sometimes, she considered the loss of Dash's child.

Considered what a different life might look like.

Thankfully, Irene behaved as if Sammy belonged to the both of them. Much like, perhaps, Rosie behaved with Palace Studios.

Indeed, Irene had developed into a top junior executive, keeping Rosie in the know at Palace Studios, negotiating contracts, watching budgets, working with distributors and the publicity office, even reading scripts. She knew more about the day-to-day studio operations than Rosie. All the same, Rosie's name was etched on the door—not to mention on the loan from Bennett and, especially, the executive papers. And Rosie had engineered the rise from the red books to the red carpet for Palace Studios over the past five years.

So, while Irene raised Sammy, Rosie raised a studio.

If only it filled her with the same sense of joy.

"Sammy looks like he's grown a yard since I last saw him." Rosie walked into the family room, down the steps to the sunken area, and sank into the white divan. She and Irene had redecorated during the filming of *Eight for Dinner*, for a promotional spread in *Photoplay*, and turned her favorite room into a white cloud with faux lambskin carpets, a white damask silk divan, and two white velveteen chairs. A gold chandelier hung over the white piano—not that anyone ever played it—and they had even reset the stone fireplace in white marble.

A spray of white orchids decorated the center of the glass table.

All of it was a fabulous attempt to turn her bombshell image into pure glamour. More of the star-making machine, but it had worked.

White became the new rage across the country.

Rosie reached up under her dress and unpinned her stockings. Then she rolled them down, past her knees, working them off her feet. "Fletcher turned into a regular beast on the set today, dressed me down in front of the entire crew."

Irene made a face. "He's terrible if he feels he's running behind. But if it were Rooney, you'd still be there, working."

"True." Rosie removed her other stocking then leaned her head back on the divan. Outside, tulips swayed in the evening breeze, the pond rippling. A black swan paddled around the pond, in the shadows. She watched Sammy sitting on the chaise near the pool, her gaze pinned to him until he moved away. She'd once suggested filling it in, but Irene wanted to teach him to swim.

Rosie still had nightmares, occasionally, of finding the child at the bottom.

"You look tired. Maybe you should take a break. No one does twenty films in four years. Fletcher will forgive you for declining the role. Besides, the studio doesn't own you anymore."

"It doesn't?" She opened an eye. "We have even more at stake now. MGM might be losing money, but Palace Studios has to stay in the black if we want to survive. Still…" She pressed her hands to her face, feeling the bones there. "I'm not sure I can carry the roles anymore." So unfair that Grayson could act until he dropped at the age of eighty, but a starlet's lifespan lasted until the next It Girl took her place.

"What do you mean?"

"You know what they say. You have three years of fame in this business, tops. And my two years, going on eight, are nearly up."

"You're an icon."

She held up a finger. "One flop, just one. But a streak of three and I'm done for. You're just being nice to suggest that *Jungle Nights* wasn't a box-office bust. We need a blockbuster if we want to stay afloat, keep ahead of Paramount and MGM and those Warner Boys."

She leaned up, running her hand around the back of her neck. "I saw Joan Crawford today, lurking around the sound studio. She's thirsty for this role with Grayson. I can feel it."

"I think she has something going with Grayson. Did you see them in *Don't Run from Love?* Sparks. Real sparks." She sighed, and Rosie might have heard something of longing in it. "The buzz is that they actually ran away together for two weeks after that film."

Rosie rubbed her forehead. "I don't want to hear about Grayson and Joan and sparks. If she's smart, she'll run as fast as her pretty legs will carry her from Grayson Clarke. His kind of sparks could turn her career to flames if gossip queen Louella Parsons gets ahold of any hint of a relationship between them. At best, she's just going to get burned."

Irene looked at her, wearing a sad smile. "Nearly eight years, and you still haven't figured out how to get Rolfe Van Horne from your heart."

Rosie stilled. Looked away.

"I'm not blind, Rosie. You barely looked at Tagg Channing last time he was here. He had to play croquet all by himself."

"He played with Janet Gaynor. He hardly suffered."

"Tagg is sweet, handsome, and just smitten enough to jump when Fletcher decides you need a date. A guy like that might make you forget Rolfe Van Horne."

Hardly. But Rolfe had all but vanished from Hollywood the day after Dash's funeral, and not even Rooney hinted at his existence. And after almost eight years she had done her dead-level best to forget him. Besides, it hadn't been love, not really. She'd simply been angry, lonely, even a little thirsty for attention. She didn't need love. Didn't even want it. It was just so…exhausting.

She had to keep reminding herself of that.

"I *have* forgotten Rolfe Van Horne, I promise."

Irene narrowed her eyes, and then she walked over and picked up a notepad off the desk near the window. "Do you want me to go over your calls? Or would you prefer to know the guest list for Sunday's barbeque."

Rosie made a face. "Oh no. The barbeque. I forgot. Please tell me that I don't have to attend."

"Ten minutes. An appearance. And by the way, Joan will be here." Irene smiled. "And Bette."

"Perfect. So they can flirt with Fletcher and steal my parts."

"Maybe you'll steal theirs. How about if I make you some tea for that throat?"

She ran a hand down it. "It sounds pretty bad?"

Irene nodded. Then she sat down on the divan. "Really. Don't you think it's time to take a break? So what if Joan lands this part?"

"And what? I say good-bye to my career?"

"You still have the studio."

The studio didn't earn her applause or fans lining the red carpet. The studio didn't tell her that she was beautiful and beloved. "How about pouring me a drink? A glass of cabernet?"

A frown creased Irene's brow, but she got up, went to the kitchen.

Rosie undid her scarf, took it off. Then she reached up and drew the wig off her head. Air, blessed, sweet air. It lifted the heat from her scalp. She couldn't help it; she drew off the hair net.

So little remained of the blond hair, she'd gotten used to the feel of her bare scalp. Now she ran a hand over it, feeling the bumps and ridges. Tiny fuzz brushed against her fingers and, along with it, a forbidden spur of hope.

Maybe, finally, it was growing back.

"Oh my—oh!"

A glass crashed, shattered, and she looked up to see Irene in the hallway, the wine puddling on the floor, shards of glass curled around her feet. Her hand covered her mouth. "I'm so sorry." Her gaze fixed on Rosie's head then to the wig and back.

Oh. Rosie drew her hand down. "I'm sorry. I—shouldn't have—"

"I—Oh, Rosie, when did it happen?"

"On the set of *Riders of the Sagebrush*. It just all came out, in huge clumps. I sat there at the mirror, my hair in my hands and—" She smiled through the burn in her chest. "It's from the bleach, they think. But, it'll be okay. I think it's growing back."

Dorian came from the kitchen. Short and dark haired, she spoke with an accent and did her best to keep Rosie regularly fighting her figure. "Mademoiselle Price, you're home." She looked at Irene. "Are you all right?"

"Can you clean this up, please?" Irene said and stepped away from the puddle of glass.

She turned away from Rosie, pressed a hand to her mouth.

Rosie hadn't really looked in the mirror since that day, not without a wig. She always managed to tuck her hair into her net before glancing at the mirror. But, it wasn't that awful, was it?

She heard feet skid across the patio, a low growl, and Rosie reached for the wig just as Sammy bounded in off the porch.

He skidded to a stop and stared at her as she scrambled to fit it on. Then his eyes widened, and he gasped.

It was enough to serrate Rosie clear through.

"Shh, Sammy, it's not polite." Irene turned him away from her.

"No, he's right. It's terrible." Rosie fitted on the wig, got up, feeling weak. "Sammy, it's okay. It'll grow back." She met Irene's gaze, hating that, for the first time, she too wanted to cry. She'd been so brave on the set, glad that Rooney had concocted the red wig for the western production. He'd likely heard about her troubles from wardrobe, but he'd spun it as a new look. A modern, redheaded look designed to turn her into a woman of the frontier.

In a white nightie, of course.

Rosie reached out to Sammy, but he flinched and backed away from her, a sort of horror in his eyes, even as he tried to hide it.

And right then, she caught sight of herself in the mirror on the wall behind Irene. She hadn't put the wig on correctly, it sat askew on her head, messy and awkward.

The face that stared back appeared sallow, her eyes gaunt, her cheekbones pronounced, the lines above her bald eyebrows faded and smudged.

She looked old. Worn.

Maybe she did need a break. Worse, maybe she should just surrender her career to Joan Crawford and Bette Davis. Maybe the flame of her stardom had already flickered out.

"I'll be in my room," Rosie said quietly, turning. But Irene caught her arm.

"I'm sorry. He didn't mean it."

Rosie shook her head. "He's just reacting exactly how my fans would react. How I would react. It's not pretty. I know it. But maybe it's who I am. I just have to face it."

"It's not who you are, Rosie."

She met Irene's eyes. Put a hand on Sammy's shoulder.

Oh, she hoped not.

But as she gathered up her hosiery, the script, and her satchel then padded down the hall to her glorious, angelic white room to hide, she realized that perhaps she didn't know who she was anymore. Really.

Or maybe, who she was supposed to be.

She nudged open her door and dropped the debris from her arms onto her bed. Stood there in the darkness.

Then she climbed onto the bed, drew up her legs, and wrapped her arms around herself in a quiet, tight embrace.

* * * * *

"Why did you come back to me? To break my heart? To destroy me?"

Rosie turned away from Grayson, kept her head up for the camera to find her face and stayed on her mark, holding her emotions taut for the close-up.

He came up behind her, sliding his hands over her shoulders. "Why do you think, Eva? Because every day I was rotting in that cell, the only thing that kept me alive was you. I kept thinking of you and the idea that, maybe, you'd be waiting for me."

She could smell his breath, close to her neck, hot and tickling her skin. Dressed in a satin bathrobe, the sweat from the soundstage lights clung to her skin and beaded down her spine. Grayson pressed her close to him, looking up for the camera to capture his angst.

"I don't love you anymore." The line came out just as she'd hoped, filled with lies, a tremor at the end. But she'd used what Rolfe taught her so long ago. Find the truth in the emotion, let it roll out into her character. "You shouldn't be here."

"I know you still love me, Eva. I know it as sure as I stand here breathing." He took her by the shoulders, turned her, lifted her chin.

She could smell a hint of his old-fashioned from lunch, the dusky scent of cigarettes. After four films, Grayson no longer turned her stomach aflutter as he stared into her eyes, no longer made her believe when he ran his thumb so sweetly down her cheek. No longer swept his name into her mind as he pulled her close and pressed his lips against hers.

But she could admit to wishing that, perhaps, one day, some man might find her, mean it. Some man might pine for her as he sat in jail for a crime he didn't commit, and crossed a country to come back to her, believing in her love despite her brutal words.

She put that longing into her response, kissing him back, making sure her face stayed beautiful and strong as she finally pushed him away. "What are you doing?"

"Making you remember all we had. Eva, you're my girl. That's never going to change."

"Get out, Patch. Get out and leave me alone!"

She pressed her hand to her mouth, turned away, again found the camera, delighted that she'd managed to conjure real tears.

She held herself there as Grayson turned. Closed her eyes as he marched stage left, toward the door.

She knew that he would turn and look at her and she let her face betray the urge to run into his arms.

Then he left, slamming the door, and she shook at the sound, visibly wounded by her own hardened heart.

"Cut!" Fletcher emerged from the darkness, where he'd been watching from one of his camera angles. He gave her a rare smile. "Well done, Roxy. Take a break, and we'll pick it up at the start of scene 123 in the café, retake what we lost yesterday."

He came over to her, indicated that Grayson should join them. "I have a few changes for the scene. We're going to start it with a shot of you, alone, cleaning tables instead of Grayson at the bar. That's when you enter, Grayson. Then the baby cries offstage and you, Roxy, rush to pick him up, exit stage left. You'll come back in, holding your baby, and Grayson, we'll do a close-up then on your realization that Roxy had your child."

Grayson cocked that irritating smile. "She's always keeping secrets from me, aren't you, doll?"

Her head had begun to pound, but she found a smile. "You deserve it."

Fletcher waved his hand for a grip, who came over with a sheaf of papers.

"Not more pages," Grayson said, taking the papers, flipping through them.

"Just a few more lines," Fletcher said. "We'll do a run-through in twenty." He turned away, heading for one of his cameramen.

She looked at the pages, running through the blocking, the stage directions, the lines in her head.

"I'll have to get Fishe to run lines with me," Grayson said. "Unless you want to give it a go."

"Why don't you ask Joan?" she snapped. She hated that the words ran out of her mouth. Grayson frowned.

"No, I didn't mean that. Sorry, Gray. I'm not feeling well." She pressed a hand to her forehead, felt the moisture there. Heat bled into her hand. Her head pounded, probably from the shouts of the grips and gaffers staging the café scene.

"Joan has nothing on you, Roxy." He gave her a smile that could woo the world. Then he tucked a hand under her elbow. "Let me get you a drink of water."

She let him steer her to her dressing room, and she sank into a canvas chair, closing her eyes. An assistant appeared with water and a plate of fruit. *"Joan has nothing on you."* After today, no. She'd prepped half the night for today's shooting, came before 7:00 a.m. with a raging headache, her throat scratchy.

No temper tantrum for her. She was an actress, and the trades wouldn't kill her career yet. Besides, as long as she showed up, Fletcher had no reason to replace her.

She opened her eyes, took an orange, and began to peel it. Her costume, a blue and white dress, now hung from a dressmaker's stand. Her hairdresser arrived to affix a scarf to her hair, waiting for her to change first.

Beyond the canvas curtains, she heard the grips moving the cameras to the café set.

She just wanted to sit here and rub her feet. Instead she finished peeling the orange, separated the sections, and bit into one. Then she took a drink. Her throat burned as it went down, still aching.

When she got up, the world turned woozy and swam before her eyes. She put a hand out, and her hairdresser caught it.

"Are you okay, Miss Price?"

She blinked, righted herself. "Yes." But the water sloshed in her stomach, turning her nausea. She slipped behind the screen and allowed the wardrobe assistant to help her with the dress, stepping out of the frilly, high-necked robe from the previous scene, and into the waitress uniform.

She drew in her stomach as the dresser zipped her and relived a memory from the days her mother made her wear a corset, her breathing arrested, her head swimming.

She kept her smile as she ventured back out and sat in front of the mirror. The makeup artist applied powder and lipstick as her hairdresser affixed a scarf around her red wig.

"Can you hand me my pages?"

They appeared in her view, and she took them, trying to commit her new lines to memory. But the world felt hot and close and slanted.

She swallowed again and winced.

"You look flushed today, Miss Price. Is everything okay?" Her makeup artist layered on another round of powder.

Her hairdresser, pinning the scarf in place, ran a bobby pin like a razor against her scalp.

"Fabulous," Rosie said. Offstage a baby began to cry—the Photophone guys working out the sound mix.

Beyond the hanging canvas curtains, she heard Grayson running his lines with Fishe, who played her part.

"I told you not to come back."

"I got halfway to Central Station and realized, I have nowhere else to go, Eva. I don't care if I have to sit here every day, watching you hate me. I'm not leaving. Not again."

She imagined the beat there, how she'd frame her expression, then mouthed the words with Fishe. "You've shouldn't have left the first time."

"I know."

"Cue the baby," Fishe said, reading the stage directions.

"What is that?" Grayson said. According to the script, she'd leave and come back with his child in her arms. "Is that—is that my child?"

Grayson had a way of delivering lines—

"Miss Roxy, are you crying?"

She looked up at her makeup artist, dark hair, petite. What was her name—Vera? Fletcher had found her in the extras' line, put her to work as an assistant.

"No, of course not." She blinked back the moisture, glanced at the script. She'd lost her place.

Vera said nothing as she dabbed at the corner of her eyes, drying them, repairing them.

"Are you ready, Miss Price?" An assistant peeked into her room. "Mr. Harris wants you on set."

Twenty minutes already? She blew out a breath, nodded. Got up. One more scene and then she'd retire to her office, look over the script that she'd fallen asleep against last night. She reached for the plate of unfinished orange, and the world churned again, this time quick and fast. She blinked against it, shook her head.

She fed herself the orange as she exited, her pages tucked under her arm.

Grayson stood on set, redressed in a white workman's shirt, rolled up at the elbows, his hair tousled, some shadow to his dark whiskers. No wonder Fletcher waited until the end of the day to shoot this scene.

She walked through the scene, moving to her blocking, stood for the camera to find the shot, then walked to the next mark.

She could nearly hear her blood pumping in her head, swooshing hot, furious through her body. Maybe she was running a fever.

"Let's run the scene," Fishe said, folding his arms and leaning against the bar. "No blocking, just lines."

She scanned her lines fast then put the script away. See Joan do that, memorize her new pages in ten minutes.

She took a breath. Smile. Be brilliant.

Grayson exited, stage left, to get his timing right.

"Cue Grayson."

He came in the door, and she looked up, as if she'd seen a ghost. "Patch, what are you doing here? I told you not to come back." Even as she said it, the words felt far away, as if they lacked power.

She saw his mouth move, heard him, but his words scrambled in her head.

He stared at her, and for a moment, her mind blanked. Then, "You shouldn't have left the first time."

But maybe she'd said the words only to herself, because Grayson was staring at her, something of a horrified expression on his face. He advanced toward her, arms out just as the world slanted.

And then, she was falling, her body simply dropping, hard.

She never knew if Grayson caught her.

Chapter 6

"I don't care what Louella says—don't believe the gossip, because Roxy Price is not finished!" Rosie didn't care that her voice echoed into the hot June air, probably loud enough for the neighbors to hear. Let the entire world hear. She wasn't ready to be forgotten. Not yet. "Last time I looked, they hadn't taken my name off the letterhead. Fletcher Harris better start returning my phone calls, or he'll find himself knocking on Jack Warner Jr'.s door!"

She slammed the receiver down on the cradle, wishing it had the effect she desired, and handed the phone back to Louise. "Wake me the minute Fletcher calls."

Louise turned away toward the house. Rosie reached out to touch her arm.

"Tell him I'm busy. He'll have to come out to the house."

Louise nodded.

"No. Wait. Set up a meeting at Musso and Frank's. See if you can get Charlie's booth. That will cause a stir, make them realize I'm not out of the game yet."

Louise paused. "Are you sure you're ready to go out?"

Rosie's hand went to her head, almost as if it had its own mind. Hmm, maybe not. She couldn't bear the thought of another moment in the wig, not after she'd managed six weeks of freedom. Besides, light brown fuzz now covered her head in tiny ringlets. Another month, and she'd have enough to style.

And, she did need to add a few pounds. Yesterday she nearly wrapped her robe twice around her frame. Sammy could almost knock her over with a hug.

She sighed. "Fine. Tell Fletcher I expect to see him after shooting tomorrow. Here. At the house." That would give her all day to prepare a response, something that reminded him that he worked for *her*.

She could handle being replaced, once, by Joan.

After all, even she could agree the show had to go on. *A Man to Hold* couldn't wait six weeks or longer for her to recuperate.

But enough was enough. She was Palace Studio's top star. So what that she had hit her thirty-fourth birthday two weeks ago? They clearly needed reminding that she wasn't just a star but a studio head. Even if the board of directors did decide to take over control during her illness, she still owned the majority shares. They couldn't shove her out of her office, couldn't keep her from entering the gates.

So, they'd managed to wrestle the reins of the studio from her. The minute the doctor slapped a diagnosis to her fatigue—mononucleosis—the board swooped in and began picking apart her hard work. If she didn't regain the helm soon, Palace Studios would turn into another version of United Artists, no actors on contract, a company that simply distributed independent films made by unknown directors.

They might not be as large as Warner Brothers, but Palace Studios could make a film that swept the nation. Maybe even the world. She just had to find the right script.

"And what shall I say to the man who keeps calling, asking to see you?" Louise said. "He says he's representing an independent film."

See? Already the word was out. "Tell him I'm resting. Or better yet, tell him that we don't take independent films. We're Palace Studios—we make our own films."

Louise nodded. "Shall I bring your mail?"

"Yes, please. And some orange juice." Rosie replaced her sunglasses, leaned back on the chaise lounge, her head wrapped in a turban, her robe cinched tight. She let the heat find her bones. The fragrances of her climbing roses that hung over her privacy fence perfumed the day. She might actually stay awake for the duration of the day instead of sinking into a fatigued slumber by mid-afternoon. See, she'd be back on her feet in days, not months.

Mostly, she needed to see her name in the press associated with something other than disaster. ACTRESS COLLAPSES ON SET. ROXY PRICE DIAGNOSED WITH FATIGUE. JOAN CRAWFORD TO ASSUME ROLE.

She would fix this. Even if she had to write a script herself.

Direct her own show.

Cast herself in the lead.

She wasn't done with Hollywood quite yet, thank you. Her public wanted her. She just needed to remind them what they were missing.

She wanted to track down Louella, that gossip for Hearst's newspaper, and—well, Hollywood Hotel wouldn't be receiving an interview from Roxy Price anytime soon.

Rosie watched Sammy as he played a game of croquet by himself in the grass. Myrna read a book in the shadows of the broad willow tree, one eye on him.

"Watch this, Roxy!" Sammy lined up the ball, sent it flying toward the pond. A white swan nestled in the grass rose and argued with him. He ran over waving his hands, and it waddled toward safety, still angry.

"You need a hat, Sammy," Rosie said. "Your nose is getting red." The late summer heat should be enough to drive both of them inside, but she longed for the warmth of the sun, the way it seeped inside her bones. She improved every day.

Still, how she had relished this last six weeks of regaining her strength, spending the days with Sammy as Irene went to work.

Almost felt like he could be her son. Except, he wasn't, and motherhood wasn't her life.

Yes, next week she'd lunch at Musso and Franks, or perhaps make an appearance at the Brown Derby. She'd have to make sure the studio sent over a makeup gal—and let that information leak to Louella. Maybe she could ring up Tagg, see if he wanted to accompany her.

The three bouquets of irises he'd sent suggested that, perhaps, Irene's words about him might be accurate. He did make a handsome and willing date, someone the paparazzi loved to capture in print. It did them both good to appear at the Coconut Grove together, and she was fond enough of him to enjoy his overtures of affection without requiring anything of her heart.

Louise returned, a glass of fresh-squeezed orange juice on a platter. Two envelopes lay beside it.

She reached for the glass, the envelopes. "Where are the rest?"

Louise made that funny shape with her mouth, looked away.

Oh.

Rosie cleared her throat. "Well, the less to answer then," she said, forcing a smile.

Two letters. How had the cascade of fan mail trickled to nothing so quickly? She opened the first. Good. An encouraging note from an admirer wishing her a speedy recovery, a picture inside of a girl about seventeen.

Probably an aspiring starlet looking for a break.

Rosie made a mental note to send her a photo. She'd sign it herself this time, add a word of thanks.

Not too much, however, because she didn't want to encourage a trip across the country only to have the poor girl end up waiting tables, praying for a tidbit role from Central Casting.

Or worse, discovering herself as easy prey on some director's casting couch.

Rosie picked up the second letter and ran her thumb under the lip. "Be careful not to hit one of those balls into the pool, Sammy!"

The edge opened, and she pulled out the letter, another photograph. Stared at the picture.

A man, dressed in suit pants and a black suit coat stood in a field beside his wife, petite with high, regal cheekbones and short, dark bobbed hair. She wore a simple dress and stared down at three children. A baby played in the grass while a little boy stood before his father, looking robust and proud. Rosie placed him at about five. And in the middle, holding a bouquet of moccasin flowers in her fist, stood a little girl, about ten years of age. Her long hair hung down in two dark plaited braids and she stared at the camera with eyes that could see into Rosie's soul.

Coco. Rosie recognized Guthrie in the little girl's expression, the ability to look right through a person and leave them undone. But Rosie saw herself in the lift of Coco's chin and the stubborn edge of her posture.

However, the unwavering confidence in her expression seemed something all her own. Pure Coco. Or perhaps Lilly had given the little girl that quality, that piece of herself.

After all, Lilly was her mother now.

Rosie's breath caught, her throat tight.

Oh.

She ran her thumb over Coco's face. She probably knew how to ride her daddy's horse. What if Lilly had taken her up in an airplane?

"Who's that?" Sammy came over, leaned against the back of her chaise lounge, his shadow draped over the picture. "They have a dog." He pointed to the black wolf-looking animal seated beside the baby. "We should get a dog."

Rosie looked up at him, blinking back the moisture in her eyes. "Maybe. Someday." She considered him a moment then suddenly reached over and pulled him down next to her, putting her arm around him.

Oddly, he leaned back against her, as if this embrace might be an everyday occurrence, picking up the tail of her robe's belt and rubbing it between his fingers. "I'd call him Harvey. Or maybe Pete."

He was warm, his body all bones, but he smelled like the grass, fresh and sweet. She missed the little-boy exuberance, but this thoughtful, considerate child won her heart just the same. She hugged him to herself as she opened the envelope, taking out the letter. "Those are good names for a dog."

Dear Rosie,

I see your movie posters showing at the Buckle Theater and I'm so proud of you. You have taken Hollywood by storm. Truman and I went to see China Knights and thought you were fabulous. We had this picture taken of our family a few weeks ago, and I thought you'd enjoy seeing how Coco has grown. She has your laughter and spunk, your love of drama. She is so smart, a delight to our lives. If you ever want to visit, the door is open.

With love,

Lilly

The door is open. Rosie drew in a shaking breath then folded the letter and tucked it back into the envelope, along with the picture.

"Mom will never let me get a dog." Sammy turned sideways in her lap. "But you could talk her into it." His dark eyes found hers, so full of hope. Myrna had risen, was walking toward him, but Rosie waved her away.

"Why do you want a dog, Sammy?"

He pushed away from her, his expression earnest. "Every kid needs a dog." Sammy said. "Nick Templeton has a dog. He sleeps with Nick every night. A dog will never leave you."

She resisted the urge to run a finger down his chubby face. "A dog it is then, Champ. As soon as we can find the right one."

He grinned at her as he got up, and she would have given him a pack of dogs. Myrna gave her a frown, but Rosie refused to acknowledge it.

Why not? Everyone deserved someone to be their friend and never leave them.

She leaned back on the chaise, closed her eyes. Traced the image of Coco in her mind. "*The door is open.*"

And what, she'd simply walk through it, right back into her daughter's life? Coco had probably long ago stopped thinking of her as her mother—in fact, she'd never known anyone but Lilly by that name. Coco had a family, a good family, and Rosie couldn't destroy that. She'd had her chance at happiness and walked away from it.

No, the door wasn't open. She'd closed it long, long ago.

She opened her eyes to the sound of splashing and spied Myrna and Sammy sitting by the pool, kicking their legs into the crystalline surface.

What if this was the end, just as Louella said? What if God had finally caught up to her, found her, and decided that this dream too should die?

She pressed her hand to her mouth as the truth slid through her. How had it come to this? A hairless, boney, wretched old mess, childless, wishing she knew how everyone else had the magic but her.

"Blessed are the meek: for they shall inherit the earth."

She wasn't sure where the words emerged from, but they tumbled around inside her.

"Do you know who the meek are, Miss Price? The ones who hope in the Lord. The ones who wait for Him. Those who allow God to set their course."

She remembered now—the words from the nurse at the hospital. But she couldn't afford to be meek. Not with the board trying to steal the studio out from under her, and Joan and Bette horning in for her parts, and even Irene dating too many Hollywood hopefuls. Someday Irene would find love again and then…

The thought burst in her chest. Then she'd take Sammy away. And this house would again be empty.

Her life would be empty.

Maybe she should have let God decide her course, her life. But last time she'd left it in His hands, her brother had disappeared across an ocean, never to return. And her husband—but wait. No. She couldn't blame God for Guthrie's death.

Not when she could have stopped it.

And she certainly couldn't blame God for her act of abandoning her daughter.

She didn't have the right to be meek, to hope in God's love for her. Not after the choices she'd made.

And not with all she had at stake.

Louise came out, holding a plate of sandwiches. She set them down on the table, called Sammy over. He sat on the metal lawn chair, gobbling a tuna fish sandwich.

"I don't want to disturb your lunch, ma'am, but that fellow from the independent film company is here." Louise handed her a plate, four-quarter sandwiches, a stem of grapes.

Rosie sat up, taking the plate. "Here? As in at the house?" She took a bite of her sandwich and washed it down with orange juice.

"He's been at the gate for ten minutes. I told him to leave, but he's simply parked out there. What shall I have him do?"

Rosie picked at a grape. Rolled it between her fingers. "Let him in. I'll hear what he has to say. Maybe he's got something the studio might pick up." How she remembered those days, when she had shown up at Dashielle's door desperate for a part. He hadn't turned her away.

Maybe she wished he had.

"Do you want your wig, ma'am—"

"She doesn't need it."

The voice, the refined, elegant accent slid through her, turning her body to fire.

It couldn't be. But yes, His Grace, Rolfe Van Horne, Duke of Beaumont walked into the sunlight, out of the shadows of the porch, as if he deserved a spotlight, dressed in a white linen suit, a straw fedora. He hadn't changed much—still wore an arrogance on his face, his blue eyes catching her, holding her fast. He stood between her and the sun, casting a shadow over her with his wide shoulders, the lean cut of his frame. As he stared down at her, for a moment the world simply stopped, the breeze stilling, the birds quiet.

She heard only his low, "Hello, Rosie."

He sounded every inch a duke, and she called herself a fool for not realizing it right off, so long ago.

And so much for forgetting the power he had over her, the way her heart thumped like a fist inside her.

Her hand lifted to her head, this time not from reflex. She swallowed.

"I heard about your collapse," he said, his eyes not leaving hers. "You look thin."

That smarted. She blinked back the sting in her eyes. "Thank you, Rolfe. You can't imagine how delightful that is to hear." She turned away from him, shaking her head.

He made a funny noise. "I didn't mean it that way."

"I've been better, yes, but I'm doing marvelously, thank you." She put her sunglasses back on, just in case he might see her eyes glistening. "What are you doing here?"

She winced at the sound of one of her metal chairs raking across the patio stones. He sat down, close enough for her to catch the spicy scent of his cologne. It scoured up memories of walking across a windy beach, the sand like icing between her toes.

"I have a proposition for you, Rosie. I've called you twice, but since you wouldn't talk to me, I decided to pay you a visit."

"I never received your call."

He took off his hat, held it between his hands, and for the first time, a chink appeared in that regal expression. "Yes, you did. I didn't tell them it was me, because…"

Oh. The independent screenwriter. Her stomach began a slow curl into a knot. "Because you knew I wouldn't see you."

He ran his finger around the inside of his hat. Then he took a breath and set the hat on the table beside her, a hardness in his jaw. "I know we parted badly, but I believe we can put that behind us for a common good, something that I think will get us both what we want."

"How do you know what I want, Rolfe?"

He looked away, toward Sammy, and a memory whisked up inside her, the image of him sitting in the sunshine, watching Rooney's airplanes do barrel rolls and loops in the sky. She loved his profile, the strong edge of his chin, even the whiskers that would soon darken his jaw.

She fought the urge to run her hand down his face, her thumb across his lips, and hated herself for even thinking it.

She simply couldn't be that fragile. Not now. She pulled her robe tighter under her chin.

"Is that Dashielle's son?"

"His name is Sammy."

"And he lives here, with you?"

"He and his mother."

His lips formed a tight line, a nod, then a curious frown. "I didn't expect that."

What did he expect? That she'd throw the poor girl into the street? She sighed. "We don't do independent films at Palace Studios, Rolfe. I'm afraid you've wasted your time."

He glanced at her, his eyes narrowing. "You've built quite an empire with Palace Studios out of the ashes of Dashielle's failure."

"I like to think of it as his legacy. He is still very much here, in spirit." Her gaze went to Sammy, playing now with an imaginary dog. She'd find one for him tomorrow, if she could. "I'm just trying to carry on what he began."

"I know. I read the trades. You've made a valiant effort." He paused.

She frowned.

"But I also hear the scuttlebutt among the studio heads. Palace Studios lives on a shoestring, and a handful of bad films could wash you under."

"We're not that desperate."

"Your board has approached Jack Warner with an option to buy."

She stilled, the breath whooshing from her as if he'd slapped her. She put her hand to her head. "No—I—they…"

His expression softened, however briefly. "I'm sorry. I wondered if they'd told you."

She met his eyes, lifted her chin. "They can't sell it. I own it."

"If you can't pay your debts, then the bankruptcy court owns it."

"We have films in production, staff writers at work—"

"You have directors like Rooney spending money hand over fist, and Fletcher overworking your extras into a lawsuit." He lowered his voice. "And Bette Davis and Joan Crawford fighting over parts meant for you."

She looked away. "Did you come here to punish me, Rolfe?"

A sparrow called from a nearby tree, the wind rustling the willow.

"No," he finally said softly. "I came here because you need me, Rosie."

Her gaze shot at him. "I hardly think that I—"

"How many times have you called Fletcher today? Has he returned even one of your calls?"

She had the terrible urge to slap him.

"There is only one director in the business willing to offer you a part. And that's me. Could you, for one moment, surrender that legendary pride and admit that maybe you could use some help?"

She folded her arms, closed her eyes.

She felt him settle on the chaise lounge at her feet.

"Rosie."

The texture of his voice made her look up. He sighed, shook his head. "Listen. I forgive you for what happened. I think we can put it behind us." He met her eyes but didn't soften his words further with a smile.

"I don't understand. Why would you—"

"Because I still believe in the actress I once knew."

She searched his face for mocking, guile, but found nothing of it in his expression. "Why would you want to help me?"

"I have a movie, Rosie. One that I wrote...for you."

"For Palace Studios?"

He shook his head. "No, for you. The part is—well, when I wrote it, I saw you playing it." For the first time, he appeared chagrined, one side of his mouth tugging up, almost a smile.

"I forgive you...."

"Why would you write a movie for me, Rolfe?"

His lips tightened into a dark line. "Because every time I sat down to write, your face appeared before me. I couldn't escape you."

He didn't sound happy about that, and she had the strange urge to apologize.

"This is your role, if you want it."

She considered him. He seemed serious, his blue eyes intent in hers. He'd lost his smile, just met her gaze.

She didn't know what to make of him, this misplaced forgiveness, this too-generous offering. She let out a harsh laugh. "Wait. I get it. It's a jungle movie, and I get to wear a sarong and end up burning at the stake, someone's dinner."

He didn't smile.

"I was kidding."

"It's a war movie called *Red Skies over Paris* about a woman who loses the man she loves, only to discover that he isn't who he says he is. She is strong and beautiful and helps save lives as she realizes who she is."

Her smile fell. "That's not a part for me."

"It's exactly the part for you, I promise. In fact, no one can play this part like you can."

She picked up her orange juice, running her thumb down the side, leaving a trail in the sweaty glass. "We'd have to run it by Fletcher, and even then, I'm not sure he'll go for it. He's got a full plate."

"I have a director already."

She looked up. "That, I'm sure won't work. Fletcher is very choosy about his directors, that is, if he doesn't take it himself."

"He doesn't have a choice. I'm paying for it, so I'm producing it."

She blinked at him. "The entire production? That could be in the millions."

He didn't look away. "I have put my estate in arrears, but I believe the sum will cover it."

She took a sip of the juice, let it cool her parched throat. "When do you want to start production? We'll have to look at the studio schedule."

"Immediately," he said. "And we don't have to fit it into the studio schedule because it will be shot on location. In Europe."

Her words sluiced out of her.

He took the orange juice from her grip, placed it back on the table. "I estimate it taking nearly a year or more, with all the location shoots, editing, and production. And then there's the promotion." He caught her hand, and she couldn't deny that, for a moment, his touch traveled all the way up her arm, into her chest, her heart.

He still had such power over her, she could almost taste her longing. She swallowed it away.

"I will rent a sound stage in Vienna for any final shots, and then you'll have to stay with me to promote the film across Europe before we bring it to America."

"And in the meantime, Fletcher and the board will steal Palace Studios from beneath me, Joan Crawford will become the next Palace starlet, and my career will be in ashes."

"No. In the meantime, you will become not only an American movie star but an international star as well. You will have billing above the title in countries where you cannot even pronounce the name of your movie. And when you return to America, you will be a woman of intrigue and acclaim. Most of all, you will bring into the coffers of Palace Studios receipts that cost you nothing. Nothing but your trust in me."

"Why would you do this, Rolfe?"

He ran his thumb over her hand. "Because I believe in the woman I saw on the set of *Angel's Fury*, the one who made an entire crew of men cry with her brilliance. Her beauty."

She couldn't breathe past the closing of her throat. Her eyes burned, and she blinked away the heat in them. "I—but I'm no longer beautiful, Rolfe."

"Let me be the judge of that, Rosie. Besides, your hair wasn't the beauty I was referring to." He pressed her hand between both of his, and for the first time, the hard edge of his eyes softened. "No one can play this role like you can. If you don't do it, I won't produce it. But if you trust me, you will get everything you've always wanted."

She stared at his hands holding hers, wanting to pull away, refraining. "You can't give me that, Rolfe. It's not possible."

He said nothing then, but she watched as he lifted her hand and pressed his lips to it. Then he smiled, something of a challenge in his eyes. "Try me."

* * * * *

"Have you lost your mind? You can't leave. Not now. Not when the board is trying to sell the studio, and all your parts are being gobbled up. An entire year, in Europe? There will be nothing left of the studio when you return. *If* you return." Irene sat on the velvet settee in the corner of Rosie's boudoir, the sun a thin, vibrant line dissecting her closed velvet drapes. She still wore her suit dress, having stormed down the hall the minute the driver left her at the door.

Sammy lounged on the floor next to her, reading another Hardy Boys mystery. "You are planning on returning, right?"

Quietly moving around them, Louise had begun to package Rosie's clothing, the elegant gowns, her day dresses, shoes wrapped in tissue, her silk undergarments in cloth bags. She hadn't traveled overseas since—since Paris. Since the year she'd fallen in love with Dash while cavorting through the streets of France.

Since the year she'd met Rolfe Van Horne while waiting to run away with Dashielle in a French park.

She should have stopped then, looked into Rolfe's eyes, and realized that he was her future. At least she hoped so.

If she ever needed a new script, something epic and beautiful and enough to remind her of why she'd fled to Hollywood and Dash's promises, it was now. She should be grateful, not terrified that Rolfe Van Horne had snuck back into her life.

Most of all, she shouldn't have spent the last four nights staring at the whitewashed ceiling, replaying their conversation, looking for nuances of his feelings for her.

She couldn't—wouldn't—fall in love with him again. Not when he'd so easily walked out of her life last time.

"I forgive you." No, that didn't mean he still loved her.

He probably just pitied her.

A job. A role. A second chance. She wouldn't let her loneliness destroy it.

Besides, if all went well, she'd have the applause of her fans to fill the lonely places.

"Of course I am coming back. And I promise, they won't sell the studio while I'm gone. Not without my say. Palace Studios is being well compensated for my absence. You should have seen Fletcher nearly salivating over his new, improved budget. He doesn't seem to care a whit about the fact that I'm leaving."

Yes, one meeting with Fletcher and Rolfe, with her standing nearly outside the conversation as they negotiated for rights to control her career, made her realize the reality of her position at the studio. Fragile at best; at worst, redundant. She refused to use the word *replaceable*, but after six weeks, Fletcher and even Irene had taken over management so skillfully, the gap of her absence now would close behind her, without even a sucking sound to signify her departure.

But Irene was right. Rosie had to return triumphant from this last film, this last tour through Europe, or she'd have no place to return to.

"Rolfe seems to think that this role could be my best. And we both know I need something to resurrect my career." Rosie leaned into the mirror of her dressing table, drawing on a line of black liner across her lid. Tonight, she'd appear on Rolfe's arm, make a splash at the Coconut Grove, before she'd leave on a flight tomorrow to New York City then board a ship to Europe.

A year with Duke Van Horne, in his presence, dodging those blue eyes.

Irene seemed to read her heart. "And the duke? Why is he doing this? Does he still care for you?"

"I don't know." She closed one eye, pasted on a line of fake lashes.

Kept her eye closed as they dried. She'd wear a bejeweled turban instead of her wig, a fashion statement. "He says it is because he couldn't stop thinking about me, or at least I thought that's what he said. But there didn't seem the faintest hint of warmth in his words. Almost as if he begrudged my appearance in his thoughts." She kept seeing the resigned, almost sad expression as he took her hand. Pity more than love, perhaps. "He said he forgave me for hurting him."

Irene leaned over Sammy's shoulder, pointed out a picture, read the words on the page. Then she looked up and met Rosie's gaze in the mirror. "I hardly think he should have to forgive you."

"I lied to him. I didn't tell him I was married."

"He didn't mention he was a duke." Irene raised an eyebrow.

Rosie pasted on the other eyelash. Kept her eye closed. "So, we both had secrets. Maybe we just start over. Colleagues."

"Is that what you want? To start over with Rolfe? You don't think you'll fall in love with him again?"

She opened her eyes, blinked. Yes, she'd be the delight of the cameras tonight. "No."

Irene frowned.

Rosie uncapped her lipstick, painted the ox-blood red onto her lips. Smacked them. Then turned to Irene. "Listen, I can admit that Rolfe is dangerous, with those blue eyes, that way he makes me long to be in his arms. But if I've learned anything in the past eight years, it's not to give away my heart. This business is fickle, and I have to look out for myself." She got up and stepped into her closet. A black evening gown, sequined straps, a low back, hung on a hanger. She let her silk dressing gown slide to the floor as Louise released the dress from the hanger. She helped Rosie into the gown, and it smoothed over her too-thin body. But she'd put on weight, even in the last four days since Rolfe's appearance.

She'd have her figure back by the time they started shooting. And someday soon, her hair.

"And what about us? We'll miss you terribly, you know."

Her gaze went to Sammy, reading on the floor, his dark hair tousled, the sun on his cheeks. A terrible knot of pain tightened in Rosie's chest.

"You'll send me pictures and visit. Please visit."

Irene got up and nudged him with her foot. "Of course we will," she said, but her words lacked vigor. She helped Sammy off the floor and didn't meet Rosie's eyes.

"What is it, Irene?"

She sighed. Then kissed the top of Sammy's head. "Run along to the kitchen, sweetheart, and ask Dorian for some sugar sandwiches."

When he'd left, Irene turned to her, her eyes red. "You're like a sister to me, Rosie, and you and Sammy are all I have. My parents have disowned me, although they love Sammy with all their hearts. If you don't come back—"

Rosie crossed the room and took Irene's hands. "I'm coming back, I promise."

"You better." Irene managed a smile. "And Rolfe Van Horne better be everything he says he is."

She leaned in and gave Rosie a quick kiss on the cheek then squeezed her hands and followed Sammy.

Yes. Their futures depended on Rolfe and his glorious plans.

She stood at the bureau mirror as Louise worked the clasp to her pearls, the ones that dangled down her open back, a memory of Dashielle and his generosity. Or more accurately, his guilt. Then she grabbed her gloves off the bureau.

"I'll have your clothing packed and shipped to the airport for tomorrow's departure," Louise said.

"Thank you." Rosie walked over to her window, hidden behind the closed drapes. She'd kept them drawn most of the summer to keep out the heat, capture the cool air. Now, she flung them open.

The late-hour sunshine poured into the room, rose-gold across the floor of her carpet, draping over the satin white sheets of her bed. Twilight bathed the neighborhood of Beverly Hills.

Yes, Rolfe Van Horne better be everything he said he was, give her everything he promised, because this was her last chance to be brilliant.

Her last chance to hear the applause.

She had agreed to meet Rolfe at the club, and she climbed into the backseat of her roadster, acquiescing to the studio's—or perhaps Rolfe's—insistence that she have a driver. She drank in the summer redolence of the manicured lawns, the English climbing roses, the sycamore trees, the towering palms along the Beverly Hills Boulevard. She loved this town and had thought, until six weeks ago, that she belonged here.

"No one can play this role like you can. If you don't do it, I won't produce it. But if you trust me, you will get everything you've always wanted."

Happiness? Peace? The sense that she couldn't lose it all, that it wouldn't slip out of her hands like sand?

She had wrapped a silk scarf around her neck, worn a small jacket for the ride over, and now held her turban in place, just in case the wind decided to take it. Still, she managed to wave to a few onlookers parked outside the Ambassador Hotel hoping to spot a starlet, or perhaps Grayson Clarke.

She allowed her driver to let her out on the sidewalk, under the long parapet that led to the Grove and couldn't help but be reminded of the night Dashielle had sold her to Rooney.

The night she'd seen Rolfe again, sitting at the table, wearing a look of disapproval.

It had vanished now as he emerged from where he waited in the corridor. He smiled at her, although she noticed it didn't quite touch his eyes. Polite, not warm. Dashing, not dear. Still, every inch a duke, in a tuxedo with tails, a top hat, a white silk scarf around his neck. He held out his elbow, his hands gloved. "You look beautiful."

"I'm too thin," she whispered as the flashbulbs splattered dots before her eyes.

He leaned down into her ear as they walked the long red carpet. "Are you ready for this?" The mood of a swing band drifted into the night, now settling like dust around them. They reached the door and he stopped at it, turning to her, searching her eyes.

She looked for the warmth and found nothing except the concern of her new director, her boss. Hoping she might hold up her end of the deal.

No, she wouldn't fall for him, not again. Because if this failed, her heart just might be the only thing that remained to call her own.

"I'm ready," she said and met his eye, giving him her starlet smile, something printable as the press caught it.

"Very good," he said. "Smile and be brilliant."

Then he opened the door into the gala of her last chance.

Chapter 7

Clearly, Rolfe saw something in her that she didn't, because this role he'd supposedly written for her didn't suit Rosie in the least.

A servant girl? From England? The script had her dressed in a dowdy uniform, buttoned up, austere and boring for the first twenty pages. Nothing of a hint of bombshell.

Not until her character escaped England for Belgium then Paris and became a courier in the underground resistance did Bridget become interesting, and even then she was tough and stubborn, not seductive and beautiful.

Certainly Rolfe didn't see Rosie as dowdy and boring?

But perhaps he did, because after that night on his arm at the Coconut Grove, and the interminable three-week trip to Paris, he'd all but abandoned her.

As if, after his initial words to woo her, he'd gotten what he'd come for.

Maybe he did pity her, his former professed love morphing into something of tragedy. Frankly, she understood that much more than his forgiveness.

Still, despite his forgiveness, or his pity, he seemed almost annoyed by her attempts to lure him into convivial conversation. She'd tried on the plane to delight him with a story of Rooney and his attempts to turn her into a jungle woman. He'd listened with what seemed a faux smile. Even as they ate together, he wouldn't look at her, preferring to stare out the window at the ocean.

Maybe he simply worried over the movie. It seemed that signing her had been his first step, instead of the last. He still had to scout locations, cast the remaining parts, meet with the director to approve the set, makeup, and costumes, and a thousand other details. No wonder he seemed tense. She should have asked more questions before her desperation made her sign away her life for a year or more.

Now, as if to confirm her growing feeling of abandonment, Rolfe had simply plunked her in this Paris apartment, her script in hand, and disappeared.

He'd also set her up with a dialogue coach, a French woman by the name of Nellie who fussed about Rosie's pronunciation of the British servant's dialect and made her walk the hall, chin up, like she might actually have to serve tea. Nellie reminded her of a thinner, more French version of her mother, but apparently Nellie Thoreau had worked with the actors from the French stage, possibly even Sarah Bernhardt, in her final days.

That made Rosie sit up and listen, take the woman's coaching to heart.

The scent of roses from the flower market on the street below made it all the way into the open window of her sixth-floor penthouse apartment, perfuming her sitting room as she lounged on the chaise, her script in a scattered mess around her. She'd begun a fresh read-through, highlighting her scenes, playing them out, before casting the pages to the floor in disgust.

It wasn't that she couldn't play the part, but rather, it just didn't suit her. She refused to be the woman destroyed by a broken heart. Even on the silver screen.

The street noise of the busy heart of Paris, at Chatelet, drifted inside, along with the coo of the pigeons on her balcony. The filmy gauze curtain fluttered in the wind, as if beckoning her to the streets below, to the nearby Garden de Tuileries, the Louvre. Rolfe must be mocking her because he picked an apartment directly facing the grand architecture of the Theatre Musicale from one bedroom balcony and the Hotel de Ville and Theatre Populaire from the other.

Paris conjured too many memories: Dash and the way he'd twisted her heart into a knot back in the day when she gave it away too easily. Lilly and the scare she gave Rosie the day she followed a Frenchman through Paris. Her mother, weeping in quiet darkness as she surrendered to the futility of the search for Jack, Rosie's brother. The epic funeral of Sarah Bernhardt, masses filling the streets, igniting Rosie's dream of the stage, stardom, the longing for applause.

"We won't be here long," Rolfe had said as they ate dinner two nights ago, when he'd taken her out to a café along the *Champs-Elysees*. So little had changed in twelve years: the flower vendors still parked on the corners selling roses, carnations, and lilies; Peugeots and Mercedes clogging the streets along with horse and carriage; newspaper boys in berets shouting the headlines as they paced the sidewalks. She should pick up a Paris *Chronicle*, see if Uncle Oliver still listed his name on the masthead as owner.

"I just have to scout a location for the final sequence of scenes," Rolfe said.

"And then to London?"

"Actually, then to Manchester. We'll be shooting at Woolshire Castle."

"Where Bridget works as a servant."

"And meets Jardin, the man she believes she loves."

"This is the man Master Colin kills, or so she believes, also." She'd read the script through once, but, "I don't understand why you make her wait so long before she realizes that her employer is trying to protect her? Don't you think it would help for her to know that Jardin was using her to obtain military secrets from her employer?"

"She has to learn to trust Colin, despite this lie she believes about him. I want her to fall in love with him despite herself."

"Do you really think that is realistic?"

He'd stared at her then, something entering his eyes, then swallowed and turned away, watching the traffic along the street. "Maybe only in the movies," he said quietly.

Only in the movies, indeed. How did he expect her to convincingly play a woman who falls in love with her betrayer? Instead she wanted to shake Bridget by the shoulders. *Don't give away your heart!*

Now, Rosie picked up her script, flipping through the pages to the epic scene where the man she loves dies, poisoned. She sank down on the red velvet divan and tried to see the scene like Nellie said, to hear the sounds of the wind in the barn, to taste the anticipation as she went in search of the man she loved.

INT: CASTLE BARN – NIGHT

The manicured paddocks of the estate horses. Clean but eerie in the darkness

JARDIN lays in a stall, in the darkness moaning, sweating. The horses are still, glassy eyes watching him.

BRIDGET *enters, searching for JARDIN. We see her delight at their clandestine meeting turn to panic as she hears moaning. She betrays horror and confusion as she finds JARDIN hiding in the stall.*

BRIDGET
(horrified)
What is the matter with you? I was waiting, where were you?

JARDIN
(coughing)
I'm so sorry, Bridget. I wasn't clever enough.

BRIDGET
I don't understand. (clawing at his clothing to find a wound.) Are you hurt? I'll get help.

JARDIN
(catching her hand)
*Shh. It's too late.
(He presses her hand to his mouth then coughs).*

BRIDGET
Are you ill?

JARDIN
Poisoned, I fear. Your master is a sly one.

BRIDGET
(disbelieving his words)
Master Colin did this to you? Why?

JARDIN
(Jardin doubles over in pain, moaning.)
Leave me, Bridget—

BRIDGET
Never—

JARDIN
(Jardin pushes her away)
Leave! Please, leave! Go!

BRIDGET
(Bridget arises, panic on her face in the dim light of her lamp.
Backs away.)
I'll never forgive him. Never!

"It's just awful."

Rosie tossed the pages across the room. She got up, walked over to the carved marble fireplace.

"That's something a writer never wants to see."

She turned and startled at Rolfe in the doorway, his eyes on her, just enough wound in them for her to taste shame. "I came by to remind you of dinner tonight, but perhaps I should stay in my hotel room, rewriting my script." He put the lilies on the table then began to pick up the pages.

In the afternoon light, with him dressed in a double-breasted linen suit, a fedora, he looked almost pedestrian, especially when he took off his hat, set it on the table, and followed with his jacket over the back of a chair. He rolled up the sleeves of his white shirt above the elbows. Then he sat on the divan, staring at the papers. Frowning.

"I'm sorry I threw them. If I had known you were standing there, I would have—"

"Lied to me?" He didn't smile, and she longed for the humor to appear in his eyes, but perhaps that had died over the ocean as well.

She folded her arms. A job. Her last chance. She swallowed. "If you want the truth, here it is. The critics are going to eat us alive, and we'll be laughed out of every theater across America."

His lips tightened in a grim line.

She couldn't surrender to compassion, not when their careers hinged on this script. Or, at least her career. He'd always be a duke, she supposed. "Listen, I've read hundreds of scripts over the past five years." She sat on one of the Louix IVX chairs. "If you must know, the romance—it's not believable. If you want me to play this role, this one you supposedly wrote for me, you have to write a convincing romance, not one built in the mind of a man."

He raised an eyebrow. "Pardon me?"

"Rolfe, you've written this story from the man's perspective. It's simply too easy. First, you break her heart, and then—" She got up, and searched through the pages on the floor, finding the right one. "You have her accepting Colin's word for the fact he's been protecting her and having her declare her love."

He shook his head. "I know you don't believe that she can fall in love with Colin after what she thinks he's done, but—"

"It's not just that. Let's start with her reactions to Jardin's death.

Do you think she'd truly believe that Colin, her master, would do this? Even if she loved Jardin, she'd have some disbelief that Colin would want to destroy her life. Even if Colin is a terrible man."

"Which he's not," Rolfe said.

"Exactly. He's her benefactor. He rescued her when her mother died, took her into his castle to live. Yes, she became a servant, but he treated her kindly, taught her to read and write. Almost as if she might be a daughter. She wouldn't believe that he would hurt her. In fact, she might blame herself before she blamed him."

Rolfe was staring at her. "Why?"

"She might tell herself that she should have never fallen in love, that if she had been stronger, then Jardin would have never been killed."

Rolfe frowned at her. "But that's absurd. It wasn't her fault Jardin was working for the Germans. It wasn't her fault that he got in over his head."

"She doesn't know that. All she knows is that Jardin died and that he blames Colin. She might blame Colin eventually, but she'll look at herself first and figure out what she did wrong." She lifted a shoulder, came over to sit beside him. Sitting this close, she smelled his cologne lifting off him, the brush of his strong arm against her. The memory of being in his embrace rose too easily, and she shoved it away. "And then, there's this part. When Colin comes to her at the end and confesses that he loves her, by this time, she's so alone she can't possibly believe that he's been there all this time, protecting her."

He seemed nonplussed by her presence next to him. "But she's seen glimpses of him. Times when he was driving away, or across a French café."

"She did?" She leaned over and paged through his script. "I didn't see that."

He looked crestfallen, for the first time, as if her words might actually mean something to him. It stirred something inside her. "Colin needs to understand the process she has to go through to understand that he loves her. See, for a man, a romance is about conquering the obstacles between himself and wooing the woman. It's about a journey to win the woman's heart. But for a woman, a romance is about accepting the truth that he loves her. Bridget accepts this too easily."

She wasn't sure where that came from, but it felt right. It took years for her to believe Guthrie loved her, and as for Dashielle, she'd been right about him, hadn't she? "The truth is, after all she's gone through, she might not accept it at all."

Rolfe was staring at the pages. "Indeed." He sighed, put the script on the table. "So how would you write it?"

She considered him a moment. "Really?"

He reached over to where her lemonade sat on the table next to the divan. "I'm listening." He took a sip of the lemonade, made a face. "I don't know how you stand it so tart."

"I like it tart, it helps my voice. At least that's what Nellie says."

He put it away. "So, Fitzgerald, rewrite the scene for me."

Was that a touch of humor? She got up, walked away from him, glanced back, hoping for a grin.

She got something enigmatic but enough to suggest he might not be kidding.

"Okay, I'm Bridget, who, having just been rescued from the clutches of the Germans, returns to her home in the Paris countryside. She is packing, ready to run again, when Colin appears on her doorstep. He's dressed in the attire of a German general, the same attire he used to spring her from the prison."

Rolfe rose. "He has had enough of her risking her life and wants to convince her to escape with him, back home to England."

"But she's found purpose in what she's doing, especially after her losses. It's the only life she has."

"But she has so much more." He shook his head. "She just can't see it."

"Maybe, but Colin will have to convince her of that," she said.

He straightened, jutted his chin.

"What are you doing?"

"Becoming a German general. I'm trying to pretend my bones have stiffened."

"Colin is regal, not stiff."

"Austere?"

"Untouchable, maybe. Especially for Bridget."

"Oh." He undid his suspenders, slouched.

And then, finally, smiled.

The effect of it took her breath away. As if she'd been parched for so long, the first gulp of water could undo her. She stared at him, nearly drinking in his smile and hating herself for her weakness.

How had she become that desperate? Moreover, how would she spend a year with this man and not want to be in his arms?

"Rolfe," she said and tried to frown.

"I'm trying to relax."

She rolled her eyes but found herself smiling back. Maybe they could be friends. Maybe this could work. She just had to keep a grip on her goals. Her heart. What she really wanted.

"Okay, starting at the top of the scene." She looked up quickly, her words taken from the script. "They already questioned me."

He stared at her, as if caught off guard. She handed him the script, pointed to his line. He read the words. "I know. I was there."

"How about a little more emotion?"

He cleared his throat. Met her eyes. "I know." He swallowed, his expression twitching as if he'd seen something terrible, something that had broken his heart. "I was there."

It seemed, suddenly, in that moment, painfully real. She closed her eyes and saw herself in a rustic French home, before a cold hearth, shoving her worldly possessions into a burlap bag, lost, afraid.

Overwhelmed.

Afraid she might throw herself at anyone who would help her, yet fighting for the courage to stand alone. Wishing that she could rewind time. If she had, would she have saved Jardin? Maybe run into the arms of Colin?

Warned herself that love would cost her everything. And more?

Maybe she could play this role. "What do you mean, you were there?" she said, her voice soft, horrified.

She opened her eyes as Colin took a step toward her. She saw him in a German uniform, his dark hair slicked black, gleaming, blue eyes on her, paralyzing her.

"I was watching as you defied them. Your courage. Even the fear that I see now in your eyes. But you don't have to be afraid of me, Bridget." He lowered the script. "I am the one who freed you."

She stood there for a beat, staring up at him.

He waited then checked the script. "Your line is, 'It was you? I can't believe it.'"

I can't believe it. It sounded right, but the words felt suddenly too easy. Not enough…truth. She shook her head. "Why would you do that?"

He stared at her, glanced at the script.

"I'm improvising," she said.

"But it says that you throw yourself into my arms."

She considered it, acting out that moment, stepping into his arms, winding her own around his neck. "No. It's not realistic. I am too hurt, too jaded. I'm not simply going to accept that you would love me after everything—"

"But that's what I wrote." He actually looked confused.

She stepped close, looked at the script. "See, here you have her breaking down. But she's not that weak. I think she pushes him away. What if she asks him where he's been all this time? What if she picks up something and throws it—" She reached for a crystal vase, and he raised an eyebrow.

"Rosie—"

"She's angry, Rolfe. She's angry that he let her go through this, that he didn't tell her the truth. She's angry that she wasn't rescued in the beginning."

"But she didn't want to be rescued then. She wouldn't let him."

"And she's not ready to be rescued now." She put the vase down. "Not by him. Not with what she's done, the sacrifices she's made. She will push him away, tell him to leave her alone."

He stared at her frowning, shaking his head. "But why? I don't understand."

"Because she doesn't trust him that this time it will be different. That she won't end up broken and alone."

That seemed to catch him, his jaw tightening a second before he stared back at the script. They'd veered so far off it, she didn't know what he might be looking for. Maybe, "She believes he pities her," she said softly. "That's why he came for her."

He looked up then, his gaze on her, as if seeing her for the first time. "That's absurd."

"Not to Bridget. She sees everything she is and can't believe he'd love her. And until he convinces her otherwise, she won't believe a word he says. She'll push him out of her life. Frankly, I'm not sure she'll ever be able to give away her heart. Or if there is anything left to give."

"What if he walks away. This time for good?"

Oh. She didn't expect that. Her voice thinned. "Then he didn't really love her, did he?"

She wanted him to refute her, give her an argument that told her that Colin would always love Bridget, despite what she did.

His words, softly spoken, came at her like a slap. "Maybe not."

She swallowed, her eyes burning. Why had she suggested replaying this scene? His version had worked just fine. But, "Why did Colin follow her, keep protecting her, even come to her if he didn't love her?"

He swallowed, his breath rising and falling. "I don't know. Maybe to convince himself to let her go. That he could live without her."

He stared at her then, and she had the crazy urge to run at him, to shove him with both hands into the hallway, slam the door. Lock it. Instead she turned around, walked to the window. Stared at the Palais de Justice, down the street, and just over the muddy Seine. She folded her hands over her chest.

"That's perfect, Rosie. You're absolutely right."

She glanced at him over her shoulder, saw him scribbling down words. "I am?"

He looked up at her, and this time managed a wry smile. "I think so."

Oh. He continued to write. "Is there any hope for Bridget and Colin?" he said softly, not looking at her.

She turned away, watching a boat part the waters of the river. "It's your script, Rolfe. You tell me. Do they have a happy ending?"

He was silent so long, she finally glanced back at him. He was staring at her, wearing an expression she couldn't read.

Say yes. She didn't know where the urge birthed from, but the words pulsed inside her, forbidden, yet hot and sweet. *Say yes.*

She nearly reached out to him, nearly surrendered to the crazy urge to run into his arms, to make him remember everything good they'd nearly had. And then what? She would tell him how she never forgot him?

Rolfe pulled her back from the precarious edge by looking down, gathering his papers. "Maybe not—at least not the one I wrote. I guess I need a more realistic ending."

Heat bit at her eyes. See, this was why she shouldn't play anyone but the bombshell seductress. This part cost her too much.

She was simply lonely and needed to pen a letter to Irene and Sammy. Rosie turned away, blinked away the moisture in her eyes. She could do better than this. *Would* do better.

He gathered his jacket. "By the way, I found you an assistant. She'll help you with your makeup, your costumes, on and off the set."

"Off the set?"

He reached for his fedora. "She'll be over later to help you get ready for tonight's dinner."

"Are we going somewhere?"

"I'd like you to meet some friends of mine." He headed toward the door and stopped with his hand on the handle. "Thank you, Rosie. I'll have to do some rewriting to get the ending I'm hoping for. Thank you for showing me the truth."

* * * * *

What truth? Rolfe's words hung in Rosie's mind all afternoon as she bathed in the claw-foot tub then toweled off her short hair, reliving their scene.

"Is there any hope for Bridget and Colin?"

Oh, she had to stop analyzing his every action, letting him wander through her thoughts. She didn't love—wouldn't fall in love with him.

Couldn't afford to. She shut her eyes, wishing she could erase his voice from her head. *"I'll have to do some rewriting to get the ending I'm hoping for."*

What ending?

Oh, she was clearly reading too much into this script. Into the lily-of-the-valley flowers he'd left for her.

She could admit that, even if she couldn't give away her heart, it didn't mean she didn't want him to fall in love with her. The thought came to her as she stared at her thin face in the mirror. He wasn't repulsed by her. Or at least, he hadn't seemed like it. Annoyed, yes, but he seemed unimpressed by her appearance. He didn't look at her as if she were a hairless waif. He still thought of her as beautiful, even.

Which meant that maybe she could woo back his admiration. Reignite that applause she longed for in his smile. She closed her eyes, remembering how he'd waited for her between takes during Rooney's filming of *Angel's Fury* so long ago when she feared dropping every line. He'd called her brilliant and made her believe it.

How she wanted him to believe it too. To dazzle him. Make him glad he'd believed in her and hired her for this crazy part.

"Hold still, Miss Price."

"Sorry, Sophie." Her makeup girl had appeared with a case of tools from face paint to fingernail polish. A petite yet curvy girl, a few years younger than Rosie, with short red hair tied up in a green scarf, brilliant blue eyes, black pants, and a white cashmere sweater, she spoke brilliant English, introducing herself as Sophie Le Blanc. She had helped Rosie paint her nails and now applied face powder and black liquid eyeliner, her fake lashes.

"You are as beautiful as your pictures, madam," Sophie said. "Even without the wig."

She'd worn a turban for her trip overseas, had left Rooney's red wig on the stand in her room at home. "I don't have a wig," she said.

Sophie smiled at her in the mirror. "Yes, you do." She disappeared into the entryway and emerged with a tall wig box. She set it on the bureau and drew off the cover.

The wig sat on a form, arranged in perfectly styled pin waves. But instead of the platinum blond, or the garish red, the color matched her own new tawny brown fluff. Sophie took it out, held it with her hands inside to give it life. "Do you like it?"

She reached out to touch the waves, the hair soft in her hands. "It's beautiful."

"The duke sent it over today, told me that he'd had it made for you."

Rolfe had it made for her? Rosie wasn't sure why, but the words tightened her throat. Oh. She turned back to the mirror, touching her soft downy hair.

"Would you like to wear it tonight?"

She forced a smile, nodded. "I think that's the point of the delivery, don't you?"

Sophie nodded then set the wig back on the stand as she covered Rosie's head with the flesh-colored nylon cap, trapping the tendrils to her skin. She looked like a skeleton, her head smooth and hairless, and she got up to find a dress as Sophie worked on the wig.

Oh, she was being so silly. Of course Rolfe wanted her to wear a wig for her public appearances. It didn't mean anything.

She picked out a black dress, the kind that dropped daringly in back, accentuated her collarbones, hugged whatever curves remained. She'd gained a few pounds on the rich French food and no longer resembled one of those starving Dust Bowl women. Sequins lined the straps that crossed in back. She retrieved her long white gloves and found a pair of black felt, heeled shoes. Sophie helped her into the dress.

She'd be beautiful for him, even with the wig, and he wouldn't be able to resist her. She sat on the settee, and Sophie arranged the wig on her head.

It hung down past her ears in gentle waves. "It looks real," Sophie said. Indeed, it seemed like it might be an extension of her own hair.

If hers were longer. Thicker.

This version turned her from quaint to elegant, she had to admit it. Now, she'd have to figure out how to get her smile to touch her eyes.

Sophie applied Rosie's lipstick then helped her into her shoes.

"You have real talent," Rosie said as she surveyed herself in the mirror.

"Thank you. It is my first job working on a real star." Sophie retrieved Rosie's fringed black shawl. "I promise to make you beautiful."

"I'm counting on it," Rosie said, slipping the shawl over her shoulders.

Rolfe waited for her in the lobby, at the foot of the long, curved staircase, like he might be a gentleman waiting for his lady. He'd transformed into royalty, wearing a pair of gray-striped tails, his hair dark and slicked back, an ascot at his neck. He watched her descend, his blue eyes on her, and she felt her stomach give a traitorous curl. Then, just when she thought she might recognize a flash of approval, something of longing alighting in his eyes, he looked away.

At the bottom, he simply put out his arm for her. "Your public awaits."

She swallowed back the bitter edge of disappointment.

Indeed, outside, a small band of photographers gathered, shooting her picture as she and Rolfe exited to a cab. Rolfe settled beside her, his face tight.

"Are you angry?" She couldn't help it and wanted to snatch the question back even as it emerged.

He stared at her, frowned. Shook his head.

Right. She folded her hands in her lap. "I was twenty the last time I visited Paris."

"I remember," he said and turned away to the window.

They rode in silence along the *Rue du Cardinal Lemoine,* past the cathedral of Notre Dame now lit up for twilight. Once upon a time, she'd walked this boulevard with Dash, had confessed to him that she'd wanted to become a star. He'd laughed at her then. But years later, he'd tried to make her dreams come true. She couldn't fault him for that.

"Where are we going?"

"Have you ever dined at *Le Pre Catelan*? It's a cabaret in the *Bois de Boulogne.*"

"Yes, in fact. I dined there with Dash, long ago." Had infuriated him, actually, with jealousy as she'd danced with his friends.

A muscle pulled in Rolfe's jaw. "I see."

He said nothing more, and she tried not to care. They pulled up to the entrance, and Rolfe helped her from the car, letting her take his arm as they entered the restaurant. For a moment, standing there in the entrance next to the dark zinc hostess stand, time whisked her back to the moment she'd seen Dash poised across the room, waiting for her at the foot of the long red-carpeted marble stairway.

Dash. Beautiful and charming. Then his memory vanished, leaving only Rolfe. She startled as he curved his hand over hers, strong, steady. "Thank you for coming to dinner with me tonight. These are important people."

His soft tone could bruise her after all this apathy, and she couldn't stop her acrid tone. "Isn't that my job?"

She smiled for the patrons who looked up from round tables, in case some might recognize her. "I'm just trying to play the role you cast for me."

Oh, she hadn't exactly meant to be so sharp, but the hurt lingered there on her tongue.

He said nothing, but his hand slipped away. "We have a table waiting for us," he said to the hostess when she greeted him. Then he slipped his hand to the small of Rosie's back and guided her into the room.

She remembered the piano in the cabaret, a white baby grand, and from it, a soft, romantic tune seasoned the air. The terrace doors remained closed, probably to protect from any hint of night breezes, but she longed to walk into the courtyard, breathe in a moment that might calm her pulse, soothe the ache inside.

She could play this better, the actress on the arm of her director, wooing their audience. Wasn't that why she was here?

Golden light from the chandelier dripped magic into the room, over men and women in evening garb, their conversation a low, distinguished hum. It paused when she passed by, like a lull in the breeze.

She saw herself in the mirrored backsplash between the columned fireplace, and her breath uncoiled from her chest, leaving only a dark burn inside.

She had deserved at least one word of acknowledgment from Rolfe.

They reached the table, and two men rose from it. The first had dark, oiled hair receding from the brow, brown eyes that fixed on her as if hungry. He wore a double-breasted suit, a black tie, and, when he took her hand, his grip pinched.

Rolfe introduced him. "Fredrik Muller, I'd like you to meet Roxy Price. Fredrik is from Germany and is currently assigned as a minister of diplomatic relations to Austria."

"Delighted," he said, and one side of his mouth rolled up, as if she might be something he had expected, something perfect and delicious. Indeed, his eyes nearly undressed her, and she looked away from him, a chill touching her spine.

"And this is my friend Wilhelm Horst. He works for the Austrian chancellor's office."

She glanced at Rolfe as he said this, noted the tenor of his voice. Something about Horst seemed to unnerve Rolfe. Maybe it was just the way Horst took her hand, cradling it in his own, moving close to look into her eyes. A man in his late fifties, Wilhelm Horst reminded her of John Barrymore, suave, attractive, easy around the women, as if used to charming them, and with his salt-and-pepper hair, his blue eyes, they might be easily wooed.

"Roxy Price. You are even lovelier in person." Wilhelm lifted her hand to his, kissed it.

Rolfe drew in a long, ever so subtle breath.

Wilhelm pulled out a chair for her, and she sat across from

Rolfe. He glanced at her, his smile wary even as the garcon attended them.

She perused the menu, but Wilhelm ordered for her. "She'll have the Fois de Gras and a gin and tonic."

Rolfe raised an eyebrow as Wilhelm lifted a glass to her. "To our American princess."

"I'm hardly royalty," she said.

Muller glanced at Rolfe then back at her. "To some, you might be. Europe is fascinated with the American cinema."

Rolfe looked at her then, and for the first time his smile seemed genuine.

"Would you care to dance?" Wilhelm asked, and she allowed him to escort her to the dance floor.

He gathered her into his arms, clearly an accomplished dancer. "What do you do, Mr. Horst?"

"Wilhelm, please. I am in charge of diplomatic relations with certain political parties. However, part of my duties seem to include granting permission for Duke Van Horne's cinematic escapades in Vienna."

Oh, no wonder Rolfe wanted to impress the man. She glanced at Rolfe over Wilhelm's shoulder, saw his gaze on her and, in a moment of unexplained camaraderie, she tried to send a smile of reassurance. But Wilhelm turned her, holding her tight, and then moved into the music. He knew how to waltz, and she resurrected her steps, tilting her head as he dipped her, her arms a flourish.

Thank you, Eleanor Powell, for those brief lessons on the set of *Born to Dance.*

"You are everything the papers say about you," Wilhelm said as the music died, and he pressed a kiss to her cheek.

She smiled, patted his ascot. "Thank you, Wilhelm." Then she pulled him close. "I look forward to dancing in Vienna." She moved back and winked before turning off the dance floor.

Wilhelm didn't take his eyes off her for the remainder of the evening.

She finally escaped after dessert, leaving Rolfe to discuss business, and exited for air.

The music followed her outside onto the white marble terrace. She sat on a bench and leaned back. Above her, the sky winked at her, a thousand brilliant eyes, as if approving.

She closed her eyes, drinking in the smells of Paris, the chrysanthemums still blooming late in the season, the night air twining through the horse chestnut trees.

"How about a dance for me?"

She opened her eyes to Rolfe standing above her. He held out a hand.

Sliding into his arms seemed so easy, but it cost her a slice of her resolve.

He smelled good, the tangy scent of cologne rich off his skin, his breath close to hers. They did something small, a foxtrot, a dance meant for conversation.

She waited for it, even as she leaned into him, wrapping her arm close to his shoulder.

"You smell good."

She leaned back, looked at him.

He met her eyes then looked away. "I guess I'm not the only one who noticed that, though."

She frowned.

He seemed to wince then at his own words. "I'm sorry. I should be thanking you. You dazzled them. Both of them."

"Muller barely looked at me all night."

"Oh, he was looking, all right. He's just married, is all, to a Belgian baroness, one with considerable wealth."

"And Mr. Horst."

"In between wives at the moment, I believe."

"Will you get your permission to film in Vienna?"

He turned her, found her eyes then. Nodded.

"Then I played my part well, didn't I?" she said softly.

"You did. You played it perfectly." He didn't break his gaze. Then it roamed over her face, as if taking her in. It stopped at her mouth.

She felt it then, the old rush of desire, the hope that he might kiss her, the longing to stay in his arms.

No. He was supposed to fall for her; she was not to allow herself to lose her heart. She broke away, backing up, running her hands over her bare arms, now covered in gooseflesh. "Then perhaps you could take me home? It's getting cold out here."

He stood there, still looking at her, the music drifting around him. Then finally he nodded. "Indeed it is."

Chapter 8

Rosie wasn't sure what she'd done to anger Rolfe, but he couldn't look at her without frowning. Or walking away.

Or making her feel as if the chill of northwest England might be emanating right from his glower.

Since that night nearly six weeks ago at *Le Pre Catelan* restaurant, he had avoided her, and she'd been forced to dine with Nellie or even Sophie until finally they traveled to England and assembled the crew.

She kept busy adding notes to nearly every page of the script, hoping that Rolfe might be doing rewrites in between his long absences. She was rewarded with an improved script two weeks before shooting.

He'd set them up in a proper castle in the middle of Manchester, just north of the RAF airfields where he'd received permission from the British military to shoot. The castle came equipped with a tower and long drafty halls adorned with tapestries from France, Germany, and Austria. The house staff kept a fire burning in the hearth constantly, and she permanently smelled of smoke, despite trying to practically bathe in the Cancan de Caron perfume she picked up in France.

They shot the main scenes on the first floor, in the dark, now unnaturally lit, kitchen, in the long hallway with the imposing portraits of previous owners, in a library with towering shelves and a long ladder that traveled the length of the room, and in the barn, outfitted with horses bred to be docile. And of course, in the English countryside, a rolling green expanse that bordered the castle. A lush forest filled with poplar and willow rose up behind the castle to whisper to her at night through the early autumn wind. In the morning, when the maid opened the sash, the scent of the climbing roses would trickle inside. It made Rosie believe that she could play her part of a smitten servant girl unknowingly in love with a traitor.

Rolfe had certainly done his part in casting a dashing Jardin. A scamp with a German accent, Spenser Hathaway had a smile that wooed a gal into trouble, the kind of wounded expression in his brown eyes a woman might like to soothe away. He wore his dark hair dangerously long, his shirts open, his sleeves rolled up to the elbows, his forearms strong as he grabbed her about the waist and held her in an embrace. In their scenes, he had an earnestness that drew her in, made the camera believe that, indeed, he loved her. He couldn't possibly be using her, betraying her.

The audiences would devour him, and weep rivers for him when he died in her arms.

Just like Grayson, Spenser was easy to work with, never demanded anything from her as an actress.

She worried, however, for Rolfe's choice for Colin. An actor named Hale Nichols, he was aloof, cocky, too confident. Sure, she'd peg him as handsome, with his wide shoulders, muscular arms, laughing green eyes, and dark brown hair, sometimes unruly when he came to the set, as if he'd enjoyed the attention of one of the scullery maid extras. He lounged around in his oxford shirt, sometimes open to his undershirt, and she'd caught him twice smoking outside the building, flirting with one of the extras, his smile too smooth, too intoxicating. But he cleaned up like royalty, and the costume designers sculpted his wide shoulders under a proper suit, slicked his brown hair back. He reminded her of Dashielle, perhaps, and maybe that accounted for why their first scene contained too much heat, the dialogue sparking off the page and veering so far off script she thought they'd have to retake it. But Rolfe ordered the shot canned and took a moment to congratulate Hale.

As if he'd done the hard work. She'd been the one carrying the scene, toeing up to her mark for the camera, adding in the believable lines. She'd been the one working late with her dialogue coach, wheedling the story into something that audiences in America might like.

Trying to be brilliant, just like Rolfe needed, to make this movie a hit.

Even if he'd neatly forgotten her. Indeed, both the leads and even the director, a short, vocal Irishman named McDuff, seemed to have more of Rolfe's attention than his so-called star.

McDuff scared her, the way he stalked up to her, cornered her with his directing instructions.

And she thought Rooney had made her hair fall out.

She still wore the wig now, every day, but at night her hair flowed out in soft waves, nearly to below her ears.

Golden brown, like baked sugar. She loved to run her fingers through it.

Now she sat in a canvas chair in one of the grand portrait rooms they'd turned into a dressing room as they adjusted her makeup, reading the pages for her next scene. Her costumes hung in a rack, gray and dowdy for this run of shots. From the walls, dour faces stared down at her, as if disapproving. She hated this room, the prying eyes.

"You're too tense."

She startled, nearly out of her chair. See, McDuff had terrifying written all over him, the way he stalked into the room then stood behind her, with hands on his hips, wearing a beret, his dark eyes on her, peering at her through the mirror. She forced a smile. "What?"

"We need more vigor, sweetheart. More tragedy. Make us believe you're in love with him."

"Colin?"

"No, Jardin. This is your first love scene, and you need to sell it." He crouched next to her. "Listen, I know it's not fair, but Spenser is a European favorite, and you're the unknown, so the pressure is on you. Make us believe in him, in you. Break our hearts with your love for him."

He gave her shoulder a squeeze, as if that might temper the way he barked; then he walked away.

She picked up her script. She'd gone over it with Nellie a dozen times, playing the swooning servant girl, caught in the embrace of her clandestine love, Jardin.

"Break our hearts with your love for him."

She closed her eyes and stilled her thoughts, searching for that moment when she had felt the same as her character. The wonder of knowing someone saw you, believed in you.

"How do you know my real name?"

That day on the beach, so long ago swept through her. Rolfe, standing in the sand, the wind combing his dark hair, those blue eyes following her. She put her hand to her mouth, remembering his kiss, the way the world had dropped away, how, in that moment, she'd belonged in his embrace. Or wanted to. *"Rosie, you don't have to play a part with me."*

Yes, she had. Just like she would now. But she could remember that moment, use it for her scene.

She could break all their hearts.

And maybe Rolfe would stick around long enough to see it.

Even break his cold, royal heart a little.

Jardin was on set when she arrived, sitting in his canvas chair while his assistant applied fresh makeup. They'd take this scene in

Colin's office, where the lighting director had already positioned the cams, the camera boxes ready, her blocking etched out on the carpet. She knew her blocking and now ran it through her head.

Nellie stood talking with McDuff but broke away to meet her.

Rolfe stood behind her and glanced up from the knot of conversation. His gaze landed on her for a moment; then abruptly he turned away.

Yes, well, see if he could turn away after she finished this scene.

"McDuff wants to start with you entering the study, looking for Master Colin. That's when you catch Jardin in his office. He then tries to dissuade you from questioning him with his ardor." Even Nellie reddened as she detailed the scene.

"Don't worry, Nellie. I know what I'm doing." Rosie winked at her. "This isn't my first love scene."

"Of course not." Perhaps once upon a time, Rosie had blushed at the act of kissing a man not her husband. But with dozens of eyes watching, she could hardly call it intimate or romantic.

"Rosie, you don't have to play a part with me."

Perhaps that is what would make it different. For a moment, she wouldn't. She'd be the woman she'd wanted to be in Rolfe's arms. At least once upon a time.

Jardin came in, took his place, and she backed up to the door, met his eyes.

Oh, he could smolder into the camera when he wanted to. So like Grayson.

"Quiet on the set."

She refused to cast a look at Rolfe.

And then they were rolling. Two steps and she became the maid, catching the boy she loved in the act of treason. Jardin was magnificent as he stumbled around, caught, guilty before turning on the charm to will her to silence. He pulled her close, curling his arm around her waist. "You don't want Master Colin to fire me, do you?"

He trailed a finger down her cheek.

She looked into those dark eyes and saw Rafe. The flier who'd made her feel beautiful, brilliant, alive.

She shook her head, catching the collar of his shirt, unbuttoning it, running her finger into the well of his neck. Leaning into him. "No, but—"

"Shh," he said and cupped his hand around her chin. Then he lifted it, running his thumb across her cheekbone. "I love you, Bridget."

He kissed her, and she closed her eyes.

The sand mortared between her toes, the ocean air tugged at her hair, and she kissed him back. Sweetly, curving into his embrace as he held her.

Rafe. Tasting of the wind and the freedom of her youth. She wound her arms up around his shoulders, let him pull her closer.

Kissed him like she remembered. Like she wanted to again.

Spenser broke away, but she had the sense that he might not have, if the cameras weren't rolling.

"I love you too," she whispered, holding his eyes. Spenser seemed trapped, his mouth opening. She pressed her hand to his cheek, moved in toward his ear, her eyes on the camera. "I believe in you, and I belong to you, no matter what happens." She held him, found her camera and the expression she needed, a mix of desperation and disbelief.

The face believing in love, giving away her heart, heedless of the cost.

"Cut."

Jardin let her go. "Hey, I'd do that about fifty more takes." He winked at her, but something of his expression seemed undone.

Out of her peripheral, she noticed Rolfe exiting through the door.

"No," McDuff said, cutting through the thunder of her heart. "That's a wrap. I want to see it on the dailies. Let's prep for scene thirty-seven, Colin in the garden, seeing the lovers through the window."

Where was Rolfe going?

She couldn't stop herself, brushing past Nellie as she strode after him. She waited until she was in the hallway, out of earshot of the crew, "Rolfe!"

He didn't stop.

"Rolfe Van Horne, I'm talking to you."

He jerked then whirled around, and the expression on his face whisked her breath away. Anger? Frustration? The hard glint in his eyes should have been enough to slow her, but she kept coming.

To her surprise, he grabbed her by the arm and pulled her into yet another room, this time a steward's quarters, more of a closet equipped with a telephone, desk, and tiny green divan. More brooding pictures hung on the wall in dusty oval frames.

She yanked her arm from his grip. "What is your problem?"

His eyes were red, his jaw tight. "What is yours?"

"Pardon me?"

"What was that in there?"

"What do you mean? A scene?"

"A love scene!"

"So?"

He held his hands up, stepped back from her. "That's not how I wrote it."

"What are you talking about? I followed the script exactly."

"Not…exactly. You were…" He pressed his lips together. Shook his head. "Ardent."

Ardent?

"I was just doing what you taught me. Going back to a time when I felt—" No. He didn't need to know that. "I was just trying to be real."

"You were real all right. So real, I think Jardin—or Spenser—just might propose!"

"Please. I was just acting. He knows that."

He cupped his mouth with his hand. Shook his head. Wouldn't look at her. "That wasn't acting, Rosie. That was—that was…believable. Even, okay, brilliant."

"Then why are you shouting?"

He glanced toward the door, cut his voice down.

"You know what I mean."

What was his— "No, frankly I don't. Explain it to me."

He was shaking, and was scaring her a little. "I don't understand, Rolfe. What's the matter?"

He turned away from her, scrubbed a hand down his face. "Nothing." He drew a breath. "Nothing."

"This doesn't look like nothing," she said softly, her heart so loud she may not have heard her own words.

Please…

But he took a deep breath, rounded on her, and whatever played on his face had vanished, back into the expression of annoyance.

Or anger.

"Rolfe, please, talk to me."

He smiled, nothing of it real. "I apologize. You're exactly the gifted actress I hired." Then he reached for her hand, pressing it to his lips.

She stood there, turning cold.

Then he released it, meeting her eyes. "Just don't ever tell me that you have nothing of your heart left to give."

Then he brushed past her into the hallway leaving her in the quiet servant's room.

* * * * *

It wasn't quite the applause she'd hoped for, but it still warmed her as she sat in the pub, Rolfe's idea of a farewell party to his crew after this first leg of shooting.

It died too quickly as the crowd downed their toasts. From outside a patron entered, whisking in the frigid night air to the hot pub.

"You deserve it, darling," Spenser said as the crew returned to their revelry. "You mesmerized all of us with those final scenes. You could make a chap believe you actually love him." He winked and slid down beside her at the long, rough-hewn pub table, his arm staying on the back of her chair.

She tried to smile into those warm brown eyes that had inexplicably begun to follow her around the set three weeks ago, after her so-called brilliant scene, but the laughter from the table across the room caught her attention.

Rolfe, telling a story, gesturing with his hands. He wore his old flight jacket and a black sweater, which made him appear at once regal and daring, the exact mix, perhaps, of Jardin and Colin. Not once did his blue eyes glance her direction, however, and frankly, she wanted to hate him for the way he seemed unaffected by the carefully crafted emotion she layered into each scene.

She deserved the applause. His applause. Because she *had* been brilliant.

Now the cast of extras, some sitting on tables, holding pints or glasses of wine, listened to him tell his stories of flying over Germany, his face beautiful and sculpted in the lamplight of the room, every inch the heroic aviator.

She turned into Spenser's embrace. "You deserved just as much applause," she said. Indeed, Spenser as Jardin matched her beat by beat, their scenes ringing with passion. She had cried real tears when he died in her arms, nearly wanted to take a pitchfork to Colin. So what that he hadn't killed Jardin, she let herself believe his guilt and put it all into the scene.

"Did you care nothing for my happiness?"

"He was using you—he didn't love you!"

She'd slapped him then, a doozy that wasn't stage acting, and for that she owed Hale an apology. But McDuff nearly cried with joy over the drama, and Hale congratulated her on her impromptu wallop, and they put it in the can.

Her gaze traveled over to the table with Rolfe again, how he laughed and now put his arm around Sophie, her makeup girl.

Like they might be friends, or even more.

She took a sip of her cranberry juice.

"I'm over here, doll."

She made a face, turned back to Spenser. He was peering at her over the froth of his beer. "Sorry."

"Excuse me for saying so, but you hardly look like a woman about to go on a month-long holiday to Belgium. Seems to me that the phrase *castle in the country* should have you at least mildly excited."

"Castle?"

"You know, the duke's estate." He raised an eyebrow. "Or doesn't that suit your fancy, now that you're a big star in Europe?"

"It's probably not a castle. And I'm not a big star anywhere, currently. Most of all, I'd rather be going home for Christmas, to Sammy and Irene. Rolfe practically ordered me to stay behind while the rest of the crew disbands. I'm not going to a castle; I'm being held prisoner."

He smiled, just a little. "Shall I call you Rapunzel?"

"More like Beauty and the Beast." She cast another glance at Rolfe.

"Really? The duke? He's hardly a beast."

"Yeah, well, maybe not to you, but he's barely done anything but growl at me since he borrowed me from Palace Studios. Look at him over there, flirting with Sophie."

"That's flirting? With Sophie? I don't think—"

She gave him a look. "Yes, flirting."

He raised an eyebrow then took a draught of his pint. Around him, the pub crowd, mostly the crew and extras, danced and toasted the holiday. A band played in the corner, something festive that sounded decidedly Irish.

"I don't want to think about Rolfe." She raised her juice. "To you and your stardom in Germany."

His smile fell. "I'm not going back to Germany."

She frowned. "Why not?"

"I'm not allowed to work in Germany anymore. Not for German directors, that is."

She watched his hands. The way he drew his finger down the frosty glass. "Are you serious?"

He glanced at her. "I'm half Jewish. My grandfather was Jewish, although my grandmother was German, so I'm considered mixed blood. I'm not allowed to work in Germany anymore."

"You're telling me the truth?"

His mouth pursed. "Indeed. It started back in '33 when Hitler's party took over, and it's gradually gotten worse. They wanted to separate Jews from the rest of the German population, but they couldn't figure out who to label as Jewish, so they come up with the Nuremberg Laws. Anyone with Jewish parents or grandparents were included." He lifted a shoulder but looked away from her. "I was going to marry, but my fiancé was German, so they denied our permission to marry."

She touched his arm. "I'm so sorry."

He nodded, looked away from her. Shook his head. "Rolfe found out through a mutual friend that I needed to leave Germany, but they were watching Elise, and she didn't dare leave. Rolfe hired me for this film, got my visa, and hustled me out of the country."

"And Elise?"

He turned back to her. His eyes glistened. "She has moved on to someone more…suitable. I hope to forget her in America."

"That's where you're headed?"

"I have family in New York. And then to Hollywood."

"I had no idea this was happening, Spenser."

He took another sip. "It's getting worse. I hear the Nazis are eyeing Austria and Czechoslovakia and Denmark, even Poland."

"What are you talking about? War?" She shook her head. "Not after the Great War. No one has forgotten the losses."

"Indeed. Especially Germany." He covered her hand, squeezed it. "You are an amazing woman, Roxy. Thank you for letting me fall in love with you." He kissed her hand.

"You didn't fall in love with me, Spense," she said.

He raised his gaze. "Didn't I?"

She drew in a breath, smiled, tried not to hear the voices at the next table trickle over to her. Or take her gaze from Spenser, but oh, see, what was Rolfe doing bringing Sophie to the dance floor, taking her into his arms?

"You know, he isn't smitten with her."

She glanced at Spenser. "I don't care."

"Really?"

"He's just so different from the man I knew in Hollywood. He's brooding and dark—"

"And maybe still grieving."

She glanced at Spenser. "What?"

"His wife. She died about five years ago, right before Christmas, I believe."

"Wife?" *Wife?*

"You didn't know?"

"I—I—"

"How well do you know Rolfe Van Horne?"

"Clearly not well enough." She finished her cranberry juice and debated something stronger. "When did he get married?"

"I suppose about nine months before the day his wife died."

Rosie frowned.

"She died in childbirth."

Oh. Her chest tightened, though, and she couldn't breathe.

That explained a lot, really. Why he didn't reach out to her, why he'd forgiven her. He had moved on, hadn't pined for her at all. Instead, he'd fallen in love with someone else—then lost her.

Probably he didn't have anything left to give of himself either.

She watched him on the dance floor, swinging Sophie in his arms. He didn't look like a man grieving. Then again, she didn't appear to be grieving either.

Perhaps they were both brilliant actors.

"Do you want to dance?" Spenser asked.

"Maybe you should take me home."

"C'mon, Roxy, dance with me." He got up, took her hand, gave it a tug. She relented and let Spenser pull her to the dance floor. The music turned slow, sultry. He nestled her close. "If you want, we can try and make him jealous," Spenser said into her ear.

"What are you talking about?"

He grinned, gave her a kiss on the cheek. "You always put more passion into your scenes when Rolfe was on set."

"I did not!"

"Shh. I'll keep your secret. Besides, you're not the only one in love with our producer." He nodded toward Sophie.

The girl had her head against Rolfe's chest, her eyes closed as he now swayed her.

"I'm not in love with Rolfe Van Horne," she said, looking away from Sophie.

He chuckled against her ear. "Please. I'm your costar. I know when you're acting."

He held her as she tried to push away.

"Work with me, Roxy. Trust me." He began to sway with the music, turning her, dipping her, then bringing her back close.

Out of her periphery, she saw Rolfe's gaze land on them. Then Spenser turned her away, putting her back to Rolfe.

"He's watching."

She looked up at him, and Spenser smiled, winked.

Oh, he was a charmer. No wonder the audiences loved him. She smiled back.

"Want to try that again?" he whispered, his breath soft in her ear.

She giggled as she held on to his arms. "Yes, please."

He dipped her again, this time curving his body over hers then landing a kiss, something soft and intimate, on her lips.

It shocked her, and she felt a blush heat her face.

When he pulled her up, his eyes were shining. "That's wasn't just for him."

"You are a scamp," she said, but she liked the warmth that curled through her at his flirting. Especially as she watched Rolfe take Sophie's hand and pull her off the dance floor.

"Are you ready to go home now?" Spenser said as the song ended.

"Yes."

He retrieved her coat and slid it up over her shoulders. She didn't glance at the table as she left. Let Rolfe wax eloquent about his glory days. She'd heard it before.

Outside, a blanket of snow covered the thatch-roofed pub, the flakes drifting from the sky. The village lights glittered from the paned window of bungalows and storefronts, upon the evergreen-wrapped lampposts. The smell of roasting chestnuts seasoned the crisp air. Her breath spilled out, curling into the night, and she clutched her wool coat at her neck.

Spenser motioned for a driver, but she shook her head. "Let's walk."

"Are you sure?"

"It's only a little ways."

Her boots crunched in the snow, squeaking. Behind them, the raucous noise of the party spilled out of the pub, into the street as people left, laughing, some singing Irish pub tunes.

"The last time I remember walking in snow, it was in Chicago. I was pregnant with—" Oh. She glanced at Spenser, but he was staring at his feet making a trail in the snow. "I was just barely pregnant. And my husband, Guthrie, took me out to the White Sox Stadium where he played baseball, and we made snow angels." Then he'd kissed her, and pressed his hand over her belly, closed his eyes, and prayed.

Or, she thought he'd prayed. She didn't want to ask, too afraid of praying with him, afraid she'd jinx it.

But she had jinxed it all the same.

After a moment of her silence, Spenser asked, "What happened to that life, Roxy? Your husband? Your child?"

She caught a snowflake on her glove. "He died. And she—she doesn't live with me."

He walked quietly beside her. The snow floated from the sky, thick, heavy flakes.

"Since you're Jewish, do you believe in God?"

He chuckled into the night. "It's a requirement. You?"

"I used to believe." She glanced at him. "Sometimes I want to."

"And sometimes you're afraid that if you do, if you pray to God, He won't be there. He won't care, won't answer."

She nodded. "And if He does, that His answer won't be what I want."

He glanced at her, something of a wry smile on his face. "That's the problem. We ask for what we want, not what we need. And until we get that, we keep wanting."

"Maybe I don't know what I need."

He drew in a breath. Considered her for a long moment. "I think you do, Roxy. You just don't want to admit it."

Then suddenly he reached out and took her hand.

"Why did you do that?" she asked softly.

He looked up at the snowflakes, let them fall, melt on his face, turning it shiny. "Because when it's slippery out, sometimes we just need someone to hang on to until we find our footing."

She closed her hand around his as they walked into the chilly night.

Chapter 9

Had Rosie listened to her mother fifteen years ago, this castle, Rolfe's château in the rolling, wooded countryside of Belgium, would have been her home. Had she surrendered her will and simply trusted. Had she let go of her dreams, she might have found them here.

But she had to face the truth. Rolfe Van Horne hadn't come to Hollywood haunting her door with his pining heart. He had no romantic interest in her, despite her attempts to stir the old spark between them.

In fact, Rolfe might be in love with Sophie, her makeup gal, despite what Spenser had said. Hadn't Sophie and Rolfe disappeared together the minute he'd deposited Rosie at his estate like annoying baggage?

Yes, facing the truth would help her stop watching for his return and help her focus on getting through this Christmas without Sammy and Irene.

She should have insisted on returning home for the season. But she could admit that she'd held out some flimsy misplaced hope that Rolfe might, once he got her alone, finally admit that he cared for her.

Rosie stood at the frost-stained window, watching the snow fall from the sky. It seemed it had snowed every day since her arrival two weeks ago, practically entombing her in Rolfe's massive home, just her and the chamber mice, because Rolfe had instantly vanished, leaving her with a revised script, dialogue notes from Nellie, and a skeleton house staff to attend her.

After sleeping for the first four days, she'd turned adventurous and begun to explore his estate. Located in the rolling countryside outside Liege, the Chateau de Van Horne seemed plucked right out of the seventeenth century, with a gatehouse that encircled the frozen manicured gardens, the circular drive, and two medieval towers to further imprison her. She found the entrance to one, stood looking up all three stories, listening to her voice echo in the silence.

At the grand two-story entrance, a carved balustrade led up to the second floor, curving around a brilliant chandelier, with teardrops of golden light that splashed upon the whitewashed walls, the golden lamps, and carved mirrors.

She counted twenty rooms in what seemed an endless labyrinth, and she hadn't even made it to the third floor, although she suspected this was where Rolfe stashed his five house servants: the housekeeper, her maid, the cook, the footman, and the butler.

She felt like she might have stepped back in time, to her mother's house on Fifth Avenue in New York, the feeling of prestige embedded in the shiny oak-paneled walls, the scent of lavender dusting oil.

As she wandered the halls, the staff was invisible and silent, yet somehow appeared magically at her first hint of need.

She'd forgotten the sense of being pampered, *that* she'd surrendered when she'd left her mother's house to run into the grasp of the theater.

Funny, but Rolfe never seemed like a man used to being pampered. On the contrary, he seemed more like a general, a man used to fighting for what he wanted.

The Chateau de Van Horne would certainly quarter an army.

She creaked the doors open on what seemed over a dozen unused rooms. Grand, glorious chambers with Belgian tapestries of battle, or the Christ figure and His disciples, hanging on the walls. Tiled, unlit fireplaces, with frescoes of soldiers or women in repose hung over mantles, and oiled portraits—so many she'd lost count—of Van Horne ancestors.

She found Rolfe's likeness in a grandfather, dashing and robust, posing in his Belgian uniform, fringed epaulets crowning his shoulders, a rich golden sash across his chest. He stared at the artist with a lift to his chin, proud and untouchable.

Yes, she knew that posture from a Van Horne.

She counted four dining rooms, although three hosted petite tables that seated four or six. In one room, she sat so long at the barren table staring at the frescoes on the ceiling that her maid entered and asked if she would like a fire in the hearth.

No, but she would like to dine in the formal dining room at least once during her stay. The red brocade wallpaper, golden frescoed ceiling, and three crystal chandeliers bespoke grandeur, and she imagined throwing a party here, a grand Christmas ball, with a towering evergreen swagged with ribbon from the forests surrounding the estate. She'd light a blaze in the massive black marble fireplace and open the doors to the patio where the night sky could add its magic.

For that matter, she could probably hold a ball in the boudoir Rolfe assigned her. She didn't know whom it might have belonged to, perhaps one of the family's regal heiresses, but she felt it must have been someone who loved the morning light as it glided across the carpet, rich with rose reds and hyacinth blues, hints of buttercup yellow. On each wall, tapestries woven with patterns of green vines and roses cordoned off the chill, although her maid always kept the fire in the white marble hearth lit. The flames reflected off the enormous standing mirror that also captured the scrolled molding, the paneled ceiling. An acre-sized French white sleigh bed, covered in furs and lamb's wool blankets, persuaded her to curl in and stay forever.

Maybe not forever. Yet the quiet, the safety of the estate, had settled into her bones. For the first time in years, perhaps, she didn't care about the trades or the studio, or even the fact that Grayson Clarke's newest movie, *Mutiny*, might sweep the Academy Awards.

Maybe she did care a little. But next year, *Red Skies over Paris* would be in the lineup, she had no doubt.

She should probably use this time of quiet to rehearse, to find more tucked-away emotion for the next phase of filming. A woman desperate to restart her life, to do something of importance. She just might find a kinship in the role of Bridget.

Yes, she'd memorize her scenes under the comfort of a rabbit coverlet, the fire crackling, sipping tea, and she would refuse to miss Rolfe.

But she could hardly forget that she might be in the employ of a duke. For the first time, Rolfe's heritage had settled into her.

She realized all she'd surrendered by not trusting her mother.

But how was she to know that Duke Van Horne might turn out to be...

Dashing? No, aloof and frustrating.

And, even on Christmas Eve Day, absent.

She rose early, took her tea at the table in her room, and decided to venture into the village nearby, a smattering of buildings that, probably three hundred years ago, had been under the protection of the gentry, namely the Van Hornes.

She found a cloak in the closet, red, with a hood, and wrapped it around her, caught in the nostalgia of the attire.

"Would you prefer a ride, ma'am?" The butler materialized, a Mr. Yates, ready to assist her. He reminded her of Bennett, her stepfather, tall, reserved, handsome, a hint of age at his temples. He wore the butler's garb, a suit, tie, gloves. "Thank you, Mr. Yates. I think I will walk into the village." She found a muff and fur-lined boots and was just stepping outside when she turned back to him.

"You and the staff must have family or someone to spend the day with."

Mr. Yates simply stared at her, frowning. "No, ma'am. Mr. Van Horne is our family."

"And he isn't here. So I'm giving you the day off." She smiled, patted his arm. "Tell the rest of the staff they can take the rest of the day and tomorrow off."

He blinked at her. Then, "Very good, ma'am. But should you need anything, please ring."

"Merry Christmas," she said as the giant oak door closed behind her. She didn't need Rolfe's hovering staff; she knew how to care of herself, thank you.

The chill didn't even touch her as she wandered out of the grounds and onto the snowy lane. Her feet crunched on the crisp layer, the sun radiant overhead, turning the landscape to frosting upon the hills. White pine and evergreen surrounded the estate, save for an occasional winter-stripped poplar lifting bare arms to the heavens.

She heard her thoughts, sorted them out as she walked.

Tonight, she'd order a call to Irene, just in time to wish them a Merry Christmas Eve. Hopefully Sammy would have received her chess kit with British toy soldiers she'd found in London en route to Manchester. They'd probably spend the day making cookies with Dorian then decorate the tree.

She'd tell them to look for Spenser—she'd given him her address, told him to look up Palace Studios when he arrived in Hollywood.

Sometimes she could still feel his hand holding hers as they walked home that starry night. He'd left her at her door with a kiss, not asking for more. She wasn't sure what she might have said if he had pressed, and that scared her just a little, her lingering loneliness despite the applause of the evening. She kept hearing it ring inside her and, added to Spenser's words, it became a mockery. *"We ask for what we want, not what we need. And until we get that, we keep wanting."*

She didn't know what he meant about her knowing what she needed. It felt easier to let his tragedy and the horror of it incense her. Certainly he couldn't be right—the Jews couldn't be outlawed from working, from marrying? And Rolfe, did he know about these terrible laws?

And what about Hale? Was he Jewish? He didn't look Jewish, and he wasn't German as far as she knew. Dutch, she thought. She'd barely spoken to the man during the first weeks of shooting. But if Bridget was to fall in love with him, she should at least get to know him more, stir up a fondness for him.

Thankfully, she didn't have to try hard to see Hale's resemblance to Dashielle. And she'd fallen in love with him just fine. Twice, actually.

Unfortunately, just like Rolfe, Hale had vanished the moment they arrived on Belgian soil.

She supposed he had family in Europe.

She should be with her family.

Except, well—Irene and Sammy weren't exactly her family. Just… tenants, really.

Her family lived in Montana. And New York.

She closed her hands in her muff, wishing, today, she might have someone to hold on to, refusing to think what Christmas might be like with a child—her child. The sparkle of delight in her daughter's eyes, the laughter of surprise.

She probably should have sent a gift to Montana, but it felt like too little, too late. And who, really, would Lilly say it was from? It would only confuse Coco and start a conversation that might be better unspoken.

Not unlike the story of Rolfe and his bride. Spenser's words nagged at her, along with the questions. If Rolfe had married six years ago, then it would have been not too long after he'd left her, shortly after Dash's death. No wonder the man didn't want to be at home during the holidays. What painful memories might Chateau de Van Horne hold? What grief?

Apparently no one could go home this season.

She had attempted to find a photograph or an oil painting of Rolfe and his beloved bride, but no trace of her adorned the walls, the bureaus. Whoever she was, she'd died without a replica of her in the family history.

From the village, coal smoke curled up from the houses that clustered along the road, most with snow piled upon their thatched roofs, the plaster siding. The butcher, laundry, bottle shop, and constabulary sat closed, the wind nudging the signs hanging over their doors. Only the grocery and bakery appeared open, cheery wreaths hanging on their doors. She entered to the smell of bread baking in the stone oven, and her mouth nearly dripped with longing. In the case, fresh-baked cherry scones, popovers, and frosted Christmas bread, round loaves with candies pressed into the crust, looked scrumptious enough to devour right on the stoop of the storefront. A plump blond woman in her mid-fifties looked up from behind the counter where she was pulling out the Christmas bread. She set the loaf on a wooden board then wiped her hands with her apron and addressed her in French. "Can I help you?"

Rosie resurrected her rusty French. "I'm—I'll take some of that Christmas bread."

The baker gave her a sad smile. "Oh, I'm sorry. Those are all spoken for. I'm wrapping them up now. But we have scones left."

"Oh, I really wanted the bread."

The woman shook her head. "It's been purchased, earlier this morning. Perhaps a popover?"

But the bread… "Fine. The scones will do. I'll take…two. Two would be perfect." She wasn't sure why she needed two, but maybe she'd save one for tomorrow's breakfast. She hoped the cook had set aside a goose or perhaps a mutton for tomorrow's dinner, although really, why go to all that fuss for her? She didn't need more than toast and tea. After all, she had no one to celebrate with.

"Very good." The baker wrapped up the scones and handed her a paper bag. "Merry Christmas."

Rosie nodded, opened the bag to inhale the fragrance of the scones as she exited. Perhaps she could find some chocolate, melt it, and make one of her mother's favorite indulgences.

Maybe she'd call her mother also, and Finn. Listen to his voice telling her of the ice-skaters at the rink in Central Park, or the greenery in Chronicle Square. She would allow herself to miss New York City, just a little.

She stopped at the grocery and found a bar of chocolate, a bottle of milk, and considered the goose hanging in the window, but she hadn't a clue how to prepare it. Her years as Guthrie's wife demanded she learn how to cook a chicken, but a goose might be above her abilities.

And to think last Christmas Day, she'd spent it at a party in Fletcher's home, a Palace Studios soirée that made the trades.

Rolfe had better know what he was doing, or this might be the first of many lonely Christmases.

The sun had crested, already heading toward the west as she turned to home. The castle loomed foreboding in the shadows of the late afternoon. Hopefully, her maid had stirred the fire in her room—except...perhaps she'd been rash to let them go.

Rosie entered the house through the side door, off the carriage house entrance, and worked her way into the kitchen on the first floor. In her mother's house in New York, the kitchen had been in the basement, where the smells couldn't invade the house. But this kitchen was located in a chamber just off the first floor, with stairs to the wine cellar.

Taking off her cloak, muff, and boots, she laid them over a chair. The matches lay above the stove, and she fumbled for a moment then lit the gas and put on a pot of water. She rummaged around the massive kitchen before unearthing a plate and a tray, and wondered if her mother had ever set foot in her house kitchen.

She put the bag of scones on the tray along with a bowl of raspberry preserves, butter, and a knife. When the kettle whistled, she added water to the teapot then dropped in the netting of tea leaves to steep. She found a teacup and saucer, a few cubes of sugar, and took the entire tray in search of a lit fire, something to warm her bones as she waited for the operator to return her ordered call. She'd asked for 8:00 p.m., which she calculated as noon in Hollywood.

She started for her room then decided to head toward the massive dining room. So what if she dined alone. And certainly she could muster up a fire in the hearth. How difficult might that be?

For today, right now, perhaps she would pretend to be a duchess, the grand mistress of this house. She and her brother Jack had played that game, once upon a time, in her mother's grand chateau in Newport—the game of what if? What if he were Columbus and she the Queen of Spain? Or she Marie Antoinette and he Napoleon?

Their mischief at charades had probably fueled too well her imagination and sparked her desire to see herself on stage, if not on the silver screen.

Sometimes Jack could tiptoe into her mind and feel so close that she might call out his name and he'd simply appear.

Her throat tightened with the realization that she'd never given up hope, not really.

But maybe too, it was time to realize that he'd also left her. That she was alone in this big house, this big life, and had been since the day he walked out.

She drew in a breath then nudged the door open with her foot.

A fire crackled in the hearth, warm, inviting, and she stared at it, her heart thunderous in her chest.

Then, "Where on earth have you been, and what have you done with my staff?"

She jerked at the voice, turned, and the movement sent the teapot sliding off the tray.

It crashed at her feet, along with her bag of scones, soaking into the hot tea.

She looked up at Rolfe, standing there in a brown wool sweater, a pair of striped worsted wool pants, a silk ascot at his neck. He looked tired, red streaking his eyes, fatigue in the lines of his face. Even his hair seemed unkempt, almost as if he'd run his hands through it.

"What are you doing here?" she asked, and instantly regretted her tone.

Or maybe not, because he raised a glass of something amber to his lips, took a drink, then gave her a wry, almost tragic smile.

"It's Christmas, isn't it? Where else would I be?"

* * * * *

"Rolfe, have you been drinking?"

She wanted to retrieve the mess at her feet, the delicious scones now swimming in the amber liquid of her broken teapot, but she couldn't stop herself from advancing on him, from taking the glass from his hand before he could finish lifting it to his lips. "Are you okay?"

He yanked the highball from her hand, stepped away from her. "I'm fine."

But he wasn't fine. His hand shook even as he stared at the flames, flickering in the hearth.

"Did you make this fire?"

He sipped his drink and she backed away from him, bent, and retrieved the shards of the teapot, the ruined bag, and piled it onto the tray. She pulled a napkin from the table and draped it over the puddle of tea, sopping up the mess from the floor. Then she put the wet cloth on the tray and slid it onto the table.

The flames glinted against the hard set of his jaw. She stood there, staring at his back, unnerved by his silence.

"When did you get back?"

He took another sip.

"Maybe you should slow down—"

He gestured with his hand. "You should have seen this place when my mother managed the chateau. Every room had a tree, decorated with lights and ribbon, ivy, and cranberries. She spent months planning the decorations. And then, when everything was perfect, she'd invite the village over, her way of continuing the tradition of our estate. She knew all the families and would present them with gifts—trinkets, really, but something that told them that she thought of them, that she cared."

"When did she pass?" She'd seen a portrait of Lisette in the hallway with a younger Rolfe and a man she guessed must be his father.

He turned. Ran his thumb down his glass. "Mother was German, so she was a target when the Germans betrayed us and invaded Belgium in 1914. If my father had still been alive, perhaps he would have been able to protect her, but he died when I was twelve."

She stayed silent.

"I was seventeen and ready to go to university in Lueven. They invaded there in August, and ironically, ravaged the city, burned the library, all 300,000 books. They expelled the entire population of the city. My mother nearly cried with relief that I wasn't there yet."

She watched him, the way he gripped his drink with both hands. "But they didn't stop there. They pillaged our country. My mother heard about it, and in fear, she took in the families of the village, afraid of what the Germans might do. Then—" He looked up at Rosie. "Then she stood at the gate when they motored right into our gates and ordered them, in German, to leave."

Rosie realized she was holding her breath.

"They beat her." He looked away. Closed her eyes. "I watched it from the house. Two men from the village held me down, kept me from running out to the courtyard while they beat her, then—" his hand was shaking again. "A few of the villagers ran out to save her, but they were shot, leaving her to struggle on her own."

She pressed her hands around her waist, seeing him as a seventeen-year-old youth, fighting, panicked, having to be subdued.

She closed her eyes, an old memory passing through her, listening to her father terrorize her mother. Jack had held her, his strong arms around her as she shook.

Rolfe's voice dropped as he stared into his drink. "The Germans took over the chateau, used it for their headquarters."

"That's why you snuck away, learned to fly in England."

He nodded but still didn't meet her eyes.

"I'm so sorry, Rolfe."

"My mother gave her life for this village. This estate." He looked up, offered a wry smile. "She always wanted it filled with family, friends, neighbors. She came from royalty, but in her eyes, it was her job to make others feel royal. I vowed right then that I would use our title to help others. To do something with my life that might be—might be worth hiding in the castle while my mother sacrificed her life."

His hand trembled again as he finished his drink. It spilled down the front of his sweater.

Rosie picked up a cloth, came over to him, and retrieved the glass from his hand, wiping his sweater. "Come with me."

She slipped her hand into his, but he yanked it away, as if she might be on fire. "I don't need you!"

She looked up then, saw his gaze on her. Something dangerous, even pained in it.

"I know," she said softly. "I know, Rolfe. I know I'm just here to play a part. The one you wrote for me."

A muscle pulled in his jaw as he looked away. His fists clenched at his side. "I didn't mean it like that."

She had the crazy urge to press her hand to his cheek.

"Why did you go into show business, Rosie?" He looked at her. "You were an heiress. You could be in New York, married to some—"

"Duke?"

His mouth closed.

"I don't know. Why do we do anything? Because we think we can't be complete without it." She wadded up the cloth, set it on the table. "I was young, and I was in Paris when Sarah Bernhardt died. I watched the entire city mourn her. I thought, what might it be like to be mourned, to be missed so completely? And suddenly I decided to be someone the world would love."

He looked at her then, the blue of his eyes in hers. "And what if the world didn't love you? What if it was just…one man?"

His words caught her, stole her breath even as she tried to move away. But he caught her arm. "What if I were to tell you that you were missed?"

She drew in a breath. Looked at his hand on her arm and could nearly taste the longing sluice through her.

But… "You're just drunk, Rolfe. And lonely." She eased out of his grip. "You've been ignoring me for weeks, and I'm not so foolish, or desperate." She took his hand, gave him a sad smile. "I know your wife died. And I know how that grief can feel so fresh, make you say, and do, something you'll regret." She took his hand. "C'mon. You just need to sleep it off."

He stared at her, closed his eyes. "Right. Of course."

She tugged him away from the table, out of the room. He said nothing as he walked beside her.

Neither, however, did he let go of her hand.

She'd discovered his chamber during her earlier wanderings, knew it from the masculine scent embedded in the dark wood-paneled room. A fire crackled from the black-tiled hearth, evidence that he'd already attempted to ward off the chill in the unoccupied room.

His suitcase lay open on the wardrobe stand, still packed. Mr. Yates apparently hadn't heard his master return.

Then again, she'd given them the night off.

She pushed him down into a chair at the round table. "How about a drink of water?"

He nodded, and she retrieved a glass from the pitcher and brought it to him.

He caught her hand as she turned to leave. "Stay."

She eyed him.

"I just—it's Christmas Eve, Rosie. I—" He let her go. "Sit and talk to me?"

Sit and talk. To this man whom she wanted to let herself love. Who had once loved her. Maybe she owed him that much.

She sank down on a chair. "Where have you been?"

"Amsterdam. And Austria. And Berlin."

"Berlin?"

He nodded. "My mother has family there. I—they are interested in the film."

"It's going well, I think."

He nodded. "You were the right choice."

"Of course," she said, and got a real smile from him.

It caused a forbidden curl of delight inside her.

"I'm glad to hear you don't think you made a mistake."

He gave a sound that resembled a chuckle but nothing of humor appeared in his expression. "I've made too many of those." He took another sip of water, made a face.

"No, you can't have more bourbon."

He did laugh then. Something low that started a rumble inside her. "Actually, I hate the stuff. I'm not sure why—" He took another gulp. Looked at her, leaned forward, suddenly serious. He stared at the fire, his voice soft. "I didn't marry for love, Rosie."

The words, the admission reeled through her, and she had no words.

He leaned back, nodding, and took a breath, as if he'd let something go. "Bette was a distant cousin who found herself...in trouble."

"Trouble?"

"She was engaged, and unfortunately that led to a pregnancy." Rolfe put the glass on the table. "Sadly, the young man died before they could marry."

"So you did?"

He met her eyes then. "It was a few months after—well, after I came home from America, and I was...I needed something. Some*one*, maybe. So her sister came to me—she lives in Liege—and told me of Bette's predicament. Asked me for the favor of finding Bette a husband. I thought, well, perhaps I could do this one good thing."

He leaned forward then, ran his hands through his hair. "I grew fond of her, yes. But most of all, I grew fond of the idea of having a family. People to fill these halls. Maybe a son to take hunting, carry on the family name."

She waited for more, then, "Spenser said she died in childbirth."

He looked up at her, eyes freshly reddened. "Yes. Two days before Christmas."

"And the child?"

He leaned back. "A little girl. She—she survived."

"And yet she's not here?"

"My life has no room for a child."

Still, the way he said it, it came out more of a question than a statement. Like he may have made a decision he could no longer agree with.

He looked away, as if to confirm it and she refused to ask where he'd sent the child. After all, grief was a powerful motivator. "I understand."

He looked up, considered her. A frown creased his face. "I guess you do, don't you?" And in that moment, an old tenderness filled his expression. "I'm glad you're here, Rosie."

Her voice softened, and she reached out for his hand. He didn't pull it away, but let her squeeze it. "I am too."

She smiled, suddenly unable to speak.

He ran his thumb over her hand. She stared at his grip.

"Rosie. Would you—would you like to go to a party with me?"

"Tonight?"

He nodded. "I wasn't going to go, but..."

"Do I have to wear my wig?"

He looked at her, a tiny frown touching his face. Then, "No. Come as yourself."

She didn't know why her eyes burned, but she gave a tiny, quick nod. "Yes, Rolfe, I would love to go to a party with you."

Chapter 10

"I'm sorry, Mr. Yates. I thought you'd have the entire night off."

She turned so her maid could drape a fur around her shoulders, fasten it at the neck. Mr. Yates brushed off Rolfe's wool coat before helping him into it.

"It is my pleasure to serve at my master's request. I am just appalled that I wasn't on hand to greet him when he arrived." He bowed his head. "Again, my apologies, sir."

Rolfe gave him a nod. "It's all very good, Mr. Yates." He turned to Rosie, extending his hand. "Are you ready?"

Oh, he looked devastatingly handsome in full evening dress, a tailcoat in midnight blue, silk lapels and buttons, white waistcoat and tie. He wore gloves and a silk top hat and any hint of his previous precarious condition had vanished. He smelled freshly bathed, a hint of that spicy cologne at his neck. He'd shaved and slicked back his hair to perfection.

Please, let there be dancing at this party.

"You look lovely, by the way."

Thankfully, her own maid had appeared without pause when Rolfe summoned his staff into action. Her lady's maid, Miss Gwendolyn, helped her dress in a filmy light blue evening gown that she'd saved for a premiere in Paris or London. But it seemed appropriate tonight, and Gwendolyn had pinned back one side of her hair with a lovely paper flower. The rest of her hair, she left down in soft waves.

She smiled up at him, slipped her hand through his elbow. Allowed herself to lean into him as he helped her down the stairs and into the Rolls Royce. A footman closed the door behind them, and he surprised her by manning the wheel himself.

She looked out the window at the night sky, the cascade of twinkling lights.

"I heard the telephone ring. Did you get your call to America?" He pulled away from the estate and through the gates, turning onto the lane.

She nodded.

"Just for three minutes, then we lost it, but it was enough." Enough to hear Sammy's laughter. And Irene's breathless thank-you for the sapphire necklace she'd found in Garrard's in London.

"It's too beautiful to wear around the table, just Sammy and myself."

"You'll find someplace, Irene. Merry Christmas—"

Then, just as she heard a voice, something masculine, vaguely familiar, the line cut off. She hadn't been able to retrieve it.

"I'm sorry you weren't able to return home." Rolfe glanced at her, apology in his expression. But he gave no other explanation.

She drew the fur around her. "It's okay. Sammy and Irene are fine, and hopefully I'll see them in a few months, when we wrap up filming."

Again, he said nothing.

"There was a man's voice on the other end of the phone."

He glanced at her. "Is Irene dating someone?"

"Not that she's mentioned."

He slowed as they entered the village. Lights slivered onto the packed snow, evergreens wound around the lampposts. He kept driving and, in a moment, they left it behind.

The waning gibbous moon hung in the sky, the dusty side fading in the velvet expanse.

"Why did you take her in, Rosie? After she slept with Dashielle, and had his child, why did you take her in?"

She knitted her gloved hands together. "I know you didn't want to believe it, but Dashielle and I had a marriage of convenience. We were only married, in deed, the night after the premiere in New York. And I foolishly thought he loved me. By the time I met you, I realized the truth." She looked up at him, wishing he'd glance at her, but Rolfe only stared at the road, the headlights cutting a path through the darkness. "I never meant to deceive you. And I tried to tell you before— well, before I found out I was pregnant. Really."

His shoulders rose, and fell. Then, "I am sorry I didn't listen to you explain."

"You were hurt."

"I was angry." He looked at her then, but she couldn't read his expression in the darkness. "And jealous."

And now? She longed for the question to emerge from her lips, but she couldn't ask it. She didn't want to threaten their fragile cease-fire. "Irene had no one after Dash died, and I think he truly loved her. He was going to ask me for a divorce."

"Did he know about—" he paused, and his voice softened. "About the baby?"

It didn't hurt so much anymore, but she still felt the sting, deep inside. "I never told him. I was going to, but then he—he wouldn't take my calls. And after he passed, I couldn't tell Irene. She would only feel the betrayal I did."

He said nothing. But then, quietly, his hand moved over to hers, clasped in her lap, and squeezed. "You've got a kind heart, Rosie Worth. I've always known that."

The gesture, the words pooled tears in her eyes, and she looked away, blinking before they betrayed her.

"People have such a great capacity to make mistakes, to derail their entire lives." He took his hand away as he turned up a long drive to what looked like another estate house. "My hope is that God never stops forgiving mine, keeps putting me on the right track, despite my own foolish efforts to sabotage it."

She frowned but didn't have the chance to question him before they pulled into the circular drive of the two-story stone estate. "What is this place?"

"Chateau Le Blanc." He glanced at her, smiled. "Sophie's house."

She stilled. Looked at the grand estate. "I don't understand."

"You will." He got out and crossed over to the door then helped her out. "But please, don't ask me any questions until after the night is over."

He looped her hand into the crook of her arm and led her up the steps. Strange, no footman came to claim the car, no butler opened the door. Rolfe didn't knock either, just opened it and let himself in.

Darkness shrouded the foyer. "Where is the footman?"

"They have no footmen," he said, and cupped his hand over hers. From beyond the foyer, she heard the sound of voices, laughter.

Young voices.

He glanced at her, and even in the shadows, she saw him wink. "Trust me."

She gave him a shallow nod, and he led her into the next room, a sitting room of sorts with two long divans and a desk. He went straight for the door at the far end and knocked.

After a moment, it opened. Light flooded over him and with it the smells of baked bread and potatoes, roasted meat and spicy vegetables. And, blocking her entrance, Sophie Le Blanc, staring at them with wide eyes. "Rolfe! What an unexpected surprise." Sophie wore her dark hair up, pulled in a chignon, and a lovely blue dress, a strand of pearls at her neck. Her gaze landed on Rosie then, and instead of a frown, she smiled. "And Miss Price, of course. Welcome."

She opened the door and stood back and everything inside Rosie froze.

In the massive ballroom, twenty or more children sat at a long dining table in their finest attire, although from the threadbare nature of the clothing it seemed that their finest had endured dozens of Christmas Eve celebrations, maybe passed down each year. The boys ranged in age from four to fourteen, and wore all manner of dress, some in sweaters, frayed at the elbows, others in suit-jackets, and yet others in suspenders and dress pants. The girls too, from toddler to teenager, wore dresses, scarves, or holiday ribbons in their hair. Clean and smiling, their plates seemed cleared of what had been a lavish dinner. A festive red tablecloth covered the length of the table—similar to the one she'd seen in the dining room at the chateau. And, in the corner, a towering evergreen dazzled with glass ornaments. Wrapped gifts piled at the base of the tree.

A robust woman, her black hair piled up on her head, dressed in a gray wool dress and a long hanging cross necklace, rose from the end of the table. "Your Grace. What a surprise." She had flushed and now hurried toward them. "We were just about ready to serve dessert and then distribute gifts."

Rolfe removed his hat. "I'm sorry to interrupt your annual dinner. May we join you, Mademoiselle Franc?"

"Of course." She turned and directed a couple of older children, who scurried to make places for them.

Rolfe never let go of Rosie's hand, still pinched into the pocket of his arm. He leaned near her. "This is the Lady Lisette Van Horne orphanage."

Lisette. After his mother. Rosie had the strangest urge to wrap her arms around him, press a kiss to his cheek. But then a little girl, maybe five or six years old, ran up to him. She wore a pretty blue polka-dotted dress over a long-sleeved shirt, wool stockings, and a floppy ribbon woven into her long braids. "Thank you, Your Grace!" then she bent in a proper, well-trained curtsy.

He bent, caught her up, kissed her cheek. "Hello, Angelica." She giggled. He let her go, and Rosie needed to sit down.

"You know these children?"

He shook the hand of a gentleman she guessed might be about fifteen, who appeared before him, bowing his head at the neck.

"Bertrand," Rolfe said. "Nice to see you. I assume you are progressing in your studies."

"I am, sir. The Académie Royale in Brussels."

"Very good. " He turned to her. "Bertrand surprised us with a one-act soliloquy of Hamlet last spring at our annual academia show."

"Indeed," she said.

He turned to Bertrand. "Miss Price is a gifted actress, and she is starring in a film I'm producing."

"I know Miss Price, sir," Bertrand said. Was that a blush? He took her hand, bowed his head. "A pleasure, m'lady."

"I'm not a lady," she said, but Rolfe leaned in to her.

"Tonight, you are." He smiled again, and she couldn't breathe for the power of it to wind through her, undo her.

They pulled up chairs for them, and she sat beside Rolfe, aware of his presence, the rich timbre of his voice as he laughed with each child. It seemed he knew them all by name, knew about their studies in school and even their dreams.

"Nicole, have you applied to the *Conservatoire Royal de Musique de Bruxelles* yet?"

"No, Your Grace. It is quite expensive."

He took a sip of the juice Sophie had given him. She stood at the end of the table, watching the conversations like an older sister.

"Perhaps there will be a scholarship available." He lowered his voice, turned it stern. "I expect to hear of your application by the time I return in the spring."

"Yes, sir," she said, and glanced at the girl next to her, who held a hand to her mouth, giggling. Oh, of course they had a crush on Duke Van Horne. Who wouldn't?

A village woman, dressed in serving attire, emerged from the kitchen with a plate covered in cloth. Behind her, a trail of helpers followed, all with similar plates. She set hers before Rolfe and removed the cloth with a flourish.

"Well done, ma'am," Rolfe said.

The Christmas bread. Cut, presented, and ready for celebration. Rosie recognized the woman from the bakery. The woman caught her eye and smiled, ever so briefly.

Tea and bread. She was back in Paris, or perhaps New York City, dining in gloves.

Mademoiselle Franc rose. "Let us gather around the tree, read the Holy Word in remembrance of this blessed evening."

The children rose, and Mademoiselle Franc read the story from Luke, the one about Mary and Joseph and the holy infant born on this eve.

"And who remembers why the Christ child came to live among us?"

One of the little girls raised her hand, glanced at Rolfe before standing. "To redeem us from our sins." She smiled at Rolfe then at Rosie. "Because He knew that no matter what we did, we would always need Him."

"Very good, Claire," Mademoiselle Franc said. "And this holy night is the reminder that, before we even realized we needed a Savior, Christ appeared. And He came in the form of a child so that we would accept Him instead of fear Him."

Accept instead of fear. But what about God the Father? Wasn't He to be feared? Rosie had spent most, no, *all* of her life fearing the God she'd met in her Episcopal church in New York, the one who gave and took—especially took—away. The one who reminded her that no matter what she did, she'd lost His favor, and had no way to redeem herself back into His grace.

Yes, she feared God. But she hadn't, perhaps, considered the Christ child. "*Because He knew that no matter what we did, we would always need Him.*"

"We always need to remember that Jesus didn't have to come to earth—but He was trusting His heavenly Father. And His trust, His meekness, led Him to save us all. Perhaps someday, God will do something amazing through you because of your trust."

Rosie glanced at Rolfe. He had his hands clasped between his legs, his gaze beyond the children, lost somewhere.

Mademoiselle Franc turned to Rolfe. "Some music perhaps, before the gifts?"

He roused, back from his roaming, and nodded. Soon the children gathered a small ensemble of violins and flutes, playing Christmas hymns.

She sat in her chair, laughing and clapping while Rolfe directed, so much delight on his face, it could fill her right up, spilling over.

"Perhaps a song from our guest? Something from America?" Sophie asked, emerging from her corner. She smiled, nothing of malice in it. In fact, she seemed delighted at Rosie's presence.

"I can't sing—"

Rolfe stood before her. "Yes, you can. How about something simple? 'Love Me or Leave Me'?" He held out his hand.

She couldn't read him, the power of his eyes on hers stealing her breath. She started to shake her head, but he crouched before her. "Together, perhaps?"

Together.

Like they did on the beach, his arms around her, swaying to the waves. She looked at the faces of the children, heard them clapping.

"For the children," she said.

"For the children."

She got up, let him lead her to the front of the room. "I would do better with music."

He raised an eyebrow, almost in challenge.

Fine. She took a breath, "Love me or leave me...let me be lonely..."

He picked up the next line, his voice a deep, resonant tenor, just like she remembered. "You won't believe me, and I love you only...." With him staring at her like that, she might actually believe that he hadn't forgotten her, hadn't stopped loving her.

Her voice trembled, her chest tight as she sang the words back to him. "I'd rather be lonely than happy with somebody else..."

He came near her, but even as the words echoed out of her, she felt them settling into her. He sang the next stanza while taking her hand, his eyes holding her fast.

"You might find the nighttime the right time for kissing, but nighttime is my time for just reminiscing...."

She knew the next words but couldn't seem to pry them from her chest.

After a beat, he took them up himself. "Regretting instead of forgetting with...somebody else."

But that's what he'd done, hadn't he?

"I didn't marry for love, either."

Her eyes burned, too much emotion in her throat as she pressed out the lyric—"There'll be no one unless that someone is you...."

His smile faded. Silence filled the room, and all she heard was her heartbeat, then, thundering in her chest.

"I don't remember the rest," he said softly.

"I think it's something about not wanting to borrow love, not wanting to have it today only to lose it tomorrow."

He had her hand, her gaze, and nodded.

Still, silence. And then he shrugged, smiled. Turned to the audience. "That's all we have—"

The room exploded into thunderous applause. Buoyant and bright, the children rose to their feet, cheering, some of them pouncing onto their chairs.

Rolfe took her hand, and gave a bow, rich with flourish.

She couldn't move. She just pressed her hand to her chest and drank it in, letting it nourish her, filling all the empty niches of her heart. Silly tears crested at the corner of her eyes.

Rolfe squeezed her hand then stepped away, his hands out toward her.

And then all she saw was his smile, the warmth in his gaze, and the way he moved his lips to form silent words.

Merry Christmas.

She nodded and held out her hands to her audience. A few children surged forward, embraced her, and for a precious, sweet moment, she held on.

The glow of their adoration clung to her the rest of the evening as Rolfe handed out gifts to each child then danced with the girls to the melodies on a Victrola. She and Sophie danced with the boys, and she taught a few of the older boys to waltz.

The hour had turned to midnight by the time Sophie and Mademoiselle Franc ordered the children to bed.

Rolfe helped her with her cape. "Thank you," he said softly, a whisper over her skin. He helped her into the car, and she sat back, enjoying his rumpled aristocratic appearance. His tie hung askew, his gloves abandoned.

"Now the questions," he said, pulling into the night.

"Sophie is—"

"My cousin. And her family helps run the orphanage. She hosts their annual Christmas Eve party, allowing the regular staff to take the night off. She has aspirations of being in the movies, so I thought she might enjoy being your assistant."

"It wasn't fair to trick me—I treated her like a servant. Is she a duchess?"

"Her father was a baron, but she is unmarried, so her title is simply Miss."

"Miss Le Blanc."

"But Sophie will do on the set." He looked at her. "She didn't want you to know. She's a fan, and felt it rather...awkward."

"I understand. And those children. They know you."

"And I know them." He didn't offer further explanation, but it seemed that perhaps it didn't need one. He was their benefactor.

Their hero.

And, suddenly, hers. She wanted to reach across the darkness for his hand, but instead she softened her voice to something tender. "It was indeed a merry Christmas. Thank you, Rolfe."

She saw him nod as they pulled up to his château.

He got out without a word, retrieved her, and gave her his arm.

Before they reached the stoop, he paused and turned her.

Oh, he was handsome, the way the cold had burnished his cheeks. And he smelled like the revelry of the evening, a masculine redolence that made her want to lean toward him, to wrap her arms around his waist, to lift her face to him.

Maybe he could see it in her eyes, for he swallowed, his gaze landing on her lips.

Yes.

"You are so lovely, Rosie."

Oh, there were those annoying tears. She looked away, blinking.

"I know you don't believe it, not really. I know that deep inside you think you have to have others tell it to you. But if that is what I have to do, then I will." He cupped her face, turned it back to face him. "You are so beautiful that sometimes it stuns me, holds me captive."

Rolfe.

He would kiss her, and oh, how she wanted it. She even moistened her lips, lifted her face to his.

She didn't know how to grasp the emotions of the day, the loneliness, the anger, the—the delight.

Most of all, the terrible, wonderful urge to press herself into Rolfe's arms and hold on. But, "Lovely with or without my hair?"

He frowned.

She lifted a shoulder, looking away.

"Oh, Rosie." He turned her face back to his, his eyes troubled. "Don't you know?"

She blinked away the moisture gathering in her eyes.

"How many times do I have to tell you you're beautiful before you believe it?"

"I don't know."

His voice lowered. "Fine. I'll tell you every day that you're beautiful if that's what you need to hear. Because it's the truth."

She didn't ask, wanting to believe his words, and what she saw in his eyes. The way his gaze roamed over her face.

All she had to do was lean in. Lean in and then certainly he'd be kissing her. She could taste the softness of his touch on her lips.

Rolfe.

Suddenly, he seemed to catch himself. He swallowed, licked his lips, cleared his throat. "I'm so sorry about…my condition earlier this evening. I wasn't myself. And I know better than to turn to drink. I know God has a different path for me. I was just shying away from it. My Gethsemane moment, perhaps."

She frowned, not sure— "I—know that, Rolfe."

Her tone flickered on his face, the way he fashioned a smile. "I am wondering if you would do me a favor.…"

Anything. She nodded, her gaze on his blue eyes. Dark whiskers had begun to shade his face, and she wanted to run her hand down the scruff of his chin. "I must go to Vienna for a New Year's ball." He touched his hand to her face. "Please, will you accompany me?"

Vienna, to a ball? "Of course."

He smiled then, but he gave a funny little swallow, as if he might be relieved. "I need to get you inside, it's cold out here."

"I'm not cold," she said.

"Neither am I," he said. He breathed in a long breath, shook his head, wearing a strange expression. "That's the problem."

He pulled away from her then and opened the door. Mr. Yates materialized, ready to help her with her cloak, him with his wool coat.

"Thank you, Mr. Yates," he said. "Can you see Miss Price to her room, make sure Gwendolyn stirs the hearth?"

"Yes, sir."

He wasn't going to kiss her, to wrap her in his arms? To invite her—

Oh.

Had she somehow misread him on the stoop, the texture of his eyes, the way he seemed ready to take her in his arms?

He turned to her, lifted her hand, and kissed it. "Thank you, Rosie, for a beautiful Christmas Eve. As usual, you were brilliant. I look forward to Vienna with great relish." He briefly met her eyes. Then he left her standing in the hallway.

She had the strangest sense that, despite his words, she hadn't played her part right tonight, not at all.

Chapter 44

It was a night, a city, in which to fall in love. And tonight, Rosie intended that Rolfe Van Horne would remember her.

The lights of Vienna twinkled against the velvet black canopy of the night, turning the city magical on the eve of the New Year. A blanket of snow frosted the baroque statues on the monuments along the *Ringstrasse*, turned to glitter the statue of Mozart poised in front of the Imperial Building. Outside her hotel, the Grand Hotel Wein, the horses harnessed to stately carriages blew fog into the chilly air. Rolfe intended to take a carriage to the Schonbrunn Palace tonight and had left instructions, as well as a new mink stole, in her room.

If she counted only his gifts, from the fur to the richly attired suite in the Grand Hotel—a three-room suite, with the rose brocade and gilded furniture, the gleaming beech and walnut furniture, the gold chandeliers that splashed pomp and circumstance into the room—she might assume he adored her. He'd made himself virtually scarce since their arrival in Vienna three days ago, and if it weren't for Sophie to keep her occupied, Rosie would have turned around and headed back to Belgium. Or perhaps America.

"Is he angry with me?" she asked Sophie who insisted on helping her dress for the ball. "Because he's hardly spoken to me since the night at the orphanage."

"I don't believe so. Does he have any reason to be?"

Rosie shook her head. But with the exception of a few perfunctory words at breakfast, or perhaps in passing, Rolfe acted as if their moment on the steps, the warmth she felt in his arms, hadn't existed.

Tonight, she determined to revive the look in his eye, to make him see her.

To make him remember.

She simply refused to believe that the emotions she saw move through his eyes didn't belong to her. Or maybe she simply refused to believe they belonged to someone else.

"Sophie, did you know Rolfe's wife?"

Sophie stood behind her, unpinning the curls she'd set earlier. Her hair hung in soft waves, curling at the ends into a tumble of elegance. "I did."

"He told me it was a marriage of convenience."

Sophie had mentioned little about the night at the orphanage, spending her time in Austria showing Rosie the sights. They'd toured the Burgtheater and Akadamietheather, and opera house, *Staatsoper*, the *Kunsthistorisches* and *Naturhistorisches* Museums. They had taken coffee at *Zum Schwarzen Kamel*, a favorite of the composer Beethoven, and even watched a performance of the Lipizzaner stallions at the Spanish Riding School in the Hapsburg Winter Palace.

She would like to have seen all those sights on Rolfe's arm.

Sophie finished attending to her hair then reached for the dress, hanging on a silk padded hanger. She lifted it over Rosie's head. "Just because Rolfe married her because she needed him doesn't mean he didn't love her. He loved Bette very much. It just wasn't the kind of love that…" She looked away.

SUSAN MAY WARREN

That he'd had for Rosie? Rosie tried to catch her eye in the mirror, her heart suddenly in her throat.

"Why did he marry her, if he didn't love her?"

"Because she needed him. And because it is his greatest joy to help someone when they need him, even if they don't know it or accept it." Sophie seemed to be blinking away moisture from her eyes. "Rolfe is a noble man, but he's not above a broken heart. I think his wife reminded him that some things, like love, might be worth hoping for. That it was okay to long for it, even in the face of the impossible."

"Which is why he wrote the screenplay?"

"Which is why he flew to America to ask you to play the role." Sophie lifted her gaze, met Rosie's in the mirror. "Perhaps he needs to learn that just because you want something doesn't mean it's good for you."

Rosie couldn't read her expression before she slid it away, returned to her ministrations. Certainly she didn't mean that she wasn't good for Rolfe?

"This dress is so lovely on you," Sophie said, stepping back.

Indeed. Sleeveless and V-necked, it draped down to the floor and beyond in flowing white silk brocade. A sheer lace skirt overlaid the top. Her long, over-the-elbow, white gloves, and high-heeled white satin shoes completed the ensemble.

Apparently tonight's party would be a traditional Viennese Waltz, the dancers dressed in only black and white.

She almost looked like a bride.

Sophie stood behind her, met her gaze in the mirror, and smiled.

Maybe Rosie had misheard her.

"He said something about hoping God kept forgiving him for his mistakes."

Sophie frowned, glanced at her in the mirror. Her expression softened. "He's talking about Angelica, the little girl you met at the orphanage, the one who ran into his arms." She sighed, picked up the pearls and fastened them around her neck. They dangled down her back. "She's the daughter that Bette gave birth to that night."

Rosie watched her movements in the mirror, trying to comprehend her words. "Angelica is his daughter?"

"By name only."

"But then why does she live at the orphanage?"

Sophie held out a glove. "Because she is a child in need of a mother, and Rolfe can't take care of her that way."

His mistakes. No wonder he watched the child all night, his eyes shining. "She is a beautiful girl."

"He loves her dearly, just like he loves all the children at the orphanage."

"But she's his stepdaughter. Does she know?"

Sophie held out the other glove. "Yes. But she also knows he is not trying to be cruel. He's trying to protect her."

"By making her feel like she is like everyone else? That she has to earn his love?"

Sophie stepped away from her, frowning. "Angelica doesn't have to earn his love. Did it look as if she felt she needed to earn his love?"

No. Indeed, she'd run into Rolfe's open arms, overjoyed.

In fact, for a moment, Rosie had even been jealous.

Sophie picked up her cape, the dark mink, and wrapped it around her shoulders. "You will win the hearts of men tonight."

She only vied for one.

Rolfe waited for her in the lobby, again dressed in his tails, this time with white gloves, a black overcoat, a top hat. And he'd hired a carriage to carry them the short distance from the Grand Hotel to the castle.

"You look lovely," he said, but his words lacked warmth and he looked away before she could respond.

He helped her into the carriage then tucked a blanket around her. "I hope this is suitable. The drive is quite brief."

"It reminds me of growing up in New York City."

He nodded and climbed up beside her, nestling in beside her. He didn't take her in his arms, and the gulf between them felt arctic.

No, she hadn't played her role brilliantly a week ago, not at all.

Outside, St. Stephan's Cathedral glowed with the lights from the gothic tower and sprinkled starlight onto the cobbled street. Other bedazzled partygoers trotted by in open carriages.

Her throat began to burn, and she turned away. She shouldn't have expected anything but his cold shoulder, despite her attempts to catch his eye.

"Wilhelm Horst will be in attendance tonight," Rolfe said, looking ahead. "You may remember him from Paris."

She watched his words wheedle out into the air. "Of course. And your German friend? Muller?"

"Perhaps. Yes."

She studied him, saw the taut ridge of his jawline. He seemed suddenly tense, like he had that night at *Le Pre Catelan*. She couldn't help it. "Is everything okay, Rolfe?"

He surprised her with the slightest hint of fear in his expression. Or maybe she'd imagined it because it vanished in a moment.

But he reached over from under the blanket and took her hand. Squeezed. "Thank you for accompanying me tonight."

Some of the heat evaporated from her chest. "What is so important about this night?"

He didn't answer her. But he didn't let go of her hand either.

They pulled up to Schonbrunn Palace. A towering evergreen, perched on the long entrance balcony, sparkled against the night sky, bedecked with a thousand tiny white lights. Footmen in red livery opened the carriage, although Rolfe helped her down and wrapped her arm around his. "You really do look lovely," he said.

She'd never met a more confusing man.

He led her up the outside stairs, and the sounds of the orchestra twined out into the night. Another footman opened the door to the grand entrance, where she left her cape; Rolfe, his muffler. Then he led her to the ballroom.

She'd attended glorious events as the daughter of an heiress, but the grand ballroom of the Schonbrunn Palace, with the polished golden parquet floor, the massive gilded, tiered, crystal chandeliers, the arched doorways, and gold-foiled trim, stole her breath. From an anteroom off the ballroom, an orchestra played a Strauss waltz, and across the room, countless couples, the women dressed in white ball gowns and men in black tails, twirled on the dance floor.

"Look up," Rolfe said, and slipped his hand over hers.

The domed cathedral ceiling had been frescoed with paintings of warriors and chariots and horses, a canopy of battle overseeing the festive dancers, perhaps a way to remind guests of the power of the host, the former monarch of Austria.

"It's glorious."

"It's ironic."

She didn't know what he might mean by that. But for the first time, he turned to her. "One dance, perhaps, before the night begins?"

Only one? But she nodded, and he took her into his arms.

And then time vanished, and she returned to the sultry California beach, the music swelling in her head as he waltzed her onto the dance floor. The orchestra music soared with his movements, and she held on, feeling his strong grip in hers, his hand soft at the small of her back. He smelled clean, elegant, and the more she moved in step, letting him lead her, the more they became one movement, graceful and smooth. She lost herself for a moment in the heady sense of delight.

He dipped her at the end. She hadn't realized she'd been holding her breath. He was so close, she nearly leaned up to kiss him. Especially when his eyes met hers and she saw in them everything she'd hoped for.

Desire. Longing. The expression of the man she'd seen across the room that day so long ago in the hotel in Oakland. A man hoping that she might be his.

"Rolfe," she whispered then curled her hand up around his neck.

The song ended, and she might have imagined it, but even as he appeared that he might kiss her, he closed his eyes. He drew in a breath, as if gathering himself, pulled away, and righted her.

The applause lifted around them.

He stepped away adding his own applause.

"Thank you," he said. "That was perfect."

But his eyes had chilled. Then, abruptly, he left her, right there on the dance floor.

She stood frozen a moment, nonplussed. What—

"Miss Price?" She turned, and found Fredrik Muller, his obsidian eyes upon her. "I didn't realize you'd grace us with your presence this evening," he said.

He'd slicked up for tonight's event, although not in a tuxedo. Over his white shirt and tie, he wore a uniform of some kind, dark gray with gold epaulets at the shoulders and a host of honorary ribbons on his breast. On his collar, he wore patches of a three-leaf insignia and a pin with a cross in the middle.

"My escort seems to have abandoned me," she managed, shooting a glance around the room for a glimpse of Rolfe.

"That is a crime I should have him executed for," Fredrik said, winking. It felt not unlike being wooed by a reptile, pinched and scaly. And when he took her hand, moved it into the crook of his arm, she wasn't at all sure he was kidding.

"If you will permit me, I'd love to introduce you to some of my colleagues."

"Indeed," she said, searching for Rolfe. She spotted him standing in the corner, talking to an elderly woman in a tiara, long gloves, a black dress. Probably someone of Austrian royalty.

As if he might have sensed her gaze, Rolfe looked up, caught her eye. Then swallowed and looked away.

No, she didn't understand this man. Not at all.

Fine. Okay. But she could taste her heart in her throat, sour and burning.

Fredrik wove her through the crowd toward a group of four men standing in conversation, some of them holding drinks, others watching the dancers. They all wore the dark gray uniforms, some with a leather belt across the chest. "Gentlemen, I have a rare treat for you. I'd like you to meet the actress Roxy Price."

He moved his arm to clasp around her waist, even as she extended her hand to the group. A bookish-looking man with spectacles and a scratch of a moustache took her hand, bowed. "Charmed," he said, his accent heavy. "My name is Herr Himmler."

"Wilhelm Stuckart," said the next man, a bulbous man with a double chin, his hair cut so short she could see his flesh. She wanted to shrug free of his grip, shivering at the way his dark gaze traveled over her.

"Ernst Kaltenbrunner," said the third man. He had a sharp, almost pinched face, the slightest grin tipping his lips. "I'm the true Austrian," he said, winking at her.

"I'm sorry, I don't recognize your uniforms. Where are you gentlemen from?" she asked, adding an actress smile.

Fredrick still had his hand clutched to the small of her back. "We're with the German Schutzstaffel, here to provide diplomatic support for Austria."

She wanted to ask about the trouble Spenser experienced with the new Nazi party in Germany, but she said nothing as another man approached their group.

With dark blond hair and blue eyes, he stood taller than the other three, something almost regal about his bearing. He had high cheekbones, the trace of a smirk on his face, as if he might be nursing some private humor. He wore the same dark uniform, with the exception of an extra row of medals at his chest. A black iron cross hung from his pocket. She didn't know why, but she couldn't tear her gaze from him.

Fredrik noticed and tugged her closer to him. She glanced at him and frowned, but not before the stranger interjected himself into the conversation.

"Herr Muller, who is this lovely lady?" The man held a glass of champagne and now looked at her and smiled. Something about his gaze captured her, the way he looked at her then, the flicker of something akin to recognition in his eyes. "Herr Staffen. Otto Staffen," he said.

"Roxy Price," she responded.

"Of course. You're even lovelier than your press photos." His English had only the slightest accent. He took her hand, lifted it to his lips, pressed them against her hand through her glove. Then he looked up at her and smiled.

The sense of the familiar hit her so hard she gasped. But she couldn't place him, and she reeled through her past, knowing she'd seen him before. She opened her mouth to say something but he signaled to a waiter for another drink, speaking in German.

Maybe not.

Fredrik turned her. "Care to dance?"

She didn't seem to have a choice as he maneuvered her to the dance floor. She allowed him to affix her into his arms and moved with him into the waltz.

The eyes of his companions followed her. All except Otto, who had turned his back to her.

Strange, that feeling, but perhaps he simply reminded her of someone. His blond hair curled at the nape of his neck, dark, and she had the sense then that she might be seeing—

Bennett. Her stepfather.

Her brother Jack's biological father.

She tried to study the man, but Fredrick's hand on her back tightened, and she couldn't nudge him back around, regardless of her subtle attempts.

When he finally turned her again, Otto had disappeared from the group. She tried to find him in the crowd, but he'd vanished.

"Everything okay, Miss Price?"

She leaned back, smiled into Fredrik's dark eyes. "Do you know Herr Staffen well?"

"He's a war hero, served on the front in the First War. And now runs the Gestapo in Berlin. Why?"

Oh.

Well. She gave him a smile. "No reason."

When the music ended, he guided her back to the group.

"My turn, perhaps?" Ernst Kaltenbrunner asked. He bowed at the waist, and she allowed him to lead her back to the floor.

She danced in turn with each of Muller's companions, each time searching for Rolfe, or Staffen, but both seemed to have vanished.

Wilhelm Stuckart fetched her some *Millirahmstrudel* and she ate the milk cake with coffee in the massive adjoining gold-wallpapered dining room, under the hurrah of chandeliers.

Then, Muller invited her outside, to the balcony. Stars thickened with the night, and across the glittering cityscape, the St. Stephan's Cathedral shone like a beacon.

"Wait until midnight. The fireworks are quite breathtaking," Muller said. He was leaning against the balustrade of the balcony. "Are you cold?"

She ran her hands over her goosefleshed arms, glancing back into the crowd. Dance again or stand in the cold. From behind her, the orchestra had launched into another waltz, but her feet ached, and the milk-cake had settled like lard in her stomach.

And seeing this German who, for a moment, stirred up memories of her brother made her ache to her bones. She just wanted Rolfe to return, to take her home.

"Have you seen Duke Van Horne?"

Fredrick frowned. "I thought you came with him."

She drew in a breath. "I did, but he seems to have abandoned me."

Muller moved toward her, grabbing her hand. "His loss then." He pulled her toward him. "Perhaps I can help you forget the duke," he said, curling his arm around her waist.

Before she could stop him, he'd pressed a kiss to her neck. Slimy and cold, it froze her for a second before she palmed the front of his uniform. "Herr Muller, please, I—"

"There you are, Miss Price. I thought I saw you venture out here."

Rolfe's voice slid over her like a hand upon her shoulder. Muller lifted his head, put her away from him.

She reached out for the banister, her legs rubbery. She backed away from Muller even as Rolfe came up to them. "You promised me a dance, and I was searching all over for you."

She stared up at him, nonplussed.

He smiled.

Suddenly, she wanted to slap him. He abandoned her to the clutches of Herr Muller's pawing all night and now had the nerve to smile at her?

He seemed unaffected by her glower. "But you look tired. Perhaps I could see you home?"

She hated him then for the relief that sluiced through her. Her hero. Again.

Fredrik pinched his lips together then bowed at the neck. "Until we meet again, Miss Price."

"Thank you for a lovely evening," she ground out.

Rolfe watched him go, his smile dying.

He turned to her even as she rounded on him.

"Where have you been?"

"Are you all right?"

Their words crossed, and she stared at him, her mouth open. Then, "What do you care? You abandoned me! You simply left me there on the dance floor. I danced with the entire cadre of German officers tonight, and you couldn't care less."

"That's not true," he said quietly and reached out for her hand. She yanked it away.

"Just take me home." She brushed past him, but he grabbed her arm.

"Rosie, please," he started, but she whirled around and slammed her hand into his chest.

"Don't, Rolfe. Just don't act like you care. You've been ignoring me for a week—for months, really. I thought maybe we could be friends, that maybe you cared for me, and then—then you keep abandoning me. Like I repulse—"

"I can't think straight when I'm around you."

His words came out dark, even angry, and silenced her.

He closed his eyes, as if in pain. "Rosie. I never abandoned you. Don't you realize that I see everything you do? You are so far under my skin, inside me that I simply cannot think. I have to leave to keep from losing my mind."

She backed away from him, but he grabbed her arms. "I loved being with you on Christmas Eve. I—I lost myself that night. I wanted more than anything to bring you into the house, to make love to you, to rewind time, but—but we can't do that, can we?"

She could taste her heart, the way it filled her throat, but she had no words for him.

He softened his voice, reached up, and touched her cheek. "No matter how much I want it, I can't convince you to love me. I wish I could. I would give you the world, but you said it—Bridget is too wounded to give away her heart again."

Bridget? But yes, their conversation in Paris returned to her and she closed her eyes. *You tell me, Rolfe, it's your story.* A tear slipped out.

He brushed it away with his thumb, and it sent heat through her, right to her toes. She closed her eyes against the unbearable fist in her chest.

Then, abruptly, his voice softened. "But sometimes, heaven help me, sometimes I just don't care."

She opened her eyes. His eyes, so blue, were in hers, and she couldn't bear to tear away as his gaze roamed her face, finding her mouth. Stopping there with such desire she went a little weak.

And then he kissed her. Fast, as if he feared changing his mind, he pulled her to himself, covering his mouth with hers. She felt in his touch the hunger that she understood, a hunger that being near him stirred in her. *Oh Rolfe.* He tasted of the sweet champagne and the milk cake and smelled so good she could simply inhale him. She wrapped her arms around his neck and chose to mold herself to him, to give him as much of herself as she could.

No, Bridget couldn't give away her heart again. But maybe, someday, Rosie could.

And until then, she'd give him as much as she dared.

She wove her fingers into his hair, and let herself feel the strength of his arms around her. Let herself inhale the spicy elegance of his cologne, the way he deepened his kiss, held her tighter.

"Rolfe," she said as he pulled away. She caught his gaze, wouldn't release her grip around his neck. "Please don't stop kissing me."

He opened his mouth then, just a little, like a gasp, perhaps. And then he nodded, the smallest, dangerous smile across his face. "Never, Rosie," he said. "Never."

When he kissed her again the sky lit up with fireworks, a thousand explosions of celebration. The year 1938 just might be the year that everything changed.

Chapter 12

Rolfe may have her playing the role of a village resistance fighter, but he knew how to treat Rosie like a star.

Although they'd taken over the tiny nearby village of Grillendorf for shooting, Rolfe had rented rooms in the nicest hotel in the village of Berndorff, the residence of a former noble turned into a posh hotel. She could imagine herself royalty as she read her lines in the palatial estate located in the heart of town. She felt like she might be in the middle of some sort of fairy tale with the church bells ringing, the quaint white-washed houses equipped with chalet-style balconies that overlooked the town, and the lush evergreen forests ringing the surrounding hills.

Outside her window, the green dome of the St. Margareta Parish church lifted to the blue skies. A warm spell had swept through the valley, melting the last layer of snow from the red-tiled roofs, the cobbled streets.

She could live forever in her quaint two-room suite, with the green brocade wallpaper, the deep oak furniture, the claw-foot tub, pampered by too many Bavarian pastries Rolfe sent up to her suite every morning. Any more delicacies and she'd have to force herself to go hungry, like Bridget, the woman she played.

In fact, she should probably advise Rolfe to pamper her less or she'd never fit back into the role. She'd been shooting with Hale

Nichols for two weeks, struggling to feel the angst of Bridget, heart-broken, reckless, angry.

And why not? In the last three months, she'd suddenly become happy—even…well, she felt almost whole. She still didn't know why, suddenly, Rolfe had decided to take her into his arms again, why he'd become the man she remembered in California. He'd spent every free moment introducing her to Vienna and beyond. He'd taken her skiing in Salzburg before moving her and the new crew to Berndorff.

She wanted to mention that, as a studio head, she had some financial thoughts on the wisdom of rehiring the extras and too many of the crew every time they changed film locations, that perhaps letting the old crew go during the duration of the winter, between locations, might be prudent. That way he didn't have to keep them on salary, and indeed, he could let them go when they completed their set of scenes.

And, although he seemed to have no shortage of money, the cast of extras seemed excessive; he'd hired them from around Vienna, housing them for the last week in various homes around Berndorff.

She doubted if any of them had real acting ability—and why he needed to hire entire families seemed a bit overdone since he only needed a handful for village scenes and could reuse them as resistance fighters.

In fact, most of the scenes involved Bridget struggling, single-handed, to outwit the Germans who prowled the village, looking for dissent as she sabotaged the enemy.

And Hale Nichols was Colin, the benefactor that kept her alive.

He sat across from her now, in the lobby of the Berndorff Hotel, his own script in hand, reading today's rehearsal lines. They'd film outside today, a confrontation scene where she discovered Master Colin had lent his military talent to the Germans.

She wanted to like Hale, but since returning to the set, he'd turned aloof, almost angry, emotions he easily transferred into his role. He spent most of his time reading the newspaper, consulting with his dialogue coach, or even in conversation with Rolfe.

It made her miss Spenser. She hoped he'd taken her up on her offer to visit Irene and Sammy in Hollywood.

"Do you want to rehearse today's scene?" Hale said as he lowered his paper to look at her.

"I understand the scene." She picked up her script. "What I don't understand is why Master Colin is so angry when he sees her. Shouldn't she be angry with him?"

He frowned at her. "He's angry because he loves her and she is risking her life."

"But he is the one who caused her to run away. If he hadn't killed her lover—"

"He was just protecting her."

"Are you saying that Master Colin was just trying to do what was best for her, even though it hurt her?"

He lifted a shoulder.

"I disagree. How can it be in someone's best interest to break his or her heart?"

"Maybe he's given her what she wants, she just doesn't know it yet." He lifted the paper. She leaned forward suddenly caught by the headlines.

"Did you know the Nazis have annexed Austria?"

He closed the paper to read the front cover. Shook his head. "You're an amazing actress, Roxy, but you need to pay attention to the world. That happened three days ago. The Third Reich owns Austria now."

Three days ago?

Rolfe had gone to Vienna three days ago.

Hale put down the paper. "Our car is here."

She got up, gathering her wrap around her.

McDuff had transformed the tiny village located eight miles away into a Great War replica, the shots taking place either outside on the street or in her humble village cottage, where Bridget hid resistance fighters. Dressed in a peasant skirt and threadbare coat, Rosie returned from shooting most days in need of a hot bath just to feel her bones again.

Today, however, as she stepped outside, she smelled the hint of spring in the air, just enough warmth to suggest that she might not freeze today on the set.

The driver opened the door to the Rolls, and she climbed into the backseat with Hale.

He rolled the newspaper into a tight mallet in his fists.

"Are you okay?"

He shook his head, stared out the window. "I fear what our world might come to with the Third Reich taking over Austria. What country is next?"

"Germany isn't going to invade anyone. Think of what happened to them in Great War. They don't want a repeat."

Hale looked at her, frowning. "It's not a repeat. It's retaliation. Of course they haven't forgotten what happened in the Great War. The Germans will stop at nothing to make the world repay their defeat." He sighed. "I should know, I'm German."

"You're German?"

He nodded. "My family escaped after the war, but we still have family there. I was back in 1935 for the Rally of Freedom." He sighed. "More like the Rally of Death."

"What do you mean?"

He turned to her, and in his eyes she saw the age of an older man. "My best friend was killed at the *Reichsparteitage* that year. And it was my fault."

She stared at him. He looked past her as they threaded through the narrow streets of the village.

"I returned to visit my childhood chums, and we wanted to attend the rallies. Of course, I didn't have any special privileges from Himmler or the Ministry of Propaganda, so I couldn't obtain tickets, but a friend of mine managed to purchase contraband tickets from a German. I kept one and gave two to friends. One of them had been jailed as a Communist during one of the demonstrations after the war."

"Jailed?"

"As a political prisoner. He was in a concentration camp in Dachau. It happened in 1934, when Hitler took control and abolished all other political parties. Anyone with Communist leanings was imprisoned."

"I had no idea."

"Yes well, most of the world doesn't. Hans finally denounced the Communist Party, so they released him. He wanted to see firsthand what the Nazi Party planned, so I gladly gave him one of my tickets. The morning of the rally, I happened to turn over the ticket and noticed EHRENGAST printed on the back in bold gold letters."

"What does that mean?"

"It meant that the ticket was issued to a special guest. That the holder might even be seated in a place of honor, and most importantly, when I presented my ticket, the Gestapo would realize the truth— that the tickets were probably stolen."

He scrubbed his hand across his chin, his eyes suddenly bright.

"Oh no."

"I tried to find Hans, but he'd already left for the event. I knew that as soon as he presented them, he'd be arrested. Probably if he hadn't been arrested before as a left-wing conspirator, he would have been released."

He drew in a long, pained breath.

Rosie put a hand on his arm.

"I read about his execution in the paper the next morning."

"I'm so sorry."

He stared out the window. "The Nazis will make us all pay for the punishment in the Great War Treaties, you can bet on that."

She knotted her hands, watched the countryside. Please, Rolfe, return soon.

Thankfully, Hale's story served to give her exactly the fury she needed to confront Master Colin on the street, garbed in the uniform of a German officer. She played her part with such authenticity, she managed it in one take.

She found Rolfe applauding as McDuff wrapped the scene. Dressed in a long, black wool coat and his bowler, he looked tired, although he smiled, his blue eyes capturing hers.

How had she ever thought him cold? She didn't wait until they'd ducked into a discreet alley, or even her dressing room, before she flung herself into his arms. "I was so worried for you."

"Why?" He cradled her face in his hands, still cold from the spring chill.

"Because of the Nazis."

Something flickered in his eyes, sadness? Confusion? But he simply leaned down and kissed her, sweetly, assuaging her worry.

Around them, the set had gone quiet.

He seemed nonplussed by the attention and met her eyes, smiled. "Continue to be as brilliant as you were today, and you will have nothing to fear." Then he wrapped her in his overcoat. "Come. We need to hurry if we want to make the evening train."

"We're leaving?"

He nodded. "We're moving into France; our shooting here is finished."

"But we have more scenes—"

"Those also, I'm moving to France."

She broke away from him. "But that will mean more delays, rewriting—" She didn't care that everyone might be watching, including McDuff, standing amid his cameramen, poised to watch the dailies. "Rolfe, you're spending a fortune on this. At Palace Studios we'd have this movie in the can already."

"A masterpiece takes time," he said, pressing his lips to her forehead. "Trust me."

She broke away, shook her head. But when he smiled down at her, she could hardly remember her own name, let alone an argument.

"I need to pack."

"Sophie already assembled your things." He glanced at McDuff, nodding, and then steered her to the waiting car. "And the crew?"

"Coming as soon as possible. The grips have already packed as much as they can; they'll be on the morning train."

She turned, looking for Hale. He was talking to McDuff now.

"I don't understand, Rolfe."

He opened the door for her, helped her into the car. Kissed her forehead. "I'll meet you at the station. Don't worry, darling. Really."

* * * * *

A light snow had begun to drift from the darkening sky as she left the hotel. Sophie had already gone ahead with her wardrobe and personal items, leaving behind her night case and traveling clothes. Rosie changed into a pair of trousers and a cotton shirt, pulled a wool sweater over it and belted it around the waist. She added a hat, her calf gloves, and took her night case with her.

The driver brought her to the station and offered to assist her, but she declined and found Hale on the platform, searching the train for their private car.

"Have you seen Rolfe?" she asked as he took her case from her and helped her into car three.

"He's here. I saw him with McDuff; they were with some of the cast. Extras."

"He's taking them with us?"

"It seems so," Hale said. "Your car is here, I believe." He stopped at a compartment and handed her the case.

She slid open the door and set it inside. "See you at dinner."

"I don't think so," Hale said, "I feel unwell."

Indeed, he appeared white.

"Are you okay?"

"I will be when we leave Austria."

She watched him slip into a compartment only two doors down.

Down the aisle, she could see the extras assembling in the coach car, their belongings at their feet. Some still wore their village costumes, and she couldn't help but think they resembled refugees, somewhat bewildered at Rolfe's sudden uprooting of their schedule.

She felt the same way. Worse, more interruptions like this ate into their promotional budget. Someone might want to remember that her future hung in the success of this film. And without a publicity budget—well, she knew the game well enough to know that an unpromoted film turned into an unwatched film.

And a dying career.

She returned to her compartment and worked off her gloves, her coat, and pulled out the script. Maybe she'd help him rewrite a few of the scenes.

The first whistle had sounded by the time Rolfe knocked at her door. She slid it back, and he stepped inside.

He looked harried, almost undone. "We're off," he said as the train lurched forward. She grabbed his arm for balance, and he caught her against himself. Smiled. Kissed her nose.

She wound her arms up around his neck. "How long is the trip to France?"

He leaned forward, kissed her, his touch sweet, even patronizing. "Too long."

Oh. She frowned. "I was hoping it was not long enough." She molded herself to him, smiled.

He unwound her arms from his neck. Was that a blush? "I can't stay," he said. "I have to check in with McDuff. Will you be okay?"

She flipped down on the seat, picking up the script, hating the tightness in her chest. "I'm just rewriting."

When he didn't move, she looked up at him. His smile had vanished, and now he was simply watching her, something in his expression she couldn't recognize. A softness fell upon her heart, the way he stood there in the shadow of the late hour. He looked tired, and for the first time she longed to pull him down next to her, lay his head on her lap, and ease the furrows from his brow. "What is it?"

"You're so beautiful, Rosie. It takes my breath away."

Oh. The fist in her chest eased. She reached out and took his hand. "I'll be waiting for you when you come back."

He bent and lifted her hand to his lips. "I'm counting on it." Then he winked and stepped out of the compartment.

Oh, how she loved that man. The thought caught her, stilled her. No. No. She couldn't love this man. They'd made a silent, tacit agreement not to profess their love, and he'd kept his part. No, what they had, right now, would have to be enough.

She couldn't afford any more. Regardless of how many times he called her beautiful.

She flipped open to the script, began reading through the production directions, taking notes. Yes, nothing a little rewriting wouldn't fix.

The train meandered through the countryside, north toward Vienna first, and then south to Paris. Night descended around them, the houses blinking in the night like eyes as the train passed them. She took her dinner, wiener snitchzel and brioche, in her compartment, finished it with tea, and then curled up with a copy of *Gone with the Wind*, a book Irene had sent her for Christmas. She couldn't decide if she loved or despised Scarlett for her treatment of Rhett, her unending devotion to Ashley Wilkes. She did admire her spirit. "*God as my witness, I'll never be hungry again.*" According to the rumors Irene had dug up, Jack Junior was looking at it, maybe even had already optioned it. Those Warner Brothers, always one step ahead. But perhaps Palace Studios could still get their hands on it if Jack Warner couldn't find a star to wheedle into the role. She'd have to pen Irene a note and ask her to inquire.

Sometimes operations at the studio felt so far away.

She watched the lights of Vienna draw close and the landscape turn into a sparkling array of glitter. The train wound through the city toward the station. The city seemed to have transformed overnight into a hotbed of Nazi symbolism, the flag with the black swastika hanging from buildings. As they pulled into the station, a cluster of armed soldiers, helmeted and wearing the German symbol on their arms, approached the train.

Her breath tightened in her chest as Rolfe suddenly appeared on the platform. He held papers and handed them to one of the soldiers.

She watched him, his broad shoulders, the way he gestured to the train, his face solemn. The soldier shoved the papers back at him. Shook his head.

They pushed past him, approaching the train, and her stomach tightened. Something about their demeanor—

A shout, and they stopped. She saw Rolfe talking with a German officer.

Tall, dark blond, wide shoulders, a frame that suggested command. Herr...Staffen? Otto—she put the name to the face now.

He wore a military uniform—similar to the one at the New Year's ball, only this was black, and adorned with the armband.

Now, he extended his hand over his head, as if pledging allegiance to someone. She watched as Rolfe mimicked it.

"That's the Nazi salute," Hale said quietly.

She jerked, turned. "What are you doing here?"

"I—I—" He was white, however, and she reached out to him.

"Sit down, Hale. You look like you might pass out. Rolfe is talking to the Germans. I'm sure everything is in order."

"He's talking to the Gestapo, the military police." He leaned forward. "Like he knows him."

"I think he does. He has a number of friends who are—" Nazis. She looked back at Rolfe, the way he smiled, affable, easy with Otto.

Nazis.

She glanced back at Hale. He was staring at her, his breathing thick.

"Rolfe isn't a supporter of the Nazis. He's Belgian. His mother was killed by the Germans. I can guarantee you that he is not a supporter."

Hale's jaw ground tight. "Of course not."

But she pressed her hand against her stomach as she watched Otto return his papers, clamp Rolfe on the shoulder like a friend.

As Rolfe returned to the train.

As it continued its journey, out of the new Austrian Third Reich.

Rolfe knocked on her door later, after they'd escaped deep into the Austrian countryside, finally sliding it open to peer inside.

She considered him a long moment, standing there in the dusky glow of the corridor, poised at the entrance of her door. Then she put down her book, looked up, and smiled, patting the seat next to her. "Let's work on those new lines."

* * * * *

If she could, Rosie would push her hands over her ears and blunt the sounds of the machine guns, the bombs shattering the earth and desecrating the sky just beyond the farmhouse Rolfe had transformed for the finale of his film. Set in northeast France, just outside Luxembourg, on the Orne River in the Lorraine Provence, the tiny town of Etain still simmered with memories of the German Occupation.

It all felt too real, the fear in the villagers' eyes, the German military presence invading the town, the French army battling for their land against the Kaiser. The stench of gunpowder, the rawness of overturned earth, tempered the freshness of the spring air. Rolfe had simply re-opened the trenches, re-erected the barbed wire fences, and called upon the villagers to fill in as extras.

He'd let their crew from Austria go nearly as soon as they crossed the French border, it seemed. And why not? They'd spend three weeks re-creating the French countryside under siege.

All the while, Rosie helped rewrite the script, inserting into it an ending that seemed real.

Yes, Bridget did give Colin her heart, but only after he showed her that he could be trusted, that he wouldn't leave her.

Rolfe had approved it, and as she learned her lines her heart began to wrap around the truth.

If she would give her heart to anyone, it would be Rolfe Van Horne. But she wasn't Bridget, didn't have Bridget's strength, so she'd give it to Hale instead, at least on screen.

After all, Hale as Colin seemed a replica of Rolfe. Strong. Kind. Protective. Faithful.

Most importantly, Rosie knew in her heart that Rolfe could never be allied with the Nazi Germans. Not after the way he spent hours listening to the villagers recount stories, only twenty years young, of the German invasion.

"They took everything—livestock, food, everything in the factories. They left nothing but rubble, only the L'église Saint Martin and the town hall standing. People starved, children conscripted into forced labor," Pierre Leblanc told them one night while tending bar at the Hotel de'Etain.

A small man with rounded shoulders, he wore the ten-acre look of a man who knew the labyrinth of the trenches, his eyes dark, a row of tattoos on his scarred arms. "Came marching right through Luxembourg after raping Belgium and moved into Etain like they owned it. I escaped south, to Verdun." He shook his head. "The night was the worst. We'd hear the soldiers caught in No Man's Land calling out to their mothers, or begging us to finish them."

He picked up a glass, polished it, seeing the past in its reflection. "One night, a pal of mine snuck out to a farm. We found a well and drank our fill. We were sleeping when a couple of Germans snuck up on us. We watched them in the darkness, drinking from that same well. We could have shot them right there but we didn't." He set down the glass. Stared at it. "Right before dawn, a little girl, about eight came out of the house. She was filthy, as if she'd been hiding there—and she must have been, because the place was nearly decimated. She didn't see us, or the Germans, as she snuck out to the well. Must have been the pump that woke them because, in a second, they were on their feet."

Rosie could see the story in his eyes then, the horror of watching a little girl murdered.

"Then, all of a sudden, Louis simply got up and ran at them, screaming. They unloaded their guns into him, but I grabbed the girl and ran. We made it back to our trench." He looked at them. "Louis died right there, by the well."

Rosie watched memories flicker across Rolfe's face and she reached out, wove her hand through his.

He hadn't left the set, not once after they started filming. Hovering over McDuff, he seemed intent on getting every shot right. And every night he found her, asked her to sit with him in the shadows of the hotel, watching the sun surrender into the forested hills, the rolling farmland.

Sometimes, he didn't talk.

Often, he simply pulled her into his arms, held on to her.

"Someday, man will figure out that fighting is not the answer," he said into her soft hair, kissing her, running his fingers through its silky length. She still wore the wig on set, just to protect the new growth now from the hair sprays, heating irons, and peroxide.

"Until then, we'd better hope we have people like Pierre to stand in the shadows and not shoot."

She turned in his arms, cupped her hand against his cheek. "You're so much like your mother."

He stared at her then, something she couldn't read in his eyes, then pressed his lips to hers. She tasted salt in his touch.

The production had become the talk of the village—not difficult in a community of less than a thousand. Especially in a place where everyone had lost a beloved soul. Even the young adults, the ones who had been toddlers when the Germans advanced, wore the haunted eyes of the wounded.

It gave her the material she needed to bring Bridget's desperation to life. Her willingness to spy on the enemy, to house the wounded, to defy the Germans. She became Bridget, refusing to surrender.

And when Colin arrived, she embodied a woman who held on to her heart. Until...

The final scene took place in a makeshift medical tent behind French lines. They'd transformed the farmhouse into a hospital, with wounded scattered about the set. Sophie had torn her dress, matted it with mud, turned her wig to a tangled weave. Rosie layered mud down her face and staggered into camp holding the weight of a soldier she'd found hiding in a trench, blinded by mustard gas. A "beardy" they called him.

It was only after she delivered him to a doctor that the dialogue started. She hit her mark and turned to the camera, holding an expression of devastation.

In that moment, she put herself in the hospital, at Dash's bedside, and in Central Park, holding Guthrie's battered body, and even in the courtroom when Jack deserted them all. She stood there, caught in the moment when life overwhelmed, when the vastness of the destruction could choke her, and let the camera have it all.

And then she heard him. "Bridget."

She turned and found Colin broken on a stretcher, blood soaking his shirt, a bloody rag around his belly.

She ran to him, ripped away the rag. Shook her head. "Not like this."

His makeup artist had left his face intact, although dirty and sweaty with war, and now she ran her hand down his cheek, raising her voice over the din for the sound boxes. "Master Colin, what have you done?"

"I was searching for you, Bridget." He grabbed her hand. "I thought I'd lost you."

"You'll never lose me, Colin," She heard the words emerge, but they didn't feel right. Not...enough. Shallow. But they'd put too much into this scene to reshoot.

"*Everyone brings a piece of themselves to the stage. Find that piece.*"

You'll never lose me, Guthrie.

No, that didn't feel right either.

And not for Dash. But, perhaps. You'll never... Rolfe.

She stared into Hale's eyes, saw in them the blue of Rolfe's. "*I'll tell you every day that you're beautiful if that's what you need to hear.*"

She couldn't lose him. Couldn't let him slip away from her arms.

She shook her head, leaned in, put it all into her words. "Don't you dare leave me, Colin. Not now. Not after everything."

Hale frowned, jarred by her ad-lib of her lines. Around her, more bombs fell, products of the sound team. She was supposed to jump up, to get soldiers to help drag Colin to safety, but she couldn't move, caught in his gaze, the surprise in his eyes.

"You do love me," she said, pressing her hand to his face.

He nodded, as if realizing it for the first time.

A tear fell off her chin. And then, because it felt perfect, she kissed him. Curled her hand behind his neck. Touched her forehead to his. "I'll never let you go."

"Cut!"

McDuff's voice silenced the set, and for a long second, everything hushed.

She leaned back from Hale. He met her eyes. Smiled. "Beautiful," he said.

She got up and turned for McDuff. He was nodding, but her gaze fell past him to Rolfe.

He stood on the sideline, hands in his pockets, his mouth a fierce line, his eyes in hers. He wore a leather jacket, probably from his flight days, a derby, and the wind catching a white silk scarf. Strong. Stoic. Or...no, he turned away, ran a hand across his cheek before returning it to his pocket.

"That was brilliant!" Sophie ran up, throwing a jacket over Rosie's shoulders. "I was crying. I don't think there will be a dry eye in any theater in America."

Or, for her. Because as she watched Rolfe standing there, in the middle of his war-torn set, she realized he'd won the battle for her heart.

Of course she loved him. His kindness, the way he believed in her. The applause she saw in his smile, his eyes.

Yes, she loved Rolfe Van Horne. The thought caught her up, stilled her. Spread a strange heat through her.

Loved him. Not like she'd loved Guthrie, with a sort of relieved wonder, and not like Dash, a begrudging fondness, but...love. The kind that made her trust him. Believe in him.

Give him her heart.

"That's a wrap, folks. Congratulations," McDuff said.

The crew erupted in applause.

Rolfe pulled his hands from his pockets, adding to the cheer. But she couldn't deny the worry that seemed etched in his eyes.

"C'mon," Sophie said, pulling her toward her dressing tent. "You need to get out of those wet clothes."

"Is Rolfe okay?" Rosie ducked inside the tent, the ground covered in a carpet, electric lights strung over her mirror, a canvas chair the extent of the luxury. She made sure Sophie closed the door before stripping off her wet, muddy clothes. She took a towel and dried herself. "I need a bath."

"Especially before dinner tonight." Sophie pointed to an envelope on her dressing table. She picked it up and found an invitation to dinner written in Rolfe's short, crisp handwriting.

"Dinner out. I wonder why the fuss?"

Sophie handed her a robe, not meeting her eyes.

"Does he have something special planned?"

"I don't know," Sophie said. She ran a hand under her eyes.

"Sophie?"

"You know I don't profess to understand Rolfe's choices." She reached for a pair of trousers, held them out for Rosie.

Rosie stood there. "You mean me."

Sophie looked up, smiled, and a surprising warmth entered her gaze. "No. That I understand perfectly. I'm really going to miss you."

Oh. She wasn't sure why, but the words filled her up, and she tasted them, like chocolate on her lips. She leaned over and hugged Sophie. "I'm not leaving yet. We still have months of appearances and promotions to do."

Sophie didn't argue, simply held her tight. "You've surprised me, Roxy Price. Thank you for that."

After her bath, Rosie climbed into the pants then donned a cashmere sweater, a leather jacket, a knit hat, before exiting to the party.

Rolfe was nowhere to be found.

But she intended to give him an evening that would make him stick around. And perhaps, somewhere under the crystalline stars, she'd tell him the truth.

Yes, there could be a happy ending for Bridget and Colin. For her and Rolfe.

The sun hung low on the horizon before she made it back to the hotel. Rolfe had long vanished in the hum of the revelry, the champagne, the toasts, the dismantling of the set. The villagers watching the production joined in, and she spent an hour signing autographs.

The hotel clerk stopped her as she entered the lobby, the gaslights dim across the simple oak furniture. So much of the hotel had been rebuilt after the war, but the furnishings remained sparse. She'd hardly noticed.

"A car will pick you up at eight," the clerk said.

Maybe. But she knew the location of Rolfe's room. And perhaps in the privacy of his chambers she might confess that he'd changed her. That she'd give him what remained of her heart.

"Thank you."

She stared at her closet too long, not sure what to wear, finally deciding on something simple. A black silk dress, a pair of hosiery, dancing shoes. But really, where would they go in Etain?

She'd be happy simply sitting in the hotel café, drinking café au lait and eating a croissant. She debated wearing the pearls Dash had given her then left her neck bare. Checking the time, she slipped out of her room.

Rolfe had the suite at the end of the hall, a room that overlooked a private courtyard below. His also came with an outside staircase—she'd seen it one night as they'd returned to the hotel.

She padded to the end of the hall, a hum in her chest. The last time she'd felt this way, well, maybe she'd never felt this way. With Guthrie, her love for him came slowly, day by day in his arms, long after they'd married. And Dash, well, perhaps Dash didn't count. Because love wasn't a contract or an escape. Love was a surrender.

She knocked on the door and heard Rolfe's voice inside. She eased the door open, expecting him to be standing before her, a smile on his face, waiting.

Instead, he had his back to her, a private telephone to his ear. He held the base in his hand, gesturing.

And, he was talking German. She didn't know enough of it to understand it all, but the guttural sounds, the anger in his voice—she backed out of the room.

The door creaked as she began to close it and Rolfe stilled. Turned.

His eyes widened as his gaze landed on her.

"Sorry," she mouthed, but he was already hanging up.

"What are you doing here?"

It didn't sound like him. Not the way he snapped at her, the annoyance in his eyes. "I—"

"Are you ready to go?" He wore a pair of black wool pants, a dress shirt, a hunting jacket.

"I—I—" She took a breath. "I wanted to talk to you about post production. The plans for promotion."

She heard her studio voice, the one that took over when her world felt angled.

He made that strange face again, the one she'd seen on set, a fierce line to his lips. Then, he sighed. "I needed to talk to you about that. That's why I wanted to take you out for dinner."

It was? Oh. Funny, she hadn't seriously entertained any other alternatives to his dinner purposes. In fact, she'd seen…well, him proposing had flitted through her mind once or twice.

"Good. Because I have a number of ideas." Oh, shoot, now her voice trembled, because no, no, for a moment, she'd believed herself today on the set. *You do love me.*

She stepped into the room. Maybe he wanted to take her back to Belgium during post-production, to plan their tour strategy. Didn't he say it might take a year, even more? And then to America, to promote the film there.

By then, well, by then he'd realize just how much—

"I'm sending you home, Rosie."

Her mouth opened. Dried. She closed it. Found herself biting her lip. Then, a feeble, almost pitiful, "What?"

"We're done filming. It's over."

"But, we—I thought we needed to do promotion?"

"I can do that without you." He wasn't looking at her now, had picked up his derby, crunched it in his hands.

"Without me. But, I thought the plan was to make me a star in Europe and then—"

"Does everything have to be about you, Rosie?" He lifted his gaze, red in his eyes. "You know, life is more than movies. And certainly more than Roxy Price."

She closed her mouth. Felt a fist crushing her chest. "I know that."

He narrowed his eyes. Sighed. "You've played your part here and done it brilliantly, just as I asked. Now, it's over. Go home to America, Roxy. I—I don't need you anymore."

PART THREE

1938
DUCHESS

Chapter 13

Ten days of trying not to call herself a fool and still she couldn't purge Rolfe's words from her mind. *"I don't need you anymore."*

Of course not. Because, like he'd said, she was just playing a role. Including, apparently, her role in his arms.

Had he been playing a role also?

Please don't stop kissing me.

She pressed her hand to her mouth, swallowing back the ache in her throat.

She closed her eyes. "Never, Rosie," he'd said. *Never.*

More lies. She didn't know where they started and stopped with him.

At least he'd arranged her travel home. First a train to Paris then a ship across the Atlantic to New York. She'd debated stopping in to see her mother and Finn, but why? So her mother could see the destruction on her face?

Thirty-six hours and four stops on the TWA DC-2 flight, thankfully in her own sleeper berth, and in an hour she'd land on California soil, the last year a memory.

She might never forget looking out the train window from the station in Verdun and seeing Rolfe on the platform. He'd arrived conveniently after the train boarded, electing to allow Hale and

Sophie to accompany her to the train. Hale had his own compartment, heading back to the Netherlands. Sophie would take an afternoon train to Belgium.

Rolfe seemed to be dismantling their crew as haphazardly as he put it together.

He stood there, scanning the windows as if he might want to jump aboard, change his mind. She leaned away from the curtain, deciding to hate him. It felt better than the ravaging pain in her chest.

She ignored Hale's knocking and request to accompany her to dinner. She couldn't bear for her public to see her with swollen eyes. See, this was why she should never give away pieces of herself.

At least she hadn't confessed her love for him, or worse, let herself give in to their ardor. Not that he pressed, but more than once she'd wondered why she hadn't just invited him back to her room.

At least she still had that—her honor. In a way.

"Miss Price?" She heard a voice beyond her curtain and drew it back. A stewardess in a blue uniform and matching cap leaned over. "We're nearing our destination, Miss Price. May I help you back to your seat?"

Rosie had already dressed and now climbed out of her berth and found her seat in the passenger compartment. "How much longer until we land?"

"Thirty minutes or less, ma'am. May I offer you some coffee?"

Coffee. Not café au lait. She shook her head as she belted herself into her seat.

Thirty minutes to figure out how to take back her life. She'd telegrammed ahead to inform Irene and Sammy of her arrival. The thought of seeing them could buoy her heart, remind her of what she had to return home to. And the studio—she'd dive into reading scripts, find something immediately for herself. Perhaps Fletcher had a role he needed filled.

Even if she had to take a B movie, she'd fill the gap between now and when *Red Skies over Paris* finished production.

Maybe Rolfe would call her then for a tour—

No. She wouldn't return to him. Ever. She could promote the film on her own if she had to.

"*Trust me.*"

Sure.

She watched out of the window as the landscape below slid by, the rolling hills, ranches tucked into valleys, the mountains that rimmed the ocean beyond, the lush landscape of Los Angeles, filled with palm and sycamore trees.

Yes, she'd take back her life and forget Rolfe Van Horne for good.

The heat hit her like a furnace as they opened the doors to disembark. The sun shimmered off the tarmac and the wind seared her face, whipping her scarf away from her head as she climbed down the stairs.

The sun glinted against the shiny silver hull of the plane and she reached for her sunglasses. The air smelled briny, salty, even musty after the fresh breezes of Austria and France.

A driver met her at the foot of the step, a young man in a uniform. "Miss Price?" he asked, reaching for her night case.

"And you are?"

"Clive Baxter," he said. "I'm with Palace Studios. Mr. Fletcher asked me to meet you and take you home."

"Take me to the studio, Mr. Baxter," she said, and followed him to the car, a shiny Rolls convertible baking in the sunshine. She already felt sticky in her two-day-old attire—a pair of wide-leg black silk pants, a white silk halter-top, a white thin woolen jacket. She tugged her cloche hat lower in case anyone might recognize her.

First she'd stop into her office and freshen up. Then she'd track down Fletcher and interrogate him on what remained of her studio.

Los Angeles had changed little in her year away. Clive drove her into the city, down Hollywood Boulevard, past Musso and Franks Grill, the Roosevelt Hotel, Grauman's Egyptian Theater, and finally over to Santa Monica Boulevard and onto Palace Studios.

They'd replaced the sign and gated the entrance. She didn't know the new guard, but he waved Clive through.

Fresh marigolds lined the entrance walk, and the palm trees bordering the parking lot had grown, brushing the sky with their fronds. She thanked Clive, taking her night case. "You'll send a car to the airport for my luggage?"

"Of course, ma'am," he said.

"Please have them deliver it to my house."

He nodded as she turned toward the office.

How much, really, could change in a year?

She entered the building, the fans in the windows humming through the reception area. They'd remodeled, added blue velveteen chairs, a white brocade sofa, gold standing lamps, a glass desk where sat a young woman with dark wavy hair, red pouty lips. A girl destined for the casting couch, despite her prim two-piece black suit. She looked up, smiled.

"Can I help you?"

Rosie stopped. "What's your name?"

"Jane," she said. She had a nice smile, despite her distracting curves. Perhaps she would avoid Rooney's clutches.

"I'm Roxy Price," Rosie said, extending a gloved hand. "My name is on the letterhead."

"Oh—my—" Jane stood, extended her hand. "It's an honor, ma'am."

"I'm just heading back to my office. Could you please tell Fletcher that I'm here?" She turned, heading down the hall.

"Miss Price—"

"That's all, Jane," she said, throwing up her hand in a wave.

Her door was closed, but as she grabbed the handle, it turned. Maybe they'd needed to get inside to clean it.

She opened the door and stilled.

Rooney sat in her chair, his feet up on her desk, reading. He gnawed on a cigar and a record player scratched out a tune, some dark crooner in the background.

He looked up and his mouth opened. "Darling. What are you doing here?"

"This is my office, isn't it?" She advanced into the room. Or maybe not. Rooney's pictures lined the credenza, shots of his Hawaii location hung on the wall, along with movie posters, and at least three photographs of him arm in arm with young starlets.

And the room smelled like him. Cologne, cigar smoke, and arrogance.

"Get your feet off my desk."

He drew in a long breath then complied. "Roxy, I think you and Fletcher need to talk."

She dumped her coat, her night case on the sofa. "Go find him. And get a box for your debris."

He got up, dropping the screenplay on the desk. "Listen, doll, things have changed since you were here. A year's a long time."

"Out. Get. Out." She pointed toward the door, advancing toward the desk. Her gaze fell on the screenplay. "Is that Margaret Mitchell's book? About the Civil War?"

"Roxy, you're back!"

She turned and found Fletcher in the doorway. He'd added a paunch in the last year, his hair wispy as he attempted to comb it over the expanse of his melon head. He still wore the moustache, however, and his eyes still pinched even as he feigned a smile, came over to kiss her cheek.

She endured it then pressed him away with her gloved hand. "What's going on here? Why is Rooney in my office?"

Fletcher reached for her hand, but she yanked it away, folded her arms.

He pursed his lips, all attempts at good humor, at welcome, gone. "Things have changed around here, Roxy."

"Like what?"

"Like the studio directors voted you out of power."

"You can't do that."

"You were absentee for a year. We had to start making decisions. The bylaws say that if you are incapacitated or abdicate your role—"

"I did neither."

He shook his head. "We had the votes." He reached out to her again, but she backed away.

"Where's Irene?"

"She's on leave right now. Listen, Rosie, this is for the best. You, better than anyone, know how difficult it is to get backing. We needed the pull and resources of the board to extend the studio's credit—"

"So you can finance Rooney's epic about the Civil War?" She turned and grabbed for the script before Rooney could stop her. "I thought Jack Junior optioned this."

"He let it go. One of our independent directors optioned it."

She dropped the screenplay on the desk. "I told Irene to go after this if it came available."

"And that's what we did," Rooney said. "If we distribute it, it's going to make us millions."

"Of course it is." She set her jacket and case down on the davenport. "Who are you thinking to play Rhett?"

Fletcher glanced at Rooney. Shoved his hands into his pockets. "Grayson's in the mix. Along with an actor from MGM."

"I can work with anyone. What's the shooting schedule?"

Fletcher looked away. Rooney snuffed out his cigar.

Her mouth dried. "I'm playing Scarlett," she said.

Rooney reached out for the script. "No roles have been cast yet."

"Scarlett. It's my role."

"No."

She turned to Fletcher, her jaw tight, her stomach clenching. She hated the tremor in her voice. "I found it. I love this book. I want it."

"Rosie, listen, don't be unreasonable. This is not your role."

"Who do you want for Scarlett?"

She could hear her voice reverberate down the hallway and didn't care.

"Joan screen tested for it."

She stilled, something hot and white coursing through her

"It was offered to Norma Shearer, but she just turned it down," Rooney said. "We're still looking. We've narrowed the field to a few. Maybe Loretta Young. Or Katharine Hepburn."

"And not me?"

"Not this time. Roxy, it's not a role for…a woman of maturity."

"I'm thirty-five. Grayson is two years older than me."

"It's Hollywood, darling."

She wanted to throw something at him. "And the role of Melanie?"

"We're looking at Joan Fontaine."

Her mouth opened, closed. "I'm still a star. I could play either of those roles."

"I'm sure you could. But—" Fletcher perched on the edge of Rooney's desk, folded his arms, and shook his head. "But things are different now."

"Why? What's so different from a year ago? I'm stronger. My hair is back. I'm even a better actress."

"But Roxy, you have to face the truth," Rooney said, sliding back into his chair. "It's over. You're no longer a box-office star."

* * * * *

Rosie just had to get home and talk to Irene. Irene would know what had happened with the studio, the board of directors. With the *Gone with the Wind* screenplay.

She'd know how to help Rosie resurrect her career.

Most of all, under the glow of Sammy's smile, Rosie could remind herself that she hadn't lost everything.

Clive waited for her under the shade of a palm tree in the parking lot. She climbed into the back of the Rolls and closed her eyes as the summer heat seeped into her pores, dribbled down her back.

"Where to, Miss Price?"

"Home, please." Home.

She needed the cool respite of her home, the marble floors, the white walls. Serenity. She'd sit in the garden, watch the swans, thank Dashielle for finding them their sanctuary in Beverly Hills.

He'd left her that, at least.

Clive pulled up to her circle drive and helped her out. She let him retrieve her night case and follow her to the door. The gardener had managed to keep all her lilies, hydrangeas, roses, and peonies alive, and they fragranced the entrance.

She found the door locked and had to ring the bell. She recognized Louise through the thick marbled glass of the side transom and smiled. She hadn't changed—graying hair piled upon her head, a thick girth that refuted any argument. Louise made her feel safe, if not cared for.

The housekeeper opened the door, and she received her first real smile. "Miss Price. So delightful to have you back! We were all expecting you tomorrow, I'm afraid."

"I arrived a day early to port and decided to continue on to Los Angeles without visiting my family." She stepped inside shedding her gloves, her hat. Louise took them both and gestured to Clive to set her bag in the foyer.

"Your luggage hasn't yet arrived from the airport," she said, casting a look at Clive.

"I sent a truck from the studio to retrieve it," he said.

"Very good, Clive. Thank you." Rosie said. A nice boy—he reminded her of Finn with his manners.

"The studio told me that Irene is on leave?" She unpinned her hat, set it on the bureau, followed with her hair. It fell in a long wave to her shoulders. "Is she here?"

She walked down the hall. "Sammy?"

"They're not here, ma'am."

She stared at her quiet, white living room, swallowed back the taste of her disappointment. "Where are they?" She picked up a recent photograph of Sammy and his mother, taken in the grass in the backyard.

"Ohio. Visiting her parents."

She glanced at Louise. "But Irene never accompanies him to Ohio."

"Myrna is no longer with us. And, Irene took her beau with her.

I think she's hoping to make amends should she finally decide to say yes to a proposal."

Rosie pulled off her shoes, handed them to Louise. "A proposal? Is it that serious?"

Louise gathered her shoes to her chest. "I don't ask, ma'am. But I suspect it might be."

Well, she should have expected it. Irene was beautiful and smart and wealthy.

"Who is he?" She should wander to the kitchen, find something to eat.

"An actor, I believe."

Of course he was. She smiled. "I don't think we need to worry. Irene is smarter than that. I'm going to retire to my room. Can you ask Cook to bring me something in the way of a sandwich?"

"Dorian has left us also, but I will be glad to fix you something, ma'am."

She frowned but nodded.

As she entered the room, she smelled polishing oil. Louise had indeed been preparing for her arrival, Rosie's winter clothes bagged in the closet, her sheets freshly laundered on her bed. She pulled the velvet curtains to trap the cool air, what remained of it for the day, and lay down on her bed.

"You're no longer a box-office star."

She closed her eyes. Yes, she was. The public simply needed a nudge, a reminder. Maybe she just needed to be seen out with someone of merit. Someone like Tagg Channing.

She'd call him, arrange a night out at the Coconut Grove. She angled her arm over her eyes. But first, she'd simply rest. Wait for Sammy and Irene.

Figure out how everything had gone so horribly wrong.

She awoke to darkness, hungry and sweaty, the house quiet. Rising, she changed out of her travel clothes and donned a silk gown, a pair of slippers. Then she tiptoed through the shadowed, dark house, out to the patio.

The blades of grass slid between her toes, cool and sharp. The moon hung in the sky like a spotlight, bold and white against the curtain of darkness. She sank down in the grass, watching the stars, counting each one until she watched one unhinge from the sky and plummet to earth.

She reached out her hand, as if to catch it, but it flickered out and died, leaving only a void where it had once dazzled the heavens.

It was only after she'd grown cold in the grass and headed inside to the luxury of her bedroom that she realized she'd forgotten to wish.

But perhaps her wishes were all used up.

She took her breakfast in the kitchen with Louise, who fixed her an omelet and fresh strawberries. She'd bathed, wiped her face clean of makeup, and called the studio, leaving messages for Rooney and Fletcher.

Certainly they had scripts she could read.

She had to do something.

Louise handed her a copy of the *Examiner*. "Irene's new beau likes to read it sometimes, so we have a subscription."

She opened the page to Louella's column, caught up on the gossip, and then turned to the studio news. "Warner Brothers has created some sort of cartoon with a pig and a duck." First Rin-Tin-Tin, and now moving comics. Jack Junior sounded desperate.

She closed the paper. Took a sip of her coffee.

Heard the front door open. And then, with the sound of his voice, she thought she just might survive. "Rosie?"

"Sammy!"

He came around the corner of the hallway and slammed into her, nearly full speed, his hands around her waist.

She hugged him close, inhaling the scent of him. Nine years old. How could her boy be already nine? He wore sun on his nose, and it had freckled his face. He grinned at her, and in his features she saw Dashielle, a scamp, but with so much charm he could win her heart every day. "I missed you."

"I missed you!" he said. He wore a suit, his traveling clothes, and now shrugged out of his jacket, letting it hit the tile floor.

"Pick up your jacket, Sam." Irene came in behind him. She wore a slim skirt, her hair lighter, in waves under a prim hat. She peeled off her gloves, her eyes shining. "We came as soon as we heard you were returning. I'm so sorry, but he had to take the train."

She held Rosie close. "Thank you," she said, kissed her on the cheek.

Rosie held her away. "For what?"

Irene grinned and lifted her hand. On her left finger, a ring sparkled in the light, a radiant diamond in a silver filigree setting. "I'm getting married."

Rosie kept her smile, took her hand. "It's beautiful." Oh, her voice shook. She swallowed it away. "I'm so happy for you."

Really. Yes, of course she was.

"You know, it's all because of you." Irene unpinned her hat, shook out her hair.

"Why?"

She laughed. "Because you're the one who sent him here."

Sent *who?*—and then she saw him. Coming around the corner, into the house, carrying a suitcase. "Do you want this in your room, darling?"

Spenser. He froze when his gaze landed on her, and then a smile crept up his face. "Roxy."

Oh. My. He looked good too. Tan, his sleeves rolled up over thick forearms. He still wore his hair long, although he'd cut it shorter in back, and the way he sauntered up to her, wrapped her in an embrace, that night at the tavern whooshed back to her.

She just might be blushing.

Then, wait, Irene's words clicked. *"You sent him here."*

She released Spenser. "You're marrying Irene?"

He grinned, stepped back, and wrapped an arm around her. Nodded.

Oh. She kept her smile, because she was exactly that brilliant, that talented and managed to wish them both a healthy congratulations. She even listened as Irene told her the story of how she arrived home from the studio shortly after the New Year to find Spenser sitting on their doorstep, "Like some sort of refugee."

"I was a refugee, lost, hungry, alone." He pressed her hand to his mouth and another memory flashed by Rosie. She shook it away. "And then Irene fed me."

He lost himself for a moment in Irene's smile.

Rosie took a gulp of her coffee.

"I went to Ohio to ask her father's permission to marry her," Spenser said. "I wanted to do it right."

"When is the wedding?"

"Labor Day weekend." Irene touched Rosie's arm. "I know it's soon, but Spenser just landed a role in *Wuthering Heights*. He'll be on location at the ranch for filming, and we were going to go with him." She slid her hand into his, and he entwined their fingers.

She could see their lives spooling out to a perfect happy ending in the way Spenser's eyes shone.

If anyone deserved a fresh start, it was Spenser.

And Sammy deserved a father. Maybe even a brother or sister someday.

"You can live here as long as you need to," she said quietly. Refrained from adding *please.*

"Oh no. We already have our eye on a little bungalow in Beverly Hills."

Of course they did. Rosie finished her coffee, felt her eyes burning. Oh, she wanted to be happy for Irene, for them both. But despite her happiness, she couldn't breathe.

Couldn't think.

"Excuse me, I think I'll check on Sammy. I hate him being out by the pool by himself," Rosie said.

"He knows how to swim, Rosie. He swims nearly every day with Spenser."

Of course he did. She patted Spenser on the arm as she passed by. "Thank you."

The sunlight helped. She blinked away the moisture in her eyes and slipped on her sunglasses.

Behind her, she heard Spenser's steps. Drew in a breath.

"Why aren't you in Europe, with Rolfe?"

She closed her eyes, pressed on her stomach. "He—we finished shooting."

"But you were going to stay, help him promote—"

"He was done with me. He didn't need me anymore."

"What are you talking about? You're essential to everything. He can't possibly keep sneaking Jews out of Europe without you there."

She stilled. Looked at him. "What are you talking about?"

Spenser held her gaze, a muscle pulling in his jaw. "He didn't tell you." He rubbed his hand across his forehead, shook his head. "Oh no."

"Spenser."

"I thought you knew." He stepped out into the grass. "Rolfe promised me he'd tell you."

"Tell me what?"

He sank down on the end of her chaise lounge. "The movie—it's a ploy to move Jews across the borders. First, German Jews out of Germany, and then those in Austria."

"I don't understand." She sat next to him.

"Remember when I told you about the Nuremberg Laws? It was illegal to employ Jews? It's getting worse, Rosie. And it's not just Germany rejecting the Jews. Just three weeks ago, France hosted the Evian Conference on Refugees. They decided that no country in Europe would take the Jews fleeing from German persecution. Even this country will only take 30,000 refugees."

"You mean, the world is turning their backs on the Jews?"

He drew in a breath. Nodded. "Rolfe's had a plan since the early days, in 1935, when his wife died."

"What did she have to do with this?"

He ran a hand across his face. "Her fiancé was German, and Jewish, and when it was discovered they were engaged, a gang of Hitler youth beat him to death. She barely escaped. When Bette returned to Belgium, Rolfe found out through Sophie, her cousin, and he married her."

She stilled. "No wonder Rolfe married her. He understood how it felt to lose someone to the hands of thugs."

He nodded slowly. "Is he in danger?"

"He's a noble, so he's probably not suspected. Yet. But yes, if he gets caught helping the Jews escape… And if he sent you home, then something must have gone wrong. His plan was to tour Europe and use your fame to attract attention, distract the German officials from the underground Jewish activities."

She folded her hands. "I walked in on him talking on the phone, in German. He seemed…well, very friendly with his Nazi friends."

"A game. A ruse. And I know that one of them, at least, is helping him."

"He was so angry with me, Spenser. He told me he didn't need me anymore. That my role was done."

Spenser covered his hand with hers. "I don't know why he sent you home. I suspect he feared for your life, so he turned on you, made you believe he didn't want you." He squeezed her hand. "Clearly, he played his role as brilliantly as you did."

"Are you telling me that he made me leave so I wouldn't have to watch him get caught? Be executed?"

"I'm telling you I think he feared that exact thing—and more. I think he sent you home to save your life."

"But he was using me." She slipped her hands away, got up. "He had no right to involve me in a plan like that without telling me."

"Rosie. You think he was using you, but he was giving you the opportunity to actually do something significant with your life." He got to his feet. "It's not until you lose everything that you realize what really matters. What you really have."

"And what do I have now, Spenser?" She turned away from him. "Please. Rolfe took the last bit of my life from me. If I hadn't left, I'd still have a career, a studio." Irene and Sammy. She didn't want to say it, but even Spenser's arrival could be blamed on Rolfe.

"You have hope, Rosie. That's what keeps you going. That immortal hope deep inside you."

His words stopped her. Turned her.

She'd seen this before, this expression. There, in the barn, as he lay dying in her arms. "I've never met anyone like you, Rosie. Talented, beautiful, passionate. You put everything you have into your scenes—and your life. I've never seen anyone who refuses to stay down like you."

"You don't know me that well."

"Don't I? I remember what it feels like to hold you in my arms. Yes, we were acting but I knew, even then, that you were someone who wouldn't give up. That's why Rolfe wrote the story for you, why you became Bridget. Because he knew who you were, what you had. He believed in you."

"Then he sent me away."

"Because he loves you."

His words stilled her. "Rolfe doesn't love me."

Spenser held up his hands, as if in surrender. "How blind are you? Everyone knew it. You could see it in his eyes. I even told you that."

"He abandoned me time and again on the set. Only after he got to France did he decide to stick around, watch my scenes."

"And who else was watching your scenes, Rosie? Anyone who could. Which left him able to track down and help the people hiding in the shadows. He hid them in plain sight as extras then sent them on to Israel and America armed with visas and new papers. Your acting brilliance, your willingness to trust him saved lives."

"I did it to save my career."

He got up, found her gaze. "My mother used to say, one man's candle is light for many. You were just trying to keep your candle lit.

But you lit the way for many. It reminds me of what my rabbi would say about God. He does not enjoy your suffering, but He does use it for your salvation and even, sometimes, your joy."

She shook her head. "My joy? No."

"Our lives are not accidents. God has a plan, and it's so big and so good, He can take out all the mistakes and our hurts and weave it together to bring our life to full fruition. But we have to trust Him."

"I trusted God before. He abandoned me."

"I trusted God and He sent me you."

She had no words for that.

He walked out past her, to the pond. The swans were out, paddling. Finally, he said, "Did you know that swans mate for life? They will follow each other, land on the same pond, and if one of them dies, the other grieves, just like a human."

"Rolfe and I are not swans."

He folded his arms across his chest. Nodded. Finally, "Do you remember that night when I told you that I knew what you needed?" He reached down and slipped his hand into hers. "I told you to hold on."

His grip was warm, solid.

"I think you need to know that your hope hasn't been in vain. That there will be a happy ending. That when the show is over, you will hear applause."

"Isn't that what we all need?"

He said nothing, just held her hand until Irene called him back to the house.

Chapter 14

He'd started it all. Put the dreams in her heart, made her believe she could be someone.

So she went to the cemetery and found Dashielle's marker in section seven of Hollywood Memorial Cemetery, a vast lawn of markers, with a view of the lake.

Sitting in the quiet lawn, amid lush sycamore trees, their arms in a curlicue to the sky, the fragrance of the last days of summer in the air, she imagined Dash's laughter, saw his smile.

"Your son finally has a father, Dash. He's a good man. You'd like him." He probably would like Spenser. Especially the way Spenser had held Irene's hands as they stood at their wedding altar, smiled into her eyes, and told her he'd love her forever. They'd made a private party of the reception, in the backyard off the house, inviting the sunshine and the memory of Dashielle into the day.

It had healed her too, to dive in to the wedding plans, rejoice with Irene as they found a gown, ordered the orchids, and designed an intimate guest list. Grayson came, stag, and danced with Rosie on the patio to the orchestra they'd hired. "I missed you, Rox," he said into her ear, and his tenor could always make her believe it.

Fletcher attended, and Rosie earned her own applause as she kept it cordial. "One of these days you'll have to return my calls," she said only for him as she handed him a glass of champagne. "And, I promise, you need to clear Rooney out of my office."

"Already done," he said, but she hadn't had the desire to head back into the studio.

She'd heard he'd cast Jane Fontaine's rival, her sister Olivia de Havilland, for the role of Melanie. Louella Parsons had a half-page column on the sparks between the two.

No, Rosie wasn't in a hurry to head back to the gossip, the budget arguments, the vying for roles and screenplays.

Not when her gaze fixed on the headlines in Europe. Like Germany's recent invasion of Czechoslovakia.

She'd penned a letter to Sophie but hadn't heard back.

Not that it mattered. Rosie had no intention of returning to Europe.

"I don't need you anymore."

Yes, well, she didn't need him either.

Still, Spenser's words gnawed at her.

"I think you need to know that your hope hasn't been in vain. That there will be a happy ending. That when the show is over, you will hear applause."

Maybe. Because she'd had her share of applause, but she couldn't deny she always craved more. That when the applause died, she could taste her emptiness.

It didn't help that Sammy and Irene packed up with Spenser a week ago and headed to the ranch where he'd begun to film *Wuthering Heights*. They promised to return every weekend.

Rosie missed them so much the ache could tear her asunder. The house echoed with long-ago voices, memory lingering in the corners.

She got up, pressed her hand on Dashielle's marker, and then walked down the row, reading the epitaphs. BELOVED WIFE AND

MOTHER. FRIEND. OUR LITTLE ANGEL. Some with quotes, others verses. She stopped at one, read the inscription.

BLESSED ARE THE MEEK: FOR THEY SHALL INHERIT THE EARTH.

The verse nudged a shadow inside of her.

"I knew her. Geraldine House. Wonderful lady."

She turned at the voice, found a man around her stepfather's age wearing a dark suit, a fedora, and gripping white lilies in his veined, tissue-paper hands.

"Are those for her?"

"No," he said. "My girl is down the row, four more headstones."

"I'm so sorry."

He shook his head. "She's been gone for about seven years now. But I like to remember what we had. It helps."

"And Geraldine?"

"She was a nurse at the hospital where Esther stayed during her last days. No one knew it, but she had the cancer, was nearer to glory herself. I saw her grave only a few months after I laid Esther to rest. So I visit her too." He took off his hat, stopped for a moment at the grave.

Rosie felt paralyzed, not sure if she should move.

Finally, he lifted his head. "And who are you visiting?"

She shook her head. "No one."

"Just wandering the graveyard?"

She smiled. "No. I—my, husband I guess you'd call him, is over there. Dashielle Parks."

"Parks. Yes. Nice headstone." He looked away then, his expression strained.

"What?"

"Nothing. It's just, I never see any flowers there."

She made a face. "I—I don't visit often. We weren't—I mean…" She looked away. Oh, what did it matter? "We didn't love each other."

"Mmm-hmm."

She glanced at him. "It's not like that. I cared for him. But we had other reasons for marrying."

"A child?"

She swallowed. "No. A dream."

"Oh. I see. And did your dream come true?"

"I'm not sure. I think so. But maybe it was the wrong dream."

He kneeled before Geraldine's grave, tugged out a daisy from his meager bundle. "Or maybe it's not over yet."

"Oh no, it's over."

He made a funny noise. "You're not dead yet, are you?"

She stared at him. "Excuse me?"

He stood up. Gestured to the headstone. "Do you know what that is? To be meek?"

"I heard it once, yes. About ten years ago. When I was in the hospital, a nurse—" She paused, stared at the marker. "Where did Geraldine work?"

"Over in Oakland. At Highland Hospital. I admit I was surprised to see her here, but perhaps that is God's way of reminding me of His goodness."

"His goodness? You lost your wife." She didn't mean for it to come out so sharp.

But he gave her a sad smile, the patience of a grandfather in it. "I haven't lost her. I know exactly where she is. And where I'll be, in time."

Oh.

"Why do you ask?" he gestured to the grave.

"Geraldine House. I—I think I might have met her. Maybe. I don't know. But a long time ago, a nurse at Highland Hospital said something to me, about being meek, and finding your inheritance."

He wore something of wisdom in his eyes. "Indeed. Only in the paradox of life do we find the truth."

"I don't understand."

"We believe that to find our happiness, we must control our destiny. But Christ proved the opposite. Jesus was God, and yet He became meek, humble, obedient, trusting His Father's plan even though it meant His death. But by surrendering and trusting, He saved the world, for anyone who would receive it."

A faint memory wisped up, of Christmas bread and a night of wholeness.

"Why would He do that?" She crouched before Geraldine's grave. "Why would Jesus surrender to God when He knew He'd die?"

"Who for the joy that was set before Him endured the cross."

"What joy?"

The man stared at her. "Us. We are His joy. Jesus delights in loving us. We are His inheritance, the prize He pursues."

"Jesus doesn't love me." She shook her head. "He can't."

"Why not?"

"Because I have nothing to give Him."

"Of course you don't. Do you think faith is an equation? That God only hears your prayers if you earn it? We can't possibly do enough to earn God's favor."

She stood there, her throat burning. She knew that well enough. "I don't know what I did to make God angry, but everyone I've loved has been taken from me. My father. My brother. My...husband."

"I thought you said you never loved him."

"I had a husband before Dash. Him, Guthrie, I loved."

"I see." The man looked at his bouquet, studying the flowers. "You didn't do anything to make God angry. He's not in the business of punishing His children. He might discipline them, but the suffering is for the sake of redeeming and restoring."

He stared away, past her, down the row. "I don't why you went through what you did. But I do know this: I can suffer alone, or I can hold on to God in my pain. I can be meek and trust Him to make something good out of it. Only Jesus can heal the wounds, only Jesus can fill up those dark places with light, with understanding. Only He can quench our thirst for hope."

Spenser's words drifted back to her. *"God has a plan, and it's so big and so good, He can take out all the mistakes and our hurts and weave it together to bring our life to full fruition. But we have to trust Him."*

"The nurse told me that when we inherit the earth, we inherit everything God has for us, on earth, and in heaven. His blessings. His love. His destiny."

"Yes. And the only way to inherit that is through meekness. To admit that you've made mistakes, ask for forgiveness and allow God's grace—His forgiveness—to wash over you, again and again. To let His destiny for your life take over. To change you from a person of death to a person of hope."

Hope. Yes, if she leaned hard into herself, took a good look at her past, she could see it, Spenser's words. *"You have hope, Rosie. That's what keeps you going. That immortal hope deep inside you."*

The man turned to her. "If I've learned one thing in Hollywood, it's when fame loses its attraction, and the approval of others loses its hold on your heart, when Jesus becomes most important in your life, that's when you'll hear the only applause that matters." He pulled out a lily from the bouquet, handed it to her. "Lovely to meet you, Miss Price."

She stared after him, nonplussed, as he ambled down the aisle, finally stopping at a headstone. She turned away, allowing him his privacy.

And let his words soak into her.

Admit that she'd made mistakes. Yes, oh, yes. *"People have such a great capacity to make mistakes, to derail their entire lives."* Rolfe had said that, and she knew it to be true.

She closed her eyes. She feared meekness. Because what if God let her fall? What if He betrayed her?

Hadn't He already?

Or...had she betrayed Him? She'd blamed God instead of asking for help. She'd run from Him instead of holding on. She'd rejected Him instead of trusting Him.

Destiny.

She heard Geraldine, her voice as clear as it had been nearly ten years ago, as if she walked right into her head. *"Your destiny may be more glorious than you think, Miss Roxy. You just need to let go of it. Be meek and find your inheritance."*

Yes.

She pressed her hand to her mouth as her eyes watered. Yes.

She found herself in the grass, right there before Geraldine's grave, her hands pressed to the verse scripted in the marble. *Please forgive me, Lord, for my stubbornness. For not trusting You. For all the ways I've destroyed my own destiny.*

She closed her eyes, exhaled.

Please, help me to be meek.

And right then, sitting in the graveyard, she found herself lifted, filled, a heat she'd never before experienced touching her bones, her soul.

She drank it in, let it nourish her.

So this was what inheritance felt like.

Full. Deep. Whole. Sweet. Peaceful. She let it fill her and heard as if for the first time, the cheering of the birds from the trees. The applause of the wind.

She looked up, toward the end of the row, but the man had left, only a bouquet of flowers at the base of his beloved. But the breeze shifted the flowers at the base, reaping a new fragrance into the autumn day.

* * * * *

Rosie didn't know exactly what being meek looked like, but she kept seeing Rolfe at the Christmas party, adrift on some distant thought.

And his words. *"I know God has a different path for me. I was just shying away from it. My Gethsemane moment, perhaps."*

His Gethsemane moment. A moment of doubt? Fear? Asking the question Christ asked about the need to sacrifice?

Sacrifice what?

She didn't want to guess, feeling she might already know the answer.

And it was this answer that prompted her to visit the Methodist church, where they'd held Dashielle's services, and obtain a Bible. The preacher pointed her to the Psalms, so she started there.

She read a little every day, in the morning, watching the swans.

"'Bless the Lord, O my soul: and all that is within me, bless His holy name.'"

The birds chirruped from the sycamore tree, the squirrels watched her, nuts in paws.

"Bless the Lord, O my soul, and forget not all His benefits."

She could be on stage, perhaps, reading lines. But she closed her eyes, breathed out the words, feeling them from her soul. "Who forgiveth all thine iniquities…"

Forgiveth.

"Who healeth all thy diseases…"

Like broken hearts, and tragedies.

"Who redeemeth thy life from destruction…"

Even that of her own making.

"Who crowneth thee with lovingkindness and tender mercies…"

She opened her eyes, breathed in the autumn air. Lovingkindness. She longed to believe that. Held on to it.

Even in the stillness of her house, her life.

Help me be meek, Lord. Help me trust You for my destiny.

She made a habit of dressing, taking her breakfast of toast and a bowl of strawberries, and then heading down to the studio.

Rooney had moved out of her office, leaving behind curls of dust and a stack of old scripts. She decided to read them through, just in case he'd missed something. She read production reports and budgets and listened to the screenwriters, the Epstein brothers, down the hall argue.

She took lunch in the cafeteria and talked with the new faces— Carol Lombard, who was working on a Selznick film, one of their independent producers who rented out the studios. And Virginia Bruce, starring opposite Fredric March, who'd helped bring in an Academy Award for *A Star Is Born.* They'd just wrapped up the film, were starting promotions, and poor Virginia spent nearly every day with the photographers, staging her media shots.

Rosie just hoped her blond locks didn't fall out under all that bleaching and lights.

Then there was little Andrea Leeds, working on a musical in Stage Two. Pretty and young, she had so much hope in her eyes, Rosie couldn't bear to do anything but help coach her on her lines. Especially when she learned the girl hailed from Montana.

Rosie imagined that she might be coaching her own daughter, Coco.

She spent the afternoon reading the newspapers. Hearst had limited reports on the headlines in Europe, but even the scant news she found chilled her.

The Germans had talked the French and the British into letting them take over a portion of Czechoslovakia called Sudentenland in something called the Munich Pact, agreeing that if they were allowed to invade, they'd stop the advancement of the German armies into Europe. The Nazis had invaded Sudentenland the next day, and were now poised to invade the rest of Czechoslovakia.

She couldn't help but remember Hale's words. *"The Germans will stop at nothing to make the world repay their defeat."*

Including Belgium.

She'd finally received a letter from Sophie, who said that Rolfe spent most of his time in Austria.

Rosie feared what he might be doing there.

But he'd sent her home.

He didn't need her.

And, despite Spenser's words, Rolfe had never told her he loved her. Not, at least, in so many words.

Fletcher knocked on her door as she was gathering her things. "I put a new script on your desk," he said. "*The Four Feathers.*"

He smiled, and she saw concession in it. "Thanks, Fletcher."

She waved to Clive, waiting at reception to ferry someone home.

"I took the liberty of washing the Rolls for you, Miss Price," he said. Oh, the boy wanted to be discovered. She'd try and find him a role in something. Maybe the *Feathers* movie.

"Thank you, Clive."

The security guard waved to her as she left. She found a smile for him.

Perhaps she might find a life here. Not stardom, but something of peace.

She parked in her circle drive and entered her house.

The scent of *La Castillere* met her, and immediately she knew. "Mother?"

She shut the door behind her. "Are you here?"

"In here, darling."

Why the sight of her mother, Jinx Worth, New York socialite lounging on one of her white davenports, dressed in her pearls, a corset, and reading the paper, didn't surprise her told Rosie that she'd expected this visit.

Or rather, had longed for it. "What's the occasion?" Rosie kissed her mother on the cheek, crouched before her. The woman had aged, but not so much that her fifty-plus years stole her beauty. Her dark hair streaked with white, added a pearly tone to her radiance, and her dark eyes missed nothing, sharp as ever. She'd put on weight, but held it in with the corset she would probably never discard.

"I need an occasion to visit my only daughter?"

Rosie slid onto the sofa. "When did you arrive?"

"Earlier. We took an airplane." A smile touched her lips.

"Can I get you something to eat?"

"Oh, we'll wait for the boys."

"Bennett is here?"

"And Finn, of course. He was simply dying to see Hollywood. Bennett has him out driving. Your uncle Oliver has friends in the area and they loaned us a vehicle."

"And why aren't you driving?" Her mother had been one of the first of the Newport society to take up the hobby.

"Perhaps I will, later," Jinx said, winking. "But first, I want to know why you're not in Europe with Rolfe Van Horne."

Rosie stilled then realized her mouth hung open. She closed it. "How did you know about Rolfe?"

Jinx took her hand. "If you'll remember, I was the one who tried to get you to marry him, once upon a time in France."

Rosie made a face. "I'm sorry, Mother. I should have listened to you."

Jinx raised an eyebrow. "Then, you care for him?"

Did she care for him? Did it count that she couldn't disentangle him from her thoughts, that every night he visited her in her dreams? That when she read the paper, she pressed her hands to her eyes, praying?

"Oh my," Jinx said. "You're in love with him."

"How—"

"Because I know that look. If you would have asked me how I felt about Bennett, even when married to your father, I would have given you such a look."

Her mother had married the wrong Worth brother. She'd told Rosie that years later, told her how she stole Foster, the older Worth brother from her sister, Esme, and how it wrought her nothing but heartache. How she'd fallen for his brother, Bennett, whom she was assigned to marry off one summer in Newport. How, one drunken night, she'd slept with him, and passed off his child as Foster's as a way to hide her shame and secure her life.

A life she'd despised when she realized she'd married a violent and cruel man.

"If I could, I'd return to that moment at the pier when I saw Bennett boarding his ship for France, and I would have run with abandon into his arms and never looked back."

"Mother!"

"I'm just saying, what are you doing here, when Rolfe is in Europe?"

"You still haven't told me how you know."

Jinx gave her a look. "I read the papers. And your uncle Oliver has a paper in France, you know. I am not illiterate in either language."

"They posted gossip about Rolfe and me?"

"He is a duke. And you're a movie star. What did you think, that your romance would go unnoticed by the press?"

Rosie pressed her hand to her mouth. Maybe Rolfe had been using her, had been building up a decoy.

Except, it hadn't felt that way. And of course they'd been noticed. They'd attended the opera in Vienna, went skiing in Salzburg. Hadn't exactly hidden their acquaintance.

Her mother stared at her. "Well?"

"Must I spell it out for you? Rolfe didn't want me. He sent me home."

"Pshaw. Of course he wanted you. Look at you. You're beautiful."

"*How many times do I have to tell you you're beautiful before you believe it?*"

His voice filled her ears. She shook it away.

"And he came all the way to Hollywood to ask you to be in his movie. That should matter."

"He was just using me as a decoy—"

Oops. She didn't mean to let that out.

Jinx raised an eyebrow.

"He was smuggling Jews out of the countries we filmed in. Ahead of the Nazis. They're doing something terrible to them in Europe, and Rolfe was trying to help. He used our film as a way to help them escape."

"You helped him?"

"I didn't realize it. But yes. Which meant he was using me."

"Or trusting you. It seems that he picked you because he knew he could count on you. Imagine if he'd asked Joan Crawford."

Jinx smiled.

Rosie couldn't help but smile back.

"All I know is that most people only get one chance at love, darling. You've gotten two."

Two. Guthrie and—and Rolfe. But she was trying to be meek. And unless God gave her a nudge—no, more of a full-out shove toward Europe, she couldn't go running back to Rolfe.

Because he didn't need her.

She heard the door open in the hallway, the laughter of male voices.

"We're in here," Jinx said.

Rosie got up, ready to greet them.

Finn appeared, twenty-one and handsome and suddenly everything inside her froze. Simply stopped even as he came down the steps and swept her into an embrace. "Hello, sis," he said.

His voice. His wide shoulders, his tousled blond hair, his blue eyes.

Everything about him was an exact replica of the Jack she remembered. She stepped away from him, rattled.

She looked at her mother but Jinx had turned, reaching out for Bennett.

He'd aged too, but his hair was still the blond she remembered, albeit thinner. He took Jinx's hand. "Good to see you, Rosie."

The voice. The build. She looked from Bennett to Finn, and back.

The Jack he'd become.

Sank down onto the davenport, her hand pressed to her chest.

"What's the matter with you, Rosie? You look like you've seen a ghost."

She had. In the form of Nazi Gestapo Commander Otto Staffen.

Chapter 15

The hooded train station of Vienna, with the arching girders canopying the twin tracks, cut crisscrossed shadows across the platform. Rosie wrapped her wool jacket around her, anticipating the dank chill of the foggy morning.

Perhaps even the frosty greeting she'd receive from Rolfe, once he discovered she'd returned to Vienna.

But not for him. Or, not *only* for him.

For herself. And her mother. And Bennett and Finn.

For hope, which, after twenty years, still refused to die.

The train coughed, and stilled, jolting to its final stop. Beyond the girders, the sky hung low, gray, void of cheer. She searched for Sophie one last time then gathered up her case and headed out of her compartment, joining the other passengers.

Rosie had taken little for her voyage, but she'd still require help from the porters with her luggage. She had no illusions that Rolfe would send a welcoming party. If Sophie had even told him Rosie was returning to Vienna.

Rosie stepped off the train onto the cement platform and stood there a moment, again searching. The air smelled of smoke and creosote, nothing of the grandeur of her previous stay, almost a year ago. The Nazi flag draped over the arched top of every entrance, a bloodred stamp with a spider in the center. Like bugs, the Nazis infested the city—at least that's the way Sophie described it in her letters—and already Rosie stifled a shiver.

What she knew about Hitler reminded her of Cesar Napoli, the mobster who'd once tried to own her in New York, a man who'd murdered her first husband, Guthrie.

For that reason alone, she could hate them—thugs, really. And she would plead with Rolfe to see them for the danger they were. To come back to America with her.

She'd even propose, if she had to. Lay her heart out there, even if he couldn't give her his back.

"Roxy! Over here!"

She turned to the voice and found Sophie weaving through the crowd. She wore a cloche hat, a plain brown coat, leather gloves, and threw her arms around Rosie's neck, holding her tight. "I can't believe you came."

"Me either."

The male voice wasn't who she'd expected, but it still filled her up with warmth. "Hale."

He swept her into his arms, kissed her cheek.

"What are you doing here?"

He put her away, glanced at Sophie, then, "I'm working with Rolfe."

Oh. She saw the flash of meaning in his eyes. Her smile faded. "How is it going?"

He picked up her satchel. "Do you have other bags?"

She nodded.

"I'll fetch them. We brought a car—meet me there." He glanced again at Sophie. A chill shivered through Rosie as he turned away.

"What's wrong?"

Sophie slid her arm through Rosie's. "Your timing is... unfortunate. Last night a Jewish boy from Poland shot and killed a German diplomat in his Parisian offices. It's sparked a retaliation from the Nazis."

"Here? In Vienna?"

"Yes. And I fear other places. Especially Germany."

They exited the platform and strode through the station. She paused under the Corinthian columns of the grand station in silence, staring at the cityscape.

Black smoke roiled into the sky from at least two locations, and sirens whined in the distance. The faint roar of militant crowds, of glass shattering, the shrill of distant screams rent the morning. Men and women refugees with golden stars pinned to their jackets rushed past with suitcases, gripping the whitened hands of their children, nearly dragging them along. An elderly woman bumped into her, slamming Rosie off balance.

She looked at her, a cry of pain on her lips, but the fear on the woman's face turned her silent.

Rosie found her hand tight in Sophie's. "Where's the car?"

Sophie led her around the building, to where the car, a Rolls sedan, sat at the curb. "It's Rolfe's."

"Does he know I'm here?"

Sophie shook her head.

"What's happening, Sophie? Why is Hale here?"

"He's been working on publicity for the film, planning the premiere. It is slated to be shown later this month."

Rosie looked at her, nonplussed. "Rolfe's still planning on promoting the movie?"

"Of course. How do you think he plans to keep working in Austria?"

"But certainly, the Germans have screened it—"

Sophie frowned. "You didn't hear, then. We had to edit the ending. The director of cultural affairs said that he wanted a more benevolent ending. Hale filmed a final scene where he appeared at German headquarters, confirming that he'd been a German officer all along. The Germans thought it showed their cunning. They feel it is a reminder to the Austrian people that they are watching them, even if they don't suspect it."

"Of course." Rosie tried not to let the news skewer her.

Sophie lowered he voice. "Of course, this is simply the Austrian version. He has the original ready for distribution in America, London, and Paris. And in the meantime, he will do what he must to assist the Jews escaping from the city. There are close to forty people hiding in homes here, seventeen at his apartment on the north side of the city. Jews forced from their homes and businesses, denied visas to Poland or France. Things are getting desperate, Roxy. Men arrested or beaten when they don't surrender their property. Schools and synagogues closed. Young men and women disappearing. Rolfe is planning on using the movie across Austria to distract officials, move Jews into France and then Israel."

"How?"

"I don't know, exactly. I do know there is a German he is working with, someone embedded in the Nazi Gestapo. The German has men sympathetic to the Jewish plight, soldiers willing to look the other way at the train station, even at the borders."

Otto. Her brother.

Maybe.

How she hoped, no, prayed, with every fabric of her strength that Otto was indeed Jack Worth, lost in the Great War.

Despite his German accent, his history as a German war hero. Despite the fact he might be the leader of the thugs hunting down the Jews.

Maybe he was every bit the actor she was.

She'd held on to that hope for the past month, for the three weeks her mother, Finn, and Bennett toured Los Angeles, for the week that she packed her bags and traveled with them to New York City on the train, thanks to her mother's fear of repeating her TWA experience. It only grew stronger over the few days it took to arrange passage on an Atlantic liner to Paris, the eight days on the ocean, and then the overnight train ride to Vienna.

Now, she clutched that hope as the city burned around her, the stench of rubber and oil poisoning the air. A German transport pulled up and soldiers spilled out of it, invading the train station, weapons slung over their shoulders.

Hale pushed through the throng like a man drowning, gripping her suitcase, her satchel. He moved quickly, his long legs striding up to the vehicle. "They're already arresting citizens trying to flee."

"You mean Jews trying to flee."

He shot her a look, his mouth a grim line. He opened the trunk and maneuvered the cases inside.

"I expected more baggage from a movie star," he said, apparently a sore attempt at a joke as he opened the door to the backseat.

"I'm not a movie star anymore," she said as she climbed in. "And right now I'm wondering how I can be of any use at all."

He shut the door, took the driver's seat as Sophie sat in the front. "Rolfe *is* going to lose his mind when he finds out you're here."

"Just drive."

They pulled out of the *Südbahnhof* toward the center of the city. The spires of St. Stephan's Cathedral rose like a spear above the skyline, parting the grimy smoke. In the distance, she could make out the glorious outline of the opera house, where Rolfe had finally taken her in his arms.

A haze hung over the city, however, the streets clogging with pedestrians, soldiers, crowds hunkered around vandals smashing storefronts. Glass splattered into the buildings, across the sidewalks, into the streets, jagged droplets. She saw an elderly man in an overcoat, his beard long and gray, armed with paint and a brush scribing JUDEN on the door of a building.

Their vehicle slowed as the crowds bumped it. One man slammed his hand into her window and she let out an involuntary scream.

Sophie slipped her hand over the seat to take hers.

More soldiers, their armbands designating their allegiance to the Nazi party, pushed groups of young men into a wagon, beating them with clubs. She turned away at the sight of a mob surrounding an angry teenager.

"We should stop!"

"We'll get killed," Hale snapped. "Don't look."

But how could she not look? Fire licked out of an open window of an ornate synagogue, flames breaking through the round window etched with the Star of David. A line of armed soldiers in black jodhpurs, shiny black boots, pressed ties, and military caps, held back the crowd—firefighters and onlookers watching in rapt horror. A group of rabbis knelt before the building, pistols aimed at their backs. A cadre of young men had picked up bricks, throwing them through the windows.

"Why are people doing this?"

"Anger? The Nazi propaganda has made them believe it's the Jews responsible for the economic trials of the past years. And…hatred. Evil thrives where good men do nothing," Hale said.

Down the street, a mob had destroyed the front window of a grocer, now tossed his goods into the street, canned vegetables, meats, oranges, grapefruit. The car drove through the debris, smashing the fruit into the cobblestones.

Sophie squeezed her hand. "We'll find Rolfe and leave. Immediately."

Please, God, protect him. She could taste her desperation, sour and acrid, as she mouthed the prayer.

She caught sight of a young woman pushing a pram down the street and her breath left her as a trio of teenage men turned, and began to run after the woman.

"Stop the car."

The boys had caught up, grabbed the back of the woman's coat. She stumbled, slapped at them, screaming.

"Stop, Hale!"

"No!"

They pushed the woman up against the building. She kicked out at them, and one of bullies slapped her.

Another turned to the pram.

Rosie grabbed his shoulder, shook Hale. "Stop right now!" Then she reached for the door handle.

Hale slammed on the brakes and she nearly hurtled out of the car. "Stop!"

Her voice—in English, stunned them. They turned toward her, briefly silenced. Hale, God bless him, leapt from the car, came at them with enough menace for them to scatter.

She was already at the pram, pulling the child—a baby girl judging from the pink knitted cap—free from the blanket. She clutched the wailing child to her chest.

"Get into the car," she ordered the mother.

She needed no translation. The woman fled to the car without a word. Rosie shoved the screaming baby into her arms and climbed in beside her.

She wore a yellow star on her coat, panic in her eyes.

"You can trust us," she said in English, and Sophie translated.

"But first, let's get that heinous star off you." She reached up to tear it from the jacket, but Sophie caught her arm.

"It's forbidden," she said. "She could be arrested and executed for removing it."

Rosie lowered her hand. The woman closed her eyes, drew her screaming child close.

"Hurry, Hale," Rosie said.

They cut through alleyways and side roads, weaving through the raucous city to the north side. They drove past the university steps, where soldiers barred the doors, lining up across the steps.

"They won't let Jews attend class," Hale said.

Next to her, the woman watched, tears trailing down her cheeks. She said something in German and Sophie translated. "Her brother attends school there."

Hale's hands whitened on the steering wheel. They drove in silence past the university, finally leaving the center for the suburban area, where apartment houses lined tree-anchored streets. Even here, the Nazis invaded, and she watched as a family stood on the sidewalk while soldiers tossed clothing out of windows, furniture onto the street.

She found her hand clutched in the woman's.

"Ava," she whispered.

"Rosie."

Another German transport thundered by, passing them, soldiers hunkered down in the back. They glared down at her car, and she had the urge to press her hand over the star, hide it.

Fear took control of her hands, turned them slippery.

She smelled the acrid smoke even as they came upon the crowd, men and women in the street, some of them in their housecoats, others in overcoats and slippers, as if they'd been pulled from their beds to watch as the building across the street blazed.

She followed their gaze to a three-story apartment house surrounded by a wrought-iron fence, faded, trampled chrysanthemums at the base of the columns and a cobbled drive. Fire crashed out of the top windows, the lower ones thick with belching smoke.

A stack of fine art leaned against a transport truck near the scene, armed soldiers protected it from looters. Or, perhaps, from the rightful owners.

"Oh no," Hale said, and she stiffened. He stopped the car. "Stay here."

"Why." She leaned forward, but even Sophie got out, her hand cupped over her mouth.

No.

Rosie shucked off her coat and handed it to Ava. "Put this on." She got out and shut the door. The heat bled into the morning, and she heard the screams, the murmurs of horror as more glass exploded out, spraying the onlookers, who moved back, away from the onslaught of the flames.

Hale forged ahead searching the crowd. She sidled in behind him, grabbed the back of his jacket. He looked down at her, eyes wide. "Not a word," he said softly then gestured ahead.

She pressed her hand over her mouth to stifle a scream. Armed soldiers surrounded a group of stocking-footed men, women in bathrobes, a small child, most of them crying as they watched the house burn. And standing in the middle, his face tight, handcuffed, blood trickling down his forehead—

Rolfe.

Chapter 16

"It used to be the most beautiful hotel in Austria. Built for the Vienna World Exposition, it's filled with atlantes and statues of women, massive Corinthian columns. And there is a glass floor."

Sophie stood on the edge of the *Morzinplatz*, her hands in her pockets, staring at the Hotel Metropole, a four-story magnificent building that meant death for anyone who entered it. A giant flag with a Nazi swastika, as Sophie called it, fluttered in the crisp air, as if waving.

No, taunting.

"Since the Anschluss, the Nazis have turned the Metropole into Gestapo headquarters. Rolfe is in there," Sophie said.

Rosie wore a headscarf, her mink collar lifted around her ears. The other coat she'd let Ava keep and had the woman secured in her hotel suite at the Imperial Hotel.

She experienced too much satisfaction as she'd walked Ava right past the German dignitaries lodged at the Imperial, there, turning her into her German nanny, while she, Roxy Price, toured Austria.

She'd garnished a few curious looks, every gaze falling on her and conveniently sliding right past Ava.

Suddenly, Rolfe's plotting made sense. Even if it had come to a fiery end.

"They wouldn't kill him, would they?" She'd finally stopped trembling when Hale gave his report of Rolfe's whereabouts. He'd been shipped off to Gestapo headquarters with the rest of the Jews who were labeled as political prisoners.

"I don't think so. Not if he tells them who he is. I think he could say he didn't know his tenants were Jews and they might release him. The problem is, they found the travel papers, fake documents intended to scurry them out of the country. Even if he escapes, the rest of them are headed for Dachau."

She frowned.

"A concentration camp in Germany. Some say it's a death camp."

Death camp?

She had glanced toward the closed door of her suite, where Ava tended to her child, probably singing her to sleep.

Sophie had asked about her husband, and the poor women simply burst into tears.

Rosie wanted to do the same thing. She'd spent the night pacing. Writing a story in her head.

Conjuring up her own script.

But it all hinged on her leading man, Otto Staffen. Subordinate Chief of the Gestapo in Austria, Head of Department IV, Section B4, the department that oversaw the management of the "Jewish problem."

"Staffen handles the Schutzhaft, or what they call 'protective custody'," Hale had said. "And he's as loyal as a Schnitzel. I can guarantee that Staffen is *not* Rolfe's contact."

"I saw them together in Vienna, when we left the day the Germans marched into Austria. Rolfe gave him something, and he let us pass. If Rolfe was transporting Jews from Austria and Otto knew it, why didn't he search the train?"

"Perhaps they're friends. Rolfe had to cultivate many faux relationships for his plan to work."

She refused to believe she belonged in that category. "*I don't need you anymore.*"

But, see, he did.

"I still think this is crazy," Sophie said now as they stood across the street. "What if you're wrong? You can't just go in there and ask Otto to release him."

"I'm not going to ask him to release Rolfe. I'm going to ask him to a party." She turned to Hale, whose mouth tightened into a dark line.

"This will work. I know it will." Oh, please. "After all, I'm Roxy Price, aren't I?"

Sophie let a smile tip her lips. Swallowed. Nodded.

Rosie hid her shaking hands in her pocket as she crossed the plaza toward the hotel. This wasn't a movie. She had no script to guide her. But if she wanted to free Rolfe, she had to play her role perfectly.

She untied her scarf as she entered the doors, shook out her hair, and sashayed into the reception area, a cavernous room with glass tiles in the marble floor.

She flashed a starlet smile at the youngster at the desk, clean-shaven, short-clipped blond hair. He looked about fifteen. "I'm here to see Commander Staffen, please."

The boy looked at her. She smiled, knowing she'd spoken in English. She leaned down, resting a hand on his desk. "Tell him that Miss Roxy Price is here."

He swallowed, his eyes wide, and he nodded as he picked up the phone.

The reception area housed two long, wooden benches along the cavernous hallway, a bust of Hitler perched between them along with more draped Nazi flags. Her gaze connected with two women sitting on the bench, disheveled, fatigue lining their faces.

They stared at her with such grief she had to turn away.

Please, God, let this work.

She hadn't told Sophie and Hale everything—how could she? Even to her own ears her story sounded impossible. Her brother, who'd run away at the age of seventeen to the Great War somehow ends up as a Gestapo commander in Hitler's Third Reich?

But, what if...

Her courage nearly failed as she stood at the desk, despite her fur coat, Dash's pearls around her neck. She could hear the faint echo of noise beyond the wooden doors, and the stench of fear and smoke still coated her nose.

Thirty-six people had lost their lives last night, thousands more imprisoned in schools around the city. She feared their destination.

She heard boots against marble, and then the door opened.

She expected Otto, his blue eyes, some smile of familiarity. Instead, another guard greeted her, this one small with shiny black hair, a pinched face, too much seriousness in his eyes, about the age of Finn. He glanced at the receptionist and nodded toward her.

She followed him down the hallway. Portraits of Nazi leaders hung on the walls in between more flags. A stream of light through the paned, arched windows played checkerboard on the floor. In the massive hall, even the clopping of her shoes cowered.

He led her to a door then inside to an office. He gestured for her to sit, but she couldn't. Not and have any hope of standing again.

He pursed his lips then knocked on the inner door.

She heard a voice, tried to test it with her faint memories. Did it sound like Jack's? She couldn't be sure.

And suddenly, she stood before him as the man who could be her brother rose from behind his desk and held out his hand.

"Miss Roxy Price. We meet again," he said in English, his German accent thicker than she remembered. Oh, maybe she'd simply convinced herself differently.

She couldn't breathe as she met his eyes, took his hand. Indeed, he looked a younger version of Bennett, with his blond hair, thick and wavy on top. And Finn, just a hint of spark in his blue eyes. "Hello," she said. "I—I wondered if you could help me."

"Let's see," he said as he sat down.

He had a desk the size of Austria itself, expansive and polished oak. She feared asking to whom it had belonged before the Anschluss. Now, he smiled, almost kindly, as he folded his hands on his desk.

"I think there's been a mistake."

He raised an eyebrow.

"I—I, well, see, in last night's raid, my—producer was arrested."

He suggested no hint of understanding.

"The Duke, Rolfe Van Horne? He is the producer of the upcoming film, *Red Skies over Paris*. It's a Great War epic, and we spent the last year filming. Surely you remember the Austrian minister of diplomatic affairs granting us permission?"

He narrowed his eyes just enough for her to add a smile to her words. Oh yes. Smile. Be brilliant.

"The problem is, Mr. Staffen—"

"Otto, please." He smiled again, and the effect of it jolted her. Otto? Really? Why not Jack?

"Yes, Otto. Thank you. See, the problem is that our premiere is tomorrow night, and we need his help to prepare. He was wrongly imprisoned with tenants of a flat he owns here in Vienna, and we would like his release before tomorrow night's gala event. We wanted to invite you and your officers, of course."

There, it was out.

Otto simply blinked at her. Then, quietly, "I can't release Mr. Van Horne."

She had slid her hand to the armrest and now released it, forcing her body to relax. "Why not?"

"See, those weren't just tenants, Miss Price. They are Juden. And not just that, but political dissidents—"

"They're men and women, children and families. They are simply trying—"

She closed her eyes. Calmed her breathing. Opened them and smiled to his dark expression. "I beg your pardon, but I was under the impression they were simply families renting his rooms."

He leaned back, steepled his hands. Considered her. "And after we release him, after you show your movie, then what?"

She blinked at him, frowned. "Then we go to Paris, and show it there. And maybe even Amsterdam."

"And Berlin." His eyes darkened, fixed on her, sent a chill down her spine.

Oh, how could she have been so terribly wrong? This man couldn't possibly be the brother who climbed into her wardrobe with her, hiding with her those nights when her parents fought, who turned her life to sunshine with his laughter and teasing. Who made her feel whole and beautiful.

"Yes," she said softly, thankful suddenly of Rolfe's revised ending. "Of course."

"I'm sorry, Miss Price, but I don't believe you."

She opened her mouth. Closed it. Lifted her chin. "What don't you believe...Otto? That I wouldn't dare show a movie about courage and triumph and hope in the middle of a Fascist Germany?"

"Careful," he growled. "Besides, the movie is a reminder of what happens when Germany is defied."

At least the version he saw. She hid a smile.

She stood. Tugged on her gloves. "Think again, Mr. Staffen. I've had enough of bullies and lies. Our movie will premiere tomorrow night. And when it does, if Rolfe Van Horne is not on the premises, the entire world will know that he's been taken by the thugs of the Third Reich!"

She turned, strode to the door, grabbed the handle, shaking, her chest so tight she thought she might weep right there.

"You haven't changed at all, have you, sis?"

Her breath caught, even as she pressed her hand against her mouth, even as she turned.

He was on his feet, his eyes slick with moisture. He swallowed hard, his smile tremulous. "I feared you'd recognize me when I saw you at the New Year's party."

The words pulsed between them, in the thickened silence, and suddenly, he turned away, his hand tented over his eyes.

She closed the gap between them. "Jack?" She touched his arm.

He nodded, and when he turned back to her, he ran his fingers under his eyes, catching the moisture there.

Jack.

He'd aged yes, and somehow endured a terrible wound on his jaw, but the handsome scamp that wooed every girl on Fifth Avenue remained in his blue eyes, the wide shoulders, the regal cut of his jaw-line. "Jack."

He caught her up then, his arms around her waist, pulling her to himself. She could feel him tremble, even as he pressed his face into her neck. "I never thought I'd see you again."

She closed her arms around his neck, breathing in the wholeness of him. The strong, bold, courageous even brash Jack she knew, the reality of her brother, here embedded—

"You're a Nazi." She untangled her arms from his neck, backed away. "You're a *Nazi*. A Gestapo commander. What—?"

He pressed his hand over her mouth. "Shh. Listen. Of course I am—it's been the plan all along."

"What plan all along?"

"The one that Army Intelligence conjured after they liberated me from a German labor camp."

"What?"

"Yes. For me, the war had just begun. I had picked up the language so well, and...I felt I had nothing to go home to. So, we invented a story for me and I returned to the string of captives, this time as a German. I continued to live as a German and feed information to the army for the past twenty years, working my way into the military, up the channels, and by God's providence, I am exactly where I'm supposed to be."

"But you're responsible for— People *died* last night, Jack."

"And I'm trying to keep people alive. That's why I arrested Rolfe and his tenants—if I hadn't, mobs would have found them and who knows what might have happened? Of course I know what he's doing. I'm helping him."

"I knew it."

He smiled. "I couldn't believe it when I saw you that night. I knew you were in Europe, but I never thought we'd cross paths. How did you meet Rolfe?"

"Mother set us up. Or, well, it's a long story."

But his face had fallen on her mention of Jinx. "How is she?"

"She's married to Bennett."

His lips formed a tight, dark line.

"You have to forgive her, Jack. You know what she lived through—what we all lived through with Father. And Bennett is a good man. Nothing like Father."

He turned, staring out the window. "I believe that I was supposed to be here, for this moment in history. But getting here seems more painful than it had to be."

"Maybe it was the only way to get you here," she said quietly, her words landing on the own soil of her heart. "Maybe you wouldn't have stayed if you felt you could go home."

He said nothing.

"And you're not the only one who has suffered. Mother cried herself to sleep for years. She still holds out hope that, someday, you'll come home." She touched his back. "You have to tell her you're alive."

He tensed. "I can't. Not yet."

"Jack—"

He rounded on her, his eyes cracked with red. "You don't understand. I can't leave. I am here for a reason, and if I leave, who else do they have?"

"But if you're found out—"

"I'm very careful." A smile slid up his face, something of recklessness that she recognized from long ago. "You're not the only one in the family who can act."

She tried to match his grin, but she just wanted to weep.

"Don't you dare get killed, or Mother will—" She closed her eyes then pressed a hand over her mouth before a sob escaped. "Please stay alive, Jack."

He drew her close again. Leaned down to whisper into her ear. "If I perish, I perish. But I'll do it with fewer regrets. Now, at least."

He lifted her chin, kissed her on the nose. "Tell Mother you found me, tell her I love her."

"She can't bear losing you again."

"All right. Then wait. I promise that, should I survive, I will come home to you."

She read his face, the truth in his eyes. "I'll wait. And hope."

Because that's what she did best. She took his hands. "Now it's your turn to trust me. Will you free Rolfe? Please?"

"It's not just Rolfe I'm worried about."

"Me either. Get ready for one of Mother's society bashes because I, too, have a plan. And we're not just going to rescue Rolfe. Darling brother, it's time for you to go to the movies."

Chapter 17

"What kind of crowd do we have out there?"

Rosie dropped the curtain from the window, effectively hiding her presence in the entrance hall of the Theater an der Wien.

"I can't tell in the dusky light, but it looks significant. Mostly uniforms, but civilians also."

She turned to Hale, who approached her across the parquet floor, looking every inch a movie hero in his fresh haircut, his black tails, a silver silk scarf around his neck. "How angry is he?"

His expression gave her the only answer she needed.

"Did you tell him I was here?"

"I'm desperate but not crazy." Hale lifted the curtain at the doorway. Nodded. "This just might work."

"Is everything in Austria ornate?" she pointed to the arched frescoed ceiling of the theater hallway, the Romanesque moldings along the walls. "Why did they close the theater?"

"I don't know, but be glad, because it was the only place I could get on such short notice. You look gorgeous, by the way."

She smiled at him. "Sophie dug out the wig. It looks so much like my own hair."

"And the dress?"

"We bought two, same style."

Indeed, Sophie looked just as fabulous in the gown, the silky satin black dress flowing over her curves just as well as Rosie. Rosie wore the long pearls Dashielle had gifted her and long black gloves and turned into the starlet seen pasted on the banners and leaflets around Vienna.

Jack, just like his mother, knew how to advertise a party.

And she, Rosie Worth, knew how to throw one.

Now, she hoped Roxy Price might show up to dazzle—and blind—them all.

"Is Sophie ready?" Hale asked. He glanced again outside, his fingers fumbling with his cuff links. She put a hand on his arm.

"This will work, Hale."

He gave her a tight smile, pressed his hand on hers. "I wish I had your hope."

Well, hope was about the only thing holding her together. "It's time."

He caught her hand, pressed it to his lips.

"I'll see you on the red carpet."

Jack's cadre of workers—how could they know they were committing an act of treason—managed to carry out all her orders, from the printed movie posters that flanked the entrance, to the model airplanes used as props in the film, now hanging inside the grand four-story theater. The airplanes dangled like mobiles from the first balcony tier. Along the backdrop on stage, a small task force had erected a giant cinema screen.

She'd seen the drama once already and had nearly wept with the beauty of the film.

In addition to changing the ending, Rolfe had added Technicolor.

If it ever made it to America, she might actually become a star again.

Not that she cared. Not after today. After today, she just wanted them all to survive.

And someday, to bring Jack home.

The secret might burn a hole clear through her if she returned to New York City and looked her mother in the eyes.

Rosie stood in the empty theater for a moment, imagining the Nazi officials seated, mesmerized, in the floor and balcony seating. An ornate two-headed eagle hung at the apex of the stage. She had no doubt a Nazi banner would soon replace it.

She'd never seen a more glorious theater. The perfect place to show her last film.

She expected an ache, but something of relief swept through her. Last film.

And tonight, her last, and best performance.

She headed toward the side doors then to the alleyway and found Sophie there, smiling. Sophie handed her the fur coat. Kissed her on the cheek. Her Rolls waited, a German soldier at the wheel, and Rosie slid inside, relaxing against the plush velvet, relishing the quiet of the moment.

Releasing into the hands of the Almighty the outcome of her drama.

Meekness. Trust. So she might help others.

It was a glorious night for a movie. The stars twinkled like spotlights overhead, the air finally clearing after the fires.

A glorious night to save lives.

They pulled out, around the block, and headed down the street toward the theater. The crowd pressed in, hoping for a glimpse of her, and she couldn't help but compare the faces to those she'd seen throwing bricks and rocks and chasing Jewesses down the street.

Smile. Be brilliant.

She waved even as her driver pulled up.

The door opened, and she slipped out, to the red carpet.

The crowd erupted, cheering. She stood there, smiling and lifted her hand in a wave.

Usually she drank in the applause, let it feed her. But tonight she had no appetite for it. Especially when she turned and saw Rolfe.

He waited at the entrance to the theater, beside Hale, who had clamped his hand on his shoulder.

Regal. Courageous. Angry. She couldn't decide which adjective described Rolfe the most as he stared at her. First a frown then his mouth closing, his jaw tight.

She kept her smile. Kept waving. Posed for the flashes. Waved again. Then she reached him and looped her arm through his.

"Darling," she said. "It's a divine night for a movie, don't you think?"

His jaw tightened.

"Smile, Rolfe. Be brilliant." She turned him, and he lifted his hand. "Really, smile. Trust me."

He glanced at her, something of heat in his eyes, but he forced a smile. The crowd erupted. Perhaps they were as hungry as she for something to make them forget.

They turned toward the entrance, and she made to withdraw her hand, but he clamped his on hers. "What are you doing here," he said under his breath.

"I'm attending our movie premiere," she said.

He glanced at her, his eyes narrowing.

"Please, trust me."

"I'm finding it difficult," he said as they entered the theater hall.

"I know how you feel."

He let her go, and she led him down the aisle to their reserved row, to the side, near the doors.

The theater filled up behind them, and she turned, watching the cadre of officials take their seats. She'd sent tickets to nearly every Nazi in Vienna. She searched for Jack but couldn't find him in the throng.

Maybe he wouldn't come. Probably he wouldn't come.

She pressed against the ache in her stomach. For this to work, she couldn't say good-bye.

Couldn't even hint that she knew him.

"Are you ill?"

Yes. "No. Just nervous." She smiled down at Rolfe, and he responded with a frown, something of real concern in his expression.

Oh Rolfe. Even when furious with her, he still cared.

She slid down into her seat. "Listen. No matter what happens tonight, please—please remember that once upon a time you believed in me."

He blinked at her. "I still do."

She was counting on that.

On the stage, the screen began to descend, and the room darkened. Nazi propaganda sputtered to life, and beside her, Rolfe tensed. She put her hand on his arm, squeezed until the reel ended and the next reel— their credits spooled across the screen.

Then suddenly, the world dropped away, and Jardin was on screen wooing her into his arms. Rosie stayed until he died; then she ducked down in her theater seat and slipped away, through the side entrance into the darkened hallway.

She felt her way to the dressing room door behind the stage and let herself in.

Everyone in the room froze. Including Rosie. Seventeen refugees: nine men, seven women, and a ten-year-old girl had transformed into high society under the deft hand of Sophie Le Blanc.

Rosie put a finger to her lips and shut the door behind her.

Sophie was finishing applying makeup to a young man still nursing a black eye.

"That's pure magic," Rosie said.

Sophie had raided the costume container from the film, and now the men wore tuxedos, some of them in bow ties, others in silvery vests and shirtwaists, the women in ornate dresses, all from scene 37, a ball held in Master Colin's estate.

Though the dresses might be out of fashion, they still blended, and with the capes attached, they would make for fine disguises.

The little girl's dress Rosie purchased at a shop she had visited with Sophie during her New Year's stay. Sophie took it in, hemmed it up, and with a bow at the waist, it fit fine. Made the girl look older—twelve, perhaps.

Sophie had done the ladies' hair, and with the faux jewelry, the assembly appeared as if the royal house of Windsor had shown up for the premiere of *Red Skies over Paris*.

"Remember to wait until after the applause. Then slip in from the side door, blend in with the crowd. There will be cars waiting at the curb. Remember, you're all my special guests. More than that, you're royalty."

She touched Ava's hand. "Especially you." Ava was still posed as a nanny, dressed in a black dress, her hair in a severe bun. Rosie leaned down and kissed the baby on the forehead, inhaling the smell.

She slipped back into the theater just as, on screen, Hale as Colin confronted Bridget with the truth.

"I was there." He looked fierce, angry, and way too handsome in his German uniform. It was a wonder Bridget didn't just throw herself into his arms right there.

But she didn't. She rounded on him. Kept her face tight for the close-up. Then, "What do you mean, you were there?"

Even though she'd said it a hundred times, the surprise, the horror in her voice seeped through her.

And then Hale stepped toward her. His voice softened, his eyes in hers. "I was watching as you defied them. Your courage. Even the fear that I see now in your eyes. But you don't have to be afraid of me, Bridget."

He reached out, touched her face. "I am the one who freed you."

Oh, silly girl. Why was she crying? She reached up to wipe her face and found Rolfe's hand intercepting hers.

He gripped it in his.

"Why would you do that?"

Hale pressed her hair back, behind her ear. "Because I love you, Bridget."

She stilled, saw Hale's mouth move— "Because I've always loved you."

Rosie turned and Rolfe was staring at her, his gaze in hers.

On the screen, Bridget was pushing Colin away, picking up a vase, about to hurl it at him. "No, you don't. You can't. Not after what you put me through—"

"I was just trying to protect you," Rolfe said softly, repeating the words on the screen. And why not—he'd written them. And suddenly, she understood. He shook his head even as the vase crashed on screen. "But I'm a pitiful man because I—I shouldn't have reached for your heart. I should have made you hate me."

How could she ever think of hating this man, this duke who'd chased her across the world, not once but twice, who believed in her so much he wrote a movie for her.

And then—and then declared his love for her through every line. She stared at Bridget as the final scenes played out. As Colin continued to protect her, to bring her food, to keep her from harm even as the Germans discovered his ploy, as they sentenced him to execution.

Rolfe was watching the screen, his face taut.

This was Rolfe. The man who loved her despite her mistakes. Who called her beautiful when she had no hair. Who wrote a part for her. Who knew she could be brilliant if she just—just... *"Everyone brings a piece of themselves to the stage. Find that piece."*

If she just gave away her heart.

To the screen.

To the role.

To Rolfe.

She didn't have unquenchable hope.

She had unquenchable love.

So much of it, she kept giving it away, hoping it would return to her. But she'd just been giving it to the wrong places. The wrong audience. The wrong man.

"If I've learned one thing in Hollywood, it's when fame loses its attraction, and the approval of others loses its hold on your heart, when Jesus becomes the most important in your life, that's when you'll hear the only applause that matters."

Meekness wasn't about losing control. It was handing over her heart, her destiny to the one who loved her. Jesus.

And maybe He'd sent her Rolfe to remind her of that. That no matter how many times she pushed Him away, He kept showing up. Not because He needed her.

But because He loved her.

"Don't you dare leave me, Colin. Not now. Not after everything."

Rolfe turned to her, searched her face.

"You do love me," Bridget said.

The movie flashed to the final scene, but she didn't watch the travesty demanded by the German censors. Instead she caught Rolfe's eyes, those beautiful blue eyes. "You do love me," she repeated softly.

But right then, the audience burst into applause, the screen dark as the final credits rolled. She wanted to pause it, to hold his eyes with hers, to make him hear her. But people rose to their feet around her, and Hale reached over and pulled her up, taking her hand. They turned, waved, and as she looked down at Rolfe, he was looking away.

As if pained.

Hale led her up the aisle, and she prayed Sophie heard the thunderous applause, was already scampering toward her position.

"Don't forget Rolfe," she said to Hale as they entered the foyer. The crowd pressed in behind them, on their way out of the theater, and she glad-handed fans, waving as she let him go, and spilled out into the street.

There, the line of Rolls Royces. And under Hale's direction, their cadre of nobles just might make a clean getaway.

She climbed into the first one.

"So, how did it go?" Sophie asked.

Rosie managed a smile. "Drive," she said, and gasped when her driver turned around.

"Finally giving me directions," McDuff said. He wore a derby and a tweed jacket. "Sophie told me about the premiere. I didn't want to miss it."

"I'm so sorry. I would have telegraphed you—"

"I've seen the movie a hundred times in production." He turned away. "But it seems I'm not the only one who can direct."

He pulled out into the street, and Rosie pulled off her wig, handed it over to Sophie. Sophie pulled off her black wig, cut at the neck and covered in pin curls, and fitted it on Rosie.

Rosie adjusted hers onto Sophie, turning her into a brunette. Then she unclasped her pearls and placed them around Sophie's neck. "Sell them if you have to. They were from Dashielle. It's about time his fortune went to good use."

"They're beautiful."

"He gave them to me the night of my first premiere."

She nodded. "It's a glorious movie, Roxy. I wept."

Rosie squeezed her hand.

Sophie pulled on long black gloves while Rosie stripped hers off and unzipped her dress. She glanced at McDuff, but he seemed unaffected about the activity in the backseat.

Rosie wiggled into a new white evening gown, fur at the neck. Worked on a pair of long white gloves. Then she helped Sophie into her fur coat.

They pulled into the train station. McDuff parked and Sophie pressed on a layer of blood red lipstick then closed her compact. "Do I look like a movie star?"

"Do I look like a duchess?"

Sophie pulled her into a hug. "You'll always be a duchess to me."

Then, as McDuff opened the door, Sophie as Roxy Price climbed out of the car and into her public. McDuff followed Sophie/Roxy to the train.

Rosie watched as Sophie lifted her hand to wave to her audience, pulling her fur collar up around her face, as if chilly. She hustled toward the train, to the private cars they'd rented, one for Hale, the other for herself.

Hale emerged from the other Rolls, waved to the gathering crowd. Around them, the other Rolls and Bentleys arrived, carrying the contraband nobles.

But they emerged with airs, playing their role, heading for the train cars, the elite society of Austria headed for a private party with Hale Nichols and Roxy Price.

Rosie held her breath as they all moved past the guards, showing their tickets to the conductor before they boarded.

Roxy Price stood at the rail of her car, waving, welcoming them aboard. Hale stood at the other car, doing the same.

Her car door opened and Rolfe slid in. Stared at her. Glanced at the waving Roxy.

"Sophie always said she wanted to be in the movies."

"What are you doing?"

"I'm staying here. With you."

He shook his head. "No, Rosie, you can't. It's too dangerous."

"In Vienna, yes. But not in Belgium."

He opened his mouth, but she pressed her finger over it. "Listen to me. What you don't know is that your friend Otto is more than just a Jewish sympathizer. He's—he's my brother. My brother, Jack."

Rolfe seemed not to know how to digest that information, frowning, shaking his head, then, "I thought he died."

She nodded. "He's been here since the Great War. Working with Army Intelligence. And now, providentially placed to help us. He'll do the work here in Austria and send the refugees to our estate in Belgium. We'll get them visas and papers out of Europe."

Rolfe swallowed, as if unable to understand her words.

"Please, say something."

Outside, the train was pulling from the station, the whistle blaring.

It jolted him, and he seemed unraveled. "You did this? You did *all* this?"

"The train will take them nonstop to Paris. Jack arranged it."

"Jack…" he made a soft noise, like a groan, then leaned over and cradled his head in his hands.

And then, suddenly, his shoulders were shaking.

"Rolfe?"

He didn't answer her. Just shook his head, his hands over his face.

"Rolfe, you're—you're scaring me. I thought you'd be happy…."

He looked up then, his face unreadable, his eyes reddened, his cheeks stained. "I—Rosie, you undo me. One moment I want to choke you, the next you take my heart right from my chest. I can't breathe around you sometimes with the force of you in the room. And yet, when you're not here, I think I'm going to suffocate."

Oh. She swallowed away the bitter acid of disappointment in her throat. Looked away.

"No, you don't understand. I love you, Rosie. Since that day I saw you in the park, and every minute on the set of *Angel's Fury*, and all the moments in between, dying a little every time I saw your face on screen. I wrote the movie in the wild hope you'd agree to play the role, wishing you could see me the way I saw you."

Oh. *Oh.* "I did see it, Rolfe. On the screen. In Hale's eyes."

"In my eyes," he said quietly. "You are brave and beautiful and—and brilliant." He put his hand to her cheek. "And I prayed every day that I could figure out a way to show you that. That someday I'd earn the right to have your heart."

She leaned into his hand.

He wove it behind her neck, bent down, and kissed her. His touch was everything she remembered, everything sweet and full and perfect. He tasted of coffee, and the strength of a man who knew both hard work and privilege. And he smelled good. Too good for a man who'd spent two days in captivity. But perhaps that's what made him perfect too—the fact that he suffered without complaint, his candle lighting the way for others.

In his arms she sighed, full, whole. Applause in her heart.

And right then, she understood. She knew.

She didn't need applause. She needed this. Love. The kind that didn't leave, the kind that she could surrender her heart to.

The kind Jesus offered her. The kind he showed her through Rolfe.

And maybe she would have found it sooner, if she'd been meek, so many years ago, but God in His grace had brought her right back to her destiny.

Rolfe pulled her closer, holding her to himself, deepening his kiss, as if he had exhaled something he'd been holding on to far too long. He broke away to meet her eyes. "I love you, Rosie Worth."

"Enough to allow me to go to Belgium with you? To help you?"

"It's so dangerous," he said, his face somber. "I couldn't ask—"

"You didn't. Maybe God did, I don't know. But I am trusting Him, wherever He takes me. And I'm hoping that's Belgium."

"I should have told you what I was doing. I'm so sorry. I didn't really think you were in danger. Until Otto called me that day in France and told me that Gestapo in Berlin planned to send a man on the promotional tour with us. Otto thought they might suspect us, and I couldn't— I couldn't risk you."

"I know," she said quietly. "I understand."

He was searching her eyes, as if for confirmation, when a knock at the window jerked her away. She shrank back into the plush shadows of the seat as Rolfe rolled it down.

Fredrik Muller stood at the door. She saw the flash of his uniform, his pinched face. He peered into the car.

Her heart filled her throat. No. He could still turn the train around. Arrest everyone this time. Sophie and Hale, Rolfe...

Jack?

"Can I help you, Herr Muller?" Rolfe said, blocking his view of Rosie.

She pulled up the collar of her coat, holding her breath. Please let Rolfe's arrest have escaped Muller's attention.

"Your Grace. I saw you here. I thought you'd be on the train with your party."

She breathed, just a little.

"Thank you, Fredric. We're just leaving."

Rolfe got out, closed the door behind him.

Fredric bent down, peered into the window. Frowned. Looked over at the departing train. "Is Roxy Price in there with you?"

She heard Rolfe's silence, and her chest tightened further.

"No. That's…"

She opened her door, got out, her back to Fredric. Affected the London accent Rooney taught her. Prayed that Sophie adjusted the wig correctly. "Dahling. I'm cramped and tired. Please, can we dispense with these frivolities and return to the hotel? After all, we are on our"— she turned, holding her collar at the nape of her neck, hiding her face, adding allure to her eyes—"honeymoon."

She glanced at Fredric. "I don't believe we've met. Her Serene Highness, Duchess of Beaumont."

Fredric looked at her, frowning. Back at Rolfe. Who grinned at him, cheeky and with too much vigor.

He'd never be an actor. Daredevil, stuntman, however—yes, she saw all of those things in his grin.

"Congratulations," Fredric said quietly as Rosie slipped back into the car.

Rolfe got in, closed his door. Hung his hands on the steering wheel, breathing just a little too hard.

But then he glanced at her. Raised a brow. "Duchess?"

"I think it might be my greatest role." She swallowed. "If you'll have me."

"Have you? Or have your heart?"

He swallowed as the question lay there, in the silence.

She found the truth, nothing of the stage in her answer. "How about both, Your Grace."

His smile was slow and sweet and beautiful. He lifted her hand to kiss it. "Brilliantly played once again, m' lady."

Christmas 1945

Rosie had forgotten what it felt like to be a duchess. Or maybe she'd never truly known it. After all, she'd only lived two short years at Rolfe's chateau before the Nazis invaded Belgium. Thankfully, Jack's sources alerted the stash of Jews in transit, and by the time the Gestapo rolled into the circle driveway, Rolfe had them re-identified and en route to Israel.

But Jack couldn't prevent the Van Hornes' deportation to Germany, where they lived in house arrest, under guard until the Germans finally deported them to Switzerland until the war officially ended.

They'd returned only six months ago, to find the château destroyed, the royal portraits and tapestries stolen, the china, chandeliers, and molding chipped and desecrated, the floors scuffed, the fireplace mantels singed.

But maybe being royalty had nothing to do with place. Or title. Maybe it birthed from something inside.

Something rich and miraculous.

"She's so beautiful, darling." Rolfe leaned over the bassinette, the trauma of the past seven years seemingly erased from his face. His hair bore streaks of white, evidence of the bleak living conditions of their imprisonment. And the knowledge that he'd left his work unfinished.

Until, perhaps, now.

He reached in and pulled out the swaddled baby, cradled her close to his body.

Something about seeing Rolfe, his big aviator hands holding their child, his regal smile cast upon the cherub face of their three-month-old, could make Rosie weep in gratitude at their miracle.

A child born in her late years, conceived during war. Rosie prayed in earnest every day as she lay in bed, determined not to move.

Determined not to let it all vanish. Believing that, after all this time, hope wouldn't die.

The child squirmed in his arms, hiccoughed, frowning, working her tiny fists out of the blanket.

"I think she's hungry," Rolfe said.

"Of course she is. She spends nearly every waking hour eating." But Rosie took her into her lap, nestled her close.

"Can you check on the staff, see if Mr. Yates has brought in the tree—"

"Shh, Rosie. Everything is set. Yates and his staff have bedecked the halls just as you directed. The tree in the ballroom is up and sparkling, ready for tomorrow's gala, and he's erected another in the children's wing, even more glorious. The presents are tucked at its base and all the rooms prepared for the orphans." Rolfe pressed a kiss to her forehead. "Relax. Everything is ready. I'm going to meet the train now. And Sophie and Hale will be bringing the children after dinner. Everything is going to be perfect."

She caught his hand, delivered him a smile right before he closed the door.

Perfect. Maybe. But it didn't have to be perfect.

Because what she had was enough. More than enough.

Indeed, by her meekness, she'd inherited more than she could have asked or imagined.

Outside, falling snow drifted against a gray pallor, the glow from the windows upon the drifts. A fire flickered in her tile fireplace, sending warm, fragrant heat through the chamber.

She fell asleep with the child in her arms, rocking her, and woke to the voices in the foyer, lifting the two stories and tumbling down the hallway. She left the baby sleeping and changed into a short, double-breasted black dress with a high collar. She'd finally lost her baby inches, although she'd never regain her curves, not without a corset.

But those had died with the war, and she no longer worried about competing with the likes of Joan Crawford or Bette Davis, or the new-comers, Donna Reed, Lana Turner, and Ingrid Bergman.

In fact, with Rooney and Fletcher at the helm of Palace Studios, she merely watched it blossom as a movie-making machine, Spenser finally landing the lead roles he deserved.

Take that, Nazi Germany.

And her film—the original version of *Red Skies over Paris*—had hit America just in time for them to start to wake up to the Nazi atrocities, their takeover of Europe. She liked to think that, alongside her Academy Award for Best Picture, she'd helped awaken America to the threat of the resurging German empire.

But she never returned to America to claim her award. Or that life. Not when she had this rich, perfect, new one. She found the slew of letters from Irene waiting for her in Belgium, received and cared for by Sophie. Sammy had grown into a strapping sixteen-year-old, and Rosie could only thank God the war ended before he turned eighteen. They had a daughter, Dinah, age four, who sported Spenser's eyes, his dark curly hair.

She piled her long hair up on her head, pinned it in place, and wished she still had her pearls, or any jewelry to hang around her neck. But she'd given it away to Sophie long ago, and Sophie used it to ransom the lives of refugees smuggled out of the Third Reich.

After checking on the baby, she closed the door behind her and made her way down the hall. Yates and his footman had already begun to transfer the luggage to the rooms. The laughter, deep and thick, trickled up along the stairway and quickened her heartbeat.

She found Finn already ascending the stairs, searching for her. He watched her, grinning, as she descended. He looked so much a man, she could hardly recognize him. But that's what the military and four years flying for the Navy did to a boy. He wore his dark blond hair short, and age filled out his shoulders, his chest broad and strong.

"Sis!"

She tumbled into his arms, and he swung her around, set her down on the landing.

"I didn't think you'd come," she said, catching his face in her hands.

"And miss my niece's christening?"

"But the newspaper—?"

"Oliver certainly hasn't forgotten how to run the *Chronicle*. In fact, he reminds me nearly every day of that. The man can't seem to remember he's retired. He's in his glory, back at the office."

"How was your trip?" She looked past him, searching for her other guests.

"Mama went to sit down, Bennett with her. His eyesight is going, so it's better if they stay together."

She leaned past him, glimpsed her mother in the sitting room. Lowered her voice. "How is she?"

He leaned close. "She calls me daily with a list of eligible women for me to court. I fear I won't see another bachelor year."

Rosie reached up, patted his cheek. "You could do worse than listen to her."

The door opened behind him, ushering in the chill, and Rolfe entered, shaking off the snow from his coat. He caught Rosie's eyes. "Look who's back from boarding school."

A willowy twelve-year-old with luminous blue eyes and dark hair edged out from behind him, carrying a carpetbag, wearing a wool coat, a red cashmere scarf.

"Angelica." Rosie drew her into her arms. "How was your first term?" When Rosie discovered just who the little girl at the orphanage truly was, she insisted Rolfe bring his stepdaughter home, at least during the summer months, and she'd spent the entire glorious month of August discovering a young lady who could capture her heart.

Angelica surrendered in her arms then stepped back and curtsied. "Very good, m' lady."

Finn raised an eyebrow.

"We talked about this, darling. You don't have to be shy with me. Call me Rosie."

She managed a shy smile. Nodded. But Rosie knew how overwhelming it felt to step into so much grace, so much love.

"The housekeeper has made up your room, Angelica." Rolfe said. He turned to Rosie. "Truman and Lilly are getting settled in their rooms, said they'd be down for dinner."

"Please don't start with your war stories at dinner, Rolfe. Save them for your cigars."

"I am sure even Truman doesn't want to relive our aerial battles over a dinner of roast goose." He allowed one of the footmen to relieve him of his coat, his hat.

She stepped close to him. She didn't want to ask, afraid of too much hope blooming in her voice.

"Coco is here. And she looks just like you." He pressed a kiss to her forehead. "I fear we may have another starlet on our hands." He winked at her.

Lilly had left the door of communication open, allowing Rosie to write to her daughter, to reacquaint her with her heritage. Chilly at first, Coco's letters had warmed over the past year.

She caught Rolfe's hand, squeezed.

He nodded. "His train gets in tonight, after dinner."

That felt like an eternity, but he'd kept his promise after all. That should be enough.

She entered the parlor, found her mother with her shoes off, soaking her feet. "I feel that I am still rumbling, my bones rattled," Jinx said, making to rise.

"Don't get up, Mother," Rosie said and leaned down to kiss her. She wore a long black travel dress and smelled of powder, the faint scent of her French toilette. Age pearled her hair, and she wore it captured back, at the nape of her neck in a netting, Rosie couldn't ignore the skin gathered around her jawline, the years of war and worrying for Finn that embedded her eyes and lined her mouth.

By the grace of God, Finn had lived through his campaigns in the Pacific.

Bennett wore his spectacles, now bottle thick, and smiled at her. He was still handsome in his nearly seventy years, despite his thinning hair, the wrinkles etched into his face. "You're looking radiant, Rosie," he said and she couldn't help but love him all over again.

"Where is my grandchild?" Jinx asked.

"I'll fetch her," Rosie said.

"What of her nanny?"

"I haven't employed one, Mother." She glanced at Finn as she exited, hoping the baby was awake.

She was nearly at her chamber when the door across the hall opened. She stilled at the woman that appeared in the hallway. Eighteen and shapely, with amber blond hair cut short below her ears, just a little too much of the Wild West of her Montana home in her green eyes, she wore a pleated wool skirt, a long cashmere sweater, and as she paused, so did Rosie's heart. Crazy, wild tears burned her eyes.

"Hello, Coco."

The girl drew in a breath, lifted her chin. "Aunt Rosie? Nice to finally meet you." She found a smile, something tentative, and held out her hand.

Rosie caught it, let the warmth, the youth of it soak into her. The old ache revived, swept through her, and with everything inside her, she wanted to pull her daughter close, to tighten her arms around her, breathe her in, never let her go. But Coco didn't know her. Not really.

Not yet. She took a breath, and for a moment, took the stage and found the right voice. "Thank you for coming."

Silence. Rosie's breath rose and fell in her chest as Coco considered her, too much in her eyes for Rosie to discern.

Please, let me in. Let me apologize. Don't run away.

Then, "I wanted to meet my half sister," Coco said quietly.

Yes. Okay. Rosie let out a breath and nodded. "She's in here."

She opened the door to her room, heard the baby rustling in her blankets. Rosie went to the bassinet, fixed her swaddling, and pulled her into her arms.

Coco stepped close, ran a finger down her cheek. "She's beautiful."

"She looks like you." Rosie hadn't stayed long after Coco's birth, but she'd never forgotten the shape of her newborn's face or the smell of her skin.

"She does?" Coco glanced up, then, aware of her tone, glanced away.

"Yes," Rosie said softly. "She has your hair, the way it stands up in tufts, and your big eyes. And she cries like you did. Loud and stubborn."

"I'm not stubborn," Coco said, but caught her lower lip between her teeth.

"I doubt that," Rosie said, winking.

Coco grinned. Then she leaned over and kissed the baby on the forehead. "Grandma Jinx has talked of nothing but this baby for three months."

"Let's introduce them."

She brought the baby, now waking, downstairs. Jinx had replaced the pan of water with a knitted afghan. Rosie placed the child into her waiting arms.

She said nothing, just stared down at her, as if drinking her in. "She's so lovely, Rosie." She leaned close, pressed her lips to the baby's forehead. "And she smells like you."

Oh. Rosie sank down on the divan opposite her. "She does?"

"A mother never forgets," Jinx says.

Rosie glanced at Coco. No, she doesn't.

She wanted to capture this moment on film. Everyone hitting their marks, their faces stilled for all time. Coco, a younger snapshot of herself, strong, courageous, ready to dive into life, and Angelica, believing in a family, in belonging. Finn, dashing and the embodiment of grace, a blessing to them all. Jinx, her expression a sort of awe, Bennett beside her, touching the bundle of his step-grandchild. Rolfe pressed his hand to Rosie's shoulder and squeezed.

Yes, maybe a girl didn't have to be a duchess to feel royal.

And then the door opened. Feet stamped into the foyer, and everyone looked up, toward the commotion.

And time stopped.

Rosie saw it just as she'd hoped it would be. Jack, tall and covered with diamond droplets of snow glistening in his blond hair. A slight layer of whiskers at his cheeks, the evidence of his overnight train ride from Brussels where he worked with the international community tracking down German war criminals. The war had aged him, especially after the German SS discovered his covert activities and he'd escaped from the country.

Thankfully, they never connected him to Rolfe, or perhaps they too would have suffered the fate of too many anti-Nazi conspirators.

Jack closed the door behind him, swiped the derby from his head, and crunched it in his hands. Then, with only a hint of accent, "Hello, Mother."

Rosie held her breath, the secret coiled so tight inside her for the past six years she thought she might expire with the pain of it in her chest.

Jinx had turned white. Rosie got up to rescue the baby, but Rolfe beat her to it. Instead, she helped her mother to her feet.

Her hands trembled in Rosie's, her breath shuddering in her chest. She shook her head even as she managed, "Jack?"

He nodded, glanced at Rosie, as if at a loss. Then, "I'm sorry I didn't tell you earlier. I—I—"

He closed his mouth, his face twitching.

"Jack was with Army Intelligence, Mother, ever since the Great War. He lived with the Germans, pretended to be one of them, and then, when the war with Germany began again, he helped me and Rolfe transport refugees, Jews and other political prisoners, out of the country."

Jinx tightened her hands in hers. "You knew."

Jack took a step closer. "I asked her not to tell you, Mother. I—I didn't want you to lose me twice."

But Jinx was just staring at him, her chin trembling, her chest rising and falling.

The clock ticked over the mantle; the baby stirred in Rolfe's arms.

And then, "I never got over losing you the first time."

"And I never got over regretting how I left you," Jack said. He took a step into the room. "Please forgive me? I should have—I should have understood." His gaze flickered to Bennett. "I was wrong."

Jinx released Rosie's hands and turned to him. She was crying, the tears soft and bright on her face. "I forgive you, Jack, if you forgive me."

Then her arms were around him, and he caught her tight to himself, his head buried in her shoulder, shaking as he wept. "I love you, Mother."

Rosie pressed her hands to her cheeks, wiping her eyes, so much inside her she could burst.

Jinx leaned back, pressed her hands to Jack's face. "My boy."

He caught her wrists, nodding, grinning.

"I guess we should meet," a voice said, and Rosie saw Finn advance across the room, his hand extended. "Finley Jackson Worth."

Jack cast a look at Rosie. "I have a—brother?"

"You made the rules, not me."

Jack turned back to Finn, grinning. "I have a brother." Then he wrapped his arm around Finn, slapped him on the back.

The baby started to whimper. Jack freed Finn. "And I suppose this is my niece?" he said, looking at the baby.

"Actually, I'm your niece too," Coco said, rubbing her arms. "My mother—uh, Lilly told me about you." She held out her hand. "I'm Rosie's oldest daughter, with her first husband, Guthrie."

Rosie pressed her hand to her mouth as Jack took Coco's hand. "Of course you are. You look just like her."

Coco reddened, a blush streaking into her face. "I grew up in Montana with Lilly."

"She did a good job by you," he said.

"She comes from good stock," Lilly said from behind him. Rosie hadn't seen her enter. She looked older, her hair piled in a bun at the nape of her neck, looking lean and noble with her Crow heritage. A dark-haired boy stood beside her, his eyes hard on Coco. TJ, Lilly called him, if Rosie remembered correctly. Truman had his hands curled over the boy's shoulders. Lilly's daughter, Daisy, sat next to her great-aunt, Jinx, looking every inch like the cowgirl her mother had once been. How Rosie remembered Lilly's restless years in New York City.

Lilly caught her gaze.

She couldn't have picked a better mother for her daughter. *Thank you, Lilly, for the beautiful daughter you raised.*

The baby erupted in a howl, red faced and angry. Rosie took her in her arms, pulled her close, soothing her.

"She's magnificent, Rosie," Jack said, cupping his big hand against her head. "Has your personality exactly."

She narrowed her eyes at him but grinned.

"What's her name?"

Jinx took his other hand, and Rosie noticed how he wove their fingers together.

"Sarah," Rosie said. "It means princess."

"The Worth family princess," Jack said softly. He pressed a kiss to the baby's downy forehead. "Welcome to the family."

Author's Note and Acknowledgments

There is nothing better than diving into a story like this one, surrounding yourself with research and ideas, the culmination of a storyline you've been working on for two years. I loved penning this novel because I knew that after the hard beginning of *Heiress*, with so much pain and so many mistakes made by Jinx, and the bittersweet middle story, *Baroness*, where Rosie walks so far away from her inheritance, Rosie's redemption would be rich and profound. I loved watching her discover that she didn't need the world's applause she longed for—that she had it all inside, with the love of God. If you've read all three books, perhaps you noticed the themes: *"Blessed are the poor in spirit, for theirs is the kingdom of heaven."* Esme learned this in *Heiress*, as she discovered that wealth came from knowing your Savior. *"Blessed are they that mourn: for they shall be comforted."* Lilly learned this in *Baroness* as she let go of her grief and recognized the comfort of her father, Oliver, and that she couldn't outrun God's love. *"Blessed are the meek: for they shall inherit the earth."* Rosie learned this in *Duchess*, that inheriting everything she wanted—the applause of earth and heaven— was about surrender and trusting God's love. The series is named "Daughters of Fortune" not only because of their circumstances, but because I hoped readers might see what a true fortune looks like. What a true inheritance is when a person puts their faith in the Lord.

It was a joy to dive into the world of Hollywood and the Silver Screen. I learned a tremendous amount about the "creation" of movie stars. Rosie is a mix between a number of stars, but especially Jean Harlow, who died tragically after a terrible illness. A little known fact is that all her hair fell out with all the peroxide treatment, and for the last few movies of her career, she wore a wig. She also starred opposite Clark Gable in many of his early films. In those early days, stars were "owned" by studios, and worked for a weekly (albeit handsome) salary. They had little control over their careers.

I had to walk a careful line as I constructed the events surrounding *Gone with the Wind*. Warner Brothers initially wanted to secure rights to option the film, with Bette Davis in mind for Scarlett. When she turned it down, legendary independent film maker David Selznick picked it up. Although usually connected with United Artists, he turned to MGM, home of Clark Gable to distribute it. As I created Rooney, I formed him after Selznick, as well as the brash young Howard Hughes. Palace Studios is a loose rendition of United Artists, a studio formed by Hollywood icons D.W. Griffith, Mary Pickford, Charlie Chaplin, and Douglas Fairbanks. Of course, none of the characters or studios are an exact replication—I tried to find a common denominator and still keep the essence of the silver screen intact.

The German storyline is built around the increasing menace to the Jews in Europe even before the war. I tried to stay as true to actual events as possible, including *Kristallnacht*, or "The Night of Broken Glass," which took place November 9–10, 1938, and began the public persecution of the Jews. Rolfe's activities are based on actual events and people who risked their lives to help Jews leave Europe.

When I originally began this series, I knew that Jack would reappear. I conceived this series with the idea of Jacob and Esau (Jinx and

Esme) and used the biblical storyline to craft this one. I love the idea of God using for good what others might intend for evil. I loved the idea that Jack was a hero all along and that Jinx finally has her happy ending. All the same, writing these stories was my most ambitious project to date, and I put my faith in the Lord's provision. I am so grateful for so many who came beside me with both encouragement and applause as I wrote *Duchess*. Sarah Warren, thank you for letting me into your heart to write Roxy Price's starlet scenes. And Rachel Hauck, who continued to affirm me in the dark hours of the series when I felt I would never be able to put onto the page the spiritual truths roaming my heart. Thank you to Susan Downs, my amazing editor and friend— your belief in me is my treasure. Special thanks goes to James Scott Bell, amazing Hollywood tour guide who provided both car chases and rich historical anecdotes. And finally, Steve Laube, my agent, who walked with me through a few writer's block moments. Thank you also to the wonderful team at Summerside Press—Jason, Rachel, and so many others who believed in this series and worked so hard to bring it to publication. I am glad to have worked with you.

I could never write a word without the amazing support of my family, Andrew, David, Sarah, Peter, and Noah, encouraging me, cheering for and with me, and putting up with all those times I said, "Dahling, I'm a star. I don't do dishes." Thanks for making me feel like a duchess, every day.

I give this book and this series to the Lord, for His glory, with deep gratitude for the inheritance of being His child.

Thank you for reading,
Susan May Warren

About the Author

SUSAN MAY WARREN is the best-selling author of more than thirty novels whose compelling plots and unforgettable characters have earned her acclaim from readers and reviewers alike. She is a winner of the ACFW Carol Award, the RITA Award, and the Inspirational Readers Choice Award and a nominee for the Christy Award. She loves to write and to help other writers find their voices through her work with My Book Therapy (www.mybooktherapy.com), a writing craft and coaching community she founded.

Susan and her husband of more than twenty years have four children. Former missionaries to Russia, they now live in a small Minnesota town on the shore of beautiful Lake Superior, where they are active in their local church. Find her online at www.susanmaywarren.com.